Praise for *The Pain of Pleasure*

"Amy Grace Loyd's writing is intelligent and graceful, lighting up the mind and the body, reaching my brain and heart and spirit. A surprising and bold fusion of ideas and sensory detail that stimulates and illuminates."

—Charles Yu, author
of the National Book Award–winning *Interior Chinatown*

"Amy Grace Loyd has traveled deeply down into the nexus of pain and pleasure to reveal an endlessly generative pulsing heart. Akin to the style and intimate designs of Marguerite Duras with the epic smarts and atmospherics of Richard Powers, her new novel reminds me that to fully embrace life means to let go of easy binaries and enter embodiment without apology. Take the leap.
This book is thrilling."

—Lidia Yuknavitch, author
of the national bestseller *The Book of Joan*,
the story collection *Verge*, and *Thrust*

"*The Pain of Pleasure* is a vivid, beautifully written novel about the line between suffering and salvation. A smart, sensual writer, Amy Grace Loyd has created an unforgettable world in this old Brooklyn church, transformed into a clinic for headache sufferers and peopled with marvelous characters weathering the torment of their own desires."

—Jess Walter, author
of the national bestseller *The Cold Millions*
and No. 1 New York Times bestseller *Beautiful Ruins*

"With her brilliant novel *The Pain of Pleasure*, Amy Grace Loyd has invented an entirely new genre perfectly appropriate to this climatically insane age that blends science with high opera, realism with the surreality of altered states, resulting in a narrative that, for all of its uncanniness, still roils with the traditional novelistic pleasures of desperate love. It hurts so good to read it."

—Will Blythe, author
of New York Times bestseller
To Hate Like This Is to Be Happy Forever

Praise for *The Affairs of Others*

"[A] mesmerizing debut… beautifully, even feverishly described. As Celia discovers, the magnetic pull of other people's everyday experiences proves impossible to resist."

—*Entertainment Weekly*

"Loyd succeeds at the most difficult task for such a circumscribed setting—making the granular details of her characters' travails feel as though they added up to more than the sum of their parts."

—*The New Yorker*

"From start to finish, Loyd's prose flows exquisitely through the story, as she limns the depths of the protagonist's mind, the complexity of human intimacy, and the idiosyncrasies of each new character with the grace of a seasoned novelist."

—*Vanity Fair*

"Celia's journey is beautifully charted in this debut, with prose that mirrors her existence in her barely furnished apartment—confined, spare, but swirling with fierce emotion and insights."

—*People*

"Hypnotic, beautiful, and dangerously erotic, this book trembles with feeling, every sentence a breath, every sentence a seismographic wonder of observation."

—Jonathan Ames, author of *You Were Never Really Here*, *A Man Named Doll*, and *Wake Up, Sir!*

"Debut novels don't come any more sure-handed and deftly written than *The Affairs of Others*. But it's the damaged, brokenhearted Celia—Amy Grace Loyd's brave, all-in protagonist—who latches on to us and refuses to loosen her grip."

—Richard Russo, author of *Empire Falls*

The PAIN of PLEASURE

The PAIN of PLEASURE

A Novel

AMY GRACE LOYD

roundabout

roundabout

ISBN: 978-1-948072-11-3

Published by Roundabout Press

To those who gave me shelter in the various storms while I wrote this book: Suzanne and Jerry, Cody, Maggie, and the bear in my heart

But what if pleasure and pain should be so closely connected that he who wants the greatest possible amount of the one must also have the greatest possible amount of the other, that he who wants to experience the "heavenly high jubilation" must also be ready to be "sorrowful unto death"?

—NIETZSCHE

Part I

It is easier to find men who will volunteer to die than to find those who are willing to endure pain with patience.

—Julius Caesar

Every act of perception is to some degree an act of creation, and every act of memory is to some degree an act of imagination.

—Gerald Edelman
(as referenced in Oliver Sacks's *Musicophilia*)

The Doctor

The rooms hummed. A whisper in his ears. Climate control. Cycling and breathing. Necessary for a medical clinic housed in the basement of a church. The Doctor joked that he and his staff worked from the *under*ground up, and it was funny to him sometimes. Sometimes it seemed he was riding wave after wave of happenstance, and it was all okay, part of human life and its surprises, routine indignities. Not his fault. Not anyone's, really.

At other times, where he found himself now was an affront to him—a neurologist once poised at the top of his field—and it was clear to him he was failing. Again.

The rooms hummed with expensive equipment he didn't pay for. The rooms hummed, and his patients were subdued by it. Or mostly. Some wanted more air. Different air. Fresh air. They wanted things he couldn't always give them. The end of pain. He wanted that too. For them. And himself. Relief.

Through the humming of his offices he listened for the wind outside. He'd welcomed it when it arrived in late winter. He was a man who understood the need for circulation, outside on the streets and parks, up and down the East Coast, and of course in the body. Movement. The quickening of blood, oxygen. So vital to all the body's workings, but this was especially so for the nervous system and the brain, the nervous system's most complicated expression.

But the wind outside wouldn't stop, and as winter struggled to become spring or some version of it, he heard it as one would a woman crying through the walls. Disconsolate, out of reach, she kept at her crying. He could hear her now, whether in fact or in his head, it was hard to say, so constant had the gale become in the city.

Outside, people walked with their heads down, blind with their posture bent, clutching their collars to themselves.

Leaves let go, branches fell and broke other things. Umbrellas lay dead and useless everywhere. Tall buildings swayed like drunks, and construction projects were abandoned as debris took to the air and scaffolding came apart. Electrical lines kept snapping all over the city. Birds crashed into windows. Planes were often grounded.

It was the meeting of increasing extremes—high and low pressure, high and low temperatures, and other variables meteorologists tracked: the polar jet stream dipping, bringing colder air from Canada, while one bulky low-pressure system after another stalled off the Atlantic coast, their currents moving counterclockwise over the water and bringing rain and more wind that switched and often tore.

And the new weather brought in more patients, headache sufferers all. The wild shifts in barometric pressure tested sensitive systems—people who never had headaches before, who'd never sought treatment, came in like refugees. And for longtime sufferers of migraine, who represented the majority of his patients, it amplified the helplessness they already felt.

He could hear their voices outside his office now, an evening support group for chronic migraine. They were sophisticated. Specialists. And they taught each other to be. They knew so much, or as much as anyone could about an affliction that remained for the most part a mystery. But there they were, despite the weather, trying to solve it.

Only yesterday a cable broke loose on the Manhattan Bridge, falling into the power lines over the subways just as the N train rumbled past. It could have been disastrous but wasn't—not yet—and still his patients debated what foods were safe to eat, supplements to take and on what schedule, medications that worked or never worked or failed to work over time, and the approaches on offer at the clinic in low-lit room after room: biofeedback, injections of Botox and B vitamins, massage, magnesium sulfate drips, electrical nerve stimulation, acupuncture.

Some experiments, too, along with a roster of new drugs, the latest promises of a cure.

That was the idea of the clinic, or in theory. It would collaborate with certain studies. But not overly, or that's what the Doctor told Mrs. Watson, the clinic's patron and the force behind its current location. They had to be modest, lead with the patients' well-being, he explained, and Mrs. Watson, Adele Watson—*Call me Adele*—pretended to listen, watching his mouth and then looking into his eyes as if she could see a better him in there—better for her. A him that did what he was told.

He had moved his office into the old church a year ago. He'd acquiesced. Adele and the Doctor agreed it would be temporary, requiring him to overlook, when he could, all the money she was putting in to convey permanence. "A church is like any other building," Mrs. Watson said in a way that made it so, "once you chase out all the fancy."

Deconsecrated churches all over Brooklyn were being turned into condos and office buildings, just as St. Gabriel's would be. "You'll see," she'd tell him over the red wine she wasn't supposed to drink, given that it triggered the migraines he was supposed to be treating. "It will be a feat," she'd say.

How he found himself in another face-off with yet another woman he could only disappoint, he did not know.

First his mother, then his wife, then Sarah.

He locked his office door, removed his white coat, hung it evenly on its hanger, and took out the journal. Holding it was like holding Sarah, and not just in his hands but in his mind and heart. Sarah, a former patient, who had vanished. A year and a half ago, on January 13.

The press and social media feeds had already forgotten, moved on to other stories, these days about the wind and some variety of apocalypse, how the planet was rehearsing to blow its most troublesome tenants off its back at last. But he hadn't forgotten.

The journal arrived a few months after he'd begun at the clinic, delivered by a friend of Sarah's, a slip of a woman named Mathilde, *for your eyes only, please,* a small hand pressing his in the dark, *promise,* and he had. The Doctor had consented again. For Sarah, the last syllable of her name, *ah*, always recalling the relief that wanted to come but wouldn't.

Sarah

Even on your good days you're outrunning it, making these crazy negotiations with it—as it approaches, when it arrives, and after, when it finally goes, you think it can't come again, it won't, no way, not like that. You learn young to be on your guard, when you see or hear things that just CAN'T be real, and feel things that are, to you: something sharp digging into you, at the soft of the temple on one side first and at the back of your head, there where your neck becomes head and climbing, the saliva in your mouth souring, maybe your blood too? If you could taste it? And you wonder is it starting all over again? Will the pain come and crowd everything out, including me? You don't believe parts of you can turn so hard and others just too soft and without any protection at all, feeling pressures that you can't believe a body alone is generating. How can anyone's body do this without bursting or collapsing in? And how can I stop it? Now and forever?

Ruth

In the wind, blowing with her, then against her, Ruth made her way to a street that was only one block long. It connected two more trafficked streets. At the corner of it and another street that reached from the East River into the coursing of downtown Brooklyn, she stopped.

She wasn't from New York City and never wanted to be. She had to leave the place she'd called home because little by little it had become strange, warped. She was in exile even before she left.

Now the wind took her coat up high behind her, puffing out the skirt of her scrub dress, a nurse's uniform, as the job post specified. Rather than fight the weather, as she'd been doing block after block, while trying to decipher the map on her phone, she let go of her coat. On the subway there'd been too many bodies, too close. Now she couldn't see anyone seeing her, so she shut her eyes and leaned into the current. She felt it push back, take her weight. She extended her arms so the wind would hold them out, until she found strength to pull them back to her sides, then enough to continue her path to the address she'd memorized: 10 Linden Place.

She couldn't say if any of the trees on the street were lindens, but every tree she saw tossed and wheeled its branches.

So many blooms lost in the days she'd been here, in what was barely May.

At 10 Linden, the largest brownstone in a gleaming row of them, a man sat high up on the stoop. She straightened her coat and put together a smiling face for him. "Excuse me. I believe I have an appointment here?"

The man said something from behind what appeared to be a pair of motorcycle goggles, antique, tinted, and from under a shifting mass of white curls—white as in gone white—though he looked no more than middle-aged. But because the wind gusted, caught in her ears, she couldn't be sure of his reply: "What was that?"

Raising his voice over the wind: "I can see that," he said. "You wore the costume."

"The costume?"

He rested his lean arms on lean legs and hunched like a boy, while his hair moved along with the trees. Even with his odd goggles on, she could tell he was pretty in the way of rock stars just past their prime—his features were both hard and delicate. And his clothes—a linen shirt that flounced in the air, checked pants, white leather loafers—signaled that he'd probably identify himself as some kind of artist, or clown, an eccentric anyway.

"You dressed like a nurse," he said.

"I *am* a nurse."

"You looked like the Flying Nun." He pointed to the corner. "Down there. Did you want to blow away? See if you might?"

He wanted to play. She'd forgone her blue scrubs for the dress because it felt more formal, respectful. The ad had read, "Come prepared to work." Was it all a joke?

"I have an interview at this address today, at one thirty. Is it with you?"

"No."

"Do you work here?"

"Yes and no. I'm the son."

She searched in her pocket—in case her phone or its signal failed, she'd printed the e-mail confirming the appointment. She unfolded it and tried to read as it flapped madly at her. She tried to keep the impatience from her voice: "The son of a Mrs.... Mrs. Watson?"

"Orson. I am Or*son* Wat*son*. Double the son." He stood, stepped down to her, and extended his hand.

She took it, though she didn't want to, and offered, "Ruth."

"Ruth," he said, as if weighing the proportions of her name in his mouth, just as he'd weighed her hand in his before she snatched it back, then he confided, over the wind, "She's feisty today. Drinking wine. She's been listening to Pergolesi."

"She's not feeling well?"

"What ails my mother only makes her stronger… She's very… *very lively.*" He threw back his head and laughed at this, and his hair and Adam's apple bounced. Wind or no, she doubted his hair or the rest of him ever stayed in the same configuration for long. She doubted he'd want it to.

"May I ask which apartment it is? It's not included in the information I was given." And, surveying the building, she added, "What a beautiful place."

"Gothic revival, 1847. She owns the whole thing. She owns most of the block too, and that's just for starters."

He seemed to be taken with what "for starters" meant, because he moved onto the sidewalk as he said it. He was gone already, aimed in the direction from which she'd come, when he said, "I wish you luck, Ruth. With the lady of the house and the flying."

She thought she heard him talking on, but it was impossible to say with another gust between them. She held on to the railings of the brownstone's stairs. Her own hair was pinned down with dozens of pins, and in the wind they bit into her.

Petunia petals of deeply veined yellow and purple were scattered all over the top steps. The plants in massive ribbed concrete planters on either side of the entrance wouldn't last long, and whoever was in charge of them didn't care. There were clearly enough funds for replacing annuals blown bare over and over again.

Ruth tried to imagine the taxes alone on such a place, an Edith Wharton sort of house, one of many in this tony neighborhood—it was called Cobble Hill. Books and novels in particular gave her what little context she had for this city, though it was years now since she'd read one with any real attention or pleasure. What was left of her books waited for her in a storage unit, until she had the room for them and the rest of her belongings, the courage to remember what sort of person she'd been when she read Wharton's *House of Mirth* and had wondered from a safe distance at how a life like the novel's heroine, Lily Bart, could be stripped so bare: from abundance, beauty, belonging, in homes like this one, down to regret and poverty.

The place before her was old and elegant, as real and rigid as another age's belief in decorum. If it spoke at all, it spoke of history. And of money.

A place of its size in this city, it required money.

So did Ruth. She had to remember necessity and that was all.

But she didn't climb the stairs, though it was time. She seemed all wrong in this setting. Too loose a particle, as flimsy as Orson Watson took her to be. Barely a match for the weather. So much had happened in the past few years, and all the event and repercussions were still loud in her. She couldn't afford to let anyone know this or feel her discomfort in their company, yet all that had happened still resounded in her as if in an immense cavern: objects and relationships crashing, losing shape, accusations made and remade online: *bitch, whore, murderer*. Made new. They ran like a current, along with that incessant talking and speechifying, about her, to her—what she'd done, should have done, as if she was everything that was wrong in the world. It was too easy to forget how small she really was, how small everything human was or became in time. But when would time, which in these days insisted on speed and kept dragging the past into the present, feel real to her again? When would she?

It was that lack of faith in contours, her own above all, and of knowing anything for sure that helped Ruth up the stairs finally, to stand on petal after petal, and wonder at her finger's ingenuity as it pressed the bell, and at the bleat she heard, despite the wind, of vibrating metal on metal, of what sounded like an ancient, unhappy goat.

The Doctor

Sarah's journal was begun for the purpose of tracking her migraine triggers, finding patterns. The Doctor asked all his patients to do this, if they were willing. Most were, at least until certain sensitivities were revealed. When his receptionist knocked on his office door that evening, he held his finger on the page where the journal ceased to be a record of what Sarah had eaten early one day—a hard-boiled egg, dry toast, a cup of decaf, black—and how much she had slept—five and a half hours, *a night full of dreams that I can't remember*—and where she hurt—*right temple, neck turned to concrete, jaw, too, aching, hard to move*—and became, with a question addressed to him, something else.

It was over a year ago now when Sarah had written this, but the handwriting that formed the question, and was edged into the pages with the pen's pressure, still felt under his finger like it might move or jump: *Why didn't you come to see me? The day was beautiful and green and I waited for you for like an HOUR. I needed a friend, and aren't you that at least?*

Sue, the Doctor's receptionist, tapped on his door. She was a talker and a giggler but efficient, with a passion for organization and for kindness. She was pregnant again, the third time in six years. Twenty-nine, she could pass for seventeen and enjoyed explaining that she was half Korean and half Canadian, by way of Toronto, but *all* American.

"Dr. Berger," she said, "I'm going home."

Would he open the door to talk?

"Okay, be safe, Sue. The weather…" He closed his eyes, listened for the wind, but otherwise didn't move.

"Your father called," she spoke through the door.

"Once?"

"Twice."

"Did he ask for me?"

"No, for Kenneth."

Kenneth was his father's brother, the Doctor's uncle, who had died more than a decade ago. The dementia meant the Doctor had shifting names, significances, to his father.

"I'll call him."

"Goodnight then." Sue didn't quibble with the door between them—it had to be shut sometimes—and he did not quibble with her wanting to be home in time to bathe her kids and watch shows about celebrities, about which, if you betrayed the least interest, she'd tell you everything she'd learned about this or that star's mishap, marriage, divorce. Sue never had a headache of any severity, but she was sympathetic to those who did and referred to the Doctor as "one of the good guys," ignoring how he tensed when she did.

"Oh, and your wife—"

His eyes were still closed against the interruption: "My *ex*-wife."

A giggle. "Right, sorry. Your ex. She called about a patient. A consult."

"Emergency?"

"Maybe. Maybe not."

"And Mrs. Watson? Has she… ?"

"Not yet. There's a new nurse, evidently. An interview today."

He wished Sue away now. Wished that news away. *Another nurse*. He closed his eyes.

"Doctor?"

"Sue?"

"Did you eat today?"

"I did."

He forgot to eat sometimes. Sometimes, if he was lucky, he forgot himself.

"Safe home, Sue."

"There's half a sandwich in the fridge. Tuna, light on the mayo. It's all yours."

"Goodnight. Goodnight now, Sue. Be safe—the weather—"

A giggle retreated with her. Sue didn't know Sarah, but the Doctor believed they would have liked each other. Neither woman was easily distracted from what mattered most to her. Challenges made them livelier.

The questions Sarah put to him always came fast, were tilted up with hope, like a hand raised as high as it could go: "Aren't you a friend?" would reverberate with something like *Of course you are. Of course.*

"And if you're not a friend, strictly speaking, tell me, Doctor, what are you?"

"I am a doctor. *Your* doctor," he had said to Sarah and said again now to his empty office. "I am your doctor."

"*My* doctor?"

"Yes."

"That is, on my side? My team?" They'd had this conversation many times. How many? He couldn't say. He wished he could.

"Absolutely on your side."

"And that's not a friend?"

"It is. It simply has nuances—"

"Boundaries?"

"Yes."

"Because I pay you?"

"No, but I suppose that's a part—"

"I am not supposed to have boundaries?"

"Of course you are, Sarah. I took an oath." *To do no harm*, and he meant it. Couldn't she understand? "You see, I—"

"But you have said with migraines it's about the whole person—'the whole economy of an individual life,' emotional and otherwise. You have to know me well, *really* well."

"That's Oliver Sacks, a neurologist, a writer. I quoted him. You're quoting me quoting him."

"But it's true?"

"It's true enough."

"Doesn't seem fair, or equal, does it?"

"It's about health, *your* health, Sarah."

Their relationship hadn't become what it was all at once. It took time and many questions and answers, while the peach tones under her skin—gold and brown and pink—seemed to move with her thoughts. She had come to trust the Doctor so deeply, in fact, that that trust proved a burden, and only more so since she had disappeared. *The health of my patient will be my first consideration.* And it was. Still was.

Even now he was resuscitating her so that he could solve puzzles with her, and he couldn't help seeing her in Sue or Sue in her. He looked for her in his other patients too, and in strangers outside the clinic, on the streets, faceless in the wind; and in the journal, of course, that spoke to him, read itself to him even when he wished it wouldn't.

He would put the notebook away, but then he worried he was changing the words, remembering them wrong.

The day was beautiful and green and I waited for you… I wanted you to stop me from going any further with him. I can't say if he's giving me what my body needs, but so often it tells me he really is, because it's humming and humming. The pleasure.

"What weather! Oh, hello, *helloooo*! How lovely to see you!" Outside the Doctor's door a rocket of greetings from Izzy, one of the clinic's regulars, or irregulars, because her headaches were mostly under control these days. She was his employer Mrs. Watson's half sister, though the emphasis for both women seemed to be on *half*, the part that was not complete and never would be. They shared the genetic predisposition to migraine, but Izzy believed pain had its purposes, spiritual mostly. She wanted to be an example to others—"a vision," she liked to say, "of *escape*."

"Oh, *Christine*! There you are!" Izzy was voluble. "How was Italy? It's a miracle you got out, with the weather. Tell us about the *food*! The wine—*that gorgeous, gorgeous wine*!"

The Doctor couldn't hear Christine's reply, but he knew roughly what it would be. Christine, one of his longtime patients, was a statuesque redhead and semi-retired schoolteacher from St. Louis whose headaches, like Sarah's, were chronic, sometimes wiping out whole weeks from her life, and had gotten worse with age and hormonal fluctuation. She'd known Sarah, a waiting-room friend. They'd been among the patients of the pain-management practice where he had been on staff years ago, before his time at St. Mary's Hospital, and before Mrs. Watson and her converted church.

If he looked now, there on the other side of his door, just around the corner, Christine would be seated in the lounge with her flagpole posture, her chin up and her shoulders trained low and level. Her posture was a sort of religion, designed not to show the Doctor or the *goddamned migraines* when she was down. Sarah had worried for her, which was worrying for herself: Was that who she would be in twenty years? Still not knowing what to risk, which foods or drinks or smells or angles of light or turns of weather or sensation or medications, or which people—of course, people too—might trigger her? Take her away?

No, he told Sarah. No two experiences of the disorder are the same, no two nervous systems, from body to body, even day to day. The symptoms and phases of attack might share similarities, but each case was as unique as DNA or fingerprints or our changing synaptic connections, and every day becoming more so.

He had reassured Sarah at thirty-three and then thirty-four, with her dark hair cut in a jagged jaw-length bob that she hid behind when she wasn't feeling well and brushed off her face when she was. It exposed her neck and how delicate it was and how long. When she had an attack, he believed he could trace its indications there, the muscles tightening, while the meninges, the membranes that covered the brain, and the nerves there became incensed, especially the trigeminal nerve—the largest cranial nerve, with its branches reaching all over the face's territories. Sarah would fold—her body, her head—into her hands and, one day, into his.

The cool of your hand against my face. Me in your arms for however long you could stomach it.

Chronic migraine was defined as fifteen or more episodes a month. When diagnosed, even the most parsimonious of American insurance plans, like Sarah's, opened their treatment options. Sarah's mother was a research scientist, a behavioral biologist, her father a writer for TV talk shows and game shows, so Sarah had been schooled in trial and error, adaptability, and humor. She told the Doctor that her father used to tell her jokes as the migraine came. He snuck into the dark room where she was hiding from noise and light—knock-knock and old Borscht Belt jokes, throwaways whispered: *How do you make holy water? You boil the hell out of it... Did you hear about the hungry clock? He went back four seconds... Knock-knock. Who's there? Lion. Lion who? Lion on your doorstep—open up!*

The sweetness of it: as if a series of calls and responses, neat little U-turns, silly and light, could relieve physical pain.

Laughter outside now—a woman's, and a man's too.

Who was out there tonight? Adam? Only thirty, he'd survived three tours of duty in Afghanistan, and a near fatal blow to the head, and the landslide of opioids prescribed to him to treat the residual headaches. A man he had to watch carefully, manage, reassure.

Or Jeff? A local arborist who'd joined the city's ranks to save the local trees from the constant winds. Save what he could.

Without leaving his desk, the Doctor could look at the monitors now integrated into and available with a click of his mouse on his desktop computer, which was linked to cameras all over the clinic. But he didn't look, because that system was part of a larger one that acquainted him with his own scruples nearly every day.

Before you could be treated in the clinic, you were asked to sign a waiver, consenting to the cameras, and if you didn't have insurance, or particularly comprehensive insurance (as was the case with too many Americans), the cost of your care was reduced or covered entirely, provided you agreed to other things—blood taken, dental records shared, genes sifted through—to become "part of progress," as Mrs. Watson, Adele, put it. No one had to sign, he told his patients, prospective or otherwise. Or they could opt that the camera be turned off in the examination room they found themselves in.

He stressed that they had choices, within the clinic, outside it, too: other doctors, other practices, other methods.

But his solicitude only gave them more faith in him. He cared, after all, didn't he? Yes, of course. And then didn't the cameras protect them, too? Yes, maybe so, he told them, but didn't say what he knew too well: People in pain will agree to things, anything, if it means stopping the pain. All at once or over time.

He never hid his professional history from new patients. And then it was all at their fingertips anyway, online: that he'd been part of a controversial pain-management practice for six years, before leaving and making a name for himself as a headache specialist at St. Mary's Hospital, where he engaged in his own revisionist history and focused on the mechanism of pain in the head and body, at stopping the chain of events before they could form any length of chain at all. To calm cellular activity, if not to contain it.

Also part of public record: He was questioned in Sarah's disappearance, and back then, during what was a period of police and of Sarah's friends and family posting appeal after appeal and offering rewards for information through social media and the press, the pain-management practice became news again, another story line to follow. Its partnerships and approaches, its role in a larger national story. Did Sarah vanish because of overdose, suicide? Was malpractice to blame?

Patients fell for their doctors all the time, but didn't doctors fall for patients, too? And Sarah? Such a pretty girl.

There was nothing to find there, but it didn't matter: It was years since he'd left the practice, and he was still apologizing for that moment's answer to treating pain. His former wife, Jacqueline, Jackie, his only wife, also a neurologist, had insisted that he join the pain-management practice she was establishing with an old crony anesthesiologist.

The timing had been perfect, and tragic: Pharmaceutical companies had declared a "war on pain" with strong opioids, drugs that to date had largely been prescribed to cancer patients. Lavish trips were on offer for participating doctors. Jackie came home from weekends in Las Vegas and the Virgin Islands tanned and happy and *proud*, she'd say, to be a doctor, a fighter in a war in which she could wear Prada.

But the party couldn't last. It never should have started.

Of course, theirs wasn't the only practice that had been compromised and that found itself with a population of patients whose bodies were being rewritten internally. They became more rather than less sensitive to the pain in their bodies—developing something close cellularly to neuropathic pain. They couldn't function with or without the medicines, and for many, the euphoria, the pleasure, was worth whatever it cost them. Then there was the public bearing witness, increasingly outraged and sharing their outrage in every possible forum and linking it with others' until it was its own force field.

He should have walked away sooner. It didn't matter that he almost never prescribed these drugs to his patients. Even then, the majority of his patients were, like Sarah, headache sufferers, not just of migraine in all its variety, but tension, sinus, and cluster headaches and those that resulted from injuries—patients his colleagues didn't want, given how variable headaches and headache sufferers' needs could be, how hard to treat with any reliable rate of success. What was predictable was how poorly his headache patients responded to analgesic opioids.

No, his staying on at the practice was itself bound up in a greater mistake: choosing his wife not once but over and over, with every day he did not leave the practice and leave her.

Sarah had been his wife's patient first, and that fact involved Sarah in more than professional politics. She saw and heard things, watched him change practices and lives. Whenever she asked him about his wife, he'd been constrained in his replies.

"Will you remain friends after the divorce?" Sarah had asked after the separation, more than once, to check, he supposed, whether his answer would change. The Doctor said yes each time, because he was supposed to. But he and Jackie weren't friends. They'd never been. Sarah had to know that she could confess to things that he could not. And she did—she still was.

I don't think romantic love ends—I think it becomes something else if we let it. Its opposite: hatred. It can become that so easily, can't it? But to hate him? That would be way too easy, wouldn't it? No, it's me I hate. I take the blame. Because I should have known. I shouldn't have gone so far. I kept telling myself this is the last time I'll see him, and THIS is the last time, this is really the last. But it never was. Each time. It isn't. I can't stop.

Ruth

A woman answered the door to 10 Linden Place. Ruth tried not to stare at her: the cinnamon-colored skin, shorn black hair, big, lucid brown eyes, and a mouth that could sell lipstick, and how the woman hid herself behind overlarge horn-rimmed glasses, a blue dress shirt, khakis.

She didn't let Ruth in straightaway. She stepped through the entryway to make sure the door behind Ruth was closed before guiding her in through the final door.

"Forgive me. With the wind, I have to make sure this is shut before we go in. Here we go."

They stepped into the house's high foyer and into a tinkling of glass, so much of it, like the sound of a spell being cast. It was a chandelier, suspended overhead, what looked like hundreds of malformed icicles, each piece of blown glass stabbed through with lines of light.

"This is rather fragile. A gift to Mrs. Watson by an artist friend, but it does have its . . . "The woman paused, waiting for the parts of the chandelier to quiet down some: It didn't take much for vibration to have its way with it.

"Charms," the woman said softly, still looking up. "Yes," she agreed with herself, then hummed for a breath or two, as if lulling the light overhead.

"I'm here for an appointment?"

The woman looked Ruth over for the first time, from the white scrub dress to her new white sneakers. "Of course, yes. Let's get you situated. This way."

"I'm Ruth—Ruth Aitken," she told the woman's back as her sneakers squeaked on the floor down the long hall and away from the entryway and its chief feature besides the chandelier—a domineering staircase, paneled in a dark, muscular wood.

"Yes. Ruth. I recall your résumé. I'm Marie. I work for Mrs. Watson."

Ruth was led into a sitting room.

An even darker wood paneled this room, formed the ceiling, shelves, a mantel and the trim of an open-mouthed fireplace. Throughout were more pieces of blown glass of molten shapes, sizes, and colors, including a large light fixture, which called to mind a firework caught mid-explosion, a thousand wriggling arms of dimly lit golden-orange glass.

There were a few sculptures, too, some representational, others more abstract. Most conjured the body or its parts: busts, twisting torsos, legs, feet, some made of metal, others stone.

If the wind were to get into the room and introduce fragile to hard and vice versa, there would be such a smashing. But the long windows were shut and thickly curtained.

Before leaving her, Marie directed Ruth to sit in some sort of elaborately carved Asian-style chair. Another one like it was to its side. On the cocktail table between the chairs and a deep-bottomed sofa was an uncorked bottle of red wine, along with two glasses.

It took a moment for Ruth to see how the room was meant to work—that every object was acting on the wood framing the room, brightening it, bringing out the patterns in it, demanding it not be so stolid, so wooden, but as alive as it once was.

Somewhere music came on in the room, but from a sound system and speakers Ruth couldn't see. A tension of stringed instruments filling in to begin, in no hurry, and then, after an interval, one woman's voice rose in one long note, not pleading but calling, up and up without evidence of a breath taken. Then another higher voice followed, echoing the first, the strings arching under them, helping them rise. Ruth nearly gasped, so startling were the voices, so strange and lovely, stretching every second of the one or two minutes that Ruth heard. Then it was turned off. Without explanation. As if it had been an accident.

More minutes then passed, of such stark silence—except for the wind, which seemed far away in there, in the wooden or unwooden room, its pressure making the house tick at its joints—that Ruth wondered if she shouldn't leave while she still could.

Ruth stood at the sound of a girlish but commanding voice: "Please don't get up." But she would have to get up to cross to the woman, who did not cross to her, and offer her hand.

"Mrs. Watson? I'm Ruth—"

"Yes, yes, I know who you are."

Mrs. Watson, under the same curls her son had, though pulled up and piled in an elegance on her head, and wearing dark sunglasses, gave Ruth's hand more of a yank than a shake. She wasn't tall—shorter than Ruth—but the force and intention coming off her was a high-speed train's, or the sun's. What Ruth could see of her face was that it was heart-shaped in the way of actresses from the 1930s and '40s. A dagger of a widow's peak in her hairline accentuated the effect, as did the pointedness of her small chin.

"Do sit."

The lady of the house wore red capri pants and a man's white dress shirt. Strands of fat pearls draped her neck and poured down her front. She inserted herself into the corner of her plush sofa and didn't speak until her pearls had settled.

"Well, Ruth," Mrs. Watson said, as if to say, "Here you are."

There was no reply to this, but Ruth nodded anyway.

"You've been a nurse for ten years, I understand? Bedside nurse mostly? Hospitals, yes?"

"Eleven years. I worked in the neonatal intensive care unit. Before that I did oncology for a time. Gynecological."

"My. That, I must say"—Mrs. Watson curled her fingers in her pearls, round and round—"to me, that sounds like a nightmare."

"The oncology—"

"That, yes, and, well, *all* of it frankly. You must be made of sturdy stuff."

"It's the job. Stress. Some tears or a lot, but there are gifts. The women, the babies—there are miracles."

"In New Hampshire?"

"Well," Ruth laughed a little. This woman was a roller-coaster ride already. "I suppose they can happen anyplace."

"Forgive me: I mean you worked where?"

"Oh, yes, in a hospital on the coast there."

"Not much coast in New Hampshire."

"Enough, I suppose."

Eighteen miles of coast that stretched into Maine on one side, Massachusetts on the other. New England coast no matter the state it happened to be in.

"Cold sea," Mrs. Watson said, and shivered. "So *very* cold."

"The Atlantic, yes."

"The job we have available is at a headache clinic. Do you know much about headaches, or migraines in particular?"

"I know a fair amount—I've read a fair amount. And our patients often experienced headaches as a side effect of medications or the anesthesia—"

"Do you get them?"

"I've had a headache, like most—but I don't regularly."

"Lucky you. I do. Since I was a little girl. Migraines. They aren't really headaches at all. Seizures. They're a curse if, like me, you have them often enough. An oversensitivity to stimuli."

"I'm sorry."

"Don't be. I manage."

Mrs. Watson leaned forward and looked at the open bottle of wine on the table, deciding, it appeared, whether she'd pour some. Or some more; maybe she was a little drunk already.

"But the good news, Ruth, is that I have found a doctor I believe in. In fact, I believe in him so much that I'm funding a clinic, *our* clinic, just down the street."

"I'm certainly familiar," Ruth stressed, "with pain. Nurses—we have to manage patients' pain, in whatever form it comes."

"Yes, I'd imagine … " Mrs. Watson sighed, let her head fall back into the sofa. Sighed again, turned her face away. "Ruth?"

"Yes?"

"I saw you come to our door, from the window. I saw you speak with my son. May I ask what he said to you?"

"Nothing, really. He confirmed that I had the right address."

"Is that all?"

"Mainly."

"Ruth, we're not going to get along at all well if you can't be straightforward with me. I do prize that. It saves so much time, and you strike me as a practical person." She adjusted the bulky glasses on her face, squaring them and her regard at Ruth.

"He said I looked like the Flying Nun in what he called my costume. In the wind."

"You don't." Mrs. Watson swatted her hand at the comment and perhaps at her son. "Professional attire is just that. And it shows a certain willingness."

"Willingness?" asked Ruth.

"To play a part."

"I'm a trained nurse." Ruth tried not to sound indignant or petulant. Instead she sounded young, when, at thirty-four, she didn't feel young and hadn't for some time. "I'm here to work as a nurse. What sort of uniform I wear doesn't matter to me."

"I'm not saying you're not the real article. It's clear you are. You look every bit the part, *are* the part, and I'm in awe, frankly. I am. But you've come to the city because you want something different? By now? I imagine you want to be paid properly for a change? While getting away from where you've been, from all that… what?… "

When Mrs. Watson went rummaging for words, Ruth's car on the roller coaster of their conversation went up, only to drop when Mrs. Watson found what she was looking for and seized on it: "*Tragedy*. All that *tragedy*."

Ruth had heard that word too much in her life, in the corridors and rooms of the hospital, in public places whispered around her, and in her own home, trailing her too close, as if it was tied to her ankle.

"Can I offer you a glass of wine, Ruth?"

Drunk or sober, Mrs. Watson had to be testing Ruth, offering a nurse wine during a job interview in the early afternoon.

"No. No, thank you."

"I shouldn't drink it, but then this life is about reaching for the things we want, isn't it? Not indiscriminately, no, but to reach for what gives us life, to taste these things. Or else..." Mrs. Watson did not finish her sentence, so Ruth did, in her head—she couldn't help herself: *Or else become invisible? Or else crumble like leaves and blow away?*

"What else did my son say? You were out there long enough that I didn't realize you'd been shown in. I was putting on some music. A kind of medicine for me... I'm feeling a migraine coming, but then one always is."

"He called you lively."

"That's all? Well, then I got off easy today." She gave a rich laugh and removed her dark glasses to touch her fingers to her temples.

"Oh, I shouldn't laugh. The migraine: It starts on one side, then travels. And the nausea: a nasty bonus, and the weather has been no help. *None*. This *ridiculous* wind."

Mrs. Watson's eyes were the green of young ferns, the kind Ruth had walked through in the woods in Rye, the New Hampshire town where she grew up, and her brows and lashes were dark and all the darker against her light, live hair. Mrs. Watson had to be sixty-something, maybe seventy, and she was beautiful.

"But I have *my* doctor. You'll meet him. This is only part one of the interview, you see. You'll be working for both of us but mostly with him, his staff, and his patients, for whom headaches aren't just headaches. You'll report to me, however, keep me informed. He's from New England, too. So you'll have that in common. Dr. Berger, *Louis*, has ability. Great ability"—Mrs. Watson seemed to shudder and crossed her arms around herself—"so it's little wonder people fall for him. And why shouldn't they? He's good-looking and sober as a vault, so he takes in every word, you know, and with those eyes of his—it's just so powerful to heal, isn't it? There's disorder, dis-*ease*, and a good doctor or nurse—I'm not leaving nurses out—can give *ease*, order of some kind... You're no stranger to this, are you?"

"No."

"But I don't imagine you develop attachments, given your experiences?"

Ruth felt queasy. The woman had to be drunk. "My experiences? As a nurse, you mean?"

"Now, Ruth, please don't be coy. The internet gives us so much with just the right arrangement of words typed in." Mrs. Watson's fingers worked her temple as she continued: "Marie, whom you met, excels at research. You can understand we'd want some background on those whom we let into our... homes? Our lives?"

Ruth blushed, and the heat now in her throat and face burned. She hoped her private life would be allowed its privacy, that she could be new in a new place.

"We don't judge here," Mrs. Watson said.

Ruth's voice stiffened: "Then that would be exceptional."

"Well, I will take that as a compliment, Ruth. I don't see a thing wrong with what you did, I mean with your husband of course. You did what you had to do to protect yourself. We all have to fight for our lives, don't we? In one way or another? I'll answer that: *We do*. Your fight was merely more dramatic and... what?"

Ruth wouldn't answer. She wanted to stop her ears, run. She decided to leave at the first opportunity. *Murderer. Bitch. Whore.*

"Prosaic?" Mrs. Watson landed on this decisively. "Yes, at once dramatic and *prosaic*. Same old fight. I had plenty in my marriage, too. Different weapons, that's all."

Ruth stood up. "I can't discuss this. If this is part of the job, me discussing this, I'll have to decline. Thank you for your time."

A slight smile crossed Mrs. Watson's face. "How I love you New Englanders. How I *love* this reserve."

Mrs. Watson poured two glasses of wine.

"Did you hear that music? That bit of it before I came in? Isn't it glorious? It's Pergolesi's *Stabat Mater*, and that was the first movement, 'Stabat Mater Dolorosa,' about the sorrows of Mary. I'll play more of it for you if you'd like. If you'll sit."

Ruth didn't sit. She collected her coat from the back of the chair, draped it over her arm.

"Truth is, Ruth, you're the only one I'd like for this position. I wanted to see you first. You're the only one I'm interviewing today, because I think you are well suited to understand the job's... *complexities*? Yes. Its *nuances*. I'll even improve the pay, if you'll sit."

Ruth remained standing, legs locked against a scream rising in her. "Thank you for your time, but I must—"

Mrs. Watson barged through her parting line: "This wood on the walls is black walnut. Difficult not to notice it, isn't it? I was going to tear it all out when my husband died, but then I learned more about the tree and its wood. It's valuable, rare, and every day more so. When alive, it secretes a poison. But the poison is selective. It kills some things, like tomato plants or alfalfa, blueberries or rhododendron bushes, but the poison actually promotes other things, or at least doesn't harm them: beans, beets, corn, raspberries, even poison ivy. This fighting for survival is a fascination, isn't it? Right down to the... poison ivy. But you know more about it than most, don't you? You're a fighter?"

Ruth didn't answer, but she didn't leave. She'd counted on this working out. She was living on the very last of her savings. She had managed to pay for a sublet and could cover only the deposit and first month, and the salary promised for a trained nurse in the post at the clinic was more than she'd seen anywhere else in this city or beyond it.

"Taste this wine for me, Ruth? Before you go? Please? Just one sip. It's a Burgundy, 2007, pricey, a gift from one of my tenants. Now it's my gift to you, for coming. Or an apology? I can be, well, pointed—"

"I shouldn't." Ruth's anger for its suddenness left her depleted. It always happened, but now it made her feel too aware of how desperately alone she'd been for so very long. And how disoriented. She needed this to work. For *something* to.

"I'll put your glass here. You think about it, okay?" She gave Ruth a smile that Ruth felt blooming inside her even after Mrs. Watson voided her face of it, though she left it in her voice, high and lilting, a girl's, a confiding friend's.

Mrs. Watson was seducing Ruth, and they both knew it.

"Do you know your mythology, Ruth? Who Asclepius is? Or Ophiuchus?"

Ruth shook her head. Lowered herself to sit on the edge of the hard chair.

"Don't worry—no one does anymore. Or maybe you know your constellations? I imagine the stars in your part of the world are something to see?"

Ruth missed those stars that the city light deprived her of. She knew some constellations—the bears, Ursa Major and Minor, which were the Big and Little Dippers. Cassiopeia. And she could sometimes make out Scorpio in the night sky, because she was one, a child of mid-November.

"I call the Doctor 'Ophiuchus' or sometimes 'Asclepius.' He pretends not to be flattered by it, but I think he is. He knows he's the best there is, that the clinic will help to change things. He will, but he's haunted, and that can be preoccupying at the very least. I think you understand that, don't you, Ruth? That we all have our ghosts? We've earned them, haven't we? Just have a sip. Go on. There's no one here but us."

Ruth reached for the glass.

"The constellation Ophiuchus has always been associated with the healer Asclepius, the son of Apollo. Asclepius could raise the dead. But Hades, the ruler of the underworld, would be out of business if Apollo's son could bring everyone back to life, so he asked Zeus to kill Asclepius. And Zeus did, with a lightning bolt, and he was placed in the stars afterward, as a constellation. That's a hell of a lot better than a coffin—"

Ruth tasted the wine.

"How is it? Delicious?"

It was, and it gave Ruth's tongue black cherries and nutmeg and summer sidewalks after the rain. And the room, so crowded with art, was otherworldly and Ruth was too tired, years too tired now, to resist after all.

"Shall I join you? What do you think? Say yes, Ruth, say yes."

Sarah

Another doctor told me that like 95% of who you are and will be is determined by the age of two or three. He talked on and on about genes, and what happened to you inside your mother's body and what happened once you got out, if you got all the right care.

That I'm in pain so often, he told me, is out of my control—"by and large," he said flatly, like it was common sense and that was the medicine I needed. Like it could help me give in. Surrender to my "condition"—to my body, like some tomb. It didn't. The more matter-of-fact he was—that's life, he said—the more resistant I became, and right there in his Park Avenue office I resolved to make whatever home I could in the narrowness of that 5%, where there's free will for me, some remedy, for the misfires, mistakes. Life. How many of us live in that 5%? Are stretching it out into the whole world? My doctor, my friend, at least that, tell me, how do you confine hope?

The Doctor

He touched the word *hope* on the page and traced the shape of her question mark.

He had put the journal away, for weeks and weeks. Didn't touch it. Said *enough*.

Stop.

But it kept at him, kept talking. So he'd opened it again—let it come back, all the words in the right order—while outside his door someone, probably Izzy, cried, "Truffle oil! Sweet Lord! Europe's very own musk, *alive* on the tongue!"

There was more laughter.

The lights flickered once, twice, then stabilized. It happened often with the wind. It was barely noticed anymore. The phone rang. At this hour, with Sue gone, he had three rings to pick up before it went to the answering service. He looked at the caller ID: The number belonged to a medical practice. His ex-wife's. She did not like to be kept waiting. Ever. Particularly by him. But the call wouldn't be short. It wouldn't be simple. When Jackie needed him, it never was.

He shut the journal until the phone stopped ringing and then opened it again.

He never asked Sarah to confine her hope. Or her desire. That wasn't what he expected of her or any of his patients. Only balance—not to lose sight of which excesses in lifestyle or behavior could harm them. Sarah managed to self-regulate for so very long, but that had changed in the course of one night. The man, whom she referred to in her journal as P., had come into Sarah's life while the Doctor was treating her. A man sorely in need of diversion.

Regarding that change, that night, which led to other days and other nights, the Doctor couldn't stop asking himself how he might have protected her. How might he have done differently, better? He didn't know what he did now, only that she was in over her head with a man. She admitted as much to him during her last appointment. But would it have mattered if he had known once it began and she'd begun to change?

P. likes to say he is the cure for me, and I can't help but want to believe him. I haven't had a headache, <u>not one</u>, in days and days. I haven't taken anything but him, Doctor. This is evidence, isn't it? Quantifiable. Worthy of recording here. Worthy of your recording. It's been weeks now that I've felt like another woman in another woman's body.

A neuropsychiatrist the Doctor had met at a conference in Berkeley had once described the massive unlearning the brain went through when a man or woman fell in love, how neuromodulators disrupted the workings of synapses, the communicating links between neurons in the brain. Existing connections just gave way as the hormone oxytocin, a powerful neuromodulator, was released so that changes in the brain could take place on an impressive scale.

During orgasm, oxytocin drenched the brain, especially women's brains, which had more receptors for the hormone than did men's. It facilitated contraction during labor, was released during breastfeeding.

It was one of the brain's most effective painkillers, never mind how it persuaded people to pair up and keep pairing up by way of something as slight as touch and as forceful as sexual satisfaction.

He'd tried to explain this to Sarah, at that last appointment, without involving the personal or compromising anyone's privacy—how the body can fool us, betray us, through so many pathways in the brain and the chemicals that travel them, too: dopamine signaling the electric high of pleasure, adrenaline and norepinephrine making our hearts race and our palms sweat, testosterone supporting feelings of lust, and vasopressin, working with oxytocin, helping to consolidate attachment. It was science, after all, and then, in truth, it embarrassed him, how defenseless he himself had once been as a man, then a husband, in love. No different, no stronger, no better than anyone else.

If he'd told Sarah about his own experience, would it have helped at all? That he still had to make concerted efforts not to call to mind the particular scents, sounds, sensations of his married life, still there under his fingertips, alive on his tongue, the very taste of his wife?

Now he would tell Sarah, tell her everything: that how his marriage began said everything about why it lasted longer than it should have, why he agreed to things he shouldn't have.

He knew the order he'd tell it in, too, starting with medical school, where he'd had to work hard because he knew there was no going back to his life before it—the tree business with his father. He was first in the class, where Jackie wanted to be. If she couldn't beat him in class or in the lab, she'd have him in the bedroom, and she did, going to shocking lengths to stupefy him and his own susceptible brain, just as Sarah's lover had done to her.

And then he'd have to go back even further, explain he'd grown up in Bennington, Vermont, where the fifties lingered into the decades that followed, well into the eighties and nineties, when he was a boy and a teenager. Jackie reminded him of the girls he'd grown up with, many, like him, of recent French Canadian ancestry, girls who by high school had forcibly shaped themselves into cheerleaders, that stubborn American ideal of the adolescent female. It wasn't just their prettiness or, really, the approximating of pretty in high ponytails and tight letter sweaters that captivated him, but the energy—the exclamations and legs thrown in the air as if the body had no weight and never would. But these girls had found him too quiet. Mysterious maybe, but mystery took effort.

They didn't know the value of his hands. Neither did he, not yet. Jackie did. And how he wore that white physician's coat. "You *are* the coat," she'd say. When they graduated, he and his classmates, Jackie included, recited their oath together while wearing their white coats. What had been the Hippocratic Oath became the Declaration of Geneva or simply the physician's oath. *Primum non nocere*: *First, do no harm*. Always that, and for him, always this, just as they'd recited it: *The health of my patient will be my first consideration. I will respect the secrets that are confided in me, even after the patient has died. I will maintain, by all the means in my power, the honor and the noble traditions of the medical profession. My colleagues will be my sisters and brothers.*

They'd all taken it seriously then, after the endurance race they'd run and won, but he never stopped.

He ironed his own lab coats before he was married and after, and he knew that while wearing one he listened better and absorbed more fully what was related to him. There was something in it, something alchemical, that not even Jackie could take from him, though she'd tried. "Baby, baby, baby, let me in there," she would plead with him. She wanted him to understand the limits of his power, his will. "Keep the coat on, huh? For me?" And he did, with her naked beneath him. God, yes. "Heal me, baby. Heal *me*."

A wince—little by little he'd come to hear Adele Watson's voice in his wife's. They didn't resemble each other, the two women, save in their energies: thrusting, daring, and always claiming something or someone. Territory. "Mine" insinuating itself into every exchange. They were never tentative. They never asked questions that they didn't already know the answers to. "Is the doctor in?" asked Mrs. Watson, making a mockery of what little boundaries he could call his anymore and of any purity of purpose or method: If not to be a good man, then at least to be a good doctor. "Dear Ophiuchus, are you there? Or in the night sky? Can you hear me from way up there?"

Ruth

Ruth couldn't pinpoint the moment she'd become drunk from the wine. From the music—yes, that was easier. Before they'd finished their first glass, Mrs. Watson located a remote control on a side table, from behind a lamp. And from somewhere still out of view—speakers built into walls or ceiling or floor—came the instrumental introduction Ruth had heard earlier, with violins ascending and then retreating, in little licks, only to advance again.

Mrs. Watson let Ruth hear the whole of the first movement of Pergolesi's *Stabat Mater*—"Stabat Mater Dolorosa"—without any commentary or conversation. She let it swell up in Ruth, rearrange and soften her while she watched, and then asked, "Shall I play that again?"

"Yes."

"More?" Mrs. Watson offered the bottle.

Ruth lifted the glass by its stem to her hostess and angled in to see and smell the wine poured. She'd told herself she'd have only one glass with Mrs. Watson, then go, parting with an alert handshake.

Another tap on that remote and the music took over the room again. Ruth closed her eyes and tried to parse the shocks one by one, from the introduction, already hinting at how sustained flight could be achieved, to that opening note sung by one female voice, a note extending with what sounded like *star* but what she knew now must be *stah*, the first syllable of *Stabat*, from the piece's title, before the second female voice, higher in pitch (Ruth had been right about that), began, an interval behind.

Then the two voices came together—another shock—sang the lines together, singing what precisely Ruth couldn't say, only that it meant to take you up with it.

At the end of the first movement, Ruth's glass was empty again. She'd swallowed at every shock. She had never tasted anything so good.

"Sit by me," said Mrs. Watson. "You'll be more comfortable."

Ruth got up to let herself sink into the wide-bottomed couch and leaned her head back.

"Shall we hear that once more?"

"Please," Ruth said, her backbone giving in to the cushion. "*Please*."

Another bottle arrived, already opened, and Mrs. Watson talked and then did not, let the music talk, and then she talked again; she explained and confessed, whispered and sighed.

"This is the Passion. Mary is there, bearing witness to her son's fate on the cross."

Her voice trailed off and returned: "Translated from the Latin, *Stabat mater dolorosa* is 'The mother stood sorrowing,' or 'in pain,' or, if you'd rather, simply 'The sorrowful mother stood.' *Juxta crucem lacrimosa*: 'by the cross, weeping.' *Dum pendebat filius*: 'while her son was suspended there.' That is the scene, but it's the music that tells us what is *really* happening. What do you hear, Ruth?"

Ruth heard how inexhaustible meals were being made of the words, over so many syllables, how *dolorosa* went on for miles inside her.

"Is she calling to God—to end her son's suffering? Or is she expressing *I'm here* to her son, to God? It's bold, isn't it? *Hear me, see me.* How excruciating for this Mary of the story, and yet the music here lifts us—"

Ruth only nodded and nodded.

"Here is someone defying suffering with the sheer reach of her voice. It's an invitation to all of us, whether you're a believer or not, a mother or—"

The two voices came together again—*Dum pendebat filius*—and were supported by all the instruments with such volume of dimension and space that it seemed that what the composer was building was both of the earth and already above, beyond it.

"We are never more alive than when we are in pain, are we, Ruth? Never more caught in what it is to be alive?" And then Mrs. Watson drew close to Ruth's ear: "Love is pain for so many of us, yes, Ruth?"

"Yes," Ruth replied in a thick whisper before she could stop herself.

"But Pergolesi is showing just how beautiful our feeling can be, how alive we can be even in our darkness, to *transport, transcend.*"

The voices separated again, the alto trailed the soprano again before they returned to *stah*—

"My husband gave me several recordings. This is an Italian orchestra, which seems fitting to me. Pergolesi was Italian and he composed this in Italy, at a monastery in Pozzuoli, when he was ill with what they think was tuberculosis. Yes, this is the Orchestra Rossini di Napoli, and the soprano is Judith Raskin. She was from Yonkers—that's here in the city, up north. I mean, imagine! From Yonkers to Naples—"

A vowel turned a vehicle of sound—the soprano scaling up and up again. It was a cathedral or a skyscraper she was making—not made from pride but from longing.

"I don't think my husband fully appreciated the work until the end of his life. I cared for him when he became ill, like a mother would. We listened together. He was mine then. He wasn't faithful to me during our marriage. But I loved him. I did. He was a plastic surgeon. That should have been a warning, no? Dear God, that *man,* but had he done to me what yours did—"

Did she just say that—"what yours did"? Ruth wasn't sure at first, though she was soon enough, with what came next:

"I would have killed him," Mrs. Watson said. "Made sure of it."

The movement ended and the quiet between them constricted.

"Shall I play it again?"

Ruth turned her head away, closed her eyes.

"You were raised in the Christian faith, I assume? Catholic maybe?"

"Yes."

"My stepmother was Catholic. I thought her magnificent. I wanted her to myself, but that was not meant to be. Did I mention Pergolesi died at twenty-six? A child. And isn't it a wonder that this is as close to perfection as most of us are going to get? A composition by a young person, a man barely a man, and so afflicted..."

Mrs. Watson inclined again to Ruth's ear. "My son," she confided, just above a whisper, "he hates me/he loves me. He's gay/he's straight. He's happy/he's sad. He's a musician. A designer. An entrepreneur. My son tortures me by refusing to be any one thing, but I can take it. I can. You're strong, Ruth, so you understand when we must be plain, and when there are other approaches at our disposal, more indirect, to use one's resources, for everyone's..." Mrs. Watson went in search of the word she wanted as she bent to start the music again. "For everyone's *betterment*. Because left to themselves, most people want to sleep, not think, not feel anything unpleasant. It's a grave mistake to believe life is meant to be kind to us. We will get nothing done, create nothing lasting, if we can't confront—"

Mrs. Watson did not finish her sentence but exhaled slowly and touched Ruth's hand. It startled Ruth, but the music had started again and she was too entranced to jump or pull her hand away. And it occurred to her that she didn't want to—how long had it been since she'd touched anyone or anyone had touched her without making her want to run?

She wrapped her fingers around Mrs. Watson's, and soon felt the woman's hand was wet. She turned to see tears on Mrs. Watson's face, dripping from her jaw.

"It hurts," said Mrs. Watson. "It hurts more than I can say."

Ruth thought she understood: All of human life was in this music Mrs. Watson was sharing with Ruth. The struggle to love. The struggle to let go of those you love. Or to refuse to. Human striving didn't have to be so sordid and small-making. Couldn't it be as momentous as this music? As dignifying, even as it hurt?

God, yes, she wanted to cry out. *Yes.* Mrs. Watson hadn't scolded Ruth or counseled more self-restraint, as everyone else had, her friends and family. Suffering had made Ruth's mother nearly silent, except with judgment, fear. *I would have killed him.* Did Mrs. Watson really say that to Ruth? Yes, and she would have laughed at the audacity if it wasn't what she'd been needing to hear from someone. But of course none of it had been planned. She'd only reacted: given what she'd gotten from her husband, in what she judged to be the same proportion of enmity, using her hands, if she had to, and she did that day when he came running at her, swearing at her. She was all too ready to defend herself, her life, from him and his cheap, base violence, but he'd survived and was changed by his injury. He became someone else entirely, this sweet fool, and he trailed behind her still, a man reduced to a pitiable creature, whom, God help her, she loved still. And that was pitiable, too.

She took Mrs. Watson's hand, gathered it in both of hers. "Yes," Ruth said, "it does hurt. It hurts so much," and she felt she might cry, too, from relief, gratitude.

No one had ever spoken to Ruth quite like this woman was—whatever the contrivances, she cut right through the posturing and pretense. Surely Mrs. Watson wouldn't hold tears against Ruth. Weren't they two women mourning how strong they had to be, whatever their own injuries and imperfections, how hunted by circumstances that they couldn't have foreseen?

"Yes, Ruth, yes," Mrs. Watson said, "but it's my head, I mean. *It* hurts. The headache. I must call Louis, Dr. Berger. We must get Marie to bring the phone. *Now,* Ruth. *Now.* Please, Ruth."

Mrs. Watson drew her hand away and put it to her head, then over her eyes.

Taking the remote, Ruth stopped the music, and for the first time during her visit to 10 Linden Place, she heard the wind outside, trilling like a teakettle at full boil. She stood up and into that unwooden room, into all its gorgeous eccentricity. Her scrub dress was wrinkled. What had Mrs. Watson said about it? How it expressed a willingness to play a part? She wasn't entirely sober when she left to search out Marie, but as her shoes squeaked down the hall, she realized she was willing—she'd wanted to take the older woman in her arms and hold on. She'd do whatever she had to do to play this part.

The Doctor

"Wake up!" a voice called from the other side of the Doctor's door. A woman's.

Sound carried in the clinic. The church's basement was as vast as it was because it was designed with room enough not only for a crypt, but to be a safe house for as many people as might need it if the anti-Catholic, anti-immigrant sentiment in New York in the 1800s—when the church was built—became a full-scale holy war. The church's Irish Catholic architect made certain his version of Saint Gabriel's news from God would be anchored wide and deep in the ground. Then Mrs. Watson had added concrete floors and a labyrinth of treatment-room walls, off of which voices bounced and were rerouted.

"Why gamble?! *Why would you risk it?!"*

It sounded like Jane, another of the Doctor's patients. She worked for the ACLU, was Japanese American, and dyed her short hair white-blond. At twenty-seven, she was thin as a birch branch, and as stinging when wielded.

He cracked his door. It let go a breath, but the climate control hummed over it. His dreaminess was worse than usual, and he had almost no inclination to resist it.

"I said it's a trigger *sometimes*," Christine pleaded, "if I don't moderate but—"

"It's all about controlling inflammation, that's the bottom line—"

"Magnesium levels, you have to keep at—" someone put in.

"Sleep—good, regular sleep, how many hours do you—"

"That CGRP block—" someone put in hopefully.

A reference to a drug long in development and touted as a cure: a calcitonin gene-related peptide antagonist. It was no cure, but for some of those who'd participated in its trials it had reduced their attacks by half. It worked best as an injection, could cause, to varying degrees, rash, weight gain, constipation, fatigue, anxiety, and tachycardia, and could be prohibitively expensive besides. Still, if something worked for one of his patients, that patient couldn't help believe it the answer for others too. They got trapped in solution making, and never just for themselves.

"Sex. It's a big help for—"

"C'mon, Albert! *Please!* Not that shit again!"

Yelling now.

"We're all adults here—"

"Don't—" That was definitely Jane. "*Don't fucking touch me*, Albert!"

"Don't fucking touch her!" And that was definitely Adam's voice.

The Doctor reached for his coat. Once he went out to them, their privacy would be lost. So would his, but he stayed nearby through many of the support-group meetings because he knew that what often began as fellow feeling, concern, could turn like a squall into a venting of desperation, someone fighting to win not just a battle but a drawn-out war. And with the weather bearing down…

How can I stop it? Now and forever?

Like Sarah, Jane was diagnosed young, and her auras, like Sarah's, weren't the usual onslaught of jagged lines or scintillating lights. They approached hallucinations, visual and auditory: disembodied eyes and mouths, someone somewhere coughing, growling. Over the past year Jane had developed fibromyalgia and extreme allodynia, sensitization of the skin so intense during an episode that for a period after, she couldn't bear to be touched. Even her hair hurt.

"I have rage," Jane had told the Doctor at her first appointment at the clinic. Adam had it, too: He was too young to have a body and mind he couldn't trust, but he did, like so many veterans of the recent wars. The Doctor couldn't blame either of them. No one could. But he could try to contain them when it impacted the welfare of his other patients.

"I only reached for her hand!" pleaded Albert, a patient of the clinic for a year or so, with variable insurance and a painter boyfriend named Eduardo. Albert was a gregarious man and given to wearing fedoras until the new weather made that impossible.

"Can you at least take that stupid helmet off when you're inside, Albert?" Jane must have been referring to Albert's German motorcycle half helmet. Vintage head- and eyewear had become popular in the new weather.

"If Albert wants to play with the hats or the sex, and Christine wants to drink espresso, why not?" soothed Alla, a regular of the support groups. Her accent was Russian, and her way in the world, much like her figure, voluptuous. "We do not argue here. We listen, we co-misery, or shut the big, mad mouth. We are kind because the pain is not."

Someone huffed out what the Doctor took for a theatrical breath. Everyone waited until Jane said at last, her voice straining, "I'm sorry, Albert. I'm a bitch sometimes, okay? But it's that Christine's trip to Italy was ruined. *Ruined.* And it just makes me really sad, okay? Pisses me off. It just does—"

"Excuse me, but fuck this," Adam interrupted. "I'm going to find somewhere to sleep."

The Doctor heard the walls shift. Did they hear it too, the wind trying to find them, as Jane steadied herself and Adam stalked off?

"I mean, look at her: Christine is like the total package—*you are!*—and her plans keep getting—"

"You don't have to tell me, Jane. I *love* Christine," Albert hurried to say. "She's like a cross between Pink and Deborah Kerr—"

"*Derailed,*" Jane barged through. "It shouldn't be that way, okay? People like us? Sometimes we should get what we hope for, what we *want.*"

That deprivation—a story they all knew well. Someone—who?—had said it made for great artists, and doctors, too. *Heal thyself.*

"Christine went to Italy: That's her *happy fucking place*, and Jesus *fucking* Christ, what happened? The harm alarm went off, right? She just told all of us—she was *imprisoned* in her room."

During her appointment earlier in the week, Christine had described it that way to the Doctor, too. Her boyfriend was widowed, like her. After two years of dating, she looked forward to a proposal—and, yes, in her favorite place, Tuscany—but her migraines meant he went sightseeing and drinking wine alone or in the company of strangers. "And that room smelled of mildew," she told him.

"Mildew? Ah, no," he said and sighed to grieve a fact implicit between them: that migraine sufferers' sense of smell, indeed all their senses, become heightened before and during an attack and are in general more sensitive.

"That goddamned room," she said, laughing sadly, and he smiled with her. "I mean—" and she was gone remembering, regretting.

"He came back to me, but his face? He looked—"

She kept the Doctor there with her, suspended, while she saw the man she loved looking at her.

How many times would she visit and revisit that room? What a miracle it was, and what treachery that every time you summoned a memory, you changed the delicate architecture of that memory, not just in the mind's eye, but at a cellular level, from the connections between neurons, across the gaps of their synaptic clefts, to the neurons themselves. It was extraordinary: the brain's industry, its will toward subjectivity, software affecting hardware. Christine's boyfriend's face had looked bored or disappointed or both. It would never appear quite what it was before the trip, when it was a face alive with prospects for her; but, more crucially, would it ever be what it really was that day, in that moment? A man regarding a woman whose head hurt. It made her want to apologize for things in her that were further outside her control than in it.

The Doctor couldn't say how often he saw Jackie, his ex-wife, cold-water surfing on the Massachusetts coast on what was their third date, years and years ago now, but it happened more than he would wish, seeing her, as she was or must have been: wet-suited, sleek, balancing on that wave and flying it to the shore, competing not with the Doctor, who couldn't surf at the time, but with nature. "C'mon!" she yelled at it, this girl from suburban Connecticut, "c'mon!" as if nothing was testing her quite enough. How well he knew her face in any weather: the patrician nose, high, hard cheekbones, and a straight brow that mixed shadow into the blue of her eyes. Even her thick yellow hair seemed made to withstand adverse conditions, like rope used on ships.

For a whole decade he couldn't see an ocean wave of any size without thinking it was lacking without his wife riding it, yelling at it.

And he couldn't see sex on any screen, feel the impulse for it, without his desire for Jackie coming round again, begging.

I tell myself this is the last time, this is really the last…

But there was a last time for him: He knew the day, even the hour, that he stopped choosing his wife.

It happened in a hospital room. Maybe he wasn't recalling the right color on the walls—an anemic yellow—or how sharp and branching the smell of antiseptic was in his nose, but unforgettable was how, all at once, he recognized he had stopped loving her.

He came to Sarah's bedside that day. She had been admitted to the hospital for a migraine that was going on three days and unresponsive to her usual treatments. At that stage she hadn't been the Doctor's patient long—four or five months, if even. Jackie was the first one she'd seen at the clinic, but because of the Doctor's growing specialty in headaches, Jackie eventually referred Sarah to him, all while gently berating him that treating headaches was like shadowboxing or divining for water. It was like predicting and preventing earthquakes. Jackie remembered what his mentor at med school had said to him when the Doctor expressed an interest in the pathology of migraine: "So you'd rather *not* do serious medicine then, Louis? You'd rather spend your days at guesswork? Holding women's hands?"

His wife knew better. She knew the Doctor's mother had suffered from migraines, and she knew something few others did: that the Doctor himself had inherited the condition, but as an infrequent disturbance of his sight, a temporary blindness. It was why he didn't choose surgery. The occurrences he had rarely turned into pain, or if so, nothing ibuprofen couldn't correct. He was lucky, or luckier than most. Living with chronic pain, with migraine, required patience and endurance. It required faith.

Sarah had taught him much on this score. From the start she was what any doctor would want in a pain patient. But that wasn't why his wife had insisted she be consulted on Sarah's case, that she remain one of her doctors of record. It was that Sarah was young and lovely and in need. She brought out things in the Doctor that Jackie couldn't.

How Jackie beat him to the hospital that day, when Sarah was admitted—he still didn't know.

And even now he marveled that Jackie's will to best him was greater than any other impulse in her. She had no instinct to preserve appearances. To protect him from what her appearance in particular that day would say. Or confirm.

She had already ordered one of her preferred opioids be administered by IV to Sarah. At this point, Jackie was still fighting for her practice and its methods, despite the Doctor's telling her with less and less gentleness that they were on the *Titanic*. They were sinking. Couldn't she hold on to him? To anything else but her practice, locked in its current approaches and partnerships?

But there Jackie was in Sarah's hospital room: disheveled, her lips kissed raw, a hickey prospering in purple and climbing her neck from just above her collarbone. She barked at the nurse as the nurse, following protocol, entered the information into the computer station by Sarah's bed.

He knew what Jackie looked like when she'd been making love—that her hair grew in volume and rose up high at the crown, as if teased like a country singer's, that her nose and the tops of her cheeks broke out in patches of red, and that her skin became shiny as waxed fruit. She was supposed to be at the office catching up on paperwork, and perhaps that was where she'd been, fucking one of their colleagues on one of the overpriced, overstuffed office couches or handmade Amish desks. He feared this would happen. When he withdrew his support for how she treated her patients, he'd known she'd find the support elsewhere and maybe even—out of desperation or vengeance—wrap her legs around it.

"Please don't follow through on that order," he said to the nurse. "I am this patient's doctor."

"So am I," said his wife.

The Doctor nodded. "We're from the same practice. But I have privileges here, admitting and visiting, and you, unless I'm mistaken, do not."

Over the past year, the Doctor had begun to search elsewhere for a home for his work and set up the relationship with the hospital as a headache and head trauma specialist on the neurology staff, and let his patients know where they should go if they had an emergency. He'd been contacting friends, associates, and promoting himself in ways he might not deign to otherwise: He wrote a piece for a women's health magazine, titled, preposterously, "How to Hit Back When a Migraine Hits," and extolled the gifts of regular exercise: the release of endorphins and enkephalins, the brain's other naturally occurring painkillers.

And for a popular science magazine he wrote about auras: how the senses were not just heightened but hijacked, for some all the way to waking visions of little pink men, golden horses, or the floating eyes and mouths that Jane saw. There were sounds, too—a recorded piece of symphonic music falling out of tune, or voices heard, or even the persistent hum of chanting or singing.

These were the kinds of articles that employers, especially hospitals and their boards, found highly marketable.

Jackie, of course, hadn't noticed his publishing efforts or whom they were meant to woo. She hadn't bothered to learn about Sarah's triggers, either, or that she often heard and saw things that weren't there.

"I am his wife," Jackie told the nurse.

"She is."

"I'll ask you both to respect my orders," Jackie said.

"Not in this case," he said evenly, though an angry pleading rose up in him that he couldn't give voice to. But inside him he bellowed, the words making him dizzy: "We pledged to do no harm, if not to each other, at least not to her!"

"She's not responding to triptans," Jackie said.

"There's more than one to try, and she can't keep them down so they haven't had a chance to work. I can inject her. There are many routes to reliable relief here. She'll have an antiemetic immediately—"

"My way is the fastest. She's suffering."

"She called our service, yes, but then me, *directly*. I'm sorry, darling. I'm going to have to ask you to leave."

"Ask all you want. I'm not going."

Did she see his expression then as he considered dragging her out by her hair? Could she see it still? He could see her, even now: that hair, the hickey; that her blouse, semi-sheer and sleeveless, wasn't buttoned properly. She'd come in such a blaze that she forgot the trim linen jacket she'd worn over her top when she left that morning.

"You've used painkillers yourself, Doctor," she spat, "and if I remember, you found them plenty efficacious—"

"It's not about you or me. Our history, medical or otherwise. Or is it?"

She didn't answer. Only glared.

"I've explained this. I've shown you the data. Opioids are contraindicated for migraines in most cases. That's for one thing. For another, darling, are you quite sober yourself? You look cold. Are you cold in that… that *shirt*? And have you had a look at that bruise on your neck?"

The nurse stole a look at his wife, then at him.

"What are your orders, Doctor?" the nurse asked, and she looked to him, and only him, to give them.

Jackie was gone before she actually left. She stood there but ceased to be a factor. For the first time in a long time, he couldn't hear the throbbing of her, of her needs, appetites, complaints. He did hear her when she tossed at him, "You'll never get out of there, will you?" but from a far distance. She meant his mother's room, at her bedside, where he spent hours upon hours when he was young and wanted to be elsewhere, outside where he could run and make noise, where he could breathe fresh air, different air.

He couldn't say whether Jackie had already walked out when he reached for Sarah.

His hand circled her ankle through the thin of the hospital sheet. He didn't know then to whisper jokes—he didn't know any, besides. But after the nurse entered his orders, he told Sarah the story she knew well, one she had asked to hear before.

His voice became as low and modulated as a hypnotist's. It caught the nurse, stopped her just as she was leaving:

Migraine is among the most common reasons for visits to the ER.

He could feel Sarah's pulse through the sheet.

It's been described as a vascular disorder. That's a component of it, dilation and constriction, but increasingly it's understood as a central nervous system disorder.

He would situate them in the physical process. In the physical here and now. He would hold on to her as long as he could, stay as long as she needed him.

It begins with an electrical storm in the brain—a flurry of abnormal brain cell activity in the cerebral cortex, followed by a suppression of that electrical activity.

The wave of depolarization spreads across the cortex, over the parts of the brain that process sight, sensation, hearing.

We've seen it in animal models and in what human imaging we can: a seizure-like phenomenon, ending in stillness. Silence.

He could feel Sarah's pulse slowing. Or he thought he could. Could she feel his hand?

But because the brain is engineered to maintain a very specific balance, a homeostasis chemically and electrically, it corrects this inactivity by increasing blood flow—

She was cold. He wanted to wrap himself around her.

And by releasing nerve-activating chemicals—some bad actors in the form of neurotransmitters that enliven the nervous system's pain matrix and excite inflammation in the blood vessels, cranial nerves, throughout the meninges.

But that wasn't possible. Not more than this. Not here and now—

Now there are many areas of the brain suddenly in play—the posterior insula, the amygdala, the hippocampus—each performing a different job in the body. Some have argued persuasively that the brain stem is the place it all starts. We will see it before long. There will be a map.

A map into the room and out of it. For both of them.

Sarah

When I wake up some days but I'm not totally awake yet, the voices are there. Underneath the blood churning in my ears, I can hear them. Like a party gathered at what sounds to me like early evening. I say this because it's a wishful kind of living at that hour, isn't it? Those moods that come when the sun is getting low and making everything spread out in the golden haze. The people attached to the voices are waiting for me to join them. I don't know if they're friends or strangers, but it all seems welcoming, light. There's the chance I'll break free, and sometimes I do. I stop it in time, and I can hold on to some of the dream.

But when I wake up and the attack is already full-blown, unresponsive to the meds, the murmuring isn't inviting, it's mournful and echoes and sticks. Like people gathered at a wake.

The world jumps in, too tight, and I'm afraid to move, can't move, needing a dark that the aura, if it's still there behind my eyelids, won't give me. By then if I still hear the voices, they hurt. Like some sinister scene in an opera performed in these terrifying exaggerated whispers, all the s's stabbing the skin, right through the skull.

That's got to be when those lesions you've told me about, the ones in the brain's white matter, when they come? When the gray matter starts to shrink away. Has to be. Because there's no future then, only this vague sense of a past that's one accusation after another, and a present that won't stop breaking into me and making me into fragments.

The Doctor

"I get it, Jane, I do. And I know it comes from a good place," said Christine through a stop-and-go of breaths that told the Doctor she might cry, if she wasn't already.

"Oh, Christine, dear Christine!" Izzy exclaimed. "Come here." Izzy must have been sweeping Christine into her arms. "This story isn't written yet, is it? Not yet. Between you and—?"

"Prince Jeff!" Albert called out.

"No, *Tony*," Christine insisted. "The boyfriend; it's *Tony*."

"No, *look*! Look at Jeff in that crown!"

"Thought I'd let you all get a look at me in this thing—"

It was the young arborist joining them.

"I'd say *Princess* Jeff," cooed Alla, laughing.

"Well, yeah," said Jeff. "I was thinking *Star Trek* and not manly *Star Trek*. Nope."

This gave them all a laugh, and the Doctor was grateful for the sound of it and to Jeff: For a clinic study, he'd been trying a device that wrapped around the head and introduced electric impulses between the eyes, acting on the trigeminal nerve to induce a flood of endorphins and subdue any pain-making messages.

"Does it help at all?" asked Jane.

"Hard to say. Only my second time. Hurts a little. Face is a little numb on one side. But anything to stay off the pills," he told them.

"All hail our king of the trees!" Albert sent out.

Jeff was well liked in part because he seldom came to meetings, and when he did, owing as much to exhaustion as anything else, he was a man of few words, and those he chose with care. For weeks he'd been out cabling the city's bigger trees—oaks, beeches, maples, ginkgoes—against the wind and picking up after those he couldn't protect. The Doctor's father had been a tree man, too, as was his grandfather, in Vermont. The wiriness of Jeff's limbs, his sun-roughed face, the dirt stark under his fingernails, recalled family—men and trees.

Now that Jeff had diverted them all, the Doctor could retreat for the night, but before he could shut his door, a cannon of a voice reached him: "Alla! You Russian delicacy! Where have you been hiding? I need you, *more* of you—"

It was Ed Konradi, the Doctor's closest friend, a man whose every aspect ran yards ahead of him. His capacity for disruption was all through his DNA, and in the volume and size of his lungs and his great, full chest and stomach. He was a doctor, too, a neurologist, though he was on probation indefinitely. He couldn't practice, but that hadn't stopped him. Nothing could.

"Alla, tell me you love me. *Tell me.*"

"I tell you nothing, Konradi," said Alla, her mirth at a breathless crescendo now.

"And Izzy, you minx, how is the wicked sister, dear Adele?"

"Still the founder of our feast here, Dr. Konradi. Aren't you incorrigible?" Izzy chided happily.

With the Doctor's permission, Ed sometimes sat in on support groups, and he referred patients he could no longer treat to the clinic. He was becoming a fixture and a little too familiar.

The Doctor stepped out of his office, and in five long strides, they all perceived him there.

Jane actually stood up. Albert followed.

"Ah, the Doctor is *in*!" Ed sang out, grinning and running his eyes over the group. He hadn't come alone but with a patient of his own, Sam, who, like Adam, was a veteran and a recovered addict. "Do I hear an amen?"

"We weren't sure you were in," said Jane.

"Yes," said the Doctor. "Charts."

"He's got files on you," Ed teased, scanning everyone with the end of his index finger. "On all of us. And look at the tree surgeon here—the Doctor's crowned him."

Jeff, playing along, gave a slight bow.

"I think we know who the king is around here," said Adam, all six foot six of him fluid and grinning as he returned to them, not looking for any more trouble for now. "Pain, right? That's the king. And we're here to have ourselves a little revolution."

Adam slid alongside Sam, who was a full head shorter and much wider than Adam. The two young men had both been referred out by the VA when the doctors there ran out of treatment options for them; they'd become close. "How you, soldier boy?"

"Wind nearly knocked me on my ass tonight when Doc Konradi and I were on our way," Sam told Adam. "It's mad crazy out there."

"We have an appointment, no, Doctor?" Ed asked.

"We do." The Doctor had forgotten. Sarah—she made demands.

"Shall we?"

The Doctor gave a nod and smile to all assembled.

"I'll leave you all to it," called Ed as he followed the Doctor. "Keep the revolution at a boil!"

Once the office door was shut behind them, Ed clapped his ham of a hand on the Doctor's shoulder. "Lou, my friend, my friend! If I had your powers! Did you see how they stood up for you? You *are* Atticus fucking Finch. The original. No, better! *Way better!* Medical royalty. I love it, man, dear God, I do, and I *love* you."

"Ed, please"—with his back to Ed and his body blocking Ed's sight lines, the Doctor pushed Sarah's journal under the blotter on his desk—"take a seat."

"No, no, c'mon, man, it *is* a glorious thing," Ed said, straddling the chair provided him, like he might ride it out of there at the least invitation. "If I had that kind of effect on the ladies, *Christ*, on *anyone*"—he threw his head back and groaned, unleashing his huge Adam's apple and making the Doctor watch it jump—"Man." He shook his great head, with its graying sponge of a beard, and its loose, wet smile.

The Doctor couldn't miss the lacework of red that had taken over the whites of Ed's eyes. Marijuana: the reason Ed had gotten suspended from the hospital for now, perhaps permanently. But he persisted in using it and, since his suspension from the neurology department in the late fall, in dispensing it to others, without a license. Whenever the Doctor questioned the wisdom in this, Ed countered with Copernicus or Timothy Leary, Marie Curie or Darwin, or some other figure who'd thrown him- or herself headlong into conventional wisdom like a grenade. Then he was treating himself too—his own headaches that had been brought on in the past few years by exertion, sudden or intense blood flow.

"Alla, huh? She wears lace. Did you see that top? And that's got to mean lace *underthings*. She's Russian. She puts that scratchy lace right next to her skin. She doesn't give a shit about comfort. Russians haven't been comfortable for centuries. But sex? They care about that."

"She's one of my patients, Ed."

"I know. I know. Forgive me. Forgive me, buddy. How are you?"

"I see it in your eyes, Ed. You're not vaping. Your lungs—"

"No, no. Give me some credit. This I ate. All on my own. And what a meal it is!"

Ed sent his hand diving into his worn peacoat, digging around theatrically, and then, retrieving his object, he held up his big hand and opened it slowly. There in his palm was a tiny Ziploc baggie with orange lozenges in it.

"Hybrid: *indica* and *sativa*, a child of both AK-47 and Jack Herer, old standbys of medical marijuana, with some genetic enhancements. Immediate euphoria, which then calms down. It's like it sighs sweetly at you. A girl in love, you know? Next is this crazy, relaxing body high—your muscles and joints, they are relieved of gravity, and at our age that's no small thing. But you can function. You can think, and think *big*. I swear it, look at me, Lou, I am *expansive*."

The Doctor sat against the wall beside his desk and stretched his long arm over the desk's blotter. Ed placed the baggie inches from the ends of the Doctor's fingers. So far he'd resisted Ed's efforts to get him to try these newer, more refined formulations. In the past the drug had made him paranoid or lazy or both, but Ed kept campaigning for it, and what a campaign it was: He toured his friend through the research that had been done at Trinity College in Dublin, citing well-regarded work on the plant's regenerative effects on the brain, with an emphasis on the benefits of THC, the psychoactive part of the marijuana plant, not merely the cannabidiol or CBD.

There had been fine work in Spain and Brazil, too, and of course in Jerusalem, where the father of marijuana research, Raphael Mechoulam at the Hebrew University of Jerusalem, had unlocked the chemical key to the plant. Ed himself had seen, firsthand, symptoms of PTSD eased and opioid addicts like Sam relieved through controlled dosing.

"How is your head, in fact, Ed?"

"Painless, save when I go too hard on the court. Basketball. That's my game right now. I think I'm younger—I *feel* younger. That's one kind of cognitive dissonance we all want. And my libido? I tell you, I swear—"

Ed couldn't help defend the thing that had saved him and that he believed could save others. No different than the Doctor's patients and their prescriptions.

But Ed should have known better, because he knew better than anyone that it was the electrochemical conversations between neurons that provided for all of the extraordinary accomplishments of the human mind and, Ed would say, *for what makes you* you—utterly singular.

In your head now, he'd confide, looking to astonish the patient, intern, nurse, or, really, anyone who dared to wander with him into the topic, *there are more possible connections than there are atoms in the universe, and as long as you are alive, chemicals are coursing, seeping, and sparks sparking! Crackling! Up here, right here, in the space of your skull, right now, billions of neurons are making trillions of synaptic connections, like galaxies in flux, without cease, whether you're awake or asleep, happy or sad, smart or dumb, or encounter beauty—say, a lovely woman—ah, that!*

Yes, women: another of Ed's preferred subjects. Loving women, keeping them, losing them, chasing them, shaking free of them at last, only to reach for them again and again, also without cease. He'd been married four times—he'd married his second wife twice. The proceedings for that divorce were ongoing. He had five kids.

"I've got the endurance of an eighteen-year-old in the bedroom, and more than that, I'm *in*, in the dream of it, *way* in: into every inch of her skin, you know, every tiny invisible hair. Nothing can be neglected, nothing not touched or tasted. You got to try it, *please*—"

"How's Sam doing?" Their weekly meetings, at least in theory, were for comparing notes on patients.

"Ah, Sam? Okay, Doc, Sam it is: He's great. Less nightmares, less anxiety, less pain. Still clean. You know, he's been taking some meditation classes here, doing some massage and movement stuff. He likes that Jill."

Jill taught meditation, yoga, some tai-chi at the clinic. She was also a licensed massage therapist and, it was agreed by most, looked lovely in spandex.

"She dirty?"

"Ed."

"Kidding… sort of. How about just a little dirty?"

"This is expansive?" asked the Doctor.

Ed shrugged into another full-faced smile: "Can be, can be."

The Doctor looked at the lozenges: "How long after ingesting?"

"Hits in about an hour to an hour and a half, depending on heart rate, stomach contents, etc. Then there's this nice, mellow comedown. We've been adjusting the THC and upping the CBD."

CBD, cannabidiol, was the second most abundant natural component or cannabinoid in cannabis, marijuana. It had no psychoactive effects, but owing to the revered Dr. Mechoulam, many believed it had more *medicinal* benefits than any single pharmaceutical drug on the market with anti-inflammatory, anti-seizure, and neuron-protecting effects in the brain and body.

"I've told you it's all in the ratios. We can work wonders now. This, though, right here, guarantees a little fun, a little transportation. But it'll take time to gain on you: We're not small men, you and I, Doc."

Still, the Doctor did not take the lozenges.

"Nothing on the walls in here after how long now?" Ed asked. "I bet the old lady doesn't like it."

"She gave me a portrait of a composer. Pergolesi. Died young. I think she expects I'll hang it in here—"

"Fuck no?"

"Yes."

"No, wait, hang on. Pergolesi? He must look like the Little Prince?"

"Young Machiavelli. With lustrous, long hair. A wig maybe."

Ed roared, tossing his own wavy hair, which unlike his beard remained a defiant chestnut.

The Doctor began to laugh with his friend. As in all things, Ed was infectious, but bringing up Adele, Mrs. Watson, took some of the air out of the room. They both knew that a word from her to the hospital board could help Ed's case, get him reinstated. She withheld it. *For now.* The Doctor shook his head, and because the two men knew well in what direction each other's thoughts and judgments tended to run, Ed put in, "C'mon, man. I'm okay. You know I am. It's been months and look at me. Admit it: I am"—he gave the Doctor his profile, all the outcroppings of his great head—"I am *resplendent*."

"She refers to you as Falstaff, you know," the Doctor told him.

"That wonderful harpy! Of course she'd go for Shakespeare! She loves to hurl things from the high shelf! She outdoes your Jackie, doesn't she? No taming her… Oh, man." Ed wiped tears from his eyes. "Look… " Ed took some deep breaths. "I didn't want to tell you this until it looked good, but I have some funding. *Real* funding. Private funding. They can't keep me from research, and there's money coming from *everywhere* now. I might have to keep my name off the final paper or bury it in a list of other names, we'll see, but it'll keep me comfortably above water, and then a bit of cash coming in from my other endeavors—"

"Don't tell me. You know I shouldn't know."

"Right. Right, but look—" Something occurred to Ed that caused him to jump his chair, now gripped between his legs, closer to his friend. "Let's take Alexander Fleming—he changed the face of medicine forever. He was an untidy man who ran, by all accounts, an untidy lab. If one of his staph samples hadn't gotten contaminated and grown that gorgeous fucking fungus, there'd be no—what? Say it with me. No… Okay, *I'll* say it: peni-goddamned-cillin, man! One of the greatest discoveries in Western medicine! We've got to leave some room to let the accidents in, the mystery, let it in, let it be—fuck, Lou, don't make me quote the Beatles! Don't make me remind you of your own experiments. You have to admit they had their place. Once? Gave you a little liberation?"

He meant the opioids the Doctor had taken himself, at Jackie's insistence. She'd plied him with reasons—scientific, medicinal (he had knee and neck pain), and recreational—to loosen him up, and the drugs had, but now the memory made him stiffen. He'd done things he regretted bitterly while under their influence, under Jackie's.

The Doctor's computer, on his desk, issued two long electronic hoots.

"Someone's used the code to get in. The cleaning crew, probably."

"I can't believe you gave me a key."

"Neither can I," the Doctor laughed.

But he couldn't help it: He loved Ed. The two men had withstood each other over the years and how their characters often pulled them in different directions. They'd built a middle place for their friendship, between the Doctor's moderation and Ed's excess, and when they were in that place together, there were few places either man would rather be.

Ed whistled. "This clinic is costing the old lady a mint. It's a spa."

"We get outside funding for studies, the research. For the patients who can't pay, that funding helps."

"It's not just the electrical devices, the CGRP antagonists, or new experimental antidepressants. It's DNA, it's immunity. Taking blood still?"

"With their permission. Only then."

"To be pampered guinea pigs."

"Ed, c'mon."

"Don't look at me like that, I'm all for it. Nothing surprises me anymore, or not much. Not even the wind. Fuck, that *fucking wind*!"

Ed leaned back and raised his chin and eyes to the ceiling—the cue that he was about to quote something or someone: "The most human thing we do is comfort the afflicted and afflict the comfortable."

"Clarence Darrow," rejoined the Doctor. It wasn't the first time Ed had quoted the Scopes Monkey Trial lawyer.

"Afflict her a little, Doc."

"Who?"

"The old lady. She's not that old, and she's not at all bad to look at. She percolates. She's got this steam—"

"Ed, she's my patient."

"That's not all she is: She's your patron, too, and she's got you over a barrel. Why don't you bend *her* over something? Tit for tat."

"How is Jean? Doing well?"

"Ah, we're changing the subject again."

Jean was the nurse in the hospital room who had finally followed the Doctor's orders, rather than Jackie's, when Sarah was admitted, and she was already a lover of Ed's then, though the Doctor hadn't known at the time. It was Jean who'd called Mrs. Watson about the new headache doctor at the hospital. He found out later she'd described him as the "*real* thing."

"She's well. I have been contributing to her well-being about twice a week and more, if she'll let me."

"Send her my regards. Do I remember correctly that her brother is a compounding pharmacist?"

"You do. He is. Good guy—Curtis. Smart. Medicines to order. Helps that he's open to all sorts of recipes, botanicals too. He's got a green thumb."

"Will you send his info?"

"Brewing something, Doc?"

"Maybe."

"I'd like to hear just what."

"I bet you would." He flashed Ed a grin. Only briefly. Maybe Ed took this as a challenge, or maybe he'd been looking for the opportunity to mention the journal. He pointed to where it was hiding under the blotter.

"Any news of her—of Sarah?" He must have seen the Doctor hide it.

"No."

"But she's still talking to you? You still talking back? You talk to the police again? Any news?"

The Doctor reddened from the inside out. The very tops of his ears were hot and probably blazing, about to catch fire.

"Ed—"

"Hey, none of my business," Ed said, and frowned—at himself or the Doctor, it was hard to say. "But someday you'll tell me what really went on between you two."

Neither man moved or spoke while the Doctor tried to recover himself, until the phone rang and made them both jump. The Doctor grabbed for it without looking at the caller ID. When he did look, it was too late. He'd said hello, and Adele Watson's voice came weakly back: "I need you. I'm unwell. Please. Please come *now*."

"Yes, Adele. Yes, of course."

Ed stood up, knowing he was dismissed. He picked up the baggie and slipped it into the top drawer of the Doctor's desk. "Try it," he mouthed at the Doctor. Then whispered close to the Doctor's ear, "It won't hurt anyone. Promise."

The Doctor gave a distracted wave as his friend left and shut the door behind him.

"I'll be there shortly," the Doctor said to Mrs. Watson. "As soon as—" She hung up before he said, "I can."

Sarah

I thought I saw you coming toward me in the park, finally, finally. Was it you? The path curved away and there were so many people and trees and this kite suddenly, with streamers diving round and round. I looked away and you were gone. Those shoulders of yours, Doctor, your long arms and legs—it was you, wasn't it? Or did I dream you up? From wishful thinking? Or more of it? I wish so much now, all the time: I wish I'd told you how badly I needed help. I wish I'd told you the truth, that I'm afraid of him. But that's not the whole truth, either. It's me I'm afraid of: what I'll do with him now, that I'll never say no.

The Doctor

But he did not go to Adele as promised. Not right away.

Instead he looked in on the cleaning crew, three of them, two men and one woman, from an industrious Panamanian family, all wearing earbuds and so were closed off from him as they moved fluently down the corridors of empty rooms and offices used by his staff and a roster of pharmaceutical reps and researchers.

Except for the expanse that the lounge provided, the clinic was a series of turns and coves. Even under the expensive flooring and hypoallergenic carpeting, there were, Izzy had told him, a number of trapdoors to tunnels for smuggling Catholics away from Protestant nativists who'd controlled the city at the time of the church's construction. As he checked the clinic, he thought he could feel veins alive under his feet. It was history, this old place's, carved out to answer to a need for escape so real and relentless, he believed he could feel it shift under him now.

Last week, at the end of another support group, Izzy had raised the matter of a petition to help preserve the church, as an appeal to the landmarks committee. That was a tug-of-war between the two sisters the Doctor wished to avoid. Thankfully, he heard none of that now as the support group broke up—only "goodnights" and "feel betters." Reminders to breathe, keep hydrated, "find your triggers, mind your triggers."

Ten minutes had passed and still he hadn't left. He removed Sarah's journal from under his blotter and put it in the back of a desk drawer that he then locked.

The phone on his desk went off again—one ring, two, three; he let it go to the service. He knew the caller was either Adele or her Marie hurrying him, or it was Jackie, counting on his professionalism at least, impatient not to have heard back from him yet. He stood, smoothed and straightened his white coat, and then, despite himself, sat back down again, heavily, unable to locate any urgency in him to rush. When the phone rang once more, he picked it up, partly from want of delay and partly because he'd welcome being scolded if it woke him to what was expected of him.

To his hello there was no response. Only silence, or someone giving him silence. To his second hello and "Is anyone there?" came more silence. He didn't hang up. He listened to the nothing on the other side of the phone and let the caller listen to him breathe, in and out, the air making its noise through him. Once more he asked, in a whisper, confiding, "Anyone… there?" He couldn't make out the snigger of crank callers or any breaths in reply, even from the wind, always searching for him.

When the disconnecting click came, he told himself it was no one and nothing, and how relieving the thought, if he could just let himself believe it, *no one and nothing*.

He opened the top drawer of his desk, where Ed had deposited the Ziploc with the lozenges. He broke the seal of the bag. An hour, Ed had said, before the drug took effect—enough time to tend to Adele, stabilize her, and go out into the night, walk as he did most nights, until fatigue or the weather sent him home.

In his mouth the orange lozenge wasn't as hard as it looked, it chewed easily. An hour. He'd give her an hour and that was all—he'd be forced to go before the THC spread into his system. He debated whether to wear the white coat and opted for it; whatever its late-day creases—a coffee stain on the end of the sleeve—he knew the coat could be as potent as anything else.

Walking the long block to the Watson house, he fought the wind until he stood before the brownstone, catching his breath. It was hard not to admire the care Adele had taken with her home, and even her method of trapping him so that he now stood on her doorstep, then in her entryway, then inside, receiving greetings by the implacable Marie, and the glass chandelier clinking overhead, only to climb the stairs to Adele's bedroom.

Orson called to him midway up the flight of stairs, which bent this way and that.

"Doctor?"

"Good evening, Orson. I am on my way up to—"

"To her lair," said Orson.

The Doctor considered this when he shouldn't have. Orson understood the difficulty of the Doctor's position better than most. "Isn't the whole house her—?" He tried to swallow *house*, but too late.

"Did you say *house*?"

"I misspoke."

"No, you didn't. Yes, the house, the block—hell, it's the whole universe now, isn't it? It's *all* hers. It's terrifying. Can I offer you a drink, Doc? I'm drinking French vodka."

"No, Orson. No, thank you."

"Of course. Had to ask."

"I understand."

"You're a mensch, Doc."

"What's she taken, Orson?"

"Wine mostly. It was a Burgundy. She thinks the good stuff can't hurt her, despite evidence to the contrary. Otherwise, aspirin, that triptan—the zolmi–whatever it is."

"Orally?"

"Is there another way?"

"Yes, always other ways. Nausea?"

Orson shrugged. "She shooed me away."

Orson had something on his head—a headband, or glasses. Yes, glasses. He moved them down over his eyes. "What do you think?" They were motorcycle glasses with rose-colored lenses. "New twist on something old. Some survival gear for these twisty days. Top-notch materials. Very soft. Like skin. And I'm making masks—the protective kind."

"Enterprising," said the Doctor.

"Tell *her* that, would you, for me?"

"Goodnight, Orson." The Doctor made short work of the stairs and for an instant felt a bolt of something break up his stomach. It felt like euphoria, but it was too soon for the lozenge. Maybe just the thrill of having delayed the inevitable.

Adele's bedroom glowed orange in the semi-dark, thanks to a Himalayan rock-salt wall installation in a panel behind her bed. The onyx-like mass of it was illuminated from behind, giving off not only that strange light but negative ions, like the sea was said to do, or so it had been explained to him.

She lay in a ball on her immense four-poster bed, one arm over her eyes, the other hugging her knees. He extended a hand to place on her upper arm.

"You're late coming," she said with effort.

"There was a call—"

"Ophiuchus, it's a bad one."

"How much wine, Adele?"

"It was coming before the wine. The weather—"

"You know, alcohol, and wine in particular, is a trigger, Adele."

How many times had he told her how you had to stop the event of migraine before it could begin, that its qualities of seizure and its relationship to epilepsy were not accidental or incidental? And that a myriad of things in wine—the tannins, the sulfites, the histamines, the sugar and alcohol, those inflaming prostaglandins, or that ubiquitous, entirely troublesome amine tyramine—could not only trigger but also fuel an attack? He addressed himself to his own frustration: She would be who she was, who she was determined to be, and if there was reward in it—his coming to her—a reward greater than the deterrent of the pain, why would she stop?

"Don't make me argue," she hissed.

"How much Zomig did you take?"

"Ten milligrams, thirty or forty minutes ago. Maybe longer. You didn't come."

"I did. I have. I was merely delayed." His hand still on her arm.

"I may vomit."

He took off his overcoat, so that he was mostly doctor's coat, picked up the Italian-made ceramic pot, always by her bed, and moved it closer to her.

In her bedside table he kept some syringes and injectables.

He exposed her arm where he'd placed his hand and injected it with his preferred anti-nausea, kept in the drawer for this purpose. It had, he'd long observed, a curative effect not just on nausea but on the head and body pain as well. It relaxed the patient, induced sleep.

He'd slipped what he thought was a bottle of zolmitriptan nasal spray in his pocket but realized he'd grabbed a saline nasal spray instead. He leaned over and insinuated it into her nostrils. What Adele most needed from him was the sense of being tended to. He restored his hand to her arm, applying even pressure over the injection site.

"You'll stay?"

"I will."

"Lie with me."

She inched toward him so as not to trouble her head or neck, as if moving through viscous water. Then she grabbed heavily for his wrist.

"I'm here," he said, to express that this was what he could give her. He did not take his wrist from her. She'd be asleep soon enough.

"*Please.* Come here. Hold me."

"Adele…"

"I need you. Why make me beg?"

When he became her doctor and first took her case history, she'd claimed that she had to be *utterly alone and unmolested* when stricken with migraine. But somewhere in his treating her, this had ceased to be so. And he'd been complicit, by coming when called.

Before she managed to install him at the clinic, he'd gone willingly to see her. She was a trustee at the hospital, as well as a respected board member, her money legendary and deeply nourishing to the institution, and she was of course dedicated to the cause of headache and migraine research and to innovating new and personalized treatments. And he was dazzled: the force of her personality, a kind of ageless Hollywood glamour in her, the openness to new medical approaches, the house in Brooklyn, its antique grandeur set against her unabashed eccentricity, expressed by way of its art and decor. She seemed free in a way that few people were, and he was right, though he underestimated how she wielded that freedom—exercising it by depriving others of theirs.

When precisely had it occurred to her that he was an answer to what ailed her beyond the medical? Thought processes alone—even a single thought—could initiate the release of happy-making chemicals like oxytocin and dopamine in the brain, but when exactly had these begun to fire in association with him, and with such reinforcing regularity? And begun to call for whatever cocktail of sex hormones was animating her, Mrs. Adele Watson?

Human habits, especially the habit of loving and living with someone, rearrange the microstructure of the brain, creating neural networks that reinforce a basic human need for security. When Adele's husband died, she lost no time rewiring those billions of connections.

Maybe she'd been at it before then, as her husband was dying or long before, already conjuring a man who would give her what her husband, also a doctor, hadn't, because the need for novelty was that much greater in her. As it was in so many of us.

That euphoria again—another bolt through him and a spreading warmth traveling his limbs and finding his groin.

What a complete surprise it was, simple touch, and more touch, Doctor, and then, my God, the pleasure, my body giving me pleasure for once and not pain.

Ed had told the Doctor that up to thirty percent of migraine attacks were improved by sexual stimulation, all the way to orgasm. Sufferers of chronic headache often had lower levels of serotonin, but the trade-off for some, like Ed, and maybe Sarah too, was stronger libido.

How easy it would be to curl himself around Adele Watson now, place his face into the fragrance of her neck. Pull her to him. The thought slackened his joints. His jaw lost tension at its hinges, became heavy, while Sarah's journal talked on—*pleasure like I've never known*—his own neuronal network at play now, his longing, his attachments.

He'd struggled to reason himself out of his attachment to Sarah when she was still here, within reach. Why? Because he had wanted to love her from the first and he'd disallowed that love, also from the first. His ethics were not plastic, couldn't be—a professional oath had to be an oath, and then love was not reliable. You didn't need to be a doctor to know it was an exquisitely rendered trick of the brain. Complex and deranging as any drug. It rewrote us in collusion with our chemical selves to perpetuate the species, to encourage reproduction and collaboration.

Collaboration. Adele had used the word—in her bid to convince him to join her clinic. As if he had a choice—the salary, the promise of funds for research for the clinic and the hospital, with which he'd have an ongoing relationship, all the congratulations, and his own ambition.

Only later, too late, did he realize how costly working with Adele would be and how she'd armed herself with information about his past: "And this girl who's vanished? Sarah? You treated her? She depended on you, Doctor, didn't she?"

And later on, Adele edged closer to threats: "It's all very questionable, that relationship—not to me, of course," she'd said to him. "But to others? Suggestible others? We're never far from the witch hunt, are we, Louis? And white men are hardly a preferred flavor these days."

If he eased himself down next to Adele now? To feel her hummingbird circulatory system agitating against him on a bed that looked fit for a queen, and as soft. She was so small, all the more so now, so reduced. She trusted the Doctor wouldn't hurt her, turn the tables right here. Take whatever he wanted. Everyone seemed to feel it irresistible to test him, to see if he'd show something of himself that he couldn't. Not again.

You're no fucking man. I hit you, and nothing?

Jackie, stop.

Why? What will you do?

You've had too much.

And you? You took some, too.

Jackie didn't want to take the Vicodin alone, so he'd taken it for her—that pain, that pleasure. In the disintegrating days of their marriage.

He squeezed her throat long enough to make her stop berating him, to see pleasure turn to panic in her eyes.

How delicate all the bones in Jackie's neck.

And in Adele's, too, there next to him—the fine-spunness of her neck, shoulders, and exposed arms.

Bend her over something. The Doctor nearly laughed out loud. Ed. Big Ed. Dear Ed, always asserting in one form or another that life doesn't have to be so hard or approached so carefully. It can't be perfect, though some moments can come close. *Don't they, Doc?*

Dissolving softness all through the Doctor now, even through the meat of his tongue. Ed's edible had taken effect in less than an hour. In less than *half* an hour. Ed had miscalculated the Doctor's susceptibility. The Doctor, too, had underestimated just how ready he was to let go of his resistance, just as he had with the Vicodin, to travel out of the present, away from what was required of him as a caregiver: the attention that had to be paid, the discipline this required, the suspension of judgment and of his anger, impatience, desire.

You held on to my ankle, in the hospital. I was too far gone to say no. Please, don't, Doctor. I can't be touched by you or anyone now, but then I realized you were showing me a way out and if I could just really focus some feeling there and then more, out of the worst of it, and trust that you were pulling me out, I could be freed. Begin to be. It was a beginning, wasn't it? Your hand that asked for nothing from me. It was the gentlest invitation.

Sarah, in directing her attention, was directing sensation. That, many said, *was* consciousness—the brain and its many parts and systems competing to decide what their human reality would be, sifting through all the external stimuli: noise, odors, temperatures, and pressures shifting up and down on our skins, the pain and pleasure felt, fit into something like a whole, a picture with an intelligible landscape, from which we derive meaning. This required all the body's pathways, to the very ends of our tongues and fingers.

He put his other hand over Adele's. "You beautiful bitch," he whispered and tried to keep from laughing out loud. *Bend her over something.*

She didn't hear him or feel him: Her mouth was open in sleep, yet her other hand was still loosely arranged around his wrist. Here was yet another woman helpless beside him, just as his mother once was, drifting in and out of sleep.

He'd applied ice packs to his mother's forehead and wrists. When they were too cold for her to bear, he put the palms of his hands to the flats of her feet. Cool hands on feet hot from a hot room and bed. When he left his mother, how quiet he had to be, how slow, as he imagined the trees outside and how he'd climb them and how high he'd go. Once he was too far to hear her call him back, he would run, out into the spring or summer or fall to find his father, if he could, in the trees.

He wanted to run again—to leave this room, every room he'd known, every fucking duty—but he would have to be efficient and so make himself small, and his body wasn't suddenly; it reached up already and out of the room, to fresh air, new air. Brooklyn at night, late spring, the racing wind.

He couldn't hear the wind now, which added to his disorientation, and he couldn't say how long he'd been there, in the room with Adele—that was the cannabis, too: It altered perceptions of time. It could have been less than an hour, or hours, stretching and dissolving.

Time stopped that day with him, along with the pain, and I let it, and then again and again and again. Can't I be forgiven for wanting this?

He had to move or soon not be able to move at all, unwind Adele's hand from his wrist, but his mind had given itself over to eddies, moving fast then slow, turning over how the bedroom had become southern Italy at dusk, the ancient orange stucco of the buildings absorbing the slow-burning sky overhead, and how very young Adele looked when asleep and not sniffing for weakness or her advantage. And for a moment—longer, how long he couldn't say—he became Sarah's lover, the man described in such detail in her journal, the man who worked with her at a gallery, who flirted with her for weeks and listened feelingly to her description of her headaches, a man who should have been a stranger to the Doctor but who was not, not anymore, who called the Doctor names like "Doctor Love" to tease Sarah, because Sarah had told the man about that day in the hospital when the Doctor had held on to her, before she and the man had become close. Her lover had used the Doctor's hand or a facsimile of it to touch her, until he asserted his touch in ways the Doctor had not and would not. How fucking dare he, how fucking dare he go so far.

He put his hand where you had, Doctor, to start, around my ankle. I thought it was like a joke at first, but he breathed with me, over the noise of the art opening, where he should have been, where I should have been. Why wasn't his wife looking for us? I will never know.

The Doctor tried to concentrate his thoughts, stringing one to the next, on what was happening to him, how the THC was a very good forgery of a messenger molecule called anandamide and so worked like a key in the locks of a set of the brain's receptors.

It wasn't so different from what happened in a brain high on synthetic opioids, and though the receptors and which messengers were in play were different, the effects could be no less intoxicating, stimulating dopamine production in the nucleus accumbens, the brain's pleasure center.

"You see," he whispered to Adele, "it so often comes back to the dopamine."

P. let go of my ankle very carefully, as if he'd wake me or break me otherwise, as if I were made of something that could shatter. I could still feel the warmth that he left there... He held my hand in both of his, like I was his, or someone so very, very dear to him... My God, how did he know what I needed that day? How much pressure to apply?

The Doctor removed Adele's hand from his wrist; her hand weightless in sleep. So terribly, terribly soft. There were dustings of freckles on the pale skin of her exposed arm. He wanted to graze them with his fingertips. He could touch her. She wouldn't know. Unless... cameras? Even in here? She wouldn't, would she? But she would, and he laughed with a hand over his mouth at the audacity. Then he fit that hand around the thin white of her neck—what would he see in her eyes if he squeezed and roused her?

Jackie had become afraid once she realized he wasn't playing any game with her. The Vicodin had made him feel his anger as if it were another drug—inside the high and outside it, an observer, entertained. He might have killed her. When he finally let go of her, she'd hit him, kept hitting him until he fucked her. He could have fucked her all night.

And now the pulse in this lovely neck, Adele's neck, calmed, regular.

He took his hand away.

He'd mastered his rash impulses for so long that now *this* was impulse—to pull back.

Someone had to show restraint in a world so fitful. Someone had to be stoic, steadfast. As he had been consistently when Sarah was his patient, but the journal, all that Sarah asked him to know in it? And its blue cardboard cover that was soft as skin from being handled? From the oil of Sarah's hands, his own. Once he read it, he should have turned it over to the police, whatever his promise to a woman he saw only once, Sarah's messenger, who'd vanished, too. But as he read it again and again, he told himself he was protecting Sarah, and how far she went. Too far. And with others too. Her privacy, her honor. Fragmented.

But she was blameless. He was not: With every week, now months, that he didn't share the journal with the police or destroy it, stop its influence on him, he implicated himself and his desire, which grew with every reading, and gripped him, gave him life, gave him shame, but the *life*—

He tried to stand, but around him the room—glowing with an orange so full of faraway places—tilted him back into his seat. Everything in him that should be alert and solid wasn't—his legs, his mouth falling open as if with thirst—while his dick strained at his pants. How goddamned ludicrous! THC stuck in all the locks of his receptors. Just how much and for how long before traveling enzymes flushed its effect away could not be predicted.

I am an elm, the Doctor rejoiced, and managed to stand. He'd told Sarah about the great stands of elms in Bennington, where he grew up.

"When will you be free to go back home?" she asked. "To Bennington?"

"Soon. I'll go soon."

"I wish I could see those trees."

"You can. It's not far."

He gathered his overcoat, aimed for the door, and with every reeling step willed silence from the bed.

"The THC is too much, Ed. And if it has any benefit, it can't be like this, not expressed like this."

"It does. It can," Ed argued, as he always did. "It's not just recreation, it's re-creation, get it? How many times do I have to tell you, Doc—"

"Not like this. It's too dangerous—the liberty and the feeling—"

Each time he came to see me, he was waking parts of me, drawing feeling there as it hadn't been before. He waited, before moving his hand up, first to my shin, leaving it there to make an impression, then my knee. Later he put the flat of his hand high on my thigh. He waited for me to react. You see, he was occupying me. I understand now. With one hand to start.

* * *

The Doctor made it out the bedroom door. He didn't remember descending the stairs after he'd done so and would have been out the front door as automatically, but music caught him: the song "Stormy Weather"—*can't go on, everything I had is gone, stormy weather.* The notes, in the course of one word, went up and then down, and the Doctor went with them.

He followed the source of the sounds to Adele's study and looked in to see Orson, wearing his goggles still, dancing with Marie: his hand buried in her lower back, her hand draped casually around his neck, their other hands entwined, riding out in front of them. They had done this before, had practice and comfort in rocking in time. And then the music stopped and a man's voice on a soundtrack or radio attributed the track: "Lena Horne."

"We have a lot of music to play tonight. I'm not going anywhere," he reassured whoever was listening. He could outlast the wind, he said, or did he say *we* could?

"They've called this a semi-permanent weather system. It's official. Or semi-official. Either way, there's no end in sight, dear listeners."

A halting deep voice, part Cronkite but breathier, with a slow, drawn-out delivery.

"We're going to try a few versions of 'Stormy Weather' tonight: Ethel Waters. Kay Starr. Billie Holiday—can't leave her out. Call in with any other—What's this? Ah, what… is… *this*? We just received news of a billboard down on the West Side Highway—no injuries reported, but if you're heading north, consider an alternate route. Stay safe on this wicked, wicked night."

"Doc!" Orson called. "Didn't know you were down."

He rushed the Doctor. Before Orson arrived too close to the Doctor's face and breathed vodka into it, the Doctor glimpsed Marie turning her own face away. A Marie embarrassed, extending her hand for something that would lower the broadcast's volume.

"We're listening to this show, *The Wind Report*. New show, radio show. You can stream it—" Orson was too loud. Orson was drunk. "Bad out there. Should we call you a car?"

"All set," the Doctor managed to say.

"How's Medea?" Orson asked.

"Who?"

"Mother."

"All set," the Doctor said again, managing, "Asleep. Better."

"Hear that, Marie? She's okay."

"I have to get go—"

"No drink, Doctor, for another job well done?"

"No, not—"

"Man, I can see it in your eyes. You're wrecked. Go home."

The Doctor did his best with his goodbyes and the first door, then the second, then outside.

There came a wailing that he mistook for the wind and then a roaring that was the wind in fact; it covered the wailing, threw debris in his eyes, only for the wailing to return. Strident. Sirens? *Billboard down*, someone had said. A voice. A big, loud voice. Who was that? This was not a neighborhood for billboards. Before him the streetlights rattled and their light trembled. And the trees threw their canopies back and forth.

Wicked, wicked night.

Go home.

Yes, he turned that way, to go to his apartment, but instead he buttoned his coat and, moving sideways, struggled down Linden Place onto Kane Street, then north on Clinton, then west to Atlantic Avenue and onto Court Street.

And even with the wind finding him in stronger and stronger thrusts, some dim part of him kept aiming him toward the wailing.

Car traffic coursed by in the streets, but on the sidewalks only a few dark figures hurried by, each one hood- and scarf-covered and cowering at how unwelcome this landscape had become to them. May in New York, on a moonless night, neither warm nor cold.

He caught fragments of conversation, a few words said more than once: *The bridge. The bridge.* The Brooklyn Bridge? Was something wrong? Terrorists, he conjectured immediately, because it was where all New Yorkers' fears ran since 9/11. His own fear and then rage spiked and swirled up in him and as quickly dissipated as he realized that his neck and knees weren't hurting. He felt no pain. Was it true? Was it the THC or the cannabidiol? A simple compound in a plant at work, acting as an anti-inflammatory, an analgesic, and what else? What else would they discover? How tempting it was to believe it could be that simple. One thing to cure all ills. One remedy for every swelling pain. To feel something else, to let something else in. The accidents.

As Sarah had done. How could he blame her for needing it to be simple?

He found himself on Adams Street, which poured directly onto the bridge, and saw a red pulsing of fire and police vehicles obscuring the entrance. A surge of paranoia reached like a hand around his heart—would they know him? Police and reporters had filed in when Sarah was first gone, those first hours so crucial. So fast they came with their questions and free-floating suspicion, and so fast they'd left, on to the next puzzle. No, of course not: They wouldn't know him at all, or how he'd failed to help her. *Why didn't you come?* Another man had, pretending to be a cure.

Even before he got to the first squad car, blocking the bridge's entrance to any traffic, he was already reciting, with every long stride, *I am a doctor. I can help. I am a doctor. I can help. I am a doctor…*

Sarah

That ecstasy before the body turns on you. This lifting joy. Like gifts are everywhere, in places you've never noticed before. As early as me at four or five, flowers mooned at me, their stamens hanging like tongues, their petals veined with colors that shook with this need to communicate something I wanted to understand so very badly. Around every corner it felt like something was about to jump out at me, to take me away and help me make sense of this weird wonder-sick day. I remember hoping for a monster, some misunderstood, lonely thing, looking for a friend like me, five years old and as brave and as wild as any monster, in league with the nutso beauty all around me.

But then in an instant it all drained away. It was The Wizard of Oz before Oz. I couldn't see the green in the grass or the color of the sky. Or the brown of my mother's hair. "Your hair is all ashes," I told her.

Then in short order came the headache and the vomiting.

But that ecstasy, what my mother's favorite novelist, George Eliot, called feeling "dangerously well," never lasted long. And as I got older it didn't always come, or if it did, I didn't believe in it. The warping of sound and light did, though. My mother tried hard to give me courage through more examples of others who, though they were afflicted like me, were never limited, whose lives were extraordinary: Virginia Woolf, Elvis, Nietzsche, Freud, Joan Didion, Van Gogh, Hildegard von Bingen, Lewis Carroll, Darwin, and of course George Eliot, a woman, she liked to say, who defied categorization. But being a biologist, she always came back to Darwin, who throughout his life was as much in his bed as out of it.

She helped me collect my triggers, too, over time, some obvious—too much sugar, cold cuts, changes in weather—and some not. When I was a teenager I worried sex was one of them—or desire? I haven't told anyone this, not my mother, but I have to tell you now so you'll understand.

The boy's name was Bobby. He wasn't from the city, where I spent most of my childhood, but from White Lake, NY, up near Bethel, where Woodstock took place. (Everyone thinks Woodstock happened in Woodstock, but it didn't.)

My mother called him "Bobby of the Fields" because we'd found him lying in a field near the house we have up there. A lean, rangy kid, with shoulders so wide for his frame he looked like he might fold in two. He didn't talk much, but when he did, he talked about books I'd never read and what we couldn't see beyond the blue in the sky or the pinpricks of light that were the stars at night up there: the cold, the cauldrons, the black holes. He introduced me to Lovecraft, Henry Miller. I was 16, he was 18, and I was mad for him, his dirt, grass, and Ivory soap smell, the bones of his hips poking up over the waist of his pants. I didn't have much of a curfew when we were up there. My parents didn't think anything bad could happen to me in the country. So one night I lay down in the grass with Bobby of the Fields.

He brought the beer, a six-pack that didn't stay cold on that summer night. I had gum, two packs, peppermint. We chewed it while we sipped the beer. I shoved in new pieces on top of old. I thought that no boy could love a girl who didn't taste as fresh as she might feel. The gum was sweetened with artificial sweetener: aspartame. I didn't know yet that this was a trigger for me and how it sneaked its way into so many foods and drinks. It was just gum, you know? Sugar-free because I was trying to avoid too much sugar, even though I wanted it like <u>all the time</u>. I was already learning to be vigilant, but then I wanted to be free, too, feel free, at 16 going on 17.

There we were—the night was so clear and everywhere above us were stars. When did it begin? The brightest stars, one by one, making these light trails that only I could see. It seemed too big a risk to explain why I was seeing what I was seeing and what would probably come next because he was moving closer to me and telling me about a story by Lovecraft, about a man who raises this sorcerer ancestor of his from the dead, only to have that once-dead man kill him and steal his identity in order to raise other sorcerers from the dead. It was all about how you have to cultivate your own power, he explained, while these ropes of light thick as his arms were falling down around us.

My right eye began to ache, but more demanding was the knifepoint, so fine, at my right temple. That horrid fucking epicenter. I didn't want to believe in it. I wanted to believe in the beer and peppermint on his breath and lips, his seawater sweat coming from everywhere on him.

It wasn't all that hot, but it was humid—sultry, my mother says—and that sultriness swelled inside me so that his smells along with the field's there that night, the grass and pine, and skunk spray somewhere out there, were swelling inside me too, and growing spines with their own pointed edges.

I breathed shallowly as I could as he stopped talking and inched over on this hip and elbow, right next to me, to move his hand to the curve of my neck and look at me. He was blinking. He was considering me. I should have told him then. I should have run for the drugs and the dark, but I didn't do that either. I closed my eyes against all the ropes of light. He took this as readiness on my part, and he kissed me first on one cheek. He did the same on my other cheek and forehead, and where his lips had been he left this tickling, shimmering feeling that made me feel like I was shimmering and that that could be what happened that night, me becoming something so delicate and airy.

Sometimes, back then, I fought pressure with pressure. To have something else press into me. I didn't open my eyes, couldn't, but I pulled him to me. Hard. And that was all the invitation he needed, to release the 18-year-old in him, you know, more hormones than almost anything else, overwhelming how considerate and careful he'd tried to be, so that his tongue plunged in and in, fucking my mouth, and in no time he climbed on top of me and pushed up my shirt and began dry-humping me and saying my name and OH, GOD, OH, FUCK YEAH, GIRL, FUCK YEAH.

I tried to make my hips reply to his. I wrapped my legs around him, and I opened my mouth to his, but then the pain began to converge, rode my too-fast pulse all over me, and soon I couldn't move much apart from how he was moving me.

He wasn't forcing me to do anything. That's not what I mean. It's just that I wasn't me. I was pain, or my body was, and he was any man, or like a thousand men, exerting pressure, grinding bony hips and the buttons of jeans into my spread legs, him totally gone with desire. When he opened my pants but didn't pull them down enough, he hurt me searching and poking his fingers, but it didn't compare to the hurt in my head, jaw, and neck and spreading down my throat. He licked at my breasts like they were too cold and he couldn't risk his whole mouth and then he was back with his tongue diving into my mouth. I was inert, you know, until I had to shove him back with both hands with what strength I could summon, then turned my head and vomited into the grass. He jumped back and cried out, not with words—it was like an animal sound, total bewilderment and hurt, you know? When he gathered himself some more, he said, "What the fuck?" I said, "I'm sick." But it wasn't a good answer for a boy standing under a zillion stars with an erection. "What should I do?" he asked. I managed to say, "My parents." "Your parents?" he repeated. The fantasy he was living and feeling was gone for good then. "Jesus," he said and left me alone in the grass.

What Darwin said about being ill so often was that it "saved" him from what he called "amusements." He couldn't be frivolous. When he was well, he worked and worked, made up for the time he'd lost to the sick room. After he completed On the Origin of Species, he turned to human evolution and had trouble at first reconciling his theory on survival of the fittest with human behavior, especially with our giving sympathy/support to the physically weak among us. His great consolation, it's always seemed to me, was that the weak were less likely to find mates and reproduce and spread their flawed genetic material around. But somehow he didn't indict himself or his own crappy health in this. I did.

As early as my night with Bobby, I wondered if the sex thing, with me, wasn't life's way of making sure I wouldn't be repeated in anyone else. I experimented with other boys, men, but I had trouble relaxing, and they were always in a hurry or just not good at it, with me anyway, but that sound Bobby made—so totally wounded, and then his disgust and the glimpse I got of him stalking off when I managed to open my eyes—it meant I worked so very, very hard to please, to be whatever my lovers wanted me to be. Acrobatic. A smile on my face as my head bobbed in time with assembly-line thrusts. If I didn't get a headache during sex, sometimes I did after. Not always, but I waited anyway for what felt like a punishment, a warning: Not you. No, not you. But why not me? Why have I never insisted it be different until now? Why didn't I believe it could be?

Ruth

They told her the clinic shared an address with a church as an afterthought. But this church, at one end—the quieter end—of Linden Place, was no afterthought. If not for the sign for the clinic—a new sign, BROOKLYN HEADACHE CENTER at the start of a brick path, also new and studded with headless tulips—she would have thought she was in the wrong place.

With towers on either side of its front, St. Gabriel's looked like a fortress, one that could easily have been taken stone by stone from tenth-century France or Italy and then forgotten: The stone had turned dull and dirty, its mortar pocked with fissures and gaps. Boards stood in the arched windows, either to protect the stained glass or conceal that it was damaged or gone.

She followed the path down and around to a side of the church that had been gored through and turned into a wall of glass and metal, alert with a camera and intercom, a key-card slot and number pad. It was sleek, and it unsettled Ruth—a church turned set design for this very contemporary concern, hidden and not. She'd seen churches so much like it on a European tour with her parents and her sister Peggy. Her father was an architect, so they'd waited in long lines so he could point out the variety of arches, ceilings, mosaics. But it was the relics under glass—the skulls, fingers, and locks of hair of dead saints—that she and her sister most wanted to look at. When they did, they giggled and were hushed by their parents, lectured to about reverence and history, *sacred things*.

What would they make of this place? And this city so fast and forever in flux, and all the more so in the wind? Since arriving here by Amtrak from Boston two weeks earlier, she'd never had so many things caught in her eyes, hair, and throat. Never had inside been so preferable to outside, and yet never had she stood at so many doors she dreaded going through. But she couldn't go back. Not now, maybe never. And she couldn't let the camera above the entrance door see her hesitate, which was letting Mrs. Watson see. She pressed the intercom. No voice came back, only a clean click and a long, light buzz.

She stepped into a perpendicular hall that gave Ruth the impression of a moat stretched out into a stark line. Four tall potted plants stood like sentries along the length of the hall. Between the plants hung four black-and-white photos of a country landscape. It was the same landscape in each photo but in different seasons—a hill dotted with a few solitary-looking trees, and at the center an old wagon. Maybe the viewer was supposed to compare the photos and draw some conclusion about the passage of time? But there was no time now; the slate floor was already alive under Ruth's feet. The vibration originated from the next door in. As she pushed through it, another camera, high in a corner, winked its red light at her.

"There you are!" cried a voice from the far end of what was a long cavern of a waiting room. It was a tinkling voice, but not weak. It traveled.

The light inside was cool and warm, and the colors everywhere—on the walls, in the carpeting, artwork, and tables—were scrupulously muted, as if into everything was mixed some earth-loving clay or sepia.

Patients filled half of the dozen or so chairs provided. They were barrel leather chairs and so made those sitting in them look as if they were sinking.

"You have to be Ruth." The voice belonged to the cherubic face of a receptionist who wore her straight black hair in long pigtails and her mouth in a kinetic little grin.

"Mrs. Watson keeps calling to see if you've made it."

"I'm not late, am I—" She had been told to come at eleven o'clock sharp.

"No, right on time. She likes to know the wheels are turning"—the young woman leaned out of the open reception window to confide—"and the screws." She giggled, and a rose seemed to bloom in her face, which was Asian in some part, eager on the whole.

"Come round. I'll hang your coat and take you into the lounge. He's in with someone. Crazy morning so far. There's a lull now."

On the other side of reception, Ruth saw right away that the young woman was pregnant but moved like she hadn't noticed.

"I'm Sue. And, you, Ruth, look like you've come straight from central casting."

Ruth trembled as she handed her coat off; her uniform was thin in the wind anyway, and all the thinner for drawing so much unwanted attention to her.

"Oh, you're shivering! Here—" With Ruth's coat draped over one arm, Sue took Ruth's hands in hers. "You wouldn't know it's May. It's—" A slight shock went through Sue's body and she gripped Ruth's hands to brace herself. "There he goes again. Man, *this kid*."

Sue looked to be in her last trimester.

"He doesn't know it, but when he's out I'm going to kick him back." She shook Ruth's hands slightly, her eyes sharp with delight—"*I'm kidding*"—and then let go of Ruth altogether to hang up her coat and set off. "C'mon, it's through here."

"How many patients have you seen today?"

"A dozen maybe. We're a clinic, so we have quantity, you know, but the Doctor keeps it personal. His resident, Dr. Chaudhri, does a lot of the exams and follow-up appointments, but the Doctor sees them at the end to make sure his patients know he's around. He is a total peach. One of the good guys." Another giggle from Sue. "He hates when I say that."

Ruth had known many doctors in her life. Too few could be described as good, at least not to nurses. But Ruth reminded herself this had been true of the doctors where she'd worked—in a hospital, in departments that catered to serious cases, and where she found herself today was no hospital.

She was led to what felt like a large living room but was plainly a lounge, outfitted with two long midcentury-looking sofas, matching wing chairs, a surplus of throw pillows, and several more barrel chairs like those in the waiting room, some placed around the sofas and wing chairs to form a sloppy circle. There was a pile of yoga mats near a door to one of two corridors leading away from the lounge, and she noticed a largish side table against a near wall for coffee and tea that not only offered all the paraphernalia for making those beverages but a large pitcher of water with what looked like cucumbers floating in it.

A lanky pair of blue-jeaned legs stretched from one corner of one of the sofas. They were attached to someone with a blanket over his head and upper body.

Closer by, an older man sat crookedly in a leather barrel chair.

Sue let her voice drop as she nodded toward the long legs. "We have recovery rooms for resting down that hall, but people wind up in here sometimes. Have a seat. I'm sure the Doctor will be with you soon. This gentleman, Mr. Bavicchi, is a friend of the Doctor's. He's waiting to see him, too. Holler"—a soft giggle again—"if you need anything."

Once Sue was out of sight, Mr. Bavicchi motioned to Ruth to take the chair beside him. He had a strong, sloping forehead and nose in a prominent head that, like the rest of him, gave the impression of having been formed by medium-size rocks that had begun to slip. Leaning toward her as she sat, he produced a smile that was mostly a wince and confessed, "I'm not his friend. The Doctor's. I just met him last night. You work here?"

"No, but I hope to," she told him.

"He said, 'Come by today, this morning.' He made me promise. The Doctor. He said his office was here." He leaned in further. It appeared to hurt him. "I thought he was making it up. Can you believe this place?"

Ruth smiled politely. "It is unusual."

"I used to come here. As a kid. For mass. St. Gabriel's—Catholic. Or way back then it was, and for a long time. Then it wasn't. Episcopal next, I think, then Baptist. It's for the head? Head problems?"

"Headaches."

"All this for headaches?"

"The chronic kind. Very debilitating."

"I know about chronic." He held up a hand. His fingers had thickened and slanted each in their own direction, like root vegetables left too long under the soil. Arthritis. Rheumatoid, probably.

"I'm sorry."

"No, no need. Could be worse at my age. Always could be worse. But last night the doctor kept saying there was something I had to try and someone I had to meet. Don't imagine that was you?"

"No, but I understand he's a very talented doctor."

"He wasn't altogether all together when I found him last night, if you know what I mean." He began to wiggle himself forward in the chair, pushing out a breath for every increment moved. "Look, I always tell my kids and my grandkids, when they go looking for jobs, to keep their eyes open: You're interviewing them, too—eyes open. I'm Nick, by the way."

"Ruth."

Rather than shake her extended hand, he squeezed it hard and didn't let go until he drew toward her. "I should mind my own business, but I was out walking last night—my wife doesn't like it with the wind, but I need the air. And there *he* was at the end of Old Fulton, at the pier. You know where that is?"

"I'm new here."

"It's the pier closest to the Brooklyn Bridge. A boat hit the underside of the bridge last night. You hear about it?"

She shook her head.

"Nobody was hurt. There wasn't much damage, so I guess it wasn't big news. The wind, high tide. Must have affected the clearance. Maybe the captain miscalculated or had one too many—"

"Wasn't altogether all together?" Ruth put in.

"Right. And I see this guy. I figure he was drunk, had to be, because he was leaning over the railing of the pier like he might jump. Christ, I saw him throw a leg over to get closer to the commotion: police up on the bridge, police in boats under the bridge. I rush over, say, 'Hey, you, get the hell away from there. You'll fall in.' He looked back at me like he wasn't sure I was there. Do you know what he said? 'It'll be okay.' That's what he said. I corrected him. Had to yell, with the wind: 'It'll be fatal, you goddamned idiot.' The currents—they're murder out there. I grabbed him by one arm and didn't let go. He didn't mind, didn't pull away or anything. Couldn't smell anything on him. No booze. Then he looked at me. Like I was this long-lost friend all of a sudden. He really looked at me, thanked me, very polite. No kid at all—grown man. Pretty big guy, too. He noticed my hands when I was helping him down off the railing. So he wasn't as far gone as all that. He told me he was a doctor, that he could help. He made me promise to come today, and you know, truth be told, I had to come, to see if this really was St. Gabriel's he was talking about. I thought, 'This guy *has* to be kidding…'"

There was the soft pop and sigh of a door opening, and a man's voice, then a woman's, but Ruth wasn't ready to let go of the thread Mr. Bavicchi had teased out for her. She whispered to him, "But it didn't have to be booze. Did you ask him if he'd taken anything?"

But Mr. Bavicchi was distracted. "That's him there," he said. "I told you he was big."

The Doctor stood at one end of the lounge and wasn't so much big as tall, over six feet, and broad-shouldered and long-armed as a swimmer but otherwise, through his hips and waist, as narrow as a younger man, the kid Nick—Mr. Bavicchi—thought he'd seen at first in the night. The petite woman he emerged with had short white-blond hair. She wore oversize black sunglasses, which were all the blacker against her pale skin, and she kept saying no, as in "No, I can't," "not now," "no time," and the Doctor kept washing over these no's with low, caressing sounds that Ruth made out as "just for a moment," "catch your breath," and "close your eyes."

"Sue?" he called, his voice a sail surging, without any rancor or harshness in its volume. "Sue?"

He turned and saw Mr. Bavicchi, with Ruth there beside him. The full of the Doctor's face was as handsome as Mrs. Watson said, and as angular and orderly as the rest of him, if not for his eyes, such conspicuous eyes, bright yet deep and circled and recircled with shadows. It worried Ruth what had gone into the drilling in of those eyes in the otherwise temperate setting of his face, and she worried suddenly for the petite woman and the persuasion in the Doctor's long fingers there lightly on her shoulder. If Mr. Bavicchi's story was true, there had been nothing sober or safe in the Doctor's behavior the night before.

"Sir?" The Doctor didn't move his hand from the woman. "I met you last night, didn't I? My receptionist told me your—"

That receptionist arrived then, her belly in the lead. "You called?" Sue sang out.

"Jane is having an aura. Take her for a lie-down."

"I wasn't careful enough. Somehow, I don't know how..." The woman named Jane sighed through saying this, reciting what was for her an old story. "Or it's the weather? The barometric pressure? Is it falling?" When no one answered, she went on. "But I can't stay. Not now."

"Can you see?" Sue asked her, evidently practiced at this.

"The light. Not just there"—Jane pointed overhead—"but wherever it's reflecting, it's exploding. With light. Your face"—she gestured toward Ruth or maybe at Mr. Bavicchi—"is exploding with light."

Ruth touched her face reflexively while Sue put an arm around Jane's waist.

"Not so rough," Jane said, and as she was led away, there was less complaint in her voice than regret. "I can't stay."

The Doctor approached as Mr.Bavicchi wrestled himself out of the chair. When the Doctor extended his hand to shake, the older man seized it in order to get to his feet.

"I was just telling this nice young lady that you've got quite a place here. I used to attend mass here, a hundred years ago. Place has held up better than I have—"

"It's had some help, at least recently," said the Doctor while his face, which had been more grave than not, quickened. He enjoyed surprises, or at least this one, in the shape of this man.

"Well, I'm glad. It's good to know not everything is going to hell."

"And you are"—the Doctor turned to Ruth, who was standing now—"sent by Mrs. Watson. You're—?"

"Ruth. Ruth Aitken."

"Yes, of course."

Ruth was not a surprise, and his regard registered this with a cordial vacancy.

When she offered her hand, he took it into the cool firm of his but addressed himself to Mr. Bavicchi: "Another doctor, a friend and colleague of mine, I thought he could advise you, Mr. Bavicchi, is it? He's at work on some new things… And then of course there's the clinic here. It could be a place for you to—"

A "hallooo" sounded then. And "Anybody home?" from a voice unshy of its size. It was followed by a man who was corrugated and fizzing with hair in places and smooth and brightly flushed in others. This was a big man, and his beard, belly, and swagger amplified that impression.

"Sue has left you and your gate unguarded, Doc."

"She'll be right back."

"Am I late?" The man moved toward the Doctor, and with a clap of their hands, the two men pumped arms, pulling each other closer and taller.

"Mr. Bavicchi, this is the doctor I was talking about. Doctor Konradi—"

"Call me Ed."

"Yes, this is all informal," the Doctor clarified again.

"Unofficial. A chat," said Ed, "if you have the time?"

Mr. Bavicchi, clearly fascinated by this new element of oddness in what had been a rush of it since last night, said, "I've got nothing but time. I'm retired."

"Lucky man," said Ed. "And this is your nurse?"

"No," corrected the Doctor. "This is Ruth—Ruth Aitken. Sent by Mrs. Watson."

Ed turned his beam on Ruth: "Mrs. Watson's nurse, then?"

"No," Ruth said, feeling the butt of a joke and the doctors taking her measure, this Ed in particular: His eyes traveled and made trace lines all over her. Her muscles went rigid. A therapist she'd seen told her anger was an indication that she needed to assert her boundaries, as she'd so dismally failed to do in her marriage. She wanted so desperately to snarl at this man, spit, but knew better in this setting.

When Ed asked if she was from St. Mary's, the Doctor explained for her, "No. She's not from here. You're from New Hampshire, is it?"

"Ah, a country girl," Ed said.

Ruth nodded while she reached in her mind for the coast there, sea and rock, the smell of it, to take her elsewhere, anywhere else. Instead, in her head came, *Here, too, of course, even here,* in this famously progressive city: doctors setting themselves above nurses, men above women, and the past, too, bearing down on the present in every way. Who's up and who's down, who's in and who's out, who's local, who's not, this making and maintaining of tribes, hierarchies—far too much human activity, Ruth knew, was dedicated to this.

The Doctor invited her into his office, and as she turned to follow, Mr. Bavicchi called, "Nice to meet you," and then he forked two fingers up toward his eyes and toward Ruth's to remind her, *Keep your eyes open.*

Ruth brightened some, only to feel queasy walking into the Doctor's windowless office. For some time now, whenever possible, she'd avoided being alone in a room with a man, and this room was smaller than she anticipated, its walls starkly bare and shiny with the light. With the door shut, the Doctor moved to his desk chair and offered the only other chair to Ruth, but she didn't sit right away and neither did he.

"That woman—Jane, is it?—will she be all right?"

"Jane will be the best she can be under the circumstances," he said. "She's had migraines since she was a child. Migraine with aura."

"The exploding lights?"

"Yes, aura. Part of the body's alarm system, as is the headache itself, when it comes, a warning of something potentially harmful—"

Like Ruth's anger. And now her fear. Inopportune. Squeezing in, out of nowhere. He was at least a head taller than she was.

"Like the weather, or certain chemicals in food or the environment. Triggers a reaction. But the trouble for someone like Jane is that the whole system, which is more sensitive to begin with, can grow even more sensitive over time. So the process becomes more entrenched. Pain becomes the rule, rather than the exception to it... I'm being abstract, aren't I? What I mean is that pain becomes a habit. Or can." He looked to Ruth for assent. When he didn't get it, he asked her for it: "Has that been your experience?"

What on earth did he mean? Her experience as a nurse or a woman or both? Had he been told about her past or gone to the trouble of finding the stories about her on the internet, too, sniffing for a backstory that wasn't the whole story? Though that didn't matter—we all make meals of fragments.

But the expression in the Doctor's deep-set eyes now told her nothing, only that he waited on her with courtesy, and some indifference, too, of a man who always had so much to consider, to do, even now. He ignored his phone when it rang three digitized rings and then stopped.

"Won't you have a seat, Ruth?" he asked. He wouldn't sit until she did, and yet, only last night, he'd been careless, wild. She hadn't looked into him online yet, or not much: just his name, standard background, a handful of patient reviews, all glowing. She didn't want to jinx anything, and then, after her meeting with Mrs. Watson, thanks to the effects of the wine and the woman herself, she'd slept for more than a few hours for the first time in a long time. It had made her careless.

She sat.

"Pain as a habit," she repeated. "Yes. A mindset. Certainly the drugs to treat it can be habit-forming... We've all seen that."

Ruth pulled her hem over a catch in her white stockings. She would throw this pair out as soon as she could. And the uniform too, if she'd only let herself.

"I've looked at your CV, Ruth. You've never worked in neurology of any sort before?"

"No, but pain—I've had to manage it," she told him. "Over the years."

"And not just that. Life and death: You've managed that, too—"

What did he think he knew about her exactly? Was this another game?

"—when you worked in post-op gynecological oncology and then in the neonatal intensive care unit?"

"Out of nursing school," she explained, "most of us wanted labor and delivery—the babies—but you had to wait for a spot to open. Until then, they put me where they needed me."

He nodded, waited for more, and trapped her in his eyes, in the dreadful clarity of the room.

"In the post-op ward," she began, "there was a lot of pain, of course. They came in with one body, left with another one. It didn't feel like theirs to them anymore. I heard that a lot. Of course, there were headaches too, lots—"

"*A different body than the one they came in with?*" he broke in. She'd managed to raise something of interest to him. "Yes. *Exactly.* Exactly right! Recurrent pain does that, too, over time. When I say pain becomes a habit, I don't mean only psychologically but in the wiring itself, in the neural pathways, in the whole nervous system—"

The lights flickered above them. He waited till they stabilized, then said, simply and evenly, "The wind." And: "Do you know why they call neurology the queen of the medical specialties, Ruth?"

"Because of the brain? How it governs and dictates so much?"

He bent toward her, face alert. She saw the strong blue veins channeling through his temples and into the wells of his light gray eyes.

"And then it's so complicated and… " She wanted to please him now. She couldn't help it; it was his expectancy. "And mysterious?"

"Yes, *good,* yes, that gets us some of the way there—the mystery. Standard tests won't give the whole picture. Neither can imaging—not yet and maybe never, because the brain, as you know, isn't one organ that does one thing, but one made up of disparate parts working together and with the entire nervous system in ways we can't always see as it's happening. Diagnosis must be completed at the patient's bedside, in conversation and through observation. There's an elegance in the synthesizing of the information, some say a choreography. The human part just can't be avoided, not in clinical neurology, anyway."

He was showing her his passion, and it made him fall out of his straight lines, craning his neck, rounding his shoulders. His long fingers danced in the air between them.

"Is that why you chose it? As your specialty?" she asked.

"The challenge of it—yes. But then headaches and migraines in particular, how prevalent they are, nearly forty million sufferers in this country alone, and the medical community hasn't taken them seriously until recently, as if it were just hysteria, a female—"

Laughter erupted just outside. Male and loud. Like a rock hitting the door, and it startled Ruth, lifted her up out of her chair. The Doctor responded immediately—he was up and through the door and shooing Ed and Mr. Bavicchi away, into an examination room.

"Sorry, Ruth," he said, and seemed to mean it.

He sat back down. "What was I saying?"

"Hysteria? Or a female issue?"

"A female *problem*," he said. "Yes, a *problem*. You see, statistically, headache disorders favor women, but men are afflicted too, because of genetics or environmental causes or injury—traumatic brain injury."

Traumatic brain injury: Certain words in a specific order recurred in one's life, and these in this order, with very little variation, had recurred in Ruth's. Her husband hadn't recovered from his. All she'd done was push, pushed him away finally—*Get the fuck away from me*—and he fell and fell, was still falling, as if she could grab him back.

"It's pain that interests me, and how that's bound up in the patient's history, emotionally, physiologically. No two patients are the same, no two headaches." He shook his head. "If you sign on here, you'll hear me say this a lot. I'm talking too much, aren't I?"

If you sign on: He said it as if it were her choice and not his or Mrs. Watson's. And he was blushing, or starting to, the tops of his ears reddening.

"But it must be exciting, too? All that variety?" she asked him.

"Oh, yes," he said and smiled, and laughed at himself. "Very. And overwhelming at times. I imagine you know all about that?"

"Yes," she sighed and, despite herself, returned the smile.

She decided then that he was charming—by way of his curiosity and a courtliness. How deliberate or authentic it all was, she couldn't say. Only last night, he may have hovered over a river that would have taken him away. She heard him breathe in, as if with the office, the entire clinic, which churned in and out with air. She guessed it must be some sort of dehumidifying system to help them forget they were in the belly of a stone church.

"You know about plasticity, Ruth." He put a finger to the side of his forehead. "The way the brain can be remapped, the way it changes, must change, to make new connections, to learn, accommodate new information and behavior? It's thrilling, isn't it? A form of adaptability, renewal." The lights flickered again. "A miracle, but not with pain, no. The nerves that are firing and misfiring recruit other nerves. The hyperexcitability spreads—"

"Like with a wound? To protect damaged tissue? Discourage contact—"

"Yes, in a way. Yes! Wonderful, Ruth! Wonderful. With chronic pain—and not just headaches—the sensitivity endures, so what is harmless to most of us—even touch—hurts. You'll find that some of the patients here, like Jane, can barely tolerate being touched anymore, whether they're having an attack or not. Their bodies have been altered, they have a *different* body, as you said—"

At that, the lights went out completely and all the sounds of the clinic's respiration stopped. "Ah," he said.

"The wind," she said, as he had just moments before. "I can't hear it now. Can you?"

"Yes," he whispered to her, as if he must in the dark, so as not to spook her or the dark. She couldn't see him well in the windowless room as her eyes adjusted, but she knew he was listening for the wind too.

"Only faintly now, but I hear it. It could be downed wires, or a transformer," he told her. "We have a generator. It will take over. At any time now. We have emergency lights too—"

"Does this happen often?" she asked after an interval.

"Now and again—"

Sue yelled out, "I've got the manual! Someone changed the settings. I got it! Hold on, everyone!"

"Where the fuck am I?!" a drowsy male voice called.

"It's okay, Adam," Sue called back. "Go back to sleep."

When it was mostly quiet again, the Doctor, as if making sure she was still there, asked, "Ruth?"

"Yes?"

"It's rare I meet someone who does not believe that this city is the whole world, who has news from other places. Is the weather as off-kilter on the coast, in New Hampshire? I know the coast a little. Surfing towns?"

"It's blowing there now, too. Not as badly as here. In New England we're used to weather, but you're from Vermont, aren't you?"

"I was." He didn't want to talk about himself and veered back to her. "You put in your time in the NICU up there. That must be a geography all its own?"

It had been; it seemed a hundred years and several Ruths ago now. She was transferred into the intensive care unit for newborns just as her marriage ended at last. Forcibly. All while she was charged with protecting those tiny premature creatures. Born with too little protection, looking as desiccated and exhausted as very old men. Every one of them seemed a gift to her, a chance for redemption.

In the dark with the Doctor, she told him it was a kind of a prayer in the NICU—willing those babies to life, to the pink robustness promised to every mother, and willing the mothers to be strong, not to fear the lightness of their offspring. The gentleness and patience the nurses had practiced was a shock to her at first, everything done so as not to reverberate or leave a mark. They taught the mothers how to touch their babies, who could barely be touched at all; their skin wasn't fully formed. Neither were their lungs: *Listen for their breath.*

It was so vastly different from her days spent working in post-op, she told him, and increasingly from what her home life had been, though she didn't tell him that. In the gynecological surgical unit, you attacked the patients genially, hoping your energy would be catching: *Let's try to get up today, lean on me...* How those patients fought and complained and resented the sight of you. It was like holding to a musical note that might lift them, and you too: *Get up, get up, get up.*

She admitted to the effort it took to hold on to her compassion when human need could feel ever expanding.

"Yes," he agreed, again in a whisper. Maybe he nodded in the dark. "Yes."

And still she had charts to do, miles of them. That was a large part of what nurses were there for: keeping the records that might protect the hospital against liability, against human error, because the lawsuits kept coming, the naming of the names.

When the lights flared back to life, she could see the pupils of the Doctor's deep, bright eyes narrow, and that he was only looking at her, only listening.

"But I loved the work enough to stay," she told him, both because it was true and because it was appropriate to say in the light, now that they could see each other again so clearly. "You know, to stay and struggle with it and the deficiencies in the system, and in me," she assured him. "It's the kind of work that tests your mettle every day—"

The phone rang and was ignored once more, and his eyes asked her to continue and so she did, deciding that the danger with his eyes, which were worn and knowing and dug in with cares that she wouldn't dare guess at, was that you wanted to keep earning their attention. While you engaged him, you were not lacking, or Ruth wasn't, unless he looked away, but he hadn't. Not yet.

So she went further than she should have. She understood that this had to be some of why Mrs. Watson had likened him to Ophiuchus in the night sky. Ruth had managed to look up the constellation online: the image of a man forever wielding a snake. Aware of what that snake could do—bring knowledge, bring death—but the man in the sky was stalwart, unafraid. And the Doctor appeared unafraid of Ruth and what she might say to him, and so she confessed to him what he may have already known from an online search: that her work at the hospital had been taken from her. She was named in a complaint by a relation of her ex-husband's family, a woman who'd lost her baby in the NICU in its first weeks of life and needed someone to blame.

"I was already too visible in the area. My ex, he isn't, or he wasn't then, you know, a good man, or not enough, not most of the time, and there was some unpleasantness with him, and so later his family—"

The phone sounded again, and again the Doctor behaved as if nothing was sounding at all, except for Ruth, who continued, "What I'd like to do here is good, honest work—"

The phone then made a different noise, like two blows of a chirping whistle, one high, one low. It was the intercom, also ignored.

"To stay focused on the work, keep it simple and learn as much as I—"

That must have been what caused Sue to come to them, on the other side of the door, tapping and calling, "Paging the Doctor."

"We're getting acquainted here, Sue." There was irritation in his voice.

This didn't scare Sue: "You have patients, Doctor."

But he did not bark at Sue or make her jump, as Ruth expected. Instead, Ruth could see him switch gears. Give way. "So I do, Sue. So I do," and he smiled, at least with his eyes, and then at the door, and at whatever awaited him on the other side.

A yell: "Where the fuck am I?"

"*Shush*, Adam! Shush."

The Wind Report

Reports are coming in from our listeners that a flag's broken free. A big one. Here's someone—who? Lucas? Lucas says it looks like a pterodactyl soaring down Fifth Avenue. A big red-white-and-blue bird coming at you, baring its stripes? Imagine that. Thank you, Lucas. Thank you.

Who's on the line? Donna? Hi, Donna. You're calling about the flag?

"Yeah, hi. *Love, love* the show. That flag is like *huge*. It's got to be the one that goes on the G.W. Bridge. You see it on all the holidays. It's like the size of an Olympic swimming pool?"

A flag the size of a… Could that be it? No? My producer, Lakshmi, is shaking her head no. Evidently, that flag's been accounted for.

And here's a text. No name given. It says that this flag came from a residential building, 810 Fifth. That's an address I know. Grand old place? Didn't Nixon live there? Lakshmi? Yes?

Ah, here's Lucas again. He's posted a correction: Birds descended from terrestrial dinosaurs. Pterodactyls weren't dinosaurs at all, but flying reptiles. Okay, Lucas, you know your flying reptiles and I do not, I surrender… No need for the abuse, as colorful as it is…

Now I have Susan on the line. Susan, how are you?

"I'm fine, loving the show, but not this weather."

You sound a little worn out, Susan.

"I am."

You're calling about the flag?

"Sort of. I used to work on Fifth Avenue. At an advertising agency in the fifties there. I was there for twenty years, overseeing accounting, so I used to walk the avenue a lot, and the flags up and down it were so beautiful. I just wanted to say

I miss them, you know, the sight of those flags along Fifth, so many of them. At Saks, Rockefeller Center, the Plaza—"

So you're feeling nostalgic, Susan, for another time? Better weather? Before those flags had to come down? Before this one made its escape?

"Some days they looked almost lazy—"

Ah, yes, rolling and swelling, rising and falling. Mesmerizing, huh, Susan?

"And when there was a strong wind—not like these, not so constant, so destructive—those flags were up to it, they'd reach out straight. They flapped and pulled and they made this great noise—"

Ah, the halyards, yes, and those retainer rings and clips making a kind of music, and then quiet, right, Susan? Imagine that, would you, dear listeners? That moment when the wind dies. Everything's calm. We may see that again, any day now: gentle breezes out there. I don't know how long we'll have to wait, or maybe, Susan, we need to travel a little, all of us, go where the chilly winds don't blow? Nina Simone knows all about it, doesn't she? She's going where there are red roses around her door. Where someone is waiting for her, where the chilly winds don't blow. Listen to that voice, and pack up. C'mon, let's go—

Ruth

There was music again inside Mrs. Watson's house, but this time it played in the foyer, too, where Ruth stood waiting. Vocals came in a lush low register, then piano, bass, and drums dashed in to punctuate the song. A DJ intoned, "What a gift. Singer, songwriter, pianist: *Nina,* our Nina Simone. Activist, arranger, the self-described High Priestess of Soul—" This wasn't the delivery of a simple radio announcer, but a man who went in for theater.

"And this just in," he said. "Brace yourselves, my friends: A series of thunderstorms are on the way to us."

"Enough! Do you hear me?" Mrs. Watson shrilled. "Take that off the speakers down here. *Marie?!* Where are you? What is Orson doing? Tell him his aunt is leaving."

Mrs. Watson emerged from the hallway to one side of the stairs into the foyer.

"It's not too much to ask to put St. Gabriel's on the list, Adele," insisted another woman trailing behind. "It was built to be a sanctuary."

"Liability, Isabelle. And then don't act the innocent. It's tied to your other request, which you know very well is not in my best interest."

"How can you care so little for civic life, Adele? The life of this community? Or that church? You must grasp there are other interests at stake here."

The women wielded each other's names like lithe little daggers, and behind every word, especially Mrs. Watson's, there were other words, inaudible but charged with hostility and versions of past and present that differed and chafed.

"Ah, Ruth, you're here. My afternoon appointment. *Marie?!* Please! Turn it *off*!"

The broadcast, after the announcer had lovingly pronounced "flash flooding," was finally silenced, leaving a vacuum, and not the comforting sort Ruth had just known in the Doctor's office.

"Orson?! Isabelle is leaving. *Now!*"

"Ruth, this is a relation of mine," Mrs. Watson said, with *relation* sounding to Ruth's ears awfully like *contagion*. "And she's on her way *out*."

Ruth looked for a resemblance between the women. It wasn't obvious, but under Isabelle's misshapen rain hat, a few of those same white curls corkscrewed out. And the face structure was similar, but for every sharp turn in Mrs. Watson's features, the other woman had softer ones, gently padded. She was taller, too, with a great helping of bosom, and though irritation had edged into her face, she composed a look of welcome with the corners of her mouth.

"I'm Izzy—" Up close, Ruth saw that their eyes were the same shape under the same high brows, though Izzy's eyes were a pale blue. "You're here for the nurse's position at the clinic?"

"Yes. I'm Ruth—"

"I have a schedule to keep, Isabelle."

"I'm not going until I see Orson, Adele."

"I'll leave that to you and him. Ruth! This way!"

Izzy stiffened as Ruth followed Mrs. Watson, and at speed. "Be advised, Ruth," Izzy shouted after them. "Proceed with caution!"

Mrs. Watson stopped and turned and spat out, "What did you say, Isabelle?"

"I wasn't talking to you, Adele."

Mrs. Watson laughed, "Did you hear that, Ruth? She wants to protect you *from me*!"

Warnings arrived from all sides suddenly: Before Ruth had left the Doctor to come here, he'd stopped her: "One thing, Ruth, if I may." She'd worried he would chide her about discretion, maybe. She shouldn't have admitted to her troubles at the hospital or at home. It would give anyone pause. She'd nearly explained that a lawyer had filed a lawsuit on her behalf, that he thought her case was a strong one.

"It's delicate, but Adele—Mrs. Watson?" the Doctor had offered. "She'll need you to be her advocate. She'll require that." There was distaste on his face briefly. Then he thanked her for their talk and apologized again for the disruptions.

Now, seated across from her host, once again in that hard-bottomed antique chair, Ruth struggled to appear unruffled, receptive.

"She makes me laugh," Mrs. Watson said, but she was not laughing. "That was my father's other daughter. Younger than me. Her mother was not my mother. Isabelle was doted on, and it's *ruined* her. She thinks life's a fairy tale, and that she's some anointed fairy godmother making everything broken whole again with the shake of that *huge* wand up her ass. It would be hilarious if it weren't so sad and *infuriating*! Marie! *Marie!* Where is she? *Marie?!*"

Mrs. Watson located a small black box—a wireless intercom—and issued orders into it, asking for her "vitamin A" and something in Spanish, the something-something-blanco. Then she found the remote for the music system. "I'm fit to be tied. I know we have business to discuss, Ruth, and we will, we will."

Marie stole in with what had been requested and stole out again, without noise or acknowledging Ruth.

"Ice, Marie, *please*," Mrs. Watson called after her. There was strain in that *please,* anger that reverberated for an instant until, gently at first, an orchestra lifted up around them.

"Studies, studies I support—and by that I mean give funds to—have shown music can work as a pain reliever, as effectively as any pill. You've seen that yourself, yes? And maybe, Ruth, in this very room?"

Ruth nodded.

"I'm glad… I could certainly use some relief. You see, Isabelle came to me today because the city is asking that landlords volunteer space for people to gather in the inclement weather, should it get extreme, or *more* extreme. Isabelle wants *my* church on that list. But it's tied to her other mission with her friends at the historical society. She wants St. Gabriel's to be declared a historical monument, which will make any further renovations a matter of municipal committee. It will slow the entire process, and make it all *vastly* more costly. There's nothing saintly in bureaucracy, but of course she wouldn't know a thing about that. And now this? Making it a shelter? Imagine the liability!"

Marie's hand shot out to place a bucket of ice before them and then she was gone.

"It's more comfortable over here. Beside me here? Isn't it?"

Ruth got up and sat beside Mrs. Watson again.

"This right here is a delightful small-batch highlands tequila made from pure agave. The Doctor has said if I drink alcohol, I should drink the clear ones. I don't necessarily agree, but I'm trying to be good, *for him*. But this is interesting, far more so than vodka or gin. You'll taste floral notes, mint, rosemary. Hint of cinnamon, too, and pepper."

She poured the tequila into two highball glasses.

"Did you know Mother Teresa was actually rather a fiend? She withheld medicines, treatment, until people agreed to convert to Catholicism. There's a documentary about it. Have you seen it?"

Ruth shook her head.

"No, of course not. The film is banned in the U.S. No surprise there either. An Ativan, Ruth?"

"No, thank you."

"Slight dose. As needed." Mrs. Watson chased down a pill with the tequila.

"This music," Ruth said. "Is it Bach?" One violin had emerged out of the orchestra to draw its own arcing line.

"Bach, yes. My husband's favorite composer. It's the Concerto for Violin in E Major, the adagio. My husband liked Bach on the harpsichord. Bach, in fact, liked Bach on the harpsichord, but I like him better on the violin. The only time I heard this live was in Paris. That's a story I think you'd like. Should I tell you? I want to tell you, Ruth, if you want to hear? It might do us both good."

"Of course."

"Sip this for me first, won't you? One sip? It's an elixir. Or just smell it? *For me*?"

They had been here before, hadn't they? And Ruth had not only survived it but enjoyed it.

Mrs. Watson paused the music, waiting until Ruth lifted the glass to her nose. It took her to her mother's kitchen in the summer after they'd plundered their garden. With it came nostalgia for a spring that held on to its petals, and to its scents, to a time when contact with something beautiful lingered and insinuated itself into the body like a benediction. The music resumed as she drank now, her tongue confirming what she'd smelled, along with the light heat of the spice and alcohol at the back of her throat.

They listened to the whole of the adagio without a word between them.

As it set off for a second time, Mrs. Watson said, "I have loved Bach and hated him, too, for reasons having to do with my marriage, but this piece, this concerto, I've inhabited it, lived it. Music will allow that."

Ruth nodded, leaned her head back, and closed her eyes.

"Do you hear the orchestra widening out? And then that violin, so exquisite, coming in on a long-held note that could wither, but it doesn't?"

Mrs. Watson traced the side of Ruth's wrist with her finger. Ruth didn't open her eyes.

"The violin pierces the orchestration, but eventually neither the soloist nor the ripieno dominates. They become equals. How rare to live that. Monogamy so often fails us. We aren't really built for monogamy, are we, Ruth? Time and our chemistry seem to guarantee it. We spend so much time regretting this"—she circled the knuckle of Ruth's thumb with her finger, gently round and round—"when we should be celebrating the moments that we can feel as this music makes us feel...

"I promised you a story. It was the very first time I heard this piece performed live, in Paris. Let me tell you."

Mrs. Watson's Story

I wasn't meant to be at that Bach concert at all. I wasn't meant to meet Sandrine Vallonier. She'd been one of my husband's breast reconstructions and one of his lovers.

She'd had a double mastectomy as a preventative measure. She had the gene for breast cancer. That cancer killed her mother and her mother's mother, so it didn't strike her as too extreme a measure, and then she was a journalist and a realist, not to mention a true adventurer. She wasn't one to lead with worry about consequences and didn't judge her breasts all that necessary for a happily divorced woman in her mid-forties. But not very long after, she wanted something back, something as close to her own breasts as she could get. She came to my husband, from Paris. His reputation as a surgeon preceded him, here and in Europe, Asia too, and he cherished his patients, treated every one of them, young or old, with warmth. He loved women, not only to go to bed with. He was taken with everything feminine, and in breasts he saw our glory, all our capacities, and our vulnerabilities.

Oh, he could be crass as any man, but he could also be exceedingly sensitive and perceptive and kind. It was disarming. He was.

When he was diagnosed with pancreatic cancer, he asked if we could go to Paris to see a doctor friend there, a celebrated oncologist.

I left him once, came back, and was readying to leave him again—I had the most savage matrimonial lawyer on retainer. But my husband was dying, in a year, maybe two if we were lucky, and he said he wanted Paris and to pick out a French chestnut just for me in our favorite park, the Jardin du Luxembourg, and if I was good he'd get me something fanciful and very haute French. Givenchy, Dior, Chanel—it didn't matter, he'd spoil me. He meant it. He wanted me there with him, as we'd been countless times before, but the thing is, he wanted everything*: I well knew he* *would also endeavor to see a certain French woman. Sandrine had had an effect on him, one I couldn't understand until I met her.*

He scheduled a dinner with his doctor friend, just the two of them. He said I didn't need to hear the grim statistics they'd be discussing about his cancer or about all the complications of his getting into any trials at his age. I said, "Of course, of course," though I knew he was lying. I'd become expert at seeing through his deceptions. He had some digestive pain of late, so sleep had been erratic for him and he was often drowsy. After a splendid late lunch of lemon sole and capers, creamed spinach, and a good bottle of Sancerre, I crushed a few Ativans into the chamomile tea I ordered for him back at our room. (Ativan, you see, was my friend even then.) I found the ticket to the Bach concert for that evening in his wallet. Only one. The other ticket would be sent on—that was his style, to have the ticket delivered in advance of the meeting, along with a scent he'd like his date to wear or a piece of jewelry.

She was seated already, at the Théâtre des Champs-Élysées, a polished old place built in the early twentieth century, young by French standards but, because of its elegance and noted architects, a monument historique. *Then again, what isn't there? Protected and scrubbed clean, at great expense to taxpayers? The poor French: They're just choked with history and bureaucracy. They can barely make a cent. But don't let me digress. There was Sandrine.*

She wasn't what I expected—a long-limbed tomboy who chewed her nails and smelled of suntan lotion. She didn't wear much makeup: a light dusting of powder, a vivid red lipstick. She had a beaky nose and a square face, but was she lovely? Yes, oh yes—her brows were dark and heavy over these long lids and light, wide, staring eyes. She set them on you with frightful intensity, like a hawk might. All of Europe was in her face—Eastern, Western, the wide cheekbones, the high forehead, those undeniable brows. Her mother was Jewish; her father, no. Her skin took the sun well, and she'd been out in it that day, she told me later, making her glow. Her highlighted dark brown hair fell to her shoulders, and the top of it was pulled back with a pin. She wore a long, black, sleeveless shift and a necklace, silver, with a sizable rectangular chunk of turquoise as a pendant, aiming for her cleavage. My husband had chosen well. The piece was by a New Mexican designer we both liked. Simple, not showy.

She wore no other jewelry, and no bra, perhaps for him, to show him what staying power his work had, what youth it conveyed.

"My husband is not able to make it tonight. He's not well," I told her as I sat beside her. "I am going to join you."

Oh, the hawkish look I got, her intelligence working and weighing all the possibilities. I was afraid of a confrontation right there, that she would walk out, but then, no. She was too curious. She simply said, "Ah," and then, as much for herself: "Why not?"

"The necklace suits you," I told her.

"You know?" She looked at me with amazement.

"Yes, of course."

"And you are not dismayed?" Her English was wonderful, came straight from English novels.

"No."

"Not very American of you."

"You are hardly the first, or the last." I studied the program. "Do you like Bach?" I asked her.

"Of course."

She hid in her program but kept regarding me sideways.

"Does he know you're here?" she asked.

"He will soon."

This gave her pleasure. It colored and lit her face as the concert began and launched into the allegro, what the program called Bach's expression of "unconquerable joy." Right away I was bored, disliked the fast pace—my heart was carrying on a bit too wildly already—but Sandrine wasn't bored. The fingers on her hand nearest me directed and danced, and her head moved with the music's exuberant ticking, knocking more pieces of her hair loose. She'd forgotten me and my husband.

Through her I saw how even the allegro had a complexity and subtlety, despite its speed.

But I didn't agree with the program: Joy is *conquerable. It comes and goes. If you're lucky, it comes more often than it goes. But sorrow? Longing? They* do *conquer you. They're in charge.*

And it was this, this adagio we're listening to now, meant to slow us down, that confirmed this for me that evening. The violinist was a slip of a Polish girl, some blond rising vedette, playing with the French National Orchestra. As the orchestra started the adagio, like some mystical weather front rolling in, the Polish girl went slack for a moment, as if knowing what was to come, emptying herself. Then she shook herself upright and began on cue.

How Sandrine's whole body gave itself to the violin's pulses, as if that violin was touching her as it ascended, in all its flourishes and silences. Without looking, I knew her body, everywhere under that simple, inexpensive dress, was broken out in gooseflesh. I also knew then I could seduce her. I had never been with a woman before, but I would be that night, if she'd let me, in her apartment, or, if that wasn't available, in a hotel.

The final movement, the allegro assai, came at us like a brick thrown through glass after that sinuous adagio. It ran at us. Too much. That poor Polish girl was slick with sweat now.

"Let me feed you," I whispered, close to Sandrine's ear, grazing her bare arm with my fingers. "You pick the place."

I liked kissing her, it turned out, but even if I didn't, I would have kissed her anyway. Let's be honest: Sex is not always about desire. Sandrine seemed to enjoy it, because she kept giving me her mouth and neck on the sturdy little loveseat in her living room. We'd had wine, one bottle. Then another. She didn't initiate anything but gave herself to me. At first she did it, it seemed, as part of an experiment, or as a willing subject of one, a curiosity to her. Why not? She didn't look at me, she lay her head back, but eventually—because I was determined—I made her move as that adagio had. I made her see me seeing her, and I felt so very powerful.

I asked her if I could put my fingers and mouth wherever my husband had touched her—know every one of those places. She said flatly, "No, impossible," and explained to me that she liked sex but it didn't make her lose all sense. She said in that marvelous English of hers, "You must comprehend that I do not love him. His care of me, his sweetness, these are like a boy's. It is very dear. It refreshes. But his appetite for sex—it is a man's. And only a man's. It demands. It has many… persuasions."

But, you see, I was persuasive, too, and I kissed those breasts he'd given her, around them, under them, as I would want my own kissed. I traced her sternum up to her neck and chin, ears, then to her mouth. I drove myself into her until she cried out, and then, with her eyes open, looking at me, she showed me every place he had been, and how—how gently or how voraciously, how fast or slow. I knew he had done things to her he'd never done to me and never would. There was no real need or dependence between the two of them, or responsibility. It was fucking, you see, good, thorough fucking.

I tell you this, Ruth, not to shock you, but to explain how I turned the tables that evening and never went back to what had been before, to the way he and I were together before. I think it changed my whole life.

My husband, once he woke, waited for me to come back to him in the hotel. I did, of course, the next morning, in my evening attire, wearing the necklace he'd given her. She had draped it on me, fastened it, laughing. He saw it and me. We said nothing for a time, and we never spoke of what happened between Sandrine and me. What was there to say? I took the ticket and the woman, I wore the necklace as proof, and he needed me now. I would decide just how faithful or consistent I would be in the future. Understand, Ruth, I wasn't cruel. I catered to his every need while he received treatment and even when he stopped, but I'd no longer be anyone's fool, particularly not his. I loved him too much to be hurt by him anymore. I couldn't bear it. It was killing me; and in one night, with one woman, I had found a way to control it.

* * *

Ruth had sunk like a stone into Mrs. Watson's reverie; she could not move and didn't want to.

The music was still on, on to other violin music, though the volume had been turned low and only hinted at the music's effects. The day's switching bright pulsed at the top of the curtains, changing the light in the room and behind Ruth's eyes. She had kept them closed while listening. There had been sirens—never-ending sirens in that city now—and she thought she heard thunder, too, though she wasn't sure. If so, it was far off. Everything seemed to be, except the story, which might not be true, or not completely, though its very details, the hurt and hunger running through it and under it, like the music, and the authority with which it was relayed, felt so very real to Ruth, as if she could glance off it with her own fingers, until Marie's voice, and Marie with it, spoke up gently from behind them.

"Larry is here."

"My massage therapist. He's early."

"The weather," Marie said. "It may get bad. Heavy rain. Businesses are closing early. The mayor is recommending it. They may close the clinic early, but the Doctor—you know how he is."

"I do," Mrs. Watson said, and spent an instant thinking about that before she went on, "Ruth and I are not quite done here. Lawrence can wait. So can the weather. I'll need that item we discussed? Is that ready?"

"Yes," said Marie.

What *item*? Ruth didn't know, only that she'd been freed for a time from the constant tug of her own worries. The tequila, it wasn't like other liquor. Ruth's husband had called it the cocaine of booze, but he had never tasted this particular batch, mixing inside her with Mrs. Watson's night in Paris and how she had touched Ruth again, so tenderly. Once more, Ruth wanted to pull the woman closer to her.

"May I ask if you saw her again—Sandrine?"

"Yes, I've seen her. We're friends, of course."

"Did he, your husband? See her again?"

"She came to visit us, both of us. I can tell you more about that another time if you'd like. I have nothing to hide, though I would hope I have your confidence? Do I, Ruth?"

"Yes."

"Let's take care of some business now, shall we? Tell me, what was your opinion of the Doctor?"

She didn't want to think of the Doctor now, or any of the cautions given her. She wanted to stay in this room, where even the wood wasn't just wood—what had Mrs. Watson said? That walnut was selective? That it helped some things thrive and not others?

"The Doctor?" Ruth saw him again in her mind's eye—all those lines that made him, beams and columns; and those eyes sifting her.

"He seemed too good to be true."

Mrs. Watson laughed, maybe at Ruth.

"Last night he went out walking," Ruth hurried to report. "I don't think he was in his right mind. He nearly threw himself in the river."

Mrs. Watson turned a look of severity on Ruth: "How do you know this?"

"A man in the waiting room. He told me."

"A patient?"

"I think so, or potentially, but for the other doctor."

"Chaudhri?"

"No. Ed? Dr. Konrad?"

"Ah, that *other* doctor. Konradi. *That* explains a lot." Mrs. Watson's stare and manner relaxed. "But the Doctor was fine when you met?"

"Seemed to be."

"You see, Ruth, you're already of great use to me. Another pair of eyes, *new* eyes. But he *is* gifted. That's maybe the only thing my sister Isabelle and I agree on."

"My sister won't speak to me," Ruth confessed, to delay whatever had to come next, *business*, and then Ruth leaving this room. "I embarrassed her. What happened to me, my life, did—it embarrassed her."

"Then she's a fool. My sister certainly is. But we're not, are we? Not anymore."

Mrs. Watson could be on Ruth's side. Ruth could let her, couldn't she?

"Now I want to be able *to see*, see it all, Ruth, before it can hurt. Don't you? Haven't you always wanted to see, to know—by this I mean get *behind* what is being told to you, to the truth?"

Ruth nodded.

"That's why I have a request to make of you. There's a journal the Doctor has had in his possession for some time, too long now. It concerns me. It belongs to a former patient of his, a troubled girl who I fear brings out troubling things in him. I need to know if it threatens my investment in any way. I've made a considerable investment not just in the office but *in the man*. You're in a unique position to understand why I have to be vigilant, all the… *nuances*." Only yesterday, Mrs. Watson had used that word to flatter Ruth. Was she preparing Ruth for this even then? "I need you to make a copy of that journal for me. I have a key for you, a master key that overrides the codes, which we change from time to time."

That was the "item" mentioned. A key.

"You can go tonight, weather permitting. It's what I need for my security and the security of the clinic, and I'm hoping you can help, *want* to help with that. Do you? Want to?"

Though Ruth could still hear it faintly, the music was vanishing, taking Paris with it. She hesitated and managed to say, "Yes. Of course… "

"He, the Doctor, has not been as collaborative as I hoped. By now. I don't think I'm seeing the full picture. Do you understand?"

Mrs. Watson laid her hand over Ruth's. It was smaller than Ruth's, and softer, too. "And you should know whoever works for me benefits. I hope you know that. Marie has a daughter; in addition to Marie's salary, I pay for her daughter's schooling. And I have lovely apartments nearby, in Cobble Hill, Carroll Gardens, Brooklyn Heights, that I can give you for what you're paying where? Where are you staying?"

"Prospect Lefferts, on Clarkson Avenue, a sublet near the hospital there."

"My apartments are in quiet neighborhoods with good light and built-in bookshelves—you're a reader, aren't you?"

Ruth had given her assessment of a few books online, for anyone to see, on a book recommendation site. Years ago now, she'd gushed over books like *The House of Mirth*, Duras's *The Lover*, Marian Engel's *Bear*, using serial exclamation points like a girl.

"What I have would, I imagine, be something of an improvement over your current situation. I just want you to think about that. How I might help you. Will you, Ruth?"

"Yes."

"Marie has an offer sheet for you with the details of your eventual employment with us: your salary, your benefits, et cetera. Look that over carefully and let us know if it meets all your expectations. We always start with a trial run of a few weeks regardless—to see if we're a good fit. The *right* fit. That's been laid out for you as well, in the offer, in writing: the time frames here. I hope you'll be pleased. I'm certain we *all* will be. And then there's that key card. And Lawrence! I'm anxious for you to meet him. He works at the clinic, too—does massage there. It's extraordinary what his hands can do, and I'm willing to share those hands. I have so very much to share with you, Ruth."

Part II

I saw the angel in the marble
and carved until I set him free.

—Michelangelo

In the end, today is forever,
yesterday is still today, and
tomorrow is already today.

—William Saroyan

The Doctor

Last night, after taking Ed's lozenge, he had slept so deeply that it took him longer than usual to reassemble himself. He was still at it throughout the morning, into the afternoon.

Something had recalibrated inside him. He could only say that it felt like a shade had been snapped open to a view that he'd not only never seen before but never suspected was there. In the night, he didn't wake once to hear the wind keening. His knees weren't aching. All his joints, up and down, felt looser, as if he was in whole or in parts less for them to bear. We heal as we sleep: You didn't need to be a doctor to know that, but there was something more at work here—a sense he had of going far away and coming back, not merely renewed but different. He didn't dare say the word that would match the shivering feeling he had, not even to himself. And when it floated before him, tantalizing him, five syllables wanting out of his mouth—*neurogenesis*—he gave his attention to the patient in the room with him, a teacher, referred by Christine, from a private elementary school in Bay Ridge.

"A doctor in a church named for Saint Gabriel? An archangel, bearer of good news? You got good news for me, Doctor? Tell me you do." She laughed, and he did, too, but promised her nothing. That choice felt lighter too.

There was the landlord/tenant lawyer who explained he worked mostly for landlords and by and large despised them: "They don't want to make repairs. It's all cat and mouse. And they're the dumbest fucking cats. Greed makes them dumb and it gives me a headache. Sometimes I go numb on one side, just numb, like my body's giving up on me. And maybe it is. Let's you and I prescribe me a new career, huh?"

Yes, the Doctor agreed, getting out his pad. "What would you like to be?"

"Free. Or just enough to come up with a good answer to that question."

As the Doctor listened to his patients and the day progressed, time left him alone, showing up only in the form of Sue, who would buzz or be forced to knock to move things along, as she did at midday, when he'd met with Mrs. Watson's latest notion of what a nurse in the clinic should be.

He'd tried to give the young woman, Ruth—Ruth Aitken—a picture of what was at stake for so many of the clinic's patients, the complexity in treating them, even the beauty in it. He'd gone on too much, hoping to draw out not just the medical professional in her, but the person who'd chosen such hard human work.

When the electricity failed, he got that from her and more: He wanted to go wherever she wanted him to go, and he did, to a New Hampshire hospital, to a ward of post-op women whose bodies had been rearranged, and to a NICU, where everything was cushion and hush and hope for humans born too soon. Here was another view he'd never had and wanted more of, until Sue reset not only the generator but him, too—bringing news of heavy rainstorms and early office closures. But he didn't leave right away. Neither did Sue, and once Lydia and her son Aengus came in for their appointment, she left him to his own pace.

Aengus, or Gus, was one of a dozen children under age thirteen seen at the clinic and one of only three boys. Lydia, who was raising Gus alone, preferred he stick with over-the-counter pain relievers and antihistamines unless the migraine was especially severe, as hers were regularly. Children's nervous systems, still forming, didn't always respond to adult treatments and could be harmed by them. Because the plasticity of children's brains—the capacity to make new neurons and synaptic connections—was far greater, and because their cells' insulation wasn't complete yet, the whole substrate was more vulnerable. Gus was, and the Doctor meant to keep Mrs. Watson's various corporate research partners and their inquiries away from him and the other children treated there, except insofar as they factored into statistical information.

"I dust and vacuum and the wind just throws all the pollen and dust back in," Lydia lamented, "and he's not taking his allergy meds."

"They make me sleepy," Gus said.

"He eats more sugar than he should. Oreos," Lydia reported. "He hides them in his room."

"Well," the Doctor said, with a glee he couldn't control and could barely hide, "Oreos are delicious."

Lydia fixed stern eyes on the Doctor. She worked as an administrative director at an advertising agency where she had to, as she put it, "babysit creatives."

"He opens his windows at night. I close them," she said.

"Only a crack," Gus explained, and sniffled. His allergies, worse in the spring, tended to set off his migraines, that first link in the chain. "I like to hear what's happening out there. I mean, everyone complains, but on Neptune the winds are like thirteen hundred miles per hour. *Really* fast. It's an ice giant, that's what they call it. It's got fourteen moons."

"That many?" The Doctor tried to picture it, all those moons orbiting a planet made of ice.

"Saturn and Jupiter have a whole lot more. And their weather is like a disaster movie *every* day: One cyclone on Saturn measured like five thousand miles in diameter—"

"Is there an antihistamine that won't make him as drowsy?" Lydia asked.

"There was this boy in a plastic bubble. You know about him, Doctor?" Gus asked.

"Gus," Lydia protested. "I was speaking—"

"So was I, Mom."

"Yes, I remember him," the Doctor said, asking Lydia with a smile to indulge him.

"Yeah. He lived in a bubble like his *whole life*, then he died. I'm not like that. I keep telling Mom."

"No, that's right," the Doctor agreed. "You're not like—"

"David Vetter. You can google him."

"Ah, yes—he didn't live long, yes? He had no protections against infection. You've been built a whole lot tougher—"

"See, Mom? And the wind here, on this planet, it's like *nothing*. But if I could get closer, up there"—excited, he wiped his nose with his shirt and bent toward the Doctor so he could confide, between men—"it's not possible now, but someday, like a manned mission to—"

"You'll have to take your medicine," Lydia put in, "if you expect to be an astronaut. And no more Oreos—"

"*Mom!*" He side-kicked at her chair, set beside his, though not hard. Still, Lydia jumped. "That kid in the bubble is *dead*, dead! But I'm not! Don't you get it? *I have to live, God dammit!*"

Lydia reeled back, and so did Gus. He didn't have Lydia's coloring—her father had been Irish, her mother St. Lucian—but he had her high, hard forehead, dark blue, almost indigo eyes, and pointed intelligence. The Doctor's office narrowed as the boy returned his mother's glare.

"Lydia, would you mind terribly if I spoke to Gus alone?"

She got up without a word and closed the door behind her.

Gus looked at his feet, which he knocked together. "Sorry," he mumbled. There came the breathing of the climate control, nothing else, no wind for the moment or Sue knocking at the door. He let them both hear it before he spoke: "There was another boy, I recall, who was put in a similar sterile enclosure. This one had aplastic anemia, a different disorder: He couldn't make new blood cells. Did you know that aplastic anemia is nearly curable now?"

"No."

"It is. New treatments come out all the time. For viruses—stimulating the immune system, making antibodies—we've seen that lately. And there are new treatments for migraine that work in the same way. And these incredible antidepressants designed to make new neurons—new nerve cells in the brain—which is like making new life in your—"

"If I go into space there won't be any trees. Mom hates those tall trees, in rows, in the parks. London plane trees. Like in Cadman Plaza Park in Brooklyn Heights? I told her they're clones—they *clone* them. It's so *weird* and *so* great. They shed their bark in the summer like they're hot. In July. She doesn't like me in the park when they do—because of mold and whatever—but you tell her, okay? That I'm going, that those trees won't kill me?"

"I'll tell her. Of course."

The Doctor had passed the park on the way to the bridge the night before, and those very trees, in the dark, were long, singing shadows, giving in to the wind while shaking and *shhh*ing as if with the volume of the sea. He wanted to tell the boy about them and how the Brooklyn Bridge was suspended in blue and red light and how badly he wanted to get to it, feel its pulse.

"There are places I want to go, too, Gus. I can't go now, but soon I'll go. It takes some patience, that's all, and until then you keep searching from right here, travel in here—" The Doctor tapped his forehead and didn't utter what else was there in his head: *Pain makes us search for God.* Even if that search comes up with something other than God.

Darwin and Nietzsche and all the people on Sarah's long list of headache-impaired virtuosos had reached outside of what was known, into the unknown. They submitted to disorientation. They had no choice: Nietzsche returning from his episodes with a nothingness and a chance at reinvention that was as powerful as God. Darwin in bed for days and days, adrift; then, species by species, he pieced it together, the grandeur. *There is grandeur in this view of life.*

Again, the word with its five syllables swelled in the Doctor's throat like excitement: *neurogenesis.* Like he was no older or wiser than Gus. It was silly: All new experience creates new synaptic connections and sensations.

When Sue took Gus away to find pens and paper or magazines, whatever he wanted, Lydia came back, but not as she was. She'd been derailed in her energies, her sense of mission. She had the look of everything being too hard and of needing sleep, not just for an hour but days of it. Her headaches were more frequent than Gus's, more entrenched and harder to treat.

Like her son, she kept her eyes on the floor. The Doctor couldn't betray the elation he'd been feeling since he woke that morning, but he had to try to convey what he didn't just know but felt now: He asked her if she knew about nocebo and placebo—"If we believe something will harm us, we are probably helping it to do so, and if we believe something will help, it's more likely to."

"By how much? A lot? A little?" she asked.

"That depends on the patient. On you. For instance, there's probably no more vivid experience for the brain than pain, but joy comes close. I am going to prescribe joy for you, Lydia. For Gus but also for you: sleep and exercise *and joy*. I know massage has helped you in the past. But what about dancing? You were a swing dancer? You told me about dancing for entire weekends, I remember. Before you had Gus? Remember how you felt? Here?" He tapped his head again. "I'll write a prescription, make it official, and if you need a sitter, call me. I'll arrange something. I'm in charge here, or sometimes I am." He laughed. She didn't.

"I know I keep saying this, but Gus's headaches, statistically speaking, have a good chance of going away. They do for boys, more so than girls, and he's so resilient, isn't he? Determined?"

She nodded, still unmoved, so he tried another tack. He told her about a patient he'd treated off and on for years: a theoretical physicist who had acute weekly migraines. They began midweek, and by the weekend he was incapacitated.

Until Sunday night, when he wasn't just better but refreshed. A new man. On Monday and Tuesday he did his most inventive work.

"We put him on a blood pressure medicine, a beta-blocker, something we've talked about for you. And there are new medications, like the CGRP antagonist I've mentioned, but you see, Lydia, what I'm saying is, without his migraines, all this man's creativity was gone, too. If I recall right, he had no pain, but he couldn't work with any real vision, you see? Not up to snuff, for him. He needed his episodes in some way. So I guess the question is, at what cost do we want to be cured of who we are? Pain and all? Do you want to cure Gus of who he is? Or you?"

Lydia wagged her head at this and was about to say something—even to put him in his place—when there came a scratching sound on his door. It wasn't Sue or Gus on the other side, but Jane: She stood there before him at his now open door, as if she was the physical embodiment of his question: At what cost do we wish to be cured of who we are? *At any cost* appeared to be Jane's answer, her body wavering and weedy. She had come to say goodbye to the Doctor.

Lydia, startled at seeing this young woman before her—which was like seeing herself or her son or both there in the door—got to her feet and was gone before he could impress upon her the seriousness of his advice: *Joy. Why not joy?*

"Better?" he asked Jane.

"For now," she said, "but the weather, I can feel how bad it's going to be."

As a kid, Jane had been prescribed a range of medicines to stop her episodes, those for epilepsy, bipolar disorder, schizophrenia, with side effects she worried shadowed her still. She did not trust easily, but today she'd let him move her from her refusal—to shelter here. There was a chance in it. In her trust. She trusted him, as Sarah had—

How do you confine hope?

Ed saw it in the Doctor right away: what felt like hope, and it must have looked like it, too. He slipped in after Jane left and after his consultation with Mr. Bavicchi, the man who'd found the Doctor on the pier the night before.

"Something's different, isn't it? Your whole manner, Doc—"

"I slept so soundly," the Doctor marveled.

"Is that all?"

"My knees don't hurt. Not since I took the edible."

"Is that so?" Ed grinned at him like a man being told he'd been right all along, through all their debates and not just about cannabis. "You're a new man."

The Doctor didn't dare say the word, but it was there between them.

"Try more. See what happens."

"Tell me about Mr. Bavicchi."

Until he saw Mr. Bavicchi in the lounge with Ruth earlier, the Doctor had wondered if he hadn't dreamed him up—a man who knew the church before it had been abandoned and broken down, when it was vital. The Doctor wanted to swim last night, let go, then there were that man's twisted hands on him, pulling him back, with alarm and a kindness he couldn't argue with.

"What a piece of work he is, Nick, Nick Bavicchi, but he says he's got nothing to lose, so we'll try some combinations. As part of the study. I'll get a release signed. He asked me if I knew what I was doing. I told him I knew as much as anyone else can now, gave him a little Copernicus. He loved that. And he liked that Ruth, the nurse. Something to like there? I take it you two were in here in the dark? She's got an edge…"

She did, like an athlete before the gun was about to go off. Ruth's white uniform, showing a strong physique, only added to the impression, as did her hair, pinned down against any movement, and her face, bare of makeup. Her smiles didn't last long, seemed only for show, while something in her center of gravity ticked, ready to jump.

"Hard to say yet, about Ruth. If she's up to it, up to Adele." She'd be the third nurse in a year. Adele liked to test her hires and punish when they failed her, but he didn't want to talk about Ruth or Adele now. He was about to confess that the high had nearly been too much for him and ask about other ratios, without the THC, when yelling broke in. A woman's voice pitched up high with anger: "You will let me in! I am his *wife*!"

How that voice always pierced him through at his diaphragm and knocked the air out of him. "Ex-wife," the Doctor corrected in a whisper.

"I will not quiet down! This is an emergency—don't follow me. I know where his office is."

"Oh, no," said Ed.

"Yes, she's here."

Jackie didn't knock. She banged on the door with, the Doctor knew, the side of her fist, as if she were wielding a stabbing knife. She'd open the door next, but the Doctor got to it before she could, to cut off the momentum of the wave she was riding to him. He stepped toward her, out of his office, so that she would have to step back. With Jackie, he'd learned long ago, it was her limbic system to which he had to communicate first. He had to show her his real size to match her imagined size. There was no one she believed she couldn't outdo in energy and will.

She shrank back, but only for an instant. In her voice was resentment, but it was subdued by something childlike: "*Where* have you been?"

"Here," he said. "Right here."

Sue came up behind them: "I'm sorry, Doctor. I couldn't make her wait—"

Jackie spun around at Sue: "Make *me*? Who do you think you are?" Then she turned to step as close to the Doctor as she could without touching him. "Why haven't you called? I had a consult. It was serious. Did this little dolly here forget to tell you I called?"

A voice behind them spoke up: "Hey, hey, hey, you okay, Doc?" It was Adam, who'd been asleep on the couch off and on all day, standing now, stooped and half-awake. They all turned to look. "You need me, Doc?"

"What is this?" Jackie jeered. "Is he your bouncer?"

"Hey, I know you," Adam said, waking fully, pulling himself to his full height, taller than the Doctor, taller than all of them. Still a young, strong man despite all that had happened to him when he served. "*I know you.*"

"Me?" Jackie asked.

"I came to see you about my head, between tours, a couple years back. The VA referred me."

Jackie squinted at him. "I'm sorry. I see so many patients—good to see you again." She lowered her voice to the Doctor. "Can we go in?"

"You're a pusher, right?" Adam said.

"I'm sorry, *what*?"

"I couldn't get off that stuff. And not just me, my brothers, other soldiers—"

"Please," she said to the Doctor. "*Please,* can we go in?"

She looped her arm in his, pulled him into his office, and shut the door behind them, only to see Ed. "Good Christ—*Ed* is here. *Of course*. What next?"

Ed stood. "Ah, Jackie." He did not offer his hand or an embrace.

"I should have known you were here, Ed. It smells like a barn in here."

Ed gave a great laugh. "Jackie, *my,* how I've missed your nasty, *nasty* mouth."

"I need to talk to him alone. How about you graze somewhere else?"

"Gladly. This bull knows when a pasture has gone to shit."

"Fuck you, Ed."

"If only, Jackie. If only..." He winked at her with a ferocious waggle of his head. "We'll talk later, Doc?"

The Doctor nodded to see his door shut again and Jackie seated and turned away, inside herself, shy or pouting, he couldn't tell, but avoiding his eyes and catching her breath. He noticed there was a sheen of water on her. The rain that had been promised had arrived. She'd dressed for it in a short black belted trench coat and shiny black rain boots; she was stylish and trim, except for her decision to wear her thick blond hair, cut now to shoulder length, in pigtails, which gave the impression of trumpets at the ready on either side of her head.

"I have a patient with a lipoma," Jackie told him. "A teenager. History of congenital hydrocephalus. They blamed the headaches on the shunt, but her life was normal, until recently."

"How could I help?"

"The lipoma, of course: I need some help persuading the mother about surgery. It was for the girl, *a patient*, that I kept calling. Not for me." She said this without her customary hostility, and she still wasn't looking him in the eye. "That boy outside?"

"Adam?"

"TBI?" By that she meant traumatic brain injury.

"Yes."

"Is he okay?" she asked.

"He's doing much better."

"He's big. Violent?"

"He wouldn't do anything, not here—"

"*Not here?* Jesus, Louis! If he'd come to me now, to us—" There was a whine in her voice. "I mean, it's different. *Now*."

At her new practice she advertised a holistic approach and employed a naturopath, and on Fridays an acupuncturist. She'd embraced new methodologies with the zeal of a convert. It didn't hurt that she was making a profit on redemption.

"Why didn't you call me? I called and called."

"I'm sorry. It's been busy—"

"I was served yesterday."

"Served?"

"I'm being sued. The parents of a patient. Twenty-three. She died of a heroin overdose. I gave the girl painkillers after a car accident, and that's how it began, they say, with my prescription pad. But there are others, with the same lawyer. Several. I'll be served again and again. For all I know, that kid out there is one of the lawsuits—"

"You have a lawyer. And your malpractice insurance?" the Doctor asked.

"Of course I do. You know that."

"Statute of limitations?"

"Two and a half years."

"That's lucky, then. Surely you haven't been prescribing much in the last two years?"

"Not in the last year and not much before that, but—God, I don't know. Here and there. For some they work, they *can*—"

He didn't have it in him to judge her. Not today. "Any number of doctors did the same," he said.

She turned her face toward him and from under the hard level of her brow aimed her eyes into his. "Any number? *Everyone!* Even the VA doctors—the pharmaceutical companies made sure of it. And of course the pharmacies just kept filling the scripts. Billionaires, those fucking Sacklers! But *I* am being sued, *not you*, not even Jim."

Jim was her former founding partner at the pain-management clinic, an anesthesiologist, and her former lover, or one of them. He'd recently joined her new practice.

"I'll be a poster girl for it all again, like I was after that girl went missing—"

"You'll be the villain for a week or two, but then you'll be forgotten." As Sarah had been. "Now you know better and will do better, which is true, isn't it?"

"Don't make it sound so easy. Right now that boy is on the other side of this door. And those parents of the girl? They say I *murdered* their child…"

She dipped her head down, but even in shadow he saw her eyes were round with pleading.

"And I did, didn't I? In a way. I started her there. You warned me. How many times? I just didn't think… I mean, that girl was in acute pain. I didn't write her that many scripts. I didn't see her *that* often. There are too few options for us to treat pain. We *all* know that. Christ, how could I know it would come to this?"

She searched the Doctor's eyes, from one to the other, looking for something—assent?

"No, I should have known, two years ago. *You* knew. *We* did"—she wrapped herself in her arms—"Oh, God," she said, and then said it again but as a sob. She brought her legs up and pulled them to her and pressed her face into her knees like a girl. She'd always been hard to comfort when upset, though he'd been depended on to try. She'd come looking for that today, but admitting to wrongdoing? This was not like her, and he imagined its novelty had to scare her.

He put his hand on her back and could feel the heat of her even through her raincoat. With her upset and maybe because of the dampening she'd taken in the rain, he could smell her. Not just her Dior perfume—it was the oil from her skin, the sweat through her clothes, which always conjured cloves and seagrass, and candle wax, too, melting. All those years he had breathed her in. They had chosen New York together. She'd known the city better, having grown up only a train ride away. The life in her: durable, fast, irrepressible, like the city's. He'd not only admired it, he'd hungered for it. On the street that energy could overwhelm him, but up high, the views, the buildings, their boastful numbers and stories captivated him. In their apartment in the east fifties, near the East River, they lay in the dark so that the city's lights moved over their bedroom walls, gliding over them, too, changing shapes. It was erotic to them, but everything was when they were first married.

They'd known each other as parts of a larger body they shared, as home and sustenance and also torment: She required contest, and to win those contests. He had to let her, until he couldn't.

She was crying still when Sue came to the door again. "Doctor?"

"Not now, Sue, *please.*"

"The radio," Sue called, "they just announced—they're expecting flooding, so they're shutting the subways down. Cabs will be hard to come by soon, and the car services—"

"In a minute, Sue—"

"And there was an accident on the Upper East Side," Sue persisted. She kept the Doctor's addresses and knew this was where Jackie lived and worked. "Bricks off a building facade. Someone was hurt, maybe killed. Streets are closed."

Lifting her patchwork face, Jackie called through the door, "Where?"

"In the sixties, I think."

Jackie blew out a long, ragged breath and rested her head on the Doctor's outstretched arm. "I'm sorry," she said. She didn't say about what in particular, and he didn't ask her to clarify.

Could this display be part of some strategy to another game? Or maybe this was what happened when a predator was forced to be prey? A chance for humility?

"I shouldn't have come," she said.

"Should I call a car service?" Sue was still at the door. "While we still can?"

"We'll take care of it," he said. "Thank you, Sue."

"She wants me to leave. I don't blame her." Jackie blew out another breath, forcibly, for courage. "I'll go." She stood. "I'm a mess, but everything is, so who cares, right?" She was zipping her coat as she asked, "Do you think he's still out there?"

"Adam? Maybe. Probably."

"Will you?" There was the blue of her eyes. A late-day blue he knew so well.

"Yes."

He hung his white coat on the door and pulled his overcoat on, putting his cellphone, which he often forgot, in his pocket in case they needed to call a car. When she went in search of something in her purse, he felt for Ed's Ziploc bag in his top drawer and pinched out one lozenge and pocketed it, in case he needed it, even just the prospect of it.

The door opened to Sue standing there, her hands resting calmly on the round of the child inside her.

"I'm sorry," Jackie shot at her, "I was upset," and Sue nodded. Sue encountered this over and over, patients' outbursts that had nothing to do with her. She'd already let it go.

Adam approached them slowly as the Doctor directed to Sue, "Cancel the rest of the day. Send everyone home. Call car service for whoever needs it."

Adam stood just behind Sue, his eyes on Jackie.

"So you've met my wife, Adam?"

When Sue headed for reception, the Doctor stepped in front of Adam.

"Your ex-wife, Sue told me. *Ex*."

"Look, I *hate* that you had to go through all you have, okay?" Jackie said. "There just weren't many reliable methods to—"

"That and a fucking nickel will get you *zip*, Karen," Adam scoffed.

Jackie, her face red from the heat yet rising inside her, protested, "It's Jackie, and I couldn't know then what the drugs would do, to some of my patients—"

Adam sniffed and sneered, shook his head no. "To *some*? To *some*?"

While he was using heroin, Adam had beaten a man unconscious, menaced a girlfriend. He'd been arrested. Largely because of his military record, he'd been given probation, and once he detoxed and wasn't hustling for the drug, a person reemerged. Funny. Fiercely loyal. A man who never shied from a fight, especially for anyone he judged to be vulnerable, disenfranchised. Anger management would be a lifelong project for him.

He pressed nearer to Jackie: "He dumped you because you're trash."

The Doctor, who remained fixed between Adam and Jackie, gave Adam the full of his face and eyes. "Adam. Stop. There's a long history of doctors relying on these drugs—"

"*You* didn't. *You* wouldn't." Adam looked around the Doctor to continue to scowl at Jackie.

"Stop it, Adam, or else you'll have to go."

Adam's head reared back. Then, into the Doctor's face, he gave a hissing snort. He lowered his chin, as if to brandish horns, and held himself there for long seconds deciding if he'd go further, and then stormed off down the hall, which led to the exam rooms and restrooms.

The Doctor led Jackie away, past the remaining patients in the waiting room, and outside, where the rain fell hard at an angle.

"Does that jacket have a hood?" he yelled over the wind. Jackie didn't reply, just pulled herself to his side. He put an arm around her. So close, he breathed her again, felt her body's sturdiness, though she was shaking.

"God," she called out. "Dear God, when will it stop?"

"It's all right, darling."

The last time he used "darling," it had been to abuse the term, and her. We insisted to one another that no one really changed, no one could, especially when talking about forming realistic or lasting adult relationships, but was that a lie? Weren't we compelled to change with every pain, every loss, to bend, transform, reach out of ourselves for something or someone? Our soft-wiring never ceased; it couldn't. He had told Sarah this—that at age two or three our real work was only beginning—but now he imagined he held the promise of our plasticity against him in the figure of his wife. *Ex*-wife.

How he'd once loved to travel the length of her spine up to the nape of her neck with his tongue and make her shudder. If you made her feel as regal and desired as she insisted on being, she'd let you do anything. He saw her naked with her arms over her head in bed, her legs spread. Never ashamed of her appetites. And it was sumptuous to him. She was. The most exciting woman he'd ever known.

At Clinton Street, whatever Sue's forecasts for later, a yellow line of cabs surged past. He raised his arm, and when a cab stopped, he opened the door for her. But rather than go in, she maneuvered in front of him and hugged him, her head against his chest.

"Come home with me?" she pulled back to ask, her voice and face so young now. She was middle-aged and a girl. "You have no patients."

It was true—in theory he was free for the rest of the day. Reflexively he stole one hand into his pocket to finger the lozenge as he saw himself going with her, holding her hand as they navigated the blocked streets and police lights, and then, when they were alone in her apartment, he could see and begin, there on the street, to feel himself plunging into every tender bit of her. They had known so much pleasure together. And it had a cost.

I don't think romantic love ends—I think it becomes something else if we let it. Its opposite: hatred.

He'd hated Jackie long before he was able to admit it, because she lashed herself to her whims, because he could so rarely reach her. Her rules or none. She couldn't understand him over the riot of her ambitions and defenses, the gamesmanship. That he could have killed her when they got high one night was simply part of another game for her. Now hail bit into their foreheads and cheeks, and she waited on him, as vulnerable as he'd ever seen her. Winter in May.

"C'mon, man," said the driver through the open door—an accent, maybe Haitian—"you getting in or not?"

He kissed her on the mouth, lightly, as if only to taste her. She kissed him back, pressed her lips to his just as she had in the past, as if famished. He didn't feel hatred now—it was gone—and that was deliverance. He could permit himself that freedom at least, couldn't he? Let it grow and keep growing in him, and he did as he put her in the cab, shut the door behind her, and watched the vehicle merge into the torrent of yellow moving up Clinton toward the river and Manhattan.

The Wind Report

This is what weather experts call "training": The storms are moving along a track to us and promise more rain than wind. The city's suggesting folks in low-lying parts of Staten Island and the Rockaways move to higher ground. Shelters are open in every borough. If you want to suggest or volunteer a space, give us a call.

I've got Mike from City Island on the line. Hi, Mike. You heading out?

"No [beep]ing way. Let them come get me. Don't you get it? This is all man-made."

You mean climate change, Mike? Self-inflicted?

"F-[beep] no. It's weather warfare. They're targeting us, here in the city. The whole country hates us. Always has. They hate the Yankees and the gays and painted ladies in Times Square—I don't mean hookers, I mean the titties in body paint bouncing out there in broad daylight. They cried for us when the towers came down, but they never stopped hating this city's money and arrogance. They're trying to wipe us off the map—"

Who is, Mike? Who's trying?

"The military. Some [beep]ed-up wing of it, trying to take over. They've got access to the technology. Haven't you ever heard of cloud seeding or chemtrails or HAARP? That's the High-frequency Active Auroral Research Program. These are real experiments in controlling weather. I was in the military for five years, and I know these people: They run on fear—other people's. They want to rebuild the world for their own [beep]ing purposes. You think it's an accident there's another drought in California? One spark and they're burning again? They hate them too: the vegans and the tech jerk-offs. Look into it—"

All right, we will, but what about your safety, Mike?

"I got all I need here—life raft, flares, flashlights, water, NOAA radio, pepper spray. I'm not running. I'll be right here. Right [beep]ing here."

All right, Mike. But if you change your mind, there are a number of shelters out there. Okay, who do I have now? Linda? Hi, Linda.

"Yes, hi, I'm calling from Brooklyn Heights. We never get flooding up here—"

Some of the best views in the city from there.

"I have an extra bedroom with twin beds, a couch. It's no penthouse, of course, but if anyone needs it? And it's not just me—my neighbors, too, in the building—we're all opening our doors."

Thank you, Linda. Very generous of you and your neighbors. Lakshmi will take your info. Who do I have here on the line? Joe?

"Yeah, it's Joe here. Look, Mike on City Island sounds like a good guy and all, but he's *dead wrong*. It's not the military, not the government. It's another terrorist attack. It's a holy war all over again, but they're not using planes or explosives this time. They're using the weather."

Interesting theory, Joe. And tell us, where are you?

"The Bronx, and I'm staying put. Mike, if you're out there, I'm here, too. Nobody's pushing us around."

Okay, Joe. Be safe. Now here's Lucas writing on our comment board. Is this our dinosaur expert? Back again? Yes. Lucas says here that weather modification has been around forever. It's public knowledge that Beijing used cloud seeding to clear out pollution before they hosted the Olympic Games.

What about it, then, Lucas? Is this weather we're having a man-made conspiracy?

Lucas, back again, says no, and that Mike, Joe, and I are huge—ah, Lucas, you are pretty gifted when casting aspersions, I'll give you that, a maestro.

Who's this on the line? Orson? Hi, Orson. Where are you?

"Carroll Gardens, Brooklyn. People are welcome to come to our church, or what was a church. St. Gabriel's? That old stronghold on Linden Place. It's been de-flocked for a stretch now, de-flocked and locked and sealed, but no more! Do come—come one, come all! We're opening the doors *and* a few cases of excellent champagne! It's top-notch."

Champagne? Have you been making merry, Orson?

"No more than usual, but my invitation is in earnest, the real deal. There's plenty of room."

Thanks, Orson. You heard him: Try St. Gabriel's on Linden Place in Brooklyn. Champagne on ice. That's one way to brave a storm.

I'm told we're going to check back in with the accident on the Upper East Side. While we're gathering information for you, dear listeners, here's Neil Young for all of us who are "Like a Hurricane." Don't get blown away. Hang on. You hear me? Hang on, my friends. There is calm after the storm. Look for it.

Ruth

Ruth posted herself outside the church. She couldn't go in. There were too many people filing out of the clinic, and others arriving, looking like tourists blown in, surveying St. Gabriel's and shrinking under hoods and umbrellas as the hail became rain again.

Ruth walked away under her own hood to Court Street, where metal shutters, one after another, fell in preemptive bangs over storefronts. One bar, called Kings, appeared open, despite a CLOSED sign in the door. She went in, claimed a barstool.

"I'm supposed to be shutting down," the bartender told her as he approached her.

"Stranded" was all she could think to say to him, a medium-size man of indeterminate middle age with thick muscled arms, a flagrantly white shaved skull, and a JOIN OR DIE tattoo on his neck.

"That's what I keep hearing."

He shrugged. "What'll it be?"

"Tequila. Straight up."

The place was maybe half full. A group of five or six came in just after her, men and women in what looked like their thirties and forties, tossing off their wet coats to reveal short sleeves and tank tops, as if it were in fact spring and not this time out of season. The tequila served her was blunter and more bitter than what she'd had with Mrs. Watson, but she needed it to settle herself down. The revolt in her was already churning as Marie gave her the offer on paper, along with a key card to the clinic and a new cellphone, expressly for her communication with Mrs. Watson. She was to be a spy and a thief. Ruth must have hidden her shock poorly, because

Marie had stopped in her instructions to say, "It's up to you, you know. You can walk away from this."

Marie was instructing Ruth on choice? Marie who had done the research into Ruth's background and sussed out things that only family or close friends should know?

"Like you've done?" The words were sharp in Ruth's mouth, sharp leaving.

Marie shook her head and opened her mouth, closed it, then opened it again to say softly, succinctly, "I'm not you."

"Poor fucking Amy Winehouse!" bellowed a man now seated one empty stool away from Ruth's. It took her a moment to understand he was referring to the music. The group that had come in had set to dancing, in jerking, rutting motions. "Back to Black" beat through the bar now. "Like Janis. Good God, Janis Joplin, a warrior of black and blue, right?" he called over the singing, and then to the bartender, "Hey, buddy! The usual!"

Something amber-colored and neat arrived before the man. He had Superman's chin and hair, long, loose limbs, and a potbelly straining against his dress shirt.

"You dance?" he asked.

"No," she said.

In a toss he started and finished his drink. "You a nurse?"

"No," she said, trying it on for size, to be someone else entirely. Certainly not someone playing other people's games again with rules as arbitrary and changeable as the people who devised them. Marie had punctuated her advice to Ruth the way people do when they break up, go separate ways: "We all have different needs," she'd said. But what she really meant was *vulnerabilities*. Ruth's troubles with her husband had made her vulnerable in a way that left all the windows and doors of her wide open so more trouble could climb in and keep climbing in. Now she was a target, wasn't she? As she'd been at the hospital? Even for those from whom she'd needed help—God, especially them, to position and reposition.

"Actress?"

"Yeah," she said. "That's right."

"Tough, right? I mean you got to be, like, out there, you know? Buddy! Hey buddy, another one!"

"Tough life no matter what."

"What?"

She leaned over without turning her face to the man's: "Tough no matter what," she spat at him, and winced as she swallowed the last of her tequila.

"Sure, sure… Man, these people, they're going at it like it's the last day on earth."

"Could be," she said.

"Yeah, okay. Right…" He drank, his gaze pinballing around her. "Married?"

"No, never been," Ruth replied. *As if*, she thought. Her choice of one man and a life with him had landed her right here—nowhere—isolated from friends, family. She'd traveled in packs once too, and, yes, she'd danced, tossing her head and hips, laughing until she felt sick.

Her new phone vibrated with a text: "FYI. Clinic early close: 3-3:30." Was this from Mrs. Watson or from Marie? Didn't matter; they worked in step. Marie hadn't forgotten to invite Ruth to use Mrs. Watson's library, upstairs on the second floor. "You're a reader, aren't you?" Of course it was Marie who had stumbled on another version of Ruth frozen in amber online, who'd been free and foolish enough to air out her passions, who'd believed Wharton's Lily Bart was as real as she was, but Ruth had believed her life would be nothing like Lily's, who didn't have the courage to marry for love until it was too late. That dingy claustrophobic room in which Lily had died of an overdose was something of another time, a punishment that lay in wait for women who weren't strong and clear-sighted enough. Not for someone like Ruth.

"Boyfriend?"

"No," she said. It was just after four now. She'd have to leave soon. She was sober, mostly—at least as far as the tequila went. The anger was more deranging: It could overtake her until she couldn't see anything. It was horrible and it was thrilling, everything working in concert with it, even the bare arms of one of the dancers gleaming slick in the room's low light, waving to "Chain of Fools."

On the train from Boston to New York, a preppy kid, not long out of college from the look of him, had sat too close to her, tried to ask her about her trip, the game she was playing on her phone, if any. She'd been polite, explained she wanted to be left alone "with her thoughts." Here were the boundaries her therapist asked her to assert. "No offense," she'd added. "Bitch," the guy had grumbled and moved off down the aisle. What she was left with then was anger—she couldn't tell if it was hers or others'—and the voices that came with it, which she could summon faster than it took to call her a bitch.

"Have you ever done, like, sex scenes?" the sad Superman asked her now.

"Part of the job sometimes," she said.

He turned the full of his face toward her with a smirk. "You like it?"

"It's work, and, with everyone watching, not, you know, ideal."

He drank fast to get drunk fast. Violence in it. He hung his face at her again and waited a beat, two, with a slight quaking of his upper lip. "But you like"—his smirk became a sneer—"to fuck?"

She saw where this guy's handsomeness had gone—into seed and seediness. He'd chosen to give it up, like jogging. Now he was ready to be slapped or screeched at. In fact, he hoped for it. His own contempt needing others', to catch, flare. She knew this too well, that for someone like him, like her husband, it was as good as or better than the whisky or whatever else they were using to twist a day into their plaything.

"As much as the next girl," she said.

He laughed, drank again, raked his fingers through his hair, a glossy, thick chestnut. He'd have to go further to get the reaction he wanted from her.

"Nothing turns me on more than a girl in uniform." He dropped a hand on her knee, over the thin of her white stockings that were still damp.

"That so?" She kept her eyes on the mirror over the bar. Not on her face but on the glow of an exit sign on the far side of it. "What else? What else turns you on?"

"Well, you could suck me off in the bathroom."

"I suppose I could."

"I can pay. Ever been paid?"

"Sure."

"Right. I bet you have. Yeah, I could have called that. You're a performer, right? So how much?"

Ruth shouted to the bartender for a glass of water and another shot of tequila, and as soon as the tequila came she forced down half of it, as if it were a helpful antiseptic.

"You tell me. What am I worth?" She tried not to move.

"Depends... Yeah, depends on how good you are," he said, digging his fingers into her knee, not to hurt but to apply pressure.

She remembered her husband had called her a whore—*You like it, like a whore, a good whore, my whore, a pretty whore.* A joke, and then not. It was exalted dirty praise, in the heat between lovers, provoking, but later he said it to underscore her worthlessness to him: *nothing but a whore, a stupid whore, sad as a...*

Now, with the word waiting in the air between her and this unabashed creep with good hair, it was hilarious: They took up roles straight out of a shared script, and it was all the more absurd and artificial in a bar she'd never been in, in a city she didn't know. She nearly laughed out loud, so exquisite did her adrenaline feel.

"Just tell me, tell me—how much to fuck you in there? Hard."

She turned to him and smiled a game smile, knowing he was aroused now. This was what she'd been waiting for. She hadn't noticed that his striped dress shirt hung over some misshapen sweatpants and his sneakers had no laces, and as she moved her hand to his crotch she knew why Mrs. Watson had chosen her: Because she had nothing and no one to lose. Because anything was better than where she'd been for too long, without anyone's protection but her own.

Her hand moved lightly up his thigh and then she gripped the man's hard cock as tightly as she could through the fabric and twisted. She seethed in his ear, "More than you could afford, you sad fucking clown. You ass sore! You scum—"

"Christ! Fuuuh—" he cried, doubling over. *"Shit! Shit!"*

She withdrew her hand, finished her tequila.

"You fucking bitch!" He was standing now and shouting in her face, or the side of it, because she would not look at him. "You *stupid fucking* bitch!"

Hit me, she urged in her head. *I've had worse than you. I know worse.*

The bartender was on them fast, hollering at the man, brandishing a bat. "Carl! Damn it! I told you: You can't come in here anymore if you're going to make another fucking scene with the ladies—"

"She assaulted me!" The man—Carl—shrank back, but the script was done with him. "Fucking crazy bitch—"

"You were asking for it, Carl. You always are, man. I'm not afraid to use this. You know that. I shouldn't have served you—"

"I'll call the cops," Carl cried. "She could have done permanent damage!"

"Go ahead. Who will come in this shit?" The bartender turned to Ruth. "I'm sorry," he said, craning in so she could hear him. "Drinks on me." Ruth slid her coat on. "Don't go," he called as she headed for the door. "Lady, *don't*! It's *bad* out there!"

The Doctor

The Doctor's arm was up again before he realized it; a cab lurched at him and stopped and he was inside, dripping onto the cracked leather of the seat. He gave the driver an address in Lower Manhattan he'd been to before—more times than he cared to admit. The rain came steady; its force made the car's metal body a drum, beating over their heads.

The driver raised his voice to talk to him: "No tunnel today. Flooding." He made a sound of disgust and threw a hand away, only to return it to the wheel—he needed both hands to drive today. "Must be bridge. Brooklyn. Okay?"

"Yes, whatever you think."

Something vibrated in the inside pocket of the Doctor's overcoat. His cellphone. He took it out and looked—a message had been left. Not Sue or one of his patients. Private caller. The driver eyed him in the rearview.

"My wife texts, calls. 'Come home,' she says, no good out here… You going home?"

"Yes, home," he lied. This newness, this day was leading him elsewhere.

"Your family looking for you?"

"No," he said over the drumming and hesitated before admitting, "That was my work. I'm a doctor."

The Doctor was usually cautious about telling strangers what he did. It led to confessions about health matters, the need for help, diagnoses he could not give, but today was another matter.

The driver's ID on the partition between the seats read "Syed, Ahmed." Pakistani maybe. Like the clinic's resident, Dr. Chaudhri, though when asked, Chaudhri told patients he was Indian, because Americans were less suspicious of Indians, he said, thanks to yoga and Gandhi, and because Islam wasn't India's dominant religion.

"My daughter. She wants to be a doctor. She do the premed now. Many years to school. Too many."

The wind swerved, the rain blew at them sideways, and the car, merging onto the bridge, gave way, lost its lane, until the driver, Ahmed, righted it, held on, squeezed the wheel.

"You for the heart?" he hollered. He needed the small talk to calm him.

"What?"

"Heart doctor?"

"No, the brain. Headaches."

"My wife, she gets headache. Dentist helped. Then, no. You can fix?"

He stopped short of saying yes. What had been dawning on him all day, a belief in belief, the power of it, came out as "She and I, together, can, if she *trusts*—"

Trusted she had some say in the pain, in a cure in which she participated, and in him. Sarah's example had taught him at least that, hadn't it? The affliction was not a fiction, but neither was the opportunity for the brain to alter its course, about which we still knew too little. Had the driver's daughter already been trained in this? Probably. These days students were referred to the work of Ted Kaptchuk, an American doctor who'd begun as a scholar of Chinese medicine. An audacious man who knew placebo to be more powerful than we'd been ready to concede, because it seemed too facile. It relied on the strength of our expectations and on naturally occurring pain relievers in our own brains. *A veritable pharmacy up there*, Kaptchuk was known to say. *A hidden wholeness in each of us.*

"Trusts in *new* things, *new* methods," the Doctor continued as the taxi climbed to the bridge's height, which today felt too high for any boat to have ever touched.

When the lanes opened out to three, the cars picked up pace, but so did the rain. Everything suddenly turned white with water outside the taxi's windows. They could not move, because they could not see.

Ahmed put the radio on, turned up the volume to the sound of a man's voice, one that the Doctor had heard somewhere before. Static broke up his words; the noise of the rain overtook the static. Ahmed brought the side of his fist down on his dash. "This should not be!" he shouted and switched the radio off.

In long minutes, the rain slowed enough that there was visibility again. The East River below them rioted in millions of whitecaps.

They inched forward again and could hear the frantic squeak of the windshield wipers.

"You can drop me anywhere on the other side. Anywhere. As soon as we're over. Never mind the address—"

"I take you home." Ahmed looked at the Doctor again in his rearview mirror. "Then I go home. You first, then me." Then he declared, defiant, "We do not run like animals."

"Yes," the Doctor agreed, but in this city that's precisely what most had to do. This place thrived on ever faster speeds, escalating costs, and who could manage them, and yet its hazards bred an understanding among its inhabitants that seemed to come out of nowhere, and when it did, it felt a kind of benediction, an invitation. A simple humanity that wanted outlet, especially in moments when the city's conditions turned threatening or impassable, as now, and the choice of this city as a place to live seemed too improbable for creatures with so few protections apart from one another.

Ahmed tried the radio again, turned it up. There was static, but less. The Doctor did recognize the voice, a career radio voice, in conversation with another man whose voice was tauter, harried. This second man, evidently a spokesperson for the city's transit system, cataloged how many gallons of water the MTA pumped out of the tunnels on a normal day:

thirteen million. And during the last big hurricane to hit the city hard, Sandy, more than six hundred million gallons of water flooded the subways.

"The city is one island linked to another here, water's all around us. We've always been able to handle one, one and a half inches of water per hour, maybe two, but over three? That's tough, and it just keeps coming. You can't argue with it. Then the tides—water's a monster to beat—"

"I understand the MTA has installed something called Flex-Gates for each subway station?" the radio host asked.

"They're not exactly gates. They're these big pieces of waterproof fabric that cover the entrances.

"Did you say fabric?"

"But that's only one way the water gets in. We got to cover every manhole, vent, emergency exit, every loose joint, every crack… It's endless, but we don't stop. We oversee one of the busiest transit systems in the world. It doesn't stop, so we don't stop."

"And the system is closed?"

"Yes. Officially. Locked down. Gates up. Like the mayor said, *stay home*. The wind is in the gale-force range, but only moderate gale. No, it's the water today, the rain, and then with the high tide, it just keeps coming."

Ruth

The key card worked. The clinic appeared empty and was far too quiet, with Ruth's heart still beating with the man's curses and her own, and the torrent in her ears from the rain that had soaked her and would drown her if she didn't move fast.

She snapped on every light she could find on her way to the Doctor's office. A text instructed: "Left drawer, top. Blue notebook. Key under blotter if needed." It wasn't needed, and the Doctor's office wasn't locked. Why? Did the weather make Sue or the Doctor forget everyday cautions? Or was it just complacency? Did they really think they were safe here, or anywhere?

She found the notebook pushed all the way into the back of the drawer. Its cardboard cover had turned spongy, and under her fingertips its surface felt almost fleecy, the stuff of baby birds, children's earlobes. It was bound but had been opened so many times that the spine was loose.

As she paged through it, she saw rows of words that were neat and cramped; at other times, the writer's mix of cursive and print was loose and looping, surging up out of the lines on the pages. The blue ink was vaguely blurred as if it had been not only touched but breathed on and maybe breathed in. It fell open to a page that had been read and reread. Ruth caught words, read them without trying. *I was too far gone to say no. Please don't, Doctor. I can't be touched by you or anyone now, but then I realized you were showing me a way out…*

Ruth couldn't let herself read it. She didn't want to know more than she had to, form any questions or objections. But they were already coming, one after another, as she made her way to where she guessed the copy machine was—in the rear of Sue's reception area.

There were maybe eighty pages to copy. A few pages in, she'd seen the author's name, Sarah Robbins. She took in more words on the copies as they discharged from the machine or from the notebook as she flipped it, turned the page, flipped it over again.

In the early part, there were lists of foods and drinks. But the dietary log gave way to longer blocks of text and appeals: *Why didn't you come?*

Did the journal belong to the Doctor's lover? Was that it? The Doctor had seduced a patient? Doctors at the hospital had been fired for less. Mrs. Watson must have suspected and needed to assess the damage he'd done and whether he'd do it again. This man she thought so much of as a healer, and him so solicitous of Ruth? How stupid of Ruth to fall for it, in the dark between them, as if this fallibility in us wasn't always lying in wait, like a trapdoor we kept falling through and didn't always survive intact. *Before Heaven, a sin is a sin is a sin*, Ruth's mother would say, a woman who after her break with Ruth's father had become rigidly Catholic, far more fluent in the doctrine's punishments than its absolutions.

"I'll write when I get work," Ruth had e-mailed her mother when she first arrived in New York.

"I pray for you," her mother had e-mailed back—horrible drama in her use of the present tense, as if the mess of Ruth's life required that the effort be constant. Even now. Then, on its own line, she'd added, "Angels are all around you."

When Ruth and her sister were little, this was offered as comfort—invisible guardians watching over them as their mother would, but with her mother's increased piety and fear for her daughters' lack of it, especially Ruth's, it had come to feel like a threat. Like you could never keep track of all the eyes on you, visible and invisible, real or imagined. Ruth had nearly died of shame, at least twice. The sleazy Superman in the bar had surely smelled it on her, just as she had on him.

And the Doctor? Had he taken advantage of this Sarah's vulnerability?

I hoped for some monsters, even one, but not the kind that wanted to eat me. I imagined it would be some misunderstood, lonely thing, looking for a friend like me.

Ruth had to pee, the urgency gaining on her, but she couldn't stop; she was only halfway through—until a beep sounded, followed by a buzzing, then a click, the popping of a metal latch. Someone was coming into the clinic. Whoever it was, they were already through the first door.

Ruth grabbed the finished copies and the notebook and crouched behind the copier.

Voices burst into the waiting room—a man's and a woman's. They were just yards away from her.

"My God, they really closed?" the woman said.

"That's what Adele said," the man confirmed.

"I can't believe the Doctor's not here. He's *always* here."

"I'll check," he said.

"I'm so wet."

"That's how I like you."

"Shut up, Larry."

Larry? Mrs. Watson's massage therapist? Ruth had met him in passing only an hour or two earlier but had barely said hello with this chore newly set before her. He was barrel-chested, sharp-nosed, and too ready with a smile.

Ruth moved to the shorter end of the copier. If he looked through the door he wouldn't see her there, but if the woman looked through the reception window, she would.

"She'll know we're here," the woman called out again. "If she wants to know, she'll know."

Ruth thought she heard Larry pause at the door to the reception area, before he went on, presumably to search the rest of the space. He called back, "So what if she knows? We'll tell her the truth: We couldn't get home."

"I could have. I'm not that far."

"All clear," he said, returning to her. "Though a lot of lights are on. In the Doc's office too."

"He's coming back, then."

"He's staying wherever he is if he's smart. We'll lock the door to your room."

"The cameras, Larry."

"I can get the footage deleted from the Doc's computer if I need to, like last time. No one was the wiser, and the Doc doesn't even know to look at the recorded stuff. And we agreed this is the best place to ride the weather out. There's a generator, food, water, everything we could need. C'mon, baby, let me warm you up—"

Sound carried down here—just as it had earlier when she and the Doctor were alone in his office.

"I don't like being with you after you've been with her, Larry. It's—"

"I haven't *been* with her, Jill. I've been giving her therapeutic massage."

"Don't patronize. Therapeutic? Try sensual—I know how your sessions *end*."

"She doesn't touch me. I touch *her*, however she asks, with my *hands*. Just my hands, okay?" Whoever Jill was, she didn't comment on this qualification, so Larry persisted: "And you know why I'm doing it? For us, Jill. It's our insurance policy."

"You recorded it again?"

"Yep, in stereo."

"Did she—" Jill either couldn't find the words or didn't want to.

"Thank me? Yes, she practically sang. Man, she's something."

"What does *that* mean: *something*?"

"Just what I said."

"Fuck you, Larry."

"I mean she's, like… *out there*, in her very own universe."

Jill's voice dropped, as if she knew Ruth was listening. "Have you sent him the file already?"

"Not yet. All I could think of was you. Getting to you, and your skin, your beautiful skin. Let me—"

He let out an "*mmmmm*" over the suctioning sound of kissing.

"Not out here, Larry."

"Whatever you want."

"Is that what you say to her? Dammit, Larry, just *dammit*! You better make this worth my while."

"I'm at your service. Let's get you out of those wet things—"

"Stop talking," Jill said as her voice approached Ruth and moved away.

"Yes, ma'am." He followed her.

"You're still talking. Don't." Only a few paces away, she stopped and asked, "You sure it's safe?"

"No one knows we're here."

"No, the recordings—yours, when you're with her?"

"Only you and I know—"

"And him. *He* knows."

"That's why he's not going to tell. Won't work otherwise. He knows what he's about."

They moved away, probably down one of the halls to where the treatment rooms had to be.

Ruth fled to the Doctor's office. She had to put the journal back for now, in case the Doctor did come back. Larry said he could delete video footage from the Doctor's computer. How? Jiggling the mouse woke the desktop from its sleep. On the upper right of the screen was an application called C-View. She clicked on it and a grid of multiple images appeared. Only two had movement: one titled "Treatment Room 5," which gave her Larry and Jill in color, and another "Office 1," which showed half of Ruth's own back, bending toward the computer. She turned to see a small camera behind her high in the corner of the room.

On the new phone she'd been given, she texted, "Got interrupted," but the text didn't go through. Had to be the weather, affecting the cell towers.

She restored the journal to the back of the drawer and looked for a cup or bottle she might relieve herself in, and for food, even a mint or a piece of gum. She hadn't eaten in hours and didn't know where the restrooms were or if she could risk finding them now.

She found a small Ziploc full of what looked like oversize lozenges of some sort in the top middle drawer. Orange. With her body blocking the camera's view of her hands, she slipped one into her pocket.

She was able to enlarge the view of "Treatment Room 5." If she knew what was happening in there, she'd know whether it was safe for her to move.

Larry stood behind Jill. He'd stripped down to his briefs, and she to a full-body leotard, which had been rolled down and away from her breasts to sit low on her hips. The camera was closer to Jill but probably hung in a corner, giving a three-quarter view. She supported herself on her elbows on the massage table in the middle of the small room as Larry worked her lower back with sufficient rigor that her hips swayed. Ruth wondered when this scene had played out before and who else might have seen it before it could be deleted. Who else might be watching now? And who was the man Larry was recording his sessions with Mrs. Watson for? The Doctor?

Jill's head reared up and tossed back her hair, still wet and heavy at its ends from the rain. Her eyes were closed, and Ruth could even see the trace of tan lines on her shoulders and that her breasts were as full and firm and soft as infants' heads. Jill was saying something. Ruth turned the volume up enough to hear Jill breathe out, "Good boy, soooo good," as Larry kneaded her bare neck and shoulders and then had to taste where his hands had been, kissing, licking, biting. Jill said something more, but a whistling suddenly rose up, high and piercing. It was the wind, finding holes and other breaks in the stone and skirling through.

If Ruth was going to leave the clinic, she had to go soon, before the weather got even worse. She slid the stack of pages she'd copied under the back of her skirt.

When she saw Jill relieved of her leotard and thong altogether, lying back on the table now, her arms outstretched to Larry, Ruth ran for it; but as she crossed the threshold of the Doctor's office, the lights became jittery, and when she was nearly through the lounge, they went out, then on, and then stayed out. She held her breath as everything inside the clinic ceased to whir. Outside became even more audible then, it wanted in: the wind's sharp falsetto catching as if in her throat, pressure against the walls, and, somewhere nearby, sirens—always the sound of sirens in this city. She realized she could be stranded out there again, and God knows where and with whom.

She used her phone's light to search out the restrooms, down a hall that Jill and Larry may or may not have gone down, but before she could find them, she heard Larry's voice placating, through an open door, just feet away from her: "Okay, okay, I'll go check." But he didn't come out right away. He turned back to Jill: "Just wait here, okay? Jill? Please? Don't move. Just relax for me—"

Ruth sprinted for the very end of the hall—maybe there was an emergency exit there? A way out? She found herself down one step into a well of darkness before two oversize steel doors. The one marked MECHANICAL ROOM was locked, with a door handle equipped with a finger pad as well as a keyhole, but the other door, though heavy, was protected by an old Master hasp and padlock, which wasn't clicked shut. She removed it, shouldered her way in and into the darkness behind it. Had Larry heard the old door groan? She prayed, out of habit, to those angels her mother had equipped her with—please, oh, please—and waited.

The concrete floor in the room radiated the cold of earth that hadn't seen the sun. With her cellphone's light she could see shapes under cover, many the size of small children, as if they were hiding in there, too, and for a long time. This was a room where things were left and forgotten. It hadn't enjoyed the high-tech renovation of the other rooms in the basement.

A rattling of the door handle—Larry was just outside, trying one then the other of the two utility doors. But just for show. He didn't want to come in. He knew that Jill and he could just as easily make love in the dark.

Once he retreated and it seemed safe, Ruth saw that there was an old slide bolt on her side of the door—for what reason? So these things under cover could secure their own safety? At least she could secure hers: She moved the bolt across slowly. Now no one could come through that door without her letting them in.

A string connected to an overhead light hung in the air about three feet from her. She reached and tugged. The electricity must have come back, or the generator had kicked in: A raw bluish light from a sole fluorescent bulb vibrated out and gave the objects around her the illusion of movement, as if they shivered with her in the room's chill.

She had to see who else was in here with her, so she uncovered one, then two of the objects. Statuary. Religious: Mary, in marble, hands outstretched, one half of her index finger missing on one hand, a thump tip on the other. And an angel—she guessed Gabriel—taller than Mary at maybe four feet, his trumpet held aloft, wings of a hundred painstakingly sculpted pointed feathers extended behind him, done in a bronze that was patchy with gilt. He was a puzzle, with the face of a boy—a teen idol with waved hair and a tender, thin neck and big, empty eyes—set on the broad, sinewy body of a man in partial armor with a skirt revealing legs as dense and shapely as a wrestler's.

Back toward the center of the room, under the light, she saw there was a drain in the floor. She removed the copied journal pages from her backside, pulled down her stockings and underwear, squatted, and peed over it, trying not to cry out from the joy of it.

That pressure gone, her stomach spasmed with hunger. She remembered the lozenge in her pocket. She sniffed at it briefly, registered citrus but also something else, something familiar, but did not know what it was until the lozenge began to dissolve on her tongue: flavor as musty as peat, with an edge of sweet spice and skunk. Marijuana. Dear God, how she hated it! Not just for its effects, that drooling vacancy, the moronic laughing, and often the paranoia, but for how it factored into the stories of so many people in her life: her husband's, before and after his head injury, the young mothers in the NICU, with too much experience too young with intoxicants that led from one to another, then another.

But she didn't spit the lozenge out, though she had to fight her own distaste. There couldn't be much doubt what was behind the Doctor's nighttime behavior by the river now. Was no one or nothing ever who or what they seemed or advertised? But then neither was she, was she? No denying that or fighting where she'd been or that she'd already been altered today—by music and booze, then rage that came from a wellspring in her. Let the drug take her, if it could.

She pulled the rest of the covers off the objects in the storage room: a stack of fraying rattan collection baskets, a tippy wood-resin Saint Francis with yellow skin and strange painted red lips, tall altar candlesticks, and a filigreed altar crucifix that looked as much Coptic as Roman. There was also a chalky-pale plaster Jesus—he'd been removed from the cross. Maybe the cross had broken or been judged more valuable on its own. Plaster Jesus was left leaning against the wall. It looked uncomfortable, the leaning, on top of Jesus's baseline discomfort: that accusing starkness of his ribs and hip bones.

He and the other refugees in the room with her should have spooked her, but they were more familiar than anything else she'd encountered in all her days in New York so far.

She bunched up one of the covers to sit on and another to put under plaster Jesus's head after she laid him down on the floor.

The Doctor

Through the driver's-side window, rain already running down his neck, he shook Ahmed's hand, thanked him, and repeated the driver's parting words, "Safe home" and, in Arabic, "Inshallah"—God willing—as the cab sped away.

How much darker it always was down in the Financial District, where the narrow cobblestone streets of old New York were filled in with high-rises, blocking whatever daylight there was. So little today, with the sky and air swirling and whipping wet.

He stopped across the street from an old brick high-rise and counted the floors up and then windows across to an office that belonged to the man he'd come to see. A light was on. It wouldn't be hard to get up and in; he'd done so before. One time, the doorman was overwhelmed with a delivery. Another time he explained he was a doctor, doing a house call for a tenant's "friend" who was scared and alone up there, adding, "She's not his wife, you see." That was enough—to call on the fraternity of men and the necessity of discretion.

He'd seen cameras in the lobby, in the elevator, on each floor, but not inside the man's office, which was really a studio apartment, the bed he'd outfitted it with taking up far more room than the table meant to pass for a desk. In theory, the man worked on a book there. He'd joked about it with Sarah, asked her to come to him in his new "tax write-off," close to her own apartment on Water Street. Not a coincidence. Neither was the time frame in which the Doctor arrived today. Most days, the man worked here until afternoon, but never too late, not since Sarah had vanished: The cocktail hour—really hours, enjoyed at his "office" or in a nearby bar—could begin as early as two o'clock for him.

What few bodies were on the street were too set on their own routes, with their heads turned away from the rain, to see the Doctor there, including a man stuttering in his motions, hugging a bottle wrapped in a brown bag. He knew the man immediately. It had to be nearing three thirty. The closest liquor store and any bars were probably shutting down early with the rest of the city and had forced him out. It felt a good omen. Another.

In long strides, the Doctor got to the building's entryway before the man did. It took the man a moment to see the Doctor before him, blocking his way through the lobby doors. Then the man just nodded as if they were picking up a conversation where they'd last left off.

"I expected you," he said. "But you've come before, for a look at me? I mean since the last time we talked here, you came again?"

"Yes," the Doctor said. "Not in some time."

"Why now?"

Sarah asked why she'd never insisted on more and better for herself? Why didn't she believe she could? And why hadn't the Doctor? To insist on more—certainly more to be learned, confessed, from this man, this P. or Pietro or Peter, a man with too many names and each one fitting like a curse in the Doctor's mouth. He finally had to tell the man what he knew now since he'd read the journal.

"It's the weather, isn't it, Doctor? This weather. I keep thinking I hear her. You too?"

"No," the Doctor said, lying.

"Have you been calling me, Doctor, saying nothing and hanging up?"

"No," he said, though the surprise that the man had been getting those same calls may have shown on his face.

But the man didn't argue with him, only tried a new tack: "Do you want to come up? I have this." He held the bottle up, a suggestion of a smirk on his lips, briefly. He was controlling himself, playing at sobriety, though his eyes floated in a face so like a fox's, with its long pointed nose, wide-set angled eyes that were heavily lidded and thickly lashed. He wore a hat of fuzzing wool, out of season, and his skin was warm with dark golden tones—his ancestry was Latin, but even so, he had the look of having recently been in a tropical place or on a cruise, taking in the sun.

The Doctor didn't move—his back was to the building's doors, and so to the camera over the entrance.

"So no drink?" The man sighed, and then, over his shoulder, as if to the rain that rushed and slowed behind them at the end of the open entryway, he said, "I miss her too, but I don't have the right to say that, do I? You don't think I do, do you?" He stepped closer to the Doctor. "That I have the right?"

On the man's breath came the acrid smell of alcohol that had been marinating his insides for a long time.

"I'm sorry, I've had too much, much too much—" Yet still the man persisted: "But it should have been you, right? Not me—with her. Or someone like you? That's what you want to say? That you're an honorable man and I'm not. Isn't that it?"

He took off his hat, which was wet, as was his hair, which had receded, leaving a sharp point. Water clotted in his eyelashes, which made them darker; it beaded down his cheeks.

"It was all so unlikely, her and me," P. went on, "that it ever began. She was sweet, so very sweet and lovely. And so alone. How could anyone not want to be there, to help her? But that she *let me*? I still can't believe it. And she kept letting *me*."

He laughed with surprise, then sighed with the theatrical self-pity the Doctor had encountered before when he'd come here, before he'd gotten the journal. It was like a film all over the man.

"I just wanted to be gentle. But then somehow I needed her to be mine, however I asked for it. I needed her to give that to me. Devotion. Don't we all? Maybe? No? Maybe not. But that's what happened. And she tried to do that for me, to give herself away."

The man's eyes refused to land anywhere or meet the Doctor's.

"Did you hear about the reward money? That I gave some, or some *more*, for information leading to finding her? My *own* money. Not my wife's. I inherited it recently—an uncle... It should make some news. I've asked for it to be made something of, with contacts, you know, in the media. 'Married lover of missing woman.'" He coughed out another laugh. "A suspect. Yes, that will make some news. Still am, aren't I? Suspicious, you bet! Unreliable, of course!"

He got lost in the drama of his thoughts and wiped his face with the sleeve of his coat. His eyes still skittered around, drunk and cagey. He couldn't help talking too much. He couldn't help anything.

"My wife plans to divorce me. She tells me every day. *Every* day. Her father threatens me. Often. It's how he greets me, the goddamned Latvian crook. And Latvian crooks? There's nothing like them. 'In any other country you'd be dead already,' he says. Today I'm not welcome at home, so I'm here for the night. That happens... That happens *a lot*. Sarah's father e-mailed me, to thank me."

The man had to be lying. The Doctor had understood that Sarah's parents found the man as repugnant as he did.

"Not enthusiastically—I'm not saying that—but Mr. Robbins wrote and acknowledged the reward, the contribution. It's a beginning. The very least I could do." He finally set his eyes on the Doctor. They were like some Hollywood Egyptian king's. He was still testing the Doctor: playing and provoking, while pretending to be beaten. "C'mon, have one drink with me upstairs? Let's get out of this mess."

"I read the journal," the Doctor told him. "Sarah's. I know things now that I didn't know before."

The man began blinking as if caught in a camera's flash. "I could have read it," he said finally. Defensive now. "She said I could—"

"I know what you did," the Doctor said.

"I knew that she was keeping it for you." The man forced a shrug. "She was going to show me, and then—"

"And then *what*?"

"I don't know. Things turned. Then she was gone. I didn't see her again. *Haven't* seen her."

"She wrote she was coming back here—to you—some days after she'd left you and your 'activities.' Did she come back? Did you see her?"

"Someone was here. I don't know if it was her. I keep telling *all* of you: I don't know what happened to her. Do you remember what you asked me last time we met?"

The man had been sober on that occasion. He acted bereaved. Acted confused, shocked when the Doctor had asked him if he'd harmed the girl, his patient and, yes, his friend. He'd asked matter-of-factly as if it might prompt the man to answer in kind. He treated him with respect—with courtesy, anyway. He couldn't do that now. The man stepped even closer to the Doctor. There was heat coming off of him, and the alcohol combined with the weakness in him, his needful self-indulgence: It swelled in the wet air around them. It tightened the spaces between the Doctor's thoughts, where there'd been some calm and something like fresh air, the chance for a different kind of conversation. What had he hoped for in coming here? Complicity with this person? Some kind of deliverance? How many times would it take before the Doctor learned that his own idealism had no place in a world so fast, so blown apart?

"I don't know where she is, if she's dead or alive, I told you that. If you've come here to solve some murder mystery, I can't help you. But what I did do—what *we* did? We went too far, she and I both. She didn't say no. I needed her to; I couldn't. But she didn't. And I didn't, and we destroyed each other."

"She destroyed *you*? All she wanted was—" The Doctor couldn't speak for the rushing noise in his head, louder than the rain: *It just keeps coming*.

"I didn't force her—I wouldn't."

She'd wanted love. Approval. Certainly she'd wanted freedom—physical and more—but she'd settled for lust, then oblivion. One thing to cure all ills. And the Doctor couldn't give it to her, not in the way she needed it.

The Doctor was at the park that day, just as Sarah had asked. Of course. He *did* come, but when he saw her there waiting on him, agitated, expectant, rather than go to her, he went looking for the courage to meet her on her terms, whatever they'd be, walking in circle after circle around her and through crowds in the late-summer green, under a stark blue sky with that one kite overhead—he'd seen the kite too—diving up and down and away. He hated to disappoint her and himself, tell her no. It couldn't be him, if that was what she wanted. An oath had to be sacred; she was his patient; it made things unequal. It was unfair to them both—couldn't she see that? There had to be balance, and love was not balance. It was not moderation.

"Why not just give her what she wants?" Ed had said, always Ed advocating for appetite, as if there would be no consequences, particularly when "just" prefaced the advice. But once Sarah was gone, that question—all the questions the Doctor had had about her—landed differently. And then once he'd read her journal, whatever regret he had grew and grew until he was suspended in it. That day in the park, he didn't know time had been running out for her and for him. He didn't know it was a missed opportunity that he'd be missing forever—there would be no second chances, no more conversations—or what it would feel like, through all these months of worrying and wondering, to hate himself because this man standing in front of him, Peter or Pietro or whatever the fuck his name was, had gone too far.

"I'd like to see the journal if you still have it."

"I don't."

"Where did you get it?"

He wouldn't mention Mathilde, the young woman who brought the Doctor the journal. She'd briefly been the man's cleaning woman, and she'd cared for Sarah. After Mathilde had met with the police, telling them what she could of Sarah's last days before vanishing, including the affair with this man, she delivered the journal to the Doctor, per instructions Sarah had left in her apartment. Then Mathilde had disappeared, too—out of the country, it was presumed.

"It was mailed to me."

"By her?"

"I don't know."

"Where is it now?"

"I threw it out."

"I don't believe you, Doctor."

"I don't care what you believe."

"You hate me. I get it. I do."

The Doctor wouldn't answer. He couldn't look too long at the man's face.

"But it's also true that you envy me? You wished it was you, don't you?"

The man's upper lip curled. It shivered.

"I went places with her you couldn't go. Places you wouldn't—"

"You led her to danger," the Doctor hissed through his tightened jaw. "You undid all the good work she—"

"—places you wouldn't let yourself." He seemed not to hear the Doctor. "She'd laugh because you were good—an *honorable* man, she said—and we were not—"

The Doctor could no longer hear the man, because rage was in the blood that was battering his ears. If he could only master himself, the man would tell him everything. If they could go upstairs, away from the security cameras that had once recorded Sarah coming and going. Sarah and others—men, and women too, enlisted in the game, *his* game.

A tremor went through him. This man could have loved her as she deserved to be loved. She'd believed in the gentleness of that one hand placed with care just as the Doctor had done. From the first, this P. had to know she was not his equal either—not in decadence, connivance, self-loathing, lust—and yet he still put her through terrible paces. He *dared* her. Yes, the Doctor hated him; with every rereading of her journal he hated him more for what he'd done. And the Doctor kept reading for the chance he'd lost, to be better, show up, find her in the park and tell her what was in his heart and about his oath—to do no harm—because that, too, was love, offering her safety. But this man had changed her, changed the rules as the Doctor had understood them for someone as precious as Sarah, and the revulsion reached out from inside the Doctor, where it had become a habit of thought and feeling, curdling in his gut, but now it moved to his limbs, landing one hand around the man's throat.

He remembered how time seemed to slow so voluptuously before an act of violence, a split second splitting before you in which the desire is unbearable, re-forming you around it: *I want this, I'll kill him.* The threat of this man, his having reached into spaces that were not his, were never his, came now to the Doctor as a gift of this day, so plainly made from a sequence of days leading him here, surrounding him now.

Wasn't he lighter, freer, since last night?

He swore he was. Nothing interfered with the sensation as his thumb dug into the man's tracheal well, just below the Adam's apple, where only one thin layer of skin provided protection, while the Doctor's other fingers pressed into the neck's coronary arteries, where the man's blood throbbed.

At the open end of the entryway, the rain heaved again, and the Doctor didn't let go, because none of it should have been: the wind, this rain, Sarah having believed in the wrong remedy, administered by the wrong man, and that man taking her to such extremes, from which she didn't come back.

A predator, her P. was, but one so often pretending to be prey—and now? What calculation could save him? It was the end of calculation for him. The Doctor felt calm, without fear of consequence or of the man's frantic pulse or his eyes rolling back in his head or his legs loosening, until the man's lips formed a smile. Ghastly. Full of knowing, as if the man had hoped for this very outcome, to take the Doctor with him here, right here, into the fullness of his distortions.

When the Doctor let go, the man dropped to his knees and caught his breath and coughed and wheezed and then coughed out laughter. The wheezing and laughing echoed in the entryway and came at them off the walls.

Everywhere laughter.

Ruth

Sharp, stabbing, squeezing, aching, burning, biting, dull: Ruth knew the language. How often had she asked her patients, "How would you describe your pain?" Here was this young woman, Sarah Robbins, forming a resistance out of that language—*How can I stop it? Now and forever?*

Ruth was cold from the cold of the floor beneath her but didn't mind. She gathered her damp coat around her shoulders and neck and brought her knees up to support the journal pages that she couldn't keep from reading now that she was locked in indefinitely, outside the seeing of any camera. Who could it hurt? No one had to know, particularly the Doctor, for whom the journal appeared to be written.

After a few pages of listing foods, changes in weather and her moods, Sarah asked him why he hadn't met her in the park. He'd stood her up. Yet, pages later, here was Sarah describing the Doctor with his hand around her ankle.

A bad migraine had put Sarah in the hospital, stranded her in a narrow hospital bed, with the Doctor's hand there *why*? To comfort her? To comfort him?

Ruth touched her own ankle, wrapped her hand around it. It was chilled through, and it struck her she was becoming like the things in this room—turning to stone or wood and losing the right to her own temperatures at all. She liked the idea of feeling less and less, of being in storage for now, alone and not—she was with this prone Sarah, a doctor's hand around her ankle like a tether and then another man's hand entirely.

I had told him about you. That you weren't just any doctor. I told him about the hospital, how you held on to my ankle. I was too far gone to say no. Please don't, Doctor. I can't be touched by you or anyone now, but then I realized you were showing me a way out and if I could focus some feeling there and then more, out of the worst of it, and trust that you were pulling me out, I could be freed. Begin to be. It was a beginning, wasn't it? Yes, your hand, that asked for nothing from me. It was the gentlest invitation.

I told him after I'd gotten back to work, a day when we were alone at the gallery. I told him I was amazed. He said I did that well—amazement. I thought he was teasing me, but he said no. He said, "That's why my wife likes it when you write the exhibit catalogs. More alive. But you pay a price for all that life, don't you?" I explained that's why I was lucky to have you, my doctor. He—let's call him P. for now—P. said I looked like a girl in love when I talked about you. I didn't say yes or no and we joked along these lines after that. He'd ask after you pretty regularly then, called you Doctor Love.

It was the light that set it off at the gallery opening weeks later. I was already stressed with the show, then add in neon, that's what the artist worked in. She mounted it in cases, hid it in curtained booths, or shaped the electrified tubes into bare words hung on the wall. Certain letters flashed on and off. The word SEX in pink, fluttering, became EX in blue, and then the D in GOD pulsed on and off, all the letters a queasy algae yellow, so it was GO GOD that stuck in your head. By that time, his wife, my boss Nadya, had stopped tracking me with her eyes. I'd done my job: The gallery was packed; there was plenty of wine being poured by local graduate students, and the artist, Swedish and gossamery, was surrounded with admirers. So I could disappear for a while, into the back, where there was this tattered chaise lounge for nights when an artist or any of us stayed late. I could lie down for a minute and take my medicine and try to find strength for the cleanup and lockup later.

P. caught me on the arm as I crossed the room in the glow of this one piece called "Subway to Street." It was meant to capture that white and gray light of a New York morning when you climb up from underground. It was supposed to be blinding, and it was.

Be back soon, I told him.

He waited just long enough to follow me in. Long enough that I'd forgotten him. I heard him pull a chair next to the chaise.

He put his hand where you had, Doctor, to start, around my ankle. I thought it was a joke at first—maybe it was—but he breathed with me, over the noise of the art opening, where he should have been, where I should have been. Why wasn't his wife looking for us? I will never know.

"Better?" he whispered to me after a time, I don't know how much time. I couldn't say how long we'd been like that.

He let go of my ankle very carefully, as if he'd wake me or break me otherwise, as if I were made of something that could shatter. I could still feel the warmth that he left there, and I could smell him. He wasn't wearing his usual cologne. He smelled of sweat, his briny and dark chocolaty, and the Pinot Noir from the opening, still on his tongue.

He held my hand in both of his, like I was his, or someone so very, very dear to him. My God, how did he know what I needed that day? How much pressure to apply? And how long to stay with me? His fingers cupped my hand in his, not making my hand do anything in reply to his holding it because I had to stay as still as I could. "Better?" he whispered again after another long period, and I was—<u>truly</u>. The meds helped, but it wasn't just them, not like that, so soon and so complete.

He made me promise I'd call him next time I had a headache. No matter the time or place, he said, if he could get away, he'd come find me. That's what he said.

When I decided to call the first time, about a week later, it was late, and sparks crowded out the vision of my right eye. Already there was that aching stiffness in my jaw and neck, nausea coming.

I lay down, got up, half-blind. I picked up the phone, put it down. I'd embarrass myself for sure, or his wife would find out, and it was too much to hope for anyway—someone who cared, who wasn't afraid, you know, of me, in pain. He was attractive enough, but looks alone have never moved me. To me he was someone who belonged not just to another woman but to a world way too sophisticated and discerning to take any real interest in me: a dabbler, good at so many things, just ask my mother—writing, drawing, singing, playing piano—but not really accomplished at any of it. Never touching down completely because I'm always either anticipating the worst or recuperating from it, you know?

That day, I took the Maxalt and the anti-nausea stuff, but I wanted to see if his hands could do what they'd done before, to know if that was real.

When he answered, I spoke, but my voice wasn't all there. "Sarah? Is that you? Are you unwell?" I said yes and that was all it took. He came and had such seriousness about it. He sat beside my bed and took my ankle again, like I should have known.

And five days later, a Monday when the gallery was closed, I called again. A humid day for a body that doesn't do well in humidity.

Then another night.

Each time he came, he was waking parts of me, drawing feeling there as it hadn't been before. He waited, before moving his hand up, first to my shin, leaving it there to make an impression, then my knee. Later he put the flat of his hand high up on my leg. You see, he was occupying me, I understand now, with one hand to start.

You know how I've hated my body, what it makes me feel and lose: time, words, joy. But here was life. It couldn't be helped—blood following my excitement now, created between me and this man. He didn't leave until I said: Better, yes, I am better now.

He asked for a key to my place so he could get in without disturbing me, if that was okay, he said, with me.

Next time I didn't open my eyes when P. was there in my bedroom, and we didn't talk. We almost never did. He took my ankle like he had before, and after quiet settled into the room, into us, he took off my clothes.

He did it without rushing, so very tenderly, as if I were asleep and he might wake me.

His hand for the first time between my legs. He waited for me to move away, object—I didn't—then his fingers traced the shapes there to learn them, separating what was delicate from delicate.

He stopped to whisper: "We're getting the blood out of your head. Don't move if you don't want to."

His breath between my legs and then his tongue, the tip of it to me there, circling as slowly as his fingers.

I let him until I couldn't. <u>I just couldn't</u>... I thought I'd vomit. I needed to be calm. <u>Alone.</u> I pushed up, away, closed my legs, and turned to the wall. I expected him to leave me and not come back, ever. But no, he lay beside me, without touching me.

We fell asleep, both of us, for twenty minutes, an hour. "Better?" he asked. I was. No more voices, no sparks, only that residual soreness in my face and neck, a stony shadow.

"I'm sorry about not being able—" I said. He said, "I read that sex, or orgasm anyway, can be, well, therapeutic, that's why I... well... But not for you? Never for you?"

I told him about Darwin and Bobby, Bobby of the Fields.

Ruth could see the summer night Sarah then described with a boy named Bobby—the beer and gum, the wet grass and sky overhead—through the filter of a thousand of her own, had in clearings and by the sea, while her muscles loosened into that storage room's cement floor, as if it were not cement but the grass she swore she could smell. Her insides were shifting like butter warming. What had Mrs. Watson said about moments having to last so long? Ruth couldn't find the words exactly, but she didn't resist what time was doing to her now—the memories coming and misshaping her as they did, memories that were impossibly fragrant and fragile. Of her early days with Nathaniel, the man who would become her husband. *We aren't really built for monogamy, are we, Ruth?* Mrs. Watson said this like it was a fact, and it probably was, but it didn't change that she and Nathaniel had loved each other. He had been as nourishing and sustaining as anything in this life had ever been to her, and she had been to him.

Those first weeks and months, Ruth and he were learning all the details—the textures, temperatures, smells, and sounds made—breathless, high on breath, absorbing each other with every minute, into every hour, so many hours in each other's company, making each other new. Of course, they had said "love" too soon. The lust made them say it. Like they were conjuring love and had no say in this. Desperate, of course, to feel everything, in their twenties, all impulse and acres of skin, and growing yet more skin for each other to draw on.

She had not let herself remember just how easy it had been to believe they were seeing each other for who they really were. But how can you see anything through so much desire and hope? How crushing it was, to want someone and something so much, the hunger felt in every part of the body, along every nerve, through and into muscle clutching, and out into the air between you, passed back and forth, inhaled, exhaled?

He didn't undress me the next time. He didn't touch me in any way but respectfully, I swear it. I didn't take any meds but him. I swear that too. I wanted to risk it: only him. So when he came again, I undressed for him. Then it began as it always did: the ankle, then my knee, I moved his hand between my legs before he could, and he moved it away. He moved my own hand there and said, "Try," and I said yes—anything, anything.

Ruth could see herself again, standing at the window of Nathaniel's bedroom, which would become their bedroom, in Seabrook, New Hampshire.

Nathaniel's hand on the back of her neck, not forcing her to stay, only steadying her there, and giving sanction: *Let them see you,* he said. *It's okay.*

She was naked and stood only a breath from the live cold of the window glass. Outside, there in a dark without any moon or house lights or streetlights, there were inches of snow on the ground. There were other houses on the other side of bare trees that had been heavy with leaves only a month ago. They were no protection at all from anyone's or anything's eyes. *Let them see how beautiful you are,* he whispered: His hand so lightly on her neck and not reaching for the rest of her, and she shivered with wishing it would.

Do you feel them seeing you?

Yes, she nodded, and she did feel strange eyes on her, including hers and Nathaniel's, as if they were down there, too, in a warmer season, looking up to see what was happening to them now, December in Seabrook, a place that, only months before, Ruth, who'd grown up just two towns away, had rarely visited. She'd known about its accumulation of retail stores, smoke shops, and fireworks dealers—and its nuclear power plant, that quantity of tumorous concrete anchored into their slight New Hampshire coast. The news of the place had been remote to her: a dog track shuttered, jobs lost, fishing regulations imposed on a fishing town's ways of living and surviving, red tide after another red tide showing up like a curse and making for more bans and angry debates and lost income.

But now Ruth loved a man from a family of New England fishermen who cared bitterly about all of it. And she raised her hands and held on to the upper frame of the window and spread her legs. That's all she had to do to communicate *Let them see both of us,* the two of them there in the light, before the glass steamed over and closed them in and away from whatever might be hiding in the dark.

I was sure I could never give it to him, that response P. wanted from me so very badly. And I was sorry, and I tried to tell him—not me, you know? Not me.

He wanted to shock me, distract me from me, so he turned me over and put his tongue where no one else ever had in me, his face back there, pressing my ass cheeks apart. He was like totally fearless, and of course I just froze, embarrassed for both of us. I needed him to stop and let me go, but then—I have to explain this—he put his fingers inside me, too, in front, one then two fingers there, touching a spot in me that was so lucky that day, so alive, that it began to blossom outward, as with the pain, starting from one place, identifiable on the map of my body, but it wasn't as imposing as the pain that so often closes me in and away. I'm telling you that it lightened me, all of me, going through me in surges, as if my body's very shape, I swear to you, Doctor, was changing, opening out and out like water with the pleasure. And all of me was pleasure, the wells of my eyes, the top of my head, the back of my arms, pointing toes, and it kept going and going, the sensation lifting me and yet holding me down, aching and alive with its own heartbeat inside me where it began. It was terrifying to be taken in and away like this. But what choice did I have? Whatever the vulnerability, the disorientation? This body so transformed, emptying and yet filling from what source in me?

Can I tell you I was lost and found there? Lost and then found again, back and forth, and muttering nonsense, my God, my God—it takes my breath away even now—going and coming, coming wet.

Ruth remembered: what it was to be lost and found in someone else's hands, eyes, mouth, the taste and smell of her irresistible to someone else—yes, to be found beautiful when she had learned over time she wasn't, or not to everyone. She wondered if the Doctor could understand the impact of this on a young woman? That Ruth was barely visible to most people and had preferred it that way. The angels—her mother had called on them as never before when Ruth and her sister were newly teenagers. The angels can see you, and *oh, the shame of it*, the blood and the body and the longings never to be admitted.

But Nathaniel said, *Let them see you, Ruthie*: her freckles that swarmed her skin in summer; her muscular legs that meant she could jump and run and climb better than most girls, most boys, too; the hips that got fuller overnight and breasts bigger, through sizes A, B, to C, which she hid in oversize shirts; the rounded childishness of her cheeks and lips; the light red hair of her head, brows, and pubis that turned auburn, darkening every year as if with the darkening of events around her; the crinkled scar down her shin from a fall from a bike; the olive-pit-shaped birthmark on her calf.

Nathaniel took every bit of her back from ugliness to something cherished, desired. Nathaniel had shown Ruth a body and a way to be at home in it she didn't think was possible for her: It had been hidden from her. It had required breath on it to rise. Not her own, and not once, but repeatedly, as a devotion that had earned hers.

Time stopped that day, along with the pain, with him, and I let it, and then again and again and again. Can't I be forgiven for wanting this?

"Yes," Ruth said out loud, and compassion suddenly seemed to reach through her body there on that cold floor, another high lifting her. Of all the recriminations she'd endured—whether face to face or online—her own, for herself, had been the heaviest to bear.

If Sarah could be forgiven, couldn't Ruth be too? She'd lived it, too, how desire called on love, to sustain it—it courted and claimed love, didn't it? Trapped it.

And love, when shared over time, through days, nights, months, years, in room after room, on walks in woods, in cars driving away to restaurants or hotels, or home—*Let's go home, honey*, home again, with music of course, there too, inhabitable as well, his music, hers, *Listen to this, listen to me*—love forged a sense of place within every place that she and Nathaniel had been. Love lived like that became durable, real as a roof overhead, or as the ground felt underfoot, so it could not be given up easily. It lived everywhere in the body, as much as in the mind and imagination. It couldn't be reshaped or cut away abruptly at will, no matter the will... It *was* prosaic, just as Mrs. Watson said, but that fact, Ruth saw now, could absolve her. Love is a story told and retold, modified, to endure. Like life, love wants to persist, however it can.

I asked him to make love to me. It can't be love, he said. Of course, I said, I didn't mean love love, and yet, the first time we made love, he held himself up on his elbows, hanging there, sweat on his forehead already, inserting himself between my legs like his cock was as much metal as flesh, something that could cut me in two if he wasn't careful.

Ruth read and reread Sarah's pages, because her thoughts divided like branches and raced to ends, came back, drifted into memories, back to Sarah, then to the wife, this P.'s wife: Nadya. Ruth wasn't as naive as Sarah. Ruth had been a wife, too. She'd watched her husband struggle against his impulses—those pills prescribed for his back pain, the same pills that had helped him get through law school. *But I don't need them, now that I have you, Ruthie.* And he didn't need them. Or many fewer, as if they were a choice. For a while. When it came time to prepare for the bar exam: *Just a little longer. Don't make me give them up just yet, Ruthie, I can't get through without them and you.*

She was placated when she shouldn't have been. Even two years into their marriage, when she was twenty-nine, then thirty, he made her feel essential to him, studying with him, reading law cases to him until he fell asleep. Once upon a time she'd been encouraged to go to medical school rather than nursing school. Her grades were good; she tested well; she worked hard, wasn't put off by being on her feet for hours, or by little sleep. But it would take too long when Ruth wanted to leave room for a partner and children: Even before she met Nathaniel, she believed he must be on his way to her.

She worked at the hospital while he prepared for the bar exam and doubted himself and gave up. He didn't show for the exam, and then, confessing and contrite, he pledged to try again. *Next year.* He didn't want to fail, but he feared something else more: succeeding, as if out of deference to his family. He couldn't lose them or his place in their ranks, on the boats, on the scalding roofs they worked on when fishing wasn't enough, in the bars round after round. But he couldn't lose Ruth, either: *You think you're better than me? Don't you? You always have.* She never had. Not once. She thought him as miraculous as love was. To her his sweat smelled of the rain when it first mixes with the ground. He could repair anything: lamps and electrical outlets, an old boiler with a bad burner, boat engines, broken chairs, picture frames. He could pick out a few folk songs on a guitar, and he sang loudly through his nose and asked Ruth to sing with him. When he was well, before the addiction and its unpredictability took him over, they made love in the course of their day, in the shower or while getting dressed, in the car—it had to be done—the seat tilted back, him on top, then her on top, as if it were a part of their communication, unremarkable, *Feed me and I will feed you,* round and round. But it had been remarkable; they had been happy; and Ruth had taught herself not to remember it, or not fully, until today.

This Sarah had remembered for her, with her.

Nadya told him I had good posture and manners, that I was smart enough to do anything I wanted, but said I was another American baby who'd never been fucked properly and who didn't get life is a road race. It was Nadya who said, "The right man could help that girl with those headaches." It was a joke

between them, but P. decided it was a dare: He could be that right man, or maybe—he could try. He said that I wasn't cynical like he and Nadya were, so being with me was like a vacation to somewhere where nobody spoke their language. It was a break from the disparaging, the distrust, and disappointment as a reflex. For a time he could be a man he was not in his marriage. He could know sweetness. With you, he said to me, everything is possible.

Novelty. Sweetness. Yes. We all wanted it. Every single one of us, at our peril. Even Ruth's own father. Why did her mother expect anything different?

When Ruth's father wandered—once only, he said, with a young designer in training with his architecture firm—he'd confessed to it right away, gotten down on his knees, begged. He'd lost his head, his mind. A mistake. But Ruth's mother was no scientist like Sarah's mother. She was an accountant and a Catholic who in the shock of that news swapped the New Testament for the Old and refused to hear him, how sorry he was. And for Ruth every angel took on her mother's face, unsmiling and round-eyed and locked in with bitter knowledge. But what could those angels do? So cold, so far from knowing flesh—what did they know about human bodies? Sarah and her married man. Mrs. Watson and her Sandrine in Paris. Nathaniel coming home fucked up and with scents pressed into his skin that were not Ruth's, his cock yeasty as bread. Ruth's own father, during one night that he could not get back, because he wanted to taste something he'd never tasted, just once. *Prosaic...* Her father who built dollhouses and tree houses for them. Her father who came to sing outside their windows at night, when they were teenagers—"Love Me Tender," "Come Rain or Come Shine"—her father shut out by the divorce and shared custody that was never shared, serenading them. *I'm here. I'm here. I will do anything, anything.*

Yet when Ruth chose Nathaniel—not from Rye or Boston, but a boy from a fishing family in Seabrook—her father objected, steadying himself by then with a steady routine of Bombay and tonics and a new wife with two of her own daughters, younger models all around. *This boy isn't good enough for you. Can't you see that?*

She couldn't see it, only that her father had come to fear the sweetness he'd known in love and in lust. Wasn't that what Sarah was saying now? How Sarah and her lover tried *not* to love? But every time they touched each other, they risked love and their hearts changed rhythms and they couldn't breathe only to breathe again, inhale, exhale love.

And they couldn't stop talking to each other now, and to Ruth—their stories in blue ink that fogged up at times and looked wet to the touch. Was Ruth getting it all straight? The wife, Nadya, yes, and Nadya's brutal father, and poets—what was Sarah saying about money and poets? Is this what people in cities talk to each other about?

He said he got the apartment to work on his book—on Herman Melville's Civil War poetry, poems that he tells me over and over were barely discovered or understood. He has a Ph.D. in American literature, used to teach, but Nadya relies on him to make their everyday lives go, to make the gallery profitable. P. admitted he had little ambition for making money, which worked because his wife and her father—a Latvian native—had so much, but in her darker moods, which weren't infrequent, she told him he was not man enough for her, and he readily agreed: But who is, my darling? He said this to her. Who is more man than you?

She yelled at him in Latvian. He, because his mother was Chilean, yelled back in Spanish. Once he'd talked to Nadya about Melville and Neruda. He loved Neruda like a god—the love poems, of course, and the poems about the Spanish Civil War, so full of love and despair for Lorca. He needed someone to read the poems to, to help make them new again, and he shared his theories about the headaches, all the chronic pain out there that he'd been researching for me. He believed that Freud had it right. After all, Freud was a migraine sufferer too, right? And P. had read that headaches—and not just that but chronic pain in general—could all come down to unexpressed emotion festering, pain inviting more pain, he said. That we had to address all that energy in me. Keep at it. Move the blood, sync the body and mind. Like exercise. Or try, for me.

I wanted to quit the gallery, but he worried Nadya and her father might get suspicious, and the truth was it gave us a way to be together in the day-to-day. I reassured him Nadya doesn't scare me. "She should," he told me. "You have your pain and I have mine." And he held up his hand to show me his wedding ring, laughing a sad laugh.

I tried to take it off his finger. "No," he said. "Don't bother. I can't leave her. Won't. I'm sorry, what you and I are doing? It can't be love."

I told him I'd never expect it. But for me, despite what I tell him, it was love the first time he came to my apartment, with that patience and seriousness. It didn't matter his motivations, if his generosity wasn't only generosity, because he had helped. For as long as he could, and for a time it was unselfish. Please believe me.

We'd come to make love with our eyes open. We had to keep looking at each other and see how we opened and closed around each other, fluttering like these helpless things, while we held on, me steadying myself against the strength of his appetites. What appetites. My God! One day we both wound up in tears from our amazement, both of us, amazed, it was palpable, a gift, or I thought so, that we were feeling the same thing, but then he wept in earnest and said that had to be the last time.

What we were doing, it confused things too much for him. He got up and paced and pumped his hands in the air, at me, saying that it had always been for me. To help me feel better. We couldn't go backwards, but maybe we could change it up, try other things, to keep the body as alive as I could bear.

After Freud, he hauled out Winnicott. Winnicott?! He'd been thinking about it and he was ready to explain how we'd do it. He planned it out: how to keep me and let me go.

He knew my mother had taught me about Winnicott. He was one of her go-tos on parenting. So he said that I'd definitely understand better than most that it's not "I think, therefore I am." No. It's "I interact, I play, and then I feel that I'm alive. I'm here. I am." You see, he wanted others in the room with us, other people. To play. He could touch me through them. He'd be right there, a guide. It would be an experiment, but not just. It also was a test of how daring I was, how free I could be. "We have to play to be most ourselves," he said, "to be free. C'mon, Sarah. Play with me."

Nathaniel's voice back in Ruth's head: *C'mon, try it.* Nathaniel lifting the rose-gray powder to Ruth's face.

I'm not touching that shit, Nat...

C'mon, Ruthie...

She hit his hand and the heroin spread like fairy dust in the air, everywhere. No way to get it back.

You think you're better than me? Too good for this?

The violence between them began with words. His, then hers, violence in her voice, or rage anyway—*Please, don't do this to me, to us*—because he was shifting the very ground underneath their feet. The roof over their heads. Why risk them like this? After a fight, he wanted forgiveness, approval, and when she stopped giving it, had to, he pushed her. Then he hit her with a closed hand when he asked again if she thought she was better, and the answer, on that day, was yes—*and not just me, everyone is better while you use that shit, while you hide behind it. Everyone, everyone is better than you!*

Ruth left the next time, with a patch of hair torn out of her scalp, but she went back when the promises were made. Rehab. Therapy. Love—love like theirs...

It was prosaic. A battered woman. Another one. *Don't let them see—the shame of it.* But how could she hide? And where were her mother's angels then? Gone, chased away, because she knew by then that any punishments to be handed out were issued right here on earth.

"That's why they've retired you," Ruth said to that strange statue of Gabriel in the storage room with her. She wanted very much to touch his wings—each of their feathers a small dagger so painstakingly shaped—but she still couldn't move. Her blood pressure had dropped so low with the cannabis, and she was so hungry, but there was no one there to feed her. "Except you?" she said to the statue's boyish face, a picture of incorruptibility, regarding her with its blank irises. *Where have you been all my life?*

She laughed and couldn't stop, silly as the little girl she'd been, years before her parents' separation, imagining angels surrounding her like the army of stuffed animals on her bed, pressing their comforts into her. Those angels took in the rabbit warmth of her then, still tender with her own possibilities, while the angels were so very cold, made of faraway places and temperatures that they could bear but she couldn't, and so, there, next to her, they thawed and softened and wept with her for every pleasure and pain she knew and would know and for how far away they had to be.

She'd been alone when she was forced to defend herself from the man she'd loved most in the world, and, like that, Ruth's laughter turned to tears and a runny nose in that storage room. And she was wet, too, like the angels she'd imagined. But not just her face. The back of her jacket, skirt, and stockings, straight through to her skin, the cement floor under her, too, it was all wet. Water. The rain, the storm that she'd forgotten—it was taking the room now.

She had to get up, and somehow she did. It took so long to make any progress to the door. Time slipped in and out; so did her prayers and the sense that anyone was listening.

She unbolted the door and opened it. As far as she could see down the hall, there was no one, but then, overhead, she could hear the ceiling adjusting, feet moving maybe, and voices murmuring and then singing. But only one voice. Small at this distance, but ringing like a bright bell in reaching Ruth. Was she hallucinating now, like Sarah had?

When she stepped up the one step and onto the hall carpet—the expensive hypoallergenic sort she'd walked on in countless doctors' offices before—water pooled around one of her feet, then the next, smelling richly of wet wool. The basement was seeping. She had only to follow the sound of the ringing voice. Maybe this was answer to her prayers. Maybe she did not have to be so alone after all.

The Wind Report

"All it takes is a tenth of an inch. That's it—that much rain and the system starts to discharge. It's got to, to relieve the pressure. The same lines handling the rain runoff are already handling the sewage, never mind the industrial waste. Six thousand miles of pipes trying to deliver whatever they've got to the city's wastewater treatment plants—there's fourteen, not enough, not by a long shot—so you get what we call CSO, combined sewer overflow, into all the city's waterways. You're gonna get backflow in the streets, too. No way around it. So get yourself some good boots or stay inside. Look, I worked for the DSNY for sixteen years—"

That's the Department of Sanitation?

"Yeah. I still consult with them and the DEP—"

Department of Environmental Protection?

"I'm not telling any secrets here. This is all public knowledge. The city's doing some good to help, but fact is, there's no real way to fix the system without digging it all up, and no one—I mean *no one*—wants that. There'd be mass disruption. And how can the city afford it? I can tell you, it can't. No way."

So we've outgrown our infrastructure—

"I grew up in Bensonhurst. My father was an engineer. We'd walk over to Shore Road in Bay Ridge for the views, a look at the boats, the Verrazano, but after any rain, if we were over there, my father always said, 'That's the smell of a city that can't handle its own sh-[beep]' if you'll pardon my French."

We have another call? From Maureen on Staten Island. Maureen, are you there? Can you hear me?

"Yes, I can. Hi, love the show. I'm calling because we, my husband and I, we have animals in our yard."

Animals? And by that you mean…

"I mean wild turkeys, rabbits, deer. My husband saw what he thought was a gopher. But I think it was a possum. In broad daylight—a possum and raccoons, too. It's like the Bible, you know, the Ark? My husband said, 'Where's Dr. Dolittle when we need him?'"

To talk to the animals—

"Right. We live in Oakwood, behind what was Oakwood Beach that got hit so bad during Sandy? Everybody left the Beach finally, they took buyouts from the government so this could be what they're calling a buffer zone for the island, for us here. We live right on the line here. We couldn't afford to live in the Beach when we moved here. Now all the houses are gone. It's mostly reeds and animals, and I can hear them at night, things crying out, things, I guess, trying to survive. My husband says it's life. I say it's *Wild Kingdom*. And I still hear them in the wind, like they get even louder somehow, the sounds carrying. I ask my husband, 'Did you hear that?' He says, 'It's Foxy Loxy getting its you-know-what kicked.' He makes jokes. But now they're here in the yard. *Our* yard. Like they're running for their lives, you know? Because the water's back. It's back. Flooding now. In the buffer. Can you tell us if we should leave? I mean, should we be running too?"

The Doctor

The rain tested its momentum against the Doctor's. It slapped at his face and neck. It eased up, only to drive at him from another angle. But he had to walk until he regained himself. He judged he had when he was standing in front of St. Gabriel's. He saw people going into the church entrance. It was generally locked, tight as a tomb. He followed them in, and once inside he was blind from the whitewashing his vision had taken, but he heard the singing right away, even before the doors had closed out the day behind him. One young voice, playing around in the song "This Little Light of Mine," improvising: "This precious light of mine, I'm gonna let it shine, let it shine, to give you my love, *my-uh* love."

He heard people cheering and had begun to make them out in the half-light that wavered over the old stone of the columns and ribbed arches; it licked up to the arcades and the ceiling's cross-vaulting. It had the feel of midnight mass, though rather than a priest, there was a young girl in front of them with a small speaker and a mic. Her exuberance ran at odds with the state of the place. Because however romantic the light—generated by the emergency lighting, lanterns, candles—there was no concealing that the place was dingy with neglect, with waiting for its fate to be decided.

There were missing rows of pews and empty spaces where votive stands, statuary, prie-dieux, and a lectern once had been. A few feet into the right-hand transept, the Doctor made out Orson Watson, in a portion of light all his own, furnished by what looked like an LED camping lantern. He was bending over a folding card table and painstakingly filling an army of disposable cups from a bottle—one of several. Of what? Wine? He guessed there were about thirty to forty people there, strangers mostly, though it was hard to tell, because so many were still masked in their weather helmets and hoods, ponchos and zippered raincoats. Many were on their feet, clapping to what was now the thick of the song, with more impromptu lyrics. "Together, we're gonna let it shine, let it shine. C'mon raise those glasses high, we're gonna let it shine!"

He walked up the aisle, into the song, his head clearing enough to try to gauge how much time he had before the police came for him. Not right away, with the weather, but soon, surely.

"Been swimming, Doc?" A voice he knew, but thready, worn: Ed, with his windbreaker shrugged off, seated at the far end of a pew alone, an empty cup in his hand.

"Didn't plan on it, but it's a monsoon out there."

"You went walking in this? Jesus, Doc."

Ed shook his head at the Doctor like a disappointed father, one who'd been disappointed before. Right away, the Doctor imagined he could tell Ed, of all people, what he had done today, how he'd finally fallen, nosedived, off that high horse they all put him on. *Just do it*, and he had—done it. Ed would have a plan laid out in no time: Wouldn't he love to be the man to bail the Doctor out rather than the other way around? But when the Doctor sat beside Ed, he could see his friend's eyes were red and bright with tears. "Sam's relapsed," he said.

It didn't seem possible. He'd seen Sam only days ago, with Ed, during the support group's meeting. Sam was the vet, who'd been medicated for headaches, neck pain, straight into heroin addiction, like his own patient Adam, but unlike Adam, he had no brain injury and had shown less difficulty with impulse control. Save for the experiments with cannabis, Sam had been clean for two years and under Ed's care, officially and unofficially, for most of that time.

"I was out looking for him. Thought he'd come here. To the clinic maybe, but since that's closed, maybe up here, with all these people… " Ed scanned the place. "Doubt the old lady likes it, and that's no bottom-shelf shit Orson's pouring."

"How did you find out? About Sam?"

"His mom. She called a couple of hours ago. He was doing so fucking great."

It was true, and Sam had become like a son to Ed.

"I was sure he had it beat. I would have bet my left nut on it. And my right." He allowed a laugh, only one, then snuffed up a breath, rattled his head. "Who is that kid up there?"

"I've seen her before—" More than once, but the Doctor could not place where.

She began to sing a song the Doctor knew, but not in a way he'd ever heard it before. Uptempo. "Abide with Me." A hymn. Was he right? Yes, the lyrics were the same so far; the tune, too, except for its strange speed: "Abide with me; fast falls the eventide. The darkness deepens; Lord, with me abide."

There was nothing of the reverence he associated with the hymn, the quiet. It was written as a plea from a dying man, a love song, however resigned, to God. He'd heard it as a boy—not at mass, but at home. Thanks to an Episcopalian grandmother, his Catholic mother could sing all the hymns.

"Have you heard from Adam?" Ed asked. "Maybe they were together?"

"Adam was at the clinic earlier. I didn't see Sam."

It was hard to believe it was the same day. That was only hours ago, but time was not what it had been, thanks to the weather and all the event it excited and stretched.

"Adam was angry. Jackie. Evidently she treated him some years ago."

"Christ, she's got some skill for fucking up men."

"Adam just had to—" The word *control* was on his tongue, as in "control himself." The Doctor tasted his own hypocrisy in it. "I told him he would have to leave if he couldn't calm down."

"You did? And did he leave?"

"No, I did. I left. Before he did. To put Jackie in a cab. I haven't seen him since."

"This kid has swallowed the sun. Christ... Look at her."

She sang out and into the hard surfaces of the church, which made every word reverberate: "When other helpers fail and comforts flee, help of the helpless, oh, abide with me."

Whatever grim romance his mother found in the hymn, it didn't interest this girl. Her delivery came with defiance, as if everyone would be better off abiding *with* her, even God himself. She'd taken the hymn and turned it into a rousing show tune.

"Doctor!" Orson had swept in behind them, goggles up on his head, embedded in his curls. With his face flushed, eyes a little feral with excitement and surely with drink, he looked the part of a mad scientist. "I thought that was you! Champagne?" He extended a cup, spilling a portion. "Cuvée rosé, Laurent-Perrier. Lots of wild strawberries in it. Fresh, but not too! A r*efined* vinous character. I have a few cases of it here. A gift from Mother to help us all weather the storm, though, between us, she's not yet aware of her generosity. C'mon now, Doctor. Take it. It's rude to come to a party and not play."

The Doctor took the cup. "That girl, Orson: Do I know her? She looks so—"

"That's Marie's daughter. You've probably met her once or twice before at the house. Letty. Short for Violet." Orson beamed. "Isn't she perfect? A perfect little superstar. I thought it was time I took her out of hiding."

Orson let out a howl of support for the girl. Others followed. More people got up on their feet, clapping. Ed drank, and Letty repeated a verse, belting out, "Where is death's sting? Where, grave, thy victory? I triumph still, if Thou abide with me."

The Doctor made out someone, a woman repeating, "Thank you, thank you," over and over, not loud but insistently, in and around the lyrics and cheers. It was someone to one side of the empty space the altar had left, mostly in shadow. She was swaying, but raggedly, like a body that wasn't in charge of itself entirely, that maybe had too much of Orson's merrymaking.

The doors to the church opened, with more voices and thick, humid air heaving up the aisle.

"Back to greeting our guests. Don't let anyone tell you sanctuary is not hard work," Orson said as he dashed off.

Ed gave a snort at this. "Man," he said. "This life, huh?"

"He'll be okay, Ed. Sam will. He's a smart kid."

"Yeah. And big. God. And strong. Strong as an ox. And then, he's just, you know... sweet, a big, sweet man..." Ed lost his voice.

The Doctor grabbed his friend's hand and squeezed the ham and heat of it. The same hand he'd just used to choke a man.

"I promised his mother," Ed said, "to take care of him."

"You have. You did, as far as you were able."

"And we can't promise anything, Ed, only—

"But we *do*, don't we? *You* do, with everything you do for your patients. Every *fucking* day." Ed gripped the Doctor's hand hard in reply. "C'mon, buddy. Don't try to fool this fool."

The Doctor didn't have it in him to argue or pretend, and as the girl finished her song with a bow of her head, through the applause someone yelled, "Sing it again. One more time!" Others joined in, chanting, "One more time! One more time!" She complied, upping the tempo a little more this time.

"That woman there, by that side door—can you see her? Is that Ruth?" the Doctor asked.

"The nurse from earlier?"

"Yes."

"Didn't see her. Or I did but didn't make the connection. Yeah, she looks a little undone."

The Doctor sipped his champagne, passed the rest to Ed. "I'd better see if—"

The marble floor was slippery underfoot, and the song went faster still, and Ruth, he saw, tried to move faster with it. As he got closer, he saw the little girl in more detail—light mocha in her skin, big eyes, a pointed chin, an Afro of curls, little stars caught in it somehow. Her voice was strong and its tone shapely enough to hold you to her. And Ruth was held there. Her eyes were closed, and half of her hair was out of its pins, a bramble on one side of her head. She'd belted her coat too high and tight, so its skirt angled forward, the back of it sticking to the back of her. She continued on with her thank-yous, as if chanting, and when she pitched too far to one side and didn't right herself quickly enough, the Doctor did. But once his arms were around her and her momentum was interrupted, she fell into him, heavy as a corpse.

Ed had jumped up to help the Doctor with Ruth, but the Doctor warned him away. "No, *stay, stay.* See if Sam turns up."

The Doctor led her down the stairs to a treatment room. Once he had her up on a treatment table, she wouldn't let him unfasten her coat when he suggested he hang it to dry. She babbled on about the angels and then the water coming for them. He smelled the wet carpet in the clinic halls they'd passed through. That is what she must have meant—a leak somewhere. But more urgent to him, a doctor still, for now anyway, was that if she'd been drinking, she was probably dehydrated. He found water and food from the kitchen. She revived some after having a little of both, volunteering in complete sentences how good the food tasted, that she'd been so hungry—"*dying* of starvation. I was trapped when they came in."

"Who came in?" he asked. "Upstairs, in the church?"

"No, Larry and the woman."

"The woman?"

"With big breasts. Like a goddess's, that's what he said."

"Jill?"

"I hid in your office. Had to—I was sent here."

"To check on the place?"

"Mmmmm. They were *soooo* close, kissing. They don't know me—so I ran—"

"Larry and Jill?"

He'd heard they were an item.

"Kissing and plotting."

"Plotting? What do you mean? How much did you have to drink, Ruth?"

"No, no, that's not it. I just didn't eat. All day I didn't. So I took something from your drawer and ate it. I'm *sooo* sorry, Doctor. I was just *sooo, sooo* hungry, and it was all I could find in there. It wasn't normal, was it? That hard candy?"

"The candy in *my* drawer?"

The Doctor felt his adrenaline rise again, cold and heat threading through his neck and face.

"No. Not normal," he confirmed. This could be considered negligence, at least by Adele, if Ruth complained or reported him.

"I hate it—marijuana, Jesus, *weed*—God, I really hate it," she started to say.

"I am sorry, Ruth. That was personal property, a gift… for medicinal use. I didn't imagine anyone would go into my—"

"But I mean, I have to admit it, I kind of like it, too. There are things I didn't see until now. That girl. Right here. An angel. A *real* one. Can you believe it?" She closed her eyes: "I think I'll sleep now." But she kept talking, murmuring. "And she was so vulnerable. She needed real angels. Not him, but all she wanted was him or, no, how he made her feel, once anyway, once upon a time… " She snickered lightly at this.

"Who, Ruth? Not the girl? Do you mean Jill? Do you mean Jill and Larry?"

"Oh, no, no. Larry"—Ruth's voice changed to a small, seething whisper—"Larry's a spy. *He's a spy*!"

She crossed her arms over her middle, low, as if to shield it. "We have to keep her safe."

"Who, Ruth? Who are you talking about?"

She hugged herself closer and turned away to the wall. "She just wanted to feel better, not an invalid. All those headaches, since she was young, so very—"

Another spike in his adrenaline as he suddenly feared he recognized the plotline.

"Ruth?" He had to keep his anger out of his voice, his hands. "*Who* are you talking about?"

"*Ssssshhhhh*," Ruth offered. "They can see and hear. We're not alone."

"I'll be right back, Ruth."

On his way to his office, he heard the rumble of the clinic's generator at work and felt a dampness mixing with the air as he never had down here. The drawer in which he kept the journal was not locked. He must have forgotten to lock it. But the journal was right where he'd left it, pushed to the back. He could not tell if it had been touched or read through, but what else could have happened? And how did Ruth get in after closing? Adele, of course, for whom it was not enough to have acolytes—no, she wanted dependents, toadies, spies.

He looked up at the camera high in the far corner of the room, as if he were looking right at Adele or whoever might be watching.

In the entryway of that man's building, the security camera had recorded one man attacking another without any other context—the story had begun out of the device's seeing. It was the man's laughter, echoing in the long entryway and in the Doctor. The Doctor was leaving. He'd gathered his coat and breath to him, hunched his shoulders in advance of the rain, the rain coming down in sheets, but he didn't go because it had to stop. The laughter. He wheeled around. The man was kneeling now. With the momentum of his entire body, the Doctor landed his foot into the man's gut. The first kick forced his body back. When he went down, onto his side, the Doctor kicked him hard again, because he was hijacked by the rush of it. The pleasure. And that necessity: no more laughter. The man wasn't breathing, not audibly, but the Doctor was, hard, as if he'd sprinted to the moment.

Now he dropped his face in his hands, trying to gather himself once more today, and then, as calmly as he could, despite the lopsided thumping of his heart, stood on one of the chairs provided for patients and began to pull and twist the camera down.

The Wind Report

I heard that during the excavation of the World Trade Center after 9/11, they found, under the ruins of the tower, the hull of an eighteenth-century shipwreck. Is that an urban myth in the making or—

"It's no myth. It's true. They found it. That was all sea once."

And the sea wants it back? All of it?

"If you look at a map of all the flood damage to Manhattan during Hurricane Sandy and then another map of Manhattan in 1650, I mean, it's incredible: The maps match up perfectly. The parts overrun by Sandy didn't used to be there. And we keep on building right on the water's edge, like with Battery Park, right? Most of your listeners probably don't know Ellis Island was originally 3.3 acres and now it's almost 28 acres. Built on what we excavated from the subway system. From the city's own guts."

But is there any hope, Frank, for Maureen? For the rest of us here?

"They've been building a wall off of Lower Manhattan—it's really a berm, like this high ridge. It'll be covered with grass, benches, bike paths—recreational stuff. But politics, right? Construction's been stopped cold. New mayor, new governor, and a new debate about the funding and where they build next—"

And out by Maureen?

"There's that breakwater project underway down at the southern tip there. Meant to break any hurricane-sized waves. It's a start. But chances are better than good that that land buffer there—chances are it's going to protect you, okay, Maureen? And you got more than a decent chance at getting out if it gets a whole lot worse. And you heard some good weather is right behind this system? They've forecast an actual high-pressure system—"

Yes, that's right, blue skies on their way.

"Look, it won't be easy, but I think we can beat it. I have to think that way. This is New York."

That's the spirit, Frank. How about some more high spirits from a woman who beat the odds, Sister Rosetta Tharpe? The godmother of rock and roll. Elvis, Aretha, Johnny Cash? They all lifted directly from her book. Here's "Didn't It Rain?" Maureen—we lost you, but I know you're still out there—listen, in no time we'll be looking back on this and saying, didn't it rain? Under clear skies, we'll marvel at it together, how it rained and rained.

The Doctor

The Doctor's hand bled where the camera's mount cut through his finger. He set the dead camera on his desk. He wrapped a tissue around the finger and saw the red spread through the Kleenex. It transfixed him—blood on his hands. He bandaged it. He locked the journal with what remained of the lozenges in the drawer and pocketed the key.

He picked up the receiver on his desk phone—there was no dial tone, but the generator's power allowed him to access the phone's caller ID. One call from an unknown number came up. After that, Adele had called three times, and his father once.

The type of dementia his father suffered from sometimes caused him to act out his nighttime dreams, talking and walking, arguing. Recently, the caregiver the Doctor had hired for his dad told him that the impressions and story lines from those dreams endured during the day now. There was little boundary between real and imagined. He'd neglected his father in the past several months. He should have gone to him more often, but this place, his duty…

When he returned to Ruth, she looked to be sound asleep on the exam table, until he settled into a chair beside her.

"I'm just *soooo* sleepy, I could stay here forever," she sighed happily at him, like he was a figure in her own dream. "I wish I had my books now. I love, love, love being read to, don't you?"

It had been so long since that was an option for him, but for her sake, he told her yes.

"What would you read to me?"

"All we have are medical books here—"

At his apartment, he had several bookcases, and in them works by Sacks, Chekhov, Lewis Thomas, and Arthur Conan

Doyle, writers who had also been doctors or scientists. It had been years since he searched out any books that were unrelated to his field, but when he had, most of them were books by doctors too: Bud Shaw, Abraham Verghese, Lisa Sanders, Atul Gawande, Frank Huyler, Perri Klass. George Eliot was the exception.

"The pins hurt my head." Ruth touched her hair. Squinting with her whole face.

There was a camera in that room, too, but he knew that as much as he wanted to, he could not tear every one of them down. He couldn't do anything about what they recorded.

He stood and bent over Ruth, breathed her in, shampoo and sweat and her peanut butter breath from the protein bar he'd given her. One by one, he slid the pins from Ruth's dark auburn hair, trying not to tug. She let him move her head a little this way, a little that, and when he was done he shook his fingers lightly through her hair to free it and make a mane around her head. "Is that better?"

"Yes," she sighed again. "Yes. So much." She smiled at him. "Thank you, thank you, thank you," and then in no time she was asleep again.

He sat down beside her once more and closed his eyes. Only for a moment. He took off his coat, but his wet clothes clung to him. His finger was bleeding still, and he told himself to get up and rebandage it, but he began falling asleep too, as if he were drugged. And he heard Sarah in his head, as he often did, even in his dreams. Sarah explaining again what that monster had talked her into. The Doctor would tell the police when they came, if they came. He was showing them the pages now in his dream, passages that showed that her P. deserved what he got. He was a con man and a thief. *Look, look—*

I listened to him, of course I did, but I didn't think we'd ever go through with what he was proposing. We talked and talked about it, and as long as we were talking about it, we weren't doing it. And we weren't apart. And he was like a kid describing

some crazy invention. As if no one had ever thought of it before, you know?

Yeah, all right, he said, Freud might be considered pseudo-psychiatry now, sure, not everything is about sex, okay, but didn't science show us that mind and body are one more often than not, and didn't we prove it, together, he and I? That sensation itself can make for revelation? And he borrowed freely from the things you and I had talked about, that I'd shared, because how could I not tell him? About neurotransmitters, naturally occurring—he latched on to that, you know, the naturally occurring part—and asked had I ever felt so good, so free? Him on his knees beside me, Tell me. No, I hadn't. Didn't I trust him? I did. I did.

And it was barely September, but it was still beautiful. The days were so mild and still light into evening. That mattered, and then I thought we were playing a game, and so as part of the game I came up with conditions. What he was proposing couldn't happen in my apartment. It couldn't be anyone who'd compromise either of us. It couldn't be recorded, not on video, or audio. Ever. It would stop when I said stop. It would have to be safe, I said, though the word safe seemed to vibrate between us, make us both queasy, because although it had to be said, agreed on, it was already a lie.

He interviewed young men. We started with men. He told them different stories about experiments with pain and pleasure and brain chemistry. He finally landed on this one young guy about whom I asked to know totally nothing. He explained he'd be in the room and that the young man would be a surrogate, would do as he was told.

I never spoke to the young man. I never saw his face. The blindfold was my choice. P. held my hand at first before he retreated to a chair by a curtained window. It was P.'s voice that filled the room, in and around us, but it was the young man I smelled as he touched me where and how P. instructed, in the places P. had, but they might as well have been different places under these different fingers, these fumbling, against different skin. With different pressures and smells, another mouth, another tongue. Another man's deodorant. Under it, his sweat smelled of celery. I couldn't let go, so P. left the chair and spoke very close to my ear. I could smell his dark chocolate smell as he told me this was for me, for us, the pleasure, an evolution.

Part III

Plasticity… in the wide sense of
the word, means the possession
of a structure weak enough to
yield to an influence, but strong
enough not to yield all at once.

—William James

"Healing,"
Papa would tell me,
"is not a science,
but the intuitive art
of wooing Nature."

—W.H. Auden,
"The Art of Healing"

Ruth

The light hurt Ruth's eyes. It came from everywhere—from the cloudless sky, but also reflected up from the standing water, pooled along the sides of streets, at curbs, over choked storm drains. The sun was like a liberating force, an army of millions, and Ruth could not help but feel the relief loosening the city from the ground up, from what was rooted in it and strewn over it now—all the plastic bags and bottles, leaves and branches, more fallen umbrellas, those sad single shoes—to the gleaming surfaces of buildings, stories high, drawn into complete blue sky. The weather had shifted at last, a certain tension was gone.

At daybreak, she'd snuck out of the clinic and, in the traffic reasserting itself already, found a cab to take her home for a shower and new clothes. Now she had to get to Mrs. Watson and tell her what had happened last night.

But what *had* happened? What precisely? Ruth had gotten lost, gotten stoned, she wouldn't deny it, but somehow she'd found compassion—not in passing, or momentarily, but compassion that had stayed and was with her now, as completely as this light everywhere, making her eyes ache. She recognized this Sarah of those pages. Understood her too well. She had so many questions about her, so much more to know, but until then she knew, no matter how high she'd been, that she *had* seen angels, one in stone, one in the flesh, or so it felt—that girl, joyful defiance itself. And the Doctor? He'd come to Ruth's rescue, when she'd been taught the hard way that no one did; at least no one should be expected to. But he did. Catching her when she'd been where she wasn't supposed to be, going through his things, a thief. She had to tell Mrs.

Watson, and she nearly called her own mother to describe how she felt—renewed, her shame lifted because she'd read into someone else's tangle, a young woman like her, and because the Doctor did not reproach her when he could have, *should* have. But it was Mrs. Watson she had to try to convey it all to. She'd spoken to Ruth of nuances, saying that nothing was as simple as anyone wanted or needed it to be. Surely she'd hear Ruth when she explained there could be reversals, new ways of seeing things, even in the course of just one night. These could be opportunities, these detours, for Mrs. Watson as well, to pause, even for a moment. And the day—had Mrs. Watson seen this lovely, achingly new day?

Marie again came to the door, but the face she showed Ruth wasn't calm. It was tight with alarm, which Ruth worried she was somehow the cause of, until she was inside both of the brownstone's doors and heard what it was Marie was hearing—pieces of it:

"*Mine*… not yours!" Mrs. Watson's voice towered from out of sight, from the direction of the paneled sitting room. "Leave if you don't like it—you, a grown man! How?… Trust you? Trust you to *respect*… If you don't, *go*… Do you hear? *Go!*"

"Mother!" Orson's voice surfacing. "You don't let me be who I'm… I'm like a captive here to your—"

The voices moved closer, into the hall that joined the sitting room to the foyer. Orson moving toward them, and Mrs. Watson in pursuit, berating: "And dragging Letty into it, to what purpose? Turning her into a circus act when we've all agreed to proceed with discretion there? *Poor Marie!* Can you imagine if anyone had gotten hurt? Whose problem would that have been? Not yours. Certainly not *yours*!"

"Mom?" A girl—in fact the singer from last night, just a little girl today—appeared on the staircase at the landing midway. "Mom? Can I go home now? The R train is running…"

"Not yet, Letty. Go back upstairs." She shooed the girl with a hand that trembled along with all the glass parts not yet settled in the chandelier overhead.

Orson bellowed, "You know you can't bear to live alone! Every time I leave, you find a way to bring me back—"

"*I* find a way? You find a way to come back and disrupt *everything*... And I'm *not* alone here. I have Marie."

The girl hadn't gone, was still on the landing, listening too. "Go, *now*!" Marie hissed, and the girl, catching her mother's panic, flew up the stairs.

A face-off midway down the hall:

"Marie does not belong to you!" Orson boomed.

"She is a better daughter to me than you've ever been a son! She does not insist on playing the fool!"

"You go too far. You always go too far, Mother."

"I go there because I'm pushed. Now, out of my sight!"

The voices were moving again, approaching: "Gladly! And if I go, I'm taking Marie and Letty with me."

Marie looked like she'd been hit, hard, out of nowhere. Ruth stepped forward to comfort her in some way, she wasn't sure how, but Marie, with her eyes wild, reared back and ran up the stairs just as mother and son entered the foyer.

Ruth, with the sunlight still warm on her skin, was suddenly woozy with an Alice in Wonderland sensation she'd had here before. Stepping into this house was stepping into another world. A separate place. It had nothing to do with the new day outside; the place had its own weather, its own rules.

She turned to go back outside, but she wasn't fast enough. Orson's face was in hers: "Get out while you still can—*get out*!" His white curls moving, as if in a confused tide, his face red, eyes round with anger and terrible hurt—hurt she knew, when a parent takes you down to your foundations.

Ruth wanted to reach for him as she had for Marie, but some of his spit was on her chin. She opened her mouth. Nothing came out.

He threw his hands up. Stalked off. Not upstairs, but down a hall to the left of the foyer, to rooms Ruth did not know.

"Ruth—" Mrs. Watson, arriving, didn't go on. She couldn't.

Ruth gripped the shoulder bag she'd brought to hold the pages. They were evidence that she'd done as she was asked. She'd put on her old nurse's scrubs—royal blue tunic and pants—one of several sets that, with little variation, she'd worn for years at the hospital, many of which were good, productive years as a nurse.

Ruth said, "I can come back after—" After what? Work? Did she have a job, in fact, officially?

Mrs. Watson didn't hear her. She appeared immobilized, not from frailty but from trying to contain energy Ruth could sense from feet away, of a coil that might spring and bite, walls that might collapse. Ruth knew this well. Had known it here before, in this place, and in her own life: The charge in the air right before a disaster.

"Where's Marie?" Mrs. Watson asked.

"Upstairs, I think. I saw her go—"

Mrs. Watson looked up the stairs and then to where her son had gone.

"I can get her—"

"No!" Mrs. Watson took a long, ragged breath. "No." She squinted at Ruth as if through the bright light outside. "Come with me."

All the curtains were drawn in the sitting room again, this time as fully as possible. It could have been night still, winter, yesterday. They took their positions across from each other. Mrs. Watson's body breathed in and out. She reached for her sunglasses.

"Did you bring me what I asked you for?" she asked Ruth flatly.

"Yes, or half of it. I was interrupted. I texted."

The sunglasses went on like a mask. More breathing. Deliberate. Noticeable. A headache coming, maybe. Ruth wouldn't be surprised.

"Were you there last night? With them at the church?"

"I hid when people came into the clinic, in a storage room in the back. I was looking for an emergency exit. When I came out later, I heard noises overhead. I just went up to see—"

"And you couldn't contact me?"

"No, the phone—because of the weather, I think, I had no signal. And I wasn't well. I'd had little to eat, and the tequila—I'm not used to it—I'm sorry—"

"The cameras in the clinic—the power went out, and even with the generator coming on, there was a lapse in recording. One camera in particular is still down. Do you know anything about that?"

"No. I'm sorry I—"

"Stop saying you're sorry, Ruth."

She nearly said it again, because she was. Again and again.

"If you were in the storage room, you must have noticed the leak? I understand there are inches of water in there."

"I did. I left in part to tell someone, but then I heard movement upstairs, so I went up—"

"A faulty drain outside, in the back courtyard. My contractor should have been aware of that. Accountability. *Respect…*" She spat the word, its "s" stinging the air, but stopped herself and said again, softer, "Respect: It's so very crucial."

"Yes."

"Did you bring me what you have?"

"Yes. But I thought we, or—I wanted to talk to you about that, if I could?"

Dark glasses, tight mouth, Mrs. Watson's skin as ghostly-seeming as her hair. "What is there to talk about?"

Ruth's mouth went dry. She moved her tongue with difficulty. She knew it was a mistake to reason with Mrs. Watson now, but she had to try. "I don't think taking this from the Doctor, reading it, well, maybe it's not all that relevant now?" She heard her words faltering. "What I mean is this is not necessary to the clinic's health or your *respect* for the

Doctor or his very *real* respect for you, and his commitment to the work you two share. And then, as far as my participation as a professional, a nurse, it doesn't seem appropriate—"

Mrs. Watson put her hands up toward Ruth as if shielding herself. "No, Ruth. No. This is a lie, isn't it? What you are saying. You know it is, and you want me to lie, too? Not today. No more today. If you want to deal in lies, you should go."

Ruth stood, though her legs were shaking. To be back in the day again, to be as free as it felt out there... Before she could take tentative steps, Mrs. Watson began, as if reciting a list she'd recited before, "I have told you I am protecting my investment. I should not have to tell you more. This is business. And what does that mean? That it shouldn't be personal? But it is, isn't it? I know it is. You know it is. Don't lie about that, and don't ask me to. It's *all* personal."

Mrs. Watson kept her head rigid, as if she couldn't permit it any movement while she said what she had to say. "You read the pages?"

"I tried not to, but yes, some, as I copied, and in the storage room, alone, I looked—"

"Louis thinks he's in love, of course now that she's out of reach, *gone*. Not when she was here, on hand—no, of course not. Then, he was 'appropriate.'"

"Gone? You mean she's missing?"

"Going on two years. But you must already know this."

Ruth had looked online on her phone, but only briefly; she'd hurried to get here.

"Then what harm is there?" Ruth asked. "Now?"

"You want to protect him from me? Is that it, Ruth? Or is it the girl in the journal? Some notion of privacy for her?"

"It's that it seems wrong—"

"*Wrong?* Really? *Wrong?* For whom? Are you deciding that for me? Or for you?"

Ruth couldn't see Mrs. Watson's eyes but knew they had to be as disparaging in their expression as her tone was.

When Ruth didn't answer, Mrs. Watson went on: "Do you think you know him? Or her?"

"No, I can't say that, not exactly. But, I mean, I can tell he's very decent—"

She'd woken with the Doctor asleep in a chair beside her. His face slack, mouth partly opened, yet there was the solid length of him, long legs melted out in front of him. He'd left her hairpins in a little pile just above her head, where she'd be less likely to knock them over and lose them. Her hair had been left soft and wild around her like she'd fallen asleep after a long swim, and he'd been there to see her safely back to land. She was fully dressed, her jacket still tightly belted—the pages held there against her stomach. What harm could there be in his fascination with Sarah? And who could blame him for it, given what Sarah had written to him? It could crack any man's reserve, but didn't he do his job? Didn't he show up in every way he knew how? Why wasn't that enough? We all have our ghosts, as Mrs. Watson had said. *We've earned them*, she said. He had, too, yet he appeared to carry them with dignity, and whatever his upsets or losses, his default, like it or not, seemed to be this decency of his. From their first meeting she'd witnessed it, wanted to believe in it. Twice they'd been alone together, in close quarters, and twice she'd felt safer with him than she had with a man in a long time. She'd left him to sleep there—in the chair. She didn't want to disturb him any further.

Mrs. Watson sighed loudly, for show as much as from need; her shoulders twitched. "Would it help you to know that I've already read the journal? Not thoroughly, I'll admit. Just enough to know what's in it. I had to make sure he wasn't involved in that girl's disappearance or in anything else. *With or without* your help, Ruth, I could have that notebook back in my hands at any time. I could have asked someone else or I could make the Doctor give it to me, but I wanted to avoid that. Humiliating him. I had a hunch about you, that you'd understand all of this without my having to explain. I took a risk…"

Mrs. Watson paused, and a motion sickness took Ruth's whole body.

"There have been some, what… ?"

Mrs. Watson made her hang there, deciding what came next.

"Developments, yes. I have had someone look into what happened on the night that young woman was last seen and since. I'd hoped to share this with you, but first I had to know what I could ask of you. If I was to let you in… Yes, I took a risk, a calculated one. I thought"—she lifted her hands, open-palmed, toward Ruth—"we would have a genuine rapport. We've been terribly disappointed by the people we've trusted, haven't we? But you and I have something else in common. What is that, do you think, Ruth?"

Ruth hugged the bag that held the pages to her hip, but sweat ran down her arm to her hand and the fingers holding on to it. She was losing solidity. The wooden room and Mrs. Watson, they were taking it from her. She sat back in the chair.

"Don't you know? It's resiliency. Strength. I saw it in our first meeting. I thought we could collaborate together on something that could change people's lives, yours included. Of course you want to put some distance between you and your past, but how can you achieve that without keeping the lessons you've learned from that past in the fore so you don't repeat them? You aren't a fool, are you, Ruth?"

"No," she said.

"I didn't think so. You want to survive. That's why you came here—not just to New York, but to *me*. You want *more* this time, and who is offering you that? With that New Hampshire rabble at your back—accessible to any employer by a Google search? Who will take you in? Give you *this* much opportunity? *Access?* Do you think there are perfect choices out there? You know there aren't. I depended on that about you."

The room seemed to shiver then, the black walnut's grain and the twisting sculptures move, quickened by the conversation. A residual effect from the cannabis or a trick of the eye, from the glass fixture in this room, its wriggling and uneven light.

"My passion is very strong, so my pragmatism must be too. Did you hear what my son said? That I go too far? He's not wrong. But then, so does he. Even with him, I can't afford mistakes of judgment. Not now. I can't put my stock in anyone or anything without taking steps, whatever steps I need, even if they appear… extreme. You can understand, can't you? You decided in favor of sentimentality and idealism once. How did that go?"

The pile of hairpins the Doctor had left for her, his keeping her company through the night, the sounds he made as he slept, his exhaling not just breath but long murmuring sounds from deep in his chest and stomach, as if he were communicating with gentler people, in a gentler place.

"You told me your sister doesn't speak to you. Does she have kids?" Mrs. Watson persisted.

"Yes. A boy and a girl."

"What are their ages?

"Maeve is twelve. Conor is eight."

"Have you seen them?"

"Not in some time."

"Don't you want to show your sister this special resilience you have? Don't you want to see those kids?"

"Of course I do."

"I can help with that. All I ask—have to ask—is for you to be a good employee to me, work according to *my* rules. If you can't, go. Go now. I'm leaving the door wide open today to anyone who wants to go."

Ruth did not move. She couldn't say if she wanted to, only that she couldn't.

"I have questions," Ruth managed to say after a time of waiting, both of them waiting, "just a few, please, that I need to ask before—"

"Before?"

Ruth took the pages out of the bag. They curled up at each end—pressed against her body all night, under her coat, they'd molded to the shape of her.

The Doctor

It was like getting your sight back only to have it obscured by something else, a clarity that was too much for the eyes. All that sun spreading out. Unbroken by clouds. And the wind was barely perceptible. It did not roar in the ears as it had only hours ago, constantly inconstant, fragmenting your hearing. But on the streets on his way back to the clinic, he heard distinct sounds: laughter, car horns, birdsong. Carrying and complete.

And he could smell wet asphalt drying in the sun, moist earth, the minerals in it, but there was something else there, too: the smell of shit. Sulfur. He'd smelled this very combination of things in Venice once, on his honeymoon with Jackie, a city sinking and rotting.

As he entered the clinic reception area, he heard Sue and Dr. Chaudhri, his resident, disputing happily with one another.

There were no patients waiting. Unusual. Sue was at her desk, and Chaudhri was behind her, writing something on the three whiteboards high on an adjacent wall.

"That baby inside you should be listening to Mozart," Chaudhri teased Sue. "Not tales of the latest celebrity breakup."

"We both need the comic relief. You oughta try some—"

Seeing the Doctor, Sue rushed out from behind the reception area to greet him: "I was worried when I couldn't get you on your phone! Did you get my messages? Any of them?"

"Yes, some," he said, her hard, high pregnant belly hitting into him hard as she embraced him briefly, only to push him back as she reported, "There's been a leak—some minor flooding in the back of the clinic, the utility rooms, a couple of the treatment rooms. Some men are on their way to pull up the carpets, but today—the weather! It's a whole new world!" She giggled at her excitement. "And this one's writing a list—*up there.*"

The Doctor craned in through the reception window to see that Chaudhri was writing an overview of migraine triggers and causes, processes and treatments, in tight, exemplary print on the whiteboards behind Sue's desk.

"It is merely some of what we're working on here," Chaudhri said, "to focus us and for this new nurse? Some basics. There *is* a new nurse, right?"

He couldn't answer that. Ruth was gone when he woke. He didn't know where. He worried only briefly before reminding himself that what was done was done. He could do nothing if, once the cannabis wore off, she declined to work with him or, worse, intended to share with Mrs. Watson why that was so.

"Patients may see it," Sue said, using her hand to trace a line of sight to the waiting room. "I wasn't sure you'd approve."

"They are collaborating with us, right?" Chaudhri offered. "They're our partners in all this."

"Collaborating?" the Doctor repeated. The word was Mrs. Watson's. He'd heard it from her too often.

The Doctor knew that Chaudhri met with Mrs. Watson from time to time, but chief among the reasons he'd chosen Chaudhri as a resident, beyond his searching intelligence, was that he wasn't easily persuaded from his priorities: measurable progress among the clinic's patients and the research that supported that progress. If the Doctor got into any trouble, as he had to presume he would, and if he was fired, Chaudhri would be left in charge. Now he waited on the Doctor's reply, as patient as he was stubborn, as deferential as he wasn't at times. His handsome, boyish face was hidden by thick, ill-fitting glasses, and a reediness through his neck and limbs and a few dark acne scars just under pronounced cheekbones reminded you he was still young, just recently out of his twenties.

The phone rang—on one line and then another.

"I canceled our morning hours. A lot of subway lines aren't running yet—the flooding. I'm getting a zillion calls to reschedule anyway," Sue said before putting her headset back on, answering, and asking the caller to hold, but the caller refused—it was Ed, which the Doctor knew even before Sue told him, because Sue was giggling again and saying, "No, actually, I floated here. The upside to being as big as a parade float—"

He pointed toward his office and went there directly and unlocked the door.

"He's home," Ed reported to the Doctor's "Hello." "Sam. He's okay."

"Good news."

"God, yes. He was in Grand Central."

"Was he going somewhere?"

"Maybe, or maybe just waiting out the rain. He loves that place. Trains, you know? That starry ceiling. He got some pills from another vet. That's what set him off."

"Wasn't Adam, was it?"

"Sam won't say who gave him the stuff, only that it was a few nights ago. Once he got started again, you know how it goes… It was Adam who found him, brought him home."

"You going over?"

"Later. Yes. Want to give him some time. What about that nurse, is she all right? I meant to come down—"

"She needed to rest, get some liquids."

He didn't tell Ed how high Ruth had been on one of his lozenges or that they'd passed the night side by side in a treatment room. He didn't mention his visit to Lower Manhattan either, or the camera that still lay disconnected on his desk, how it had offended him, how Adele had. He would later. Or maybe. He also didn't tell him whom he'd be calling that morning, as soon as possible—the compounding pharmacist, Curtis. He had approaches to try. Several. When he woke that morning alone in the treatment room, he knew he couldn't delay anymore. He was on borrowed time.

But first he dialed his father's number, and when, after six rings, his father said hello as if testing the word out for the first time, the Doctor said, "Dad? It's me. It's me."

"Kenneth?"

"No, it's your son, Louis—"

"Dammit, when are you coming back, Ken? We have work to do. It's getting on June and everything's a mess out there—"

"Yes, yes, Dad—"

"—with the weather, we're behind—and there's Vivian with the baby, two mouths to feed. Vivian's back again, and dammit, I need you here—"

"I'll be there. Soon, I promise. I'm coming."

Ruth

Ruth put the pages on the coffee table between them, but close enough to her that she might grab them back. Part of her felt shoved off her feet and loathed the figure of the still woman across from her; another part of her told her she should be grateful. She'd forgotten how marooned she was. Mrs. Watson had reminded her.

"You *are* owed respect. Of course. And I value your directness," Ruth said. Placating Mrs. Watson was conceding to her own circumstances: She was broke. She had no support in this city, though it didn't change what had happened the night before. Her optimism had felt as real and unrestricted as the sunlight she hoped still flared outside these walls. Ruth asked, "I know it's been a trying morning. Shall I find Marie?"

"No. Not yet. Not quite yet."

In this Mrs. Watson was revealing her own strategy. Another battle may have been going on in the house right now—Orson said that if he left, he would take Marie and her daughter with him. Perhaps that was being decided now.

"I depend on Marie—" Mrs. Watson paused. Ruth knew what was coming: "She and her daughter have become family to me, *are* family." A slight cracking in her voice, an uneasy breath let go. "She must know—"

"I'm sure she does… "

"I'm curious, Ruth, where does that number of pages take us? Halfway? More?" Mrs. Watson inclined her head to the pages on the table. "What is the last thing you read?"

"She—Sarah and her lover—they're going to experiment, I think, do things that—"

"It's unbelievable, isn't it? To saddle the Doctor with this sordid story of hers, this part of her that he couldn't touch, couldn't fix? She must have known how it would affect him. She turned him into a voyeur, didn't she? It's cruel. He's not like"—*you*, Ruth almost said, feeling a stab of vengefulness—"most men. And all the crueler, given the… *new* developments, if they can be believed, if anything can."

"And what are they? If I may ask?"

"Not now, no, you may not."

How readily Mrs. Watson opened and shut doors, real and imagined. There were those recordings on Larry's phone—Ruth nearly forgot about them, too. She considered what telling Mrs. Watson about them might earn her, but those seemed as unreal to Ruth now as any bid for fairness or temperance. Instead Ruth put in, "She seemed convinced that her… *activities* with this man were helping her, well, chemistry, and she wanted the Doctor to know—"

"She's pretty, in the photos I've seen," Mrs. Watson veered, "though not in an obvious way maybe… What did she think she could teach the Doctor? That pleasure was the answer to what ailed her? Ails all of us? And what did she get? Something else entirely. She turned herself into that flunky professor's plaything."

A snort from Mrs. Watson. Sarah wasn't just a gnawing distraction to the Doctor, she was Mrs. Watson's rival. Mrs. Watson was a woman in love, and as desperately as Sarah or Ruth herself had been, and yet she defended herself from the helplessness of it with every resource she had, fitting a complicated apparatus around it, with her own flunkies.

"He didn't give the notebook to the police, which is what he should have done sooner rather than later. That wasn't like him. I knew then there was something there I needed to know. So I began to look into it. First it was to see if he'd been acting unprofessionally. Then I saw that if her whereabouts could be confirmed—her whereabouts dead *or* alive—it would relieve him… to *know* something, *anything*. And not just him, of course—her family, friends…"

And you, too, Ruth thought. *You too.*

"It's troubling. All this. But then, do you know how many people are missing in this country? Nearly 100,000 at any given moment, and that's just the reported cases. The man I've hired to find her told me that, and that many more than you'd think *want* to be missing. Some don't. Of course. People get hurt, get lost, so very many that it's like socks or I don't know what... But this girl? Efforts were made by everyone who knew and cared for her. This affair with the man: Pietro is his full name, what she probably called him—that's his legal name—or maybe she called him Peter. I've seen that in print, too—Peter. Anyway, *he* brought the other sex partners in. All very elaborate, like he was writing his own pornographic novel. *His* novel, *not* hers, no matter what he told her. And drugs were shared. That's all online, or most of it. The doctor was looked into—what he prescribed. Nothing to harm her. Nothing at all. Her family was good at keeping the press in the loop, with any leads, and then the story was so lurid anyway: the girl, the professor, and the prostitutes. One escort in particular, a man, was happy to detail what a fine time they all had... He is titillated, the Doctor. That's it, isn't it? He's not immune. How can he be?"

"I can't say—"

Now came voices yelling again. Orson. Then a woman's voice. Marie's—not so much yelling as imploring. Then Orson's again, louder. Ruth heard words from him that she thought added up to "I will take care of you! I will!... Have some faith, please!"

Mrs. Watson said nothing. She did not move. She waited until the voices fully retreated from their hearing before she continued: "That professor took full advantage. Of course he did. And who is he? No one. A part-time academic who's married to some Latvian gangster's daughter. I've been to the wife's gallery. Nothing new there, but she makes money. She's savvy enough, but what she truly is is dangerous. Latvians are worse than Russians, because they have more to prove. The women are no different—why should they be?

"And now, in the latest twist, Ruth, this Pietro or Peter has just added to the reward for information about her. There's been some news about that. Look it up. He's long been a person of interest, but he couldn't have killed her, at least not intentionally. He couldn't even handle the power Sarah gave him. He was in charge while pretending it was something else—some sort of revolution of feeling? What did you say? A change in 'chemistry'? Like it or not, we merely replace one pain for another. Too often we do—"

Marie wandered in then. Her glasses were steamed and smudged, her face pale, hollow. She stood at the end of the sofa and waited for Mrs. Watson to see her there. Mrs. Watson took off her sunglasses and looked, searching Marie's face.

"Tea?" Marie offered, her voice as done in as the rest of her. "Or something else?"

Mrs. Watson leaned over and took Marie's hand, held it a moment, patted it. Then she let go, righted herself and her posture. She was relieved, back in business anyway.

"No, not for me—" Ruth didn't want to ask anything of Marie now. "I'm fine, thank you."

"It's no trouble, is it, Marie?" Mrs. Watson cooed.

Marie shook her head and promptly left them.

Ruth did not know what had transpired, only that it was significant. Something had been lost, something gained. Somewhere in the house, not far away, a door slammed.

Mrs. Watson relaxed her back into the sofa. She didn't put her sunglasses back on.

"We listened to music together, you and I—Pergolesi. Bach," Mrs. Watson said dreamily.

"Yes."

"You enjoyed that?"

"Yes."

"Are you ready to work, Ruth?"

A wretched excitement flushed Ruth's face. "Yes," she said. "I am."

"I've spoken to Dr. Chaudhri. He will get you in the loop about all the mechanics of the clinic. He has a fine organizational mind. And you'll come to me, here, keep me in the know, with any *developments*?"

"Yes."

"Developments" hung in the air between them. It was meant to, to instruct Ruth on the lines between being in and out—adrift.

"I suppose I can tell you now, Ruth, though you must promise to tell no one, especially not the Doctor. That is very important, because nothing has been confirmed. Do I have your word?"

"Of course."

It was then that Mrs. Watson lunged and snatched the pages from the coffee table, set them beside her on the couch so that the page edges touched her hip, and gave herself back to the sofa's back.

"My investigator has tracked someone. It could be the girl. She's been seen. Or maybe. Very *definitely* maybe. Imagine that. *She* left. Wanted *out*. Out of all of it."

The Doctor

His phone call to the compounding pharmacist was made, things finally set in motion: ingredients discussed, to be procured, a timeline agreed to, a payment method provided.

The Doctor then returned to reception and Chaudhri's list. However compressed, it was detailed enough to carry from one whiteboard to another. It would lead their more alert patients to questions, which was probably Chaudhri's intention, and to conversations about some of the trials and new treatments listed in brief here: nerve stimulation, CGRP antagonists, ditans that, like triptans, work with serotonin but unlike them do not constrict blood vessels, new and established antidepressants, new imaging techniques, and of course alternative and nutrition-based therapies. Chaudhri had wandered off, likely to his office. Sue was on the phone, facing away from him, reshuffling appointments.

At the end of the list, Chaudhri had written, in slightly small print, the letters almost shrinking, "Oxytocin? Intranasal."

By this Chaudhri meant synthetic oxytocin, the function of which was to replicate the brain's own oxytocin and how that hormone and neurotransmitter soothed pain, stress, but it also encouraged feelings of attachment, intimacy. That was why the military experimented with it: It facilitated confessions. There must be some new channel of money associated with this, or the prospect of it, coming to them. The Doctor had read the studies about its potential in treating chronic pain, but, as he told Chaudhri some months ago now, too little work had been done, too few animal and human studies for headache, and Chaudhri had agreed. This was Chaudhri's way of raising the matter again.

The Doctor erased it from the list.

He couldn't write in the experiment he had begun that day. Not yet.

He had to show his patients first, before he explained it, that they had in their brain's electrochemical landscape resources that we were only beginning to know how to exploit, thanks to visionaries like Ted Kaptchuk, without synthetics, or many fewer. In the days to come, the Doctor hoped to help his patients see this by building on the trust they had in him. It had taken time, hopefully enough time to persuade them, now that it seemed time was running short for him; and if he wanted to deny this, that morning already had other ideas: He felt her there before he saw her—Ruth, floating her face through the reception window.

She'd not said a word yet, but still he startled at her there, back again—an envoy, maybe the very face of the beginning of an end for him at the clinic. Something had to give.

He motioned for her to come around toward the lounge so as not to disturb Sue.

He met her just outside the door from reception to the lounge. She was nervous. She smelled of shampoo. Except for some pieces in the front, her hair hung free, and under her coat she wore regular scrubs.

"I'm sorry—" she began and stopped herself. Then: "I'm late. I had to see Mrs. Watson."

He nodded and waited for the next blow—the upset or blame—but she only blushed and began, "I want to thank you, for last night. For being so kind…"

"Of course," he said, wondering when the show of leverage she and especially Adele had over him now would insert itself into their exchange.

"It's beautiful out. I did not know it could be beautiful here."

"A change in the weather."

"I hope so," she said, and "a brand new day," with pleading in her voice. She looked younger, as if she had unwrapped one skin, to put on another softer, looser one. Then she looked at him with an earnestness he recognized too well. "I hope you can forgive me, Doctor, for—" She looked back to Sue, still on the phone, then back to him.

"For what?"

"Last night. I shouldn't have—"

"There is nothing to forgive," he said but did not believe it.

Stepping closer to him so that Sue would not have to hear, she said, "I want to work, Doctor. I need to. Work."

Roses in her shampoo, blooming at him. Perspiration on her upper lip, at her temples. She'd admitted to him only yesterday in their interview that she'd had some rough years: a marriage that had ended badly and a patient's accusation that had pushed her out of her last job. That he'd anticipated Ruth would tell Adele about the cannabis, he saw now, was foolish. She was afraid he would banish her, not the other way around, or that Adele would, as Ruth had been before, from her life in New England. Or was she conning him? If so, she was good, her face so open to his, nothing to hide there, pleading: *a brand new day*.

He turned and walked to his office and she followed. The two of them alone again, the door shut, he told her there'd be a learning curve but that he imagined she could learn quickly. The air in and around her was alive now with a receptivity he could not have guessed at just yesterday.

"What I need now is to reassess a number of my cases, especially the harder ones. It's all in the files. I need to be reminded of what worked for them, what didn't, and what I may have missed, not just with the therapies and medications tried but in their lives. They tell me things, things that seem unrelated to migraine or their headache or pain disorder, but it's the whole pattern that matters, the whole economy of someone's life. Their habits—"

"Yes, yes, I remember you said that yesterday."

"Yes, I say it often, too much, about the whole life, but it's Oliver Sacks—"

"No, it was about habits. Pain as a habit."

"Ah, yes, the nervous system can rewire itself to become more and more sensitive to certain stimuli. And there's the emotional response, too, that becomes habitual. And very limiting. A habit of feeling and seeing things. I had a patient, a woman named Sarah… "

Ruth's eyes widened at the mention of Sarah's name, and a fist formed in his chest and pushed hard against his sternum: There could be no doubt now that she'd read the journal.

He paused only long enough to collect himself—keep calm—and went on, "She felt very deprived. Many of my patients do. Deprived of so many things—foods, their favorite activities, certain environments, a sense of freedom." The fist that his heart had become pounded inside him. "Because the pain can be triggered by these things. They fear it, expect it. Their life becomes, to their way of seeing, too narrow, without pleasure, or not without a cost to them. We tend to see things not as they are, but as we are. You've probably heard that before?"

Ruth nodded.

"This can provide for some susceptibility and some extremes—of perception, of behavior. I'd like to prevent that, if I can." His voice faltered with the blood pounding in his head. "There's a lot to keep track of, to try to understand. And I need fresh eyes and ears. I do, Ruth. To look harder for what I may have missed, before… "

He was about to say "before it's too late," but she was hanging on every word, as if it was her he was trying to save from further pain, there with her face washed clean as the air outside, faint freckles on the bridge of her nose, an unblemished rounded forehead, her lips and cheeks flush and full. She did look so very young today. Maybe the cannabis had helped, the stretch of euphoria given, detachment.

The last time he'd seen Sarah up close, in their last appointment, she'd tried to explain that the man who'd come into her life had changed *everything* for her, but that matters were getting confusing and the headaches were back and getting worse. She'd started to cry because she didn't understand what *she* had done. Not what *he* had done, had talked her into, but what she had done wrong, how she'd miscalculated. And the Doctor had put his hand to Sarah's face, as young as Ruth's now, as soft, and she folded into him, so that he had to put his arms around her to lift her up, and then he felt the dimensions of her—how slight and yet how strong as her rib cage pulsed inside her and her arms reached up and pulled him to her.

It was the Doctor who took Sarah's arms from around him, who sat her back down as if she were a child, who talked to her about how our own biology can derange and mislead us. Our own pleasure. He'd been embarrassed—when there'd been no time for that, not even then. He'd told her to be careful, but it was too late. She'd written that, hadn't she? Had Ruth read that far?

"Before," he finally said to Ruth, reddening again, "before they give up on me."

Sarah

You of all people, Doctor, must understand and try not to be too afraid for me. Somewhere in you, you must have known how much I needed this. You blushed, on your neck, up your jaw, when you explained how orgasm silences the parts of our brains that govern self-control and "vigilance." Women's brains more so than men's. The brain must have to do this, shut down in important ways, to allow us to be <u>that</u> vulnerable, right? I have to try to explain again, do it better than I could in your office, the lengths he went to for me. The patience, the gentleness. I told you he'd read me poetry, and you and I laughed because of course it sounded so totally ridiculous, me as susceptible as a girl. You told me to be careful, but it was too late.

I wanted to be mother-of-pearl, a grain of wheat, honeysuckle, water, wine, all the things he'd read to me from those beautiful poems. I wanted to be that simple. This is biology? Brain chemistry? It is. Of course. And then it's so much more.

It's the night he stayed over and I actually slept, with relief, and woke to his head between my legs, his lips on mine, unafraid of how ravenous I was there, not like any honeysuckle at all. And it's that I was stronger. I was altered, and so was he. If he had been free—I don't mean his marriage—if he had been able to love me fully, with courage enough to be vulnerable, as I was to him, take me as I took him into me, I believe he and I would have known something that could have freed us, at least for a while longer.

I couldn't climax, not just with the first man, twice, not with the second... but the third? He was not some student, but a professional, with this hairless soft skin, who didn't just do as he was told by P. but did what my body told him, too. He felt me responding, felt that wave in me—begun where? In my brain? Then through the nerves to the flesh, where this man felt it under his fingers and rode it, and then we did together and he whispered to me, about fucking me and me fucking him, it's so good, he said, you are, and I wasn't vigilant.

When the man had left P. and me alone, and I took my blindfold off, P. had tears in his eyes. He said he was glad for me, that he could give me this gift, no more Bobbys of the Fields, that was over now, but his were definitely not glad tears. I wasn't a virgin anymore, he said. I hadn't been in ages, he knew that, and I told him that of course, but he said no, "in a way you were, but now you're all your own." But I heard "on your own," and I was right in my mishearing. Things turned then in a way that meant there was no going back. I had done just as he asked and had lost him all the more by doing so.

I couldn't bring myself to tell you all this in your office. The frustration—the effort I'd have to undertake to be understood and not seem like such a fool, you see? You touched me then. The cool of your hand against my face. Me in your arms for however long you could stomach it.

Real intelligence, they say, is the ability to hold two opposing ideas in one's head at once, see merit on both sides, right? But what about two opposing feelings, each so crazily, overpoweringly strong and sick-making and weak-making, that can rip you into bits as they fight it out? That can't find peace with each other or in me? Desire and revulsion. Love and hate. Freedom (or its impression, like some reservoir that will never dry up) and shame, also endless.

Of course, I can't tell my parents about this, or my friends, but you? You say it's the whole person and his or her whole life that matters. You will try to understand now, won't you? And forgive me?

Every time I asked you if you could be your ex-wife's friend after the divorce you said yes, but I saw the change in your face, as if you'd caught the scent of something spoiled. You see, I don't think romantic love ends—I think it becomes something else if we let it. Its opposite: hatred. It can become that so easily. But to hate him? That would be too easy. No, it's me I hate. I take the blame. Because I should have known. I shouldn't have gone so far. I kept telling myself this is the last time I'll see him, and this is the last time I'll perform for him (because that's what it was, for him), this is really the last. But it never was. Each time. It isn't. I can't stop.

The Wind Report

Blue skies smiling at you. Nothing but, my friends. That was Dinah Washington, from 1954, making each phrase a song of its own. And her band? When they hit their stride? A controlled kind of combustion.

Our thanks to everyone who's called in to let us know what's happening near them. We've been told there's still a scattering of power outages below Fourteenth Street in Manhattan, some in Brooklyn and Queens, but Con Ed's generators and the pumps are working double time. Along with the sun back like a prodigal.

Yes, the waters are receding, but there remain cautions for all of us. To help us sort through these, I've got Janice Mangliano here from the Department of Health.

Welcome, Ms. Mangliano.

"It's Josephine Mangliano. Call me Jo."

Sorry, yes. You're here to remind us about some public health issues?

"We're asking all the city's residents to avoid contact with the standing storm water. If you have to guess whether you can drive through it, don't. If your car gets stuck, you're stuck."

Our listeners have been calling in about what the waters are leaving behind. There's been some unusual stuff reported to us: Someone found a sterling silver martini shaker, engraved to "My favorite drunk." A crossbow… A crossbow? Really?! Newspapers and magazines, sure—but these are from the 1940s, as if up from the silt. Isn't that something, Ms.—

"*Jo.* Please, let me stress this: Do not touch anything with your bare hands. Ask yourself what kind of water did those objects come into contact with? Flood water. That means *E. coli*, staph—"

We have a caller from Red Hook Films—Ian, is it? What's going on, Ian?

"Wanted to spread the word that we're showing some terrific outdoor films over the weekend, *Cinema Paradiso* on Friday—"

I love that film. Have you seen it, Ms.—Jo?

"No."

"And *The Birds* on Saturday."

Hitchcock? Scary and sumptuous. Set in California's Bodega Bay, whew! You've seen it, J—?

"A long time ago."

Okay, Ian, thank you. If you give Lakshmi the information, we'll link to your site… And we're getting messages about a host of other outdoor events—free yoga in Tompkins Square Park; Breakfast at Tiffany's *is showing Sunday after sundown at Brooklyn Bridge Park.*

Seems the gates are open, my friends, and the fields—the fields await. The ferries are up and running, and I understand both Liberty and Ellis Island are open for business? Service there only shut down at the height of the downpours. That's incredible, with all that rain, isn't it? Seems we passed a test, no, Jo? Most of the subway lines are up and running now, in a matter of hours. The airports. Even the Long Island Rail Road—

"We had the Army Corps of Engineers here, on the ground, because of the wind events we've been dealing with. The MTA, Con Ed, the Coast Guard—they were ready, too. We didn't get much storm surge here—that was the problem with Sandy. Yesterday's tropical storm was no hurricane, but it gave us eight, nearly nine inches of rain. We got that in less than twenty-four hours. This is just the beginning. This storm season is forecast to be one of the most active on record. It's a miracle there wasn't more damage from this event, considering—"

Thank heavens for that. Some good news there, my friends. And now we have another caller… Who? Dante? Thank you for your call, Dante. First-time caller?

"Yes, I've been following the crazy weather with you, man, and now it's the people! I mean, *they* are crazy: I'm on my way to class at John Jay on the A train, okay? And people are taking off their clothes and running. This one dude, this tall, skinny white dude, he ran through the cars, hand over his thing, and then at West Fourth he was up and out. I *had* to get a shot, so I followed him, but he wasn't alone out there—nope, he's meeting up with a bunch of nudies. They ran straight up Sixth Avenue. *Toooo* much, man. Mad crazy!"

There's some street noise there, Dante. Are you saying they're streaking? Up Sixth Avenue?

"If that's what you call this bunch of naked people running up the street here. Look out! Shit! Everybody's grilling!"

Grilling?

"*Looking*, man, they are looking! Cars are rolling up on curbs. Got to be like two fender benders just now."

How many people are, uh, participating, would you say?

"Five, six—nope, now there's more. Whoa! One girl just stripped right down and joined them. Left her clothes on the sidewalk, like that. Holy shit! Deadass, she's beautiful. Look at that. You beautiful, baby! I see you! I see you! Hey, beautiful, hey, *hold on*—"

Dante, you still there?... Dante? Did we lose Dante?

Ruth

The city's transformation dazzled Ruth. Flags and awnings unfurled; food carts appeared on nearly every street corner, spicing the air; and countless people turned out of the countless buildings, populating benches and stoops, picnicking, sunbathing, their legs and arms bare, midriffs exposed.

Many of the clinic's patients came in smelling of sunscreen or fresh air, and while there was little natural light in a clinic bunkered in the ground, it came in anyway, with the news of free events in the parks, of young and old in a fever, carousing to all hours, playing music, and taking to streaking, if reports could be believed, after so many months of confinement.

But in the days Ruth gave herself over to the rhythms of the clinic, she resisted every temptation of a landscape turned inside out. Dr. Chaudhri, having begun his supervision of Ruth, had warned her that the patients they saw had been engaged in a battle with their own bodies for a long time, some for years and years. In many cases, if they'd made their way to the clinic in a repurposed church in Brooklyn, from other boroughs, even other states, it was because other doctors and treatments had failed to help them and they were leery, sometimes cynical. There could be no disagreeing with what they felt or how poorly they believed they'd been served, and he told her what everyone in the clinic accepted as if part of a pledge they took: "Pain is what the patient says it is, *period*."

She took careful notes in her meetings with Dr. Chaudhri and when she was with patients or reading their files. For the sake of recall, she did so with pen on paper, in a notebook, which she kept with her as she moved through the offices and treatment rooms of the clinic.

Sue called her "our student nurse," giggling despite Ruth's blank face, though Ruth had to admit she half-liked the idea—as if she could be new, or at least renewed, to the profession in important ways.

Those she treated at the clinic came from backgrounds so different from hers that she often felt provincial. And while her years of experience made taking vitals or blood routine, she wanted to meet each patient as an equal: not as Nurse Marks, her married name, or Nurse Aitken, her maiden name and her legal name since her divorce. It was Ruth, just Ruth—*I'm Ruth*—who as a woman and as a nurse well understood how it could hurt: life, the body, the city, the weather in all its variation, all of it, who would listen as completely as she could in order to help however she could. Yes, there were parameters. And several nights a week, after she was done at the clinic, before going home, she had to check in with Mrs. Watson, the architect of these parameters.

Some nights Mrs. Watson was too busy to talk long, had guests or engagements to go to, and Ruth was free to leave or climb the stairs to the library, just as Marie had suggested. Some nights Mrs. Watson only wanted to charm Ruth, and she did. Other nights she wanted what she wanted, above all from Ruth: the rest of the pages owed her, more information, more loyalty, more of *everything*. And she did not let Ruth forget how fragile her position was at the clinic, as fragile as the city had felt in the wind when Ruth first arrived. Now the city felt knitted together with energy, fortified by life like she'd never quite known. It gave Ruth courage to believe she could manage it all somehow, whatever was asked of her, and make a place there after all.

Dr. Chaudhri, in those first weeks, tended to look at Ruth fixedly, without expression. Even after she answered one of his questions about her professional experience or about a patient as comprehensively as she could, he left silences and tempted her to fill them. She fought hard not to be unnerved by his methods or tell him any more about her than she had to. If he'd bothered to look into Ruth's past, knew more about her than her professional background, he didn't say so. He was good-looking, but he didn't seem to care for his beauty or about being charming at all.

When she sat in on his neurological exams, every one of the patients asked after the Doctor and whether he or she would be seeing him that day. The response invariably was yes, time permitting—that was always the Doctor's preference. And if she thought the Doctor's popularity might make Dr. Chaudhri feel jealous or diminished, she was wrong. He told her, as matter-of-factly as he said so many things, "I did not know men like the Doctor existed. I thought I could learn from him and move on. But I have seen it's more than that: a kind of grace. Our patients are comforted even if they are not cured. Because there is no cure. For now. Only treatment. For him, it's effortless.

"Nearly forty million Americans suffer from migraine. Some forty-five million complain of headache, just headache. And somehow the medical community for decades has not believed this type of affliction a puzzle worth solving. How does one measure this? Money. There has been too little devoted to it until now. Now there is a race to invest and learn, and, thanks to the Doctor, we are part of it."

Chaudhri had found a hero. It seemed all the staff had, and readily anchored themselves to him. When Sally, the nutritionist, spoke of the Doctor, she said he gave her a "sense of mission." On a page in her notebook dedicated to Sally, Ruth wrote down the names of the herbs that had proven therapeutic for many of the clinic's patients, that sounded like the stuff of spells—butterbur, feverfew, meadowsweet, skullcap, poppy, kava, pine bark—and recorded the word *mission* and circled it. For a moment Ruth heard and saw "missing" in the word—Sarah missing; so much of Ruth's life and plans missing—but *mission* was the opposite of any absence, and so was Sally, who was slim and tanned in the way of outdoors-loving people, a straight-haired brunette in her forties.

And Jill credited the Doctor with allowing her to "*journey* with so many people. *So* very many." Ruth tried not to blush in Jill's company. She had to drive off the visions of what she had seen Larry and the tall blond massage therapist do in a clinic treatment room and try not to imagine what Larry's recordings of Mrs. Watson had captured precisely.

If Larry noticed Ruth at all, in those first weeks at the clinic, it was only because she was near Jill, and when he saw Ruth at Mrs. Watson's, he gave her a smile that went as quickly as it came.

No one brought up Mrs. Watson around Ruth—no one dared to, save in bland terms, remarking that they all endeavored to make the clinic an "asset" to her—*asset* a word they all used, as if they'd agreed on it in advance.

For this reason, no one but the Doctor showed any open irritation with the cast of pharmaceutical reps and their researchers or with filling out their questionnaires or delivering whatever data or blood samples the clinic had agreed to provide for them. Ruth had trouble keeping track of the names and faces and the studies or drugs to which they were attached, but Chaudhri laid out, in financial terms, a hierarchy of who was contributing what, for what treatment or proposed treatment, none of which, he assured her, was frivolous.

But while seeing patients, it was a relief for Ruth to let go everything outside of her immediate function as a nurse. A single mother named Lydia was so exhausted that she seemed to speak to Ruth from deep in a well, or from far away. She set her big violet eyes on Ruth now but appeared not to take her in.

"I've been having too many... My son has them too. I can barely—" she began, in reply to Ruth's questions about her migraines, but stopped there. Her shoulder trembled, as if she might cry. "I'm sorry. I didn't sleep well last night."

Ruth had read her chart, but it didn't tell her what a rare loveliness and poise this woman had and that it was being depleted even as she sat there on the exam table.

"The Doctor," she pronounced with some bitterness, "he's prescribed massage and *joy*, as if…"

Ruth moved closer to Lydia and asked if she might gauge just how severe her muscle tension was. Lydia didn't refuse, and Ruth began to massage her shoulders and neck, around the jaw and temples. "I'm guessing the Doctor wants to relieve you of this. It could be adding to the problem."

They were lucky that Chaudhri didn't disturb them until Lydia's muscles had let go a little, until the two women had found some calm together.

Chaudhri then very quietly introduced a treatment he hoped Lydia would reconsider: a newer drug that decreases the release of an inflammatory peptide involved in the pain of the migraine process. "It has the potential to prevent migraine before it can start. So far we've seen it help more than half of those who've tried it here."

"Today I feel like I'd try anything. If the Doctor says it's okay—"

Would the Doctor approve? He had before, had suggested this drug to all his patients, Lydia included, as Ruth knew from looking at the files, but there were side effects, and lately he was consumed by a project with a freelance compounding pharmacist, something still newer and personalized, Ruth guessed. He'd not shared any details with Ruth yet, though Mrs. Watson was waiting on them.

"And I see we need some blood samples, from you and from your son," Chaudhri ventured on.

"From Gus?" Lydia asked.

"Yes."

"Just blood?"

"Yes."

"Just blood, then."

Before Lydia left Ruth to meet with the Doctor—with her blood taken, her arm carefully bandaged—Lydia thanked Ruth. She looked at her fully now, smiled at her with her eyes. "It's been a pleasure, Ruth," she said. "I hope you'll stay on here. I really do."

How long had it been since anyone had given Ruth any consideration, showed appreciation, without conditions or caveats? It allowed her to hope that things could become simpler, that, like Sally or Jill, she could stay on and contribute here, have her own sense of mission. Ruth had nearly forgotten what it was to be let into places so private, to be deemed worthy of trust as a caregiver. She had taken it for granted once. Did not see, as she did now, that none of us were alone in feeling as if our every window has been thrown open to every kind of weather.

It was after five thirty—Lydia was still shut away with the Doctor—when Ruth emerged into the now empty lounge and saw Sue hoist Larry's partially unzippered knapsack off one of the couches and complain of his carelessness. There were workmen coming and going, finishing the repairs from the flooding, and "all kinds of foot traffic."

"I'm leaving for the day now, Ruth, but will you tell Larry when he comes out of his session that I've put his bag in the closet in reception?"

"I'll walk out with you," Ruth said, "for a little air, then come right back. I'll be sure to let him know."

She followed Sue to that closet and noticed, as she had before, that it was just out of the nearest camera's seeing, and all the more so when the door to the closet was open, blocking the camera entirely. Once Sue gathered her things and moved aside, Ruth reached into the closet to get her own shoulder bag. Larry's phone leaned awkwardly out of an open outside pocket. It could have fallen out anywhere. It could have been snatched up by anyone.

She knew before she'd admitted it to herself that she'd take the phone. It was seamless, quick: As Sue switched off a desk lamp, Ruth palmed the iPhone, flicked the silence button with her forefinger, and slipped it into her bag. She'd need the phone only long enough to send herself the recordings. She'd have to act quickly. There'd be security on the phone to overcome; she hoped to get to a password, bypassing any facial or fingerprint recognition.

When Ruth came back to the clinic, after seeing Sue waddle off into the bright evening, she pulled a file of all the employees' information relevant to getting paid, kept in a vertical desktop organizer on Sue's desk. Now Ruth did a mime for the camera watching her there, as if checking her own form for any mistakes, but what she was looking at was Larry's form: his birthday, Social Security number, physical and e-mail addresses. She needed to memorize the details only long enough to get back to the small office given her, where she could write it all down, see if she could glean his password from it, open the phone, and hear whatever it was Larry had on their employer, so that Ruth might use it for insurance, too, if it came to that.

The Doctor

May was a little more than halfway through, but already it was overfull with event: Larry's phone had gone missing, and when he realized it, he went off like an alarm. The Doctor had taken him for a calmer man, but he wouldn't be dissuaded from his claim that the phone had been stolen, even after he tracked it to the clinic and it was found by the cleaning crew, just hours after it was lost. It prompted Sue to take inventory over a few days. Unaccounted for were a dozen samples of meds—triptans and NSAIDs, Narcan nasal spray for reversing opioid overdose—along with some food, pieces of flatware, a few reams of paper.

The Doctor assured everyone, especially Adele, that he wasn't overly concerned about what was missing. It hadn't interfered with clinic business and had likely happened over time. Under no circumstances, he stressed, should the police be called. "We're among friends here, aren't we?"

He asked Sue to acquaint him with the camera program linked to his desktop computer, so that he could see what the cameras had been seeing. Though she teased him about losing his "tech cherry," she explained that from his computer the system allowed him to go back only ten days. Anything before that—say, the day of the rainstorm—would be archived elsewhere, on a base system at Adele's brownstone, and Adele had her security guy looking through that footage now.

There was only one camera view the Doctor was really interested in: He'd given Ruth a key to his office for the research he'd tasked her with, and after his lesson from Sue, he was able to make her figure jump like an automaton as he fast-forwarded her going in and out of his office, some two dozen times in ten days, as she pulled and replaced files. But one morning, before the Doctor had arrived, and then again late another evening when he'd left for the day, she attempted to open a locked desk drawer, where he knew she'd found the journal once before.

On the computer screen, he watched as she sat in his chair, organizing the contents of a file, making a few notes, then she stopped and appeared to search for something she needed for her work—a pen, a paper clip, a Post-it with which she may have wanted to tab information in a file. No apparent incursion at all, her hands sweeping the surface of his desk, then lifting the blotter to look there, where, incidentally, he usually stored the key to his desk.

It was then the Doctor finally typed Ruth's full name and "New Hampshire" into his laptop's browser. Nothing came up at first, until he found her married name—Marks. This led to a few lines from a Seabrook newspaper's police log from two years earlier—Ruth had been arrested for domestic battery. An article dated several weeks later, this time from the website of a paper called *The Portsmouth Herald*, reported that the charges against Ruth had been dropped. The full article was hidden behind a paywall, but enough about the incident—that she'd critically injured her husband, and the authorities' response, a determination of self-defense—was available for internet eternity.

It was in the comment section of another article over a year later, on the same website, about a young woman suing a hospital and naming Ruth for the wrongful death of her premature baby, that Ruth's difficulties were laid bare for the Doctor. Whatever favorable public opinion Ruth had once had as a woman who'd been victimized by her husband—a violent addict, by all accounts—was lost in this latest misfortune. Locals vilified her, called her heartless, a bitch, a sociopath, and—in a hyperbolic callback to her prior troubles with her husband—a murderer, in fact a serial killer, though the word was spelled "cereal."

Anything resembling her side of the story of what had happened at the NICU didn't come up in the Google search, not on the first page, the second, or the third, and that mattered in a time when stories were made in an instant but stuck for so much longer.

After she disappeared and the story of her affair, or affairs, came out, Sarah also had been the subject of plenty of speculation online: that she'd asked for it, was a slut, had been shamed into hiding. The Doctor had sifted through these over and over, even before Sarah's journal came to him. He'd been looking for clues about when and how Sarah might reappear. But there were none, and none of the comments about her had taken on an anger that, from one rash comment (jittery with its missing or marred punctuation and spelling) to the next had become infectious, self-perpetuating, certain usernames recurring and recruiting others. The last comment written directly to Ruth had been posted only a month ago: "Justice is coming for U."

She hadn't been forgotten by her detractors.

Adele had to be aware of this, was probably trading on it, but did she know or care if Ruth was a good nurse? Perhaps Ruth's good education and tenure as a hospital nurse working in more extreme conditions than existed at the clinic told Adele all she needed.

The Doctor, however, did know. He had watched Ruth work. From the first, she never hurried or argued with a patient; she showed concern but never pity. He was told the pinch was barely felt when she took blood. Jane referred to her as a pro, and Lydia called her an angel, and Chaudhri, as early as her first week, said, "She gets it, and fast." And when a patient vomited, which was not infrequent with headaches and the nausea they caused, Ruth was there first, on her knees, cleaning up the mess before anyone else could.

With her every helpful interaction as a nurse, the Doctor suspected she meant to loosen her past's hold on her. *A brand new day.*

Christine twice mentioned that Ruth reminded her of someone, but she couldn't place who. The Doctor pretended not to know, though he had his own idea: It would do no good to share it, because of course Christine couldn't know about Sarah's journal, with the soft blue cover and its contents, or that Ruth had decided to carry one so very like it—blue, too, and written in, at times, in blue ink.

To replace Ruth would take time that the Doctor was not sure he had to give and probably produce someone less talented and who was no less Adele's creature. As long as Ruth was Adele's ears and eyes, he'd make use of it. He'd be as transparent with Ruth as he could be, act as he would with any colleague, including giving her access to his office.

He'd disposed of the lozenges, and as for Sarah's journal, he'd been carrying it with him.

Of course, he also searched for any news of the man he'd assaulted and found nothing. If the Doctor had managed to kill the man, there would have been some item somewhere, and the cameras he'd lost sight of in his anger that day would have been witness enough to what the Doctor had done. Unless the electricity had gone out by then? Or was it that P. had decided not to report him to the police? This seemed impossible, knowing what he did about the man and how his self-loathing was matched only by his self-pity. Unless he was wrong? Could he be? Could he be that lucky?

Not knowing interfered with his sleep, as did the spring nights coming through his windows, loud with the city back at work and play, gloriously and wretchedly alive.

Merely imagining having to surrender Sarah's notebook to strangers and strange hands—should the police come back into the frame—made the floor buck under him, made him want to run. But hadn't he taken all he could from it? And hadn't he begun to enact it with his patients in the only way he knew how—give them one thing, one remedy, even if it was cover for something at once simpler and more complex than they could have anticipated?

That's why it was crucial that patients and staff all saw the compounding pharmacist, Curtis, in his own white lab coat, when he came to the clinic—two, three times and counting—though the two men never talked specifics at the clinic, only outside of it or by phone. He explained to Ruth, without going into any detail, that he and Curtis were formulating something especially for the clinic's patients. Let her and Adele be distracted by what that could mean and by what had to matter most: the work of the clinic.

She was often lingering by his door when she wasn't with patients. She had observations to share, mostly useful, he had to admit, and questions of course, many practical, but sometimes she was simply there, waiting.

Today, when he opened the door, she said she hoped they could discuss gut health—its link to headaches. Dr. Chaudhri had given her an NIH study about it. "Have you read it?" she asked excitedly.

Her hair was unpinned again. It hung to her shoulders. Her posture was leisurely, her eyes bright. That is, until Ed came up alongside them, with his size and extravagance, all the familiarity he assumed, and she tensed. She didn't trust Ed. She didn't have to. She—and Adele—needed only to consider there was more to him and his approaches than they could know, and if anything happened to the Doctor, which it might, anytime now, Ed could help. He would help. He should never be underestimated.

Ed's eyes looked clear, but there was something in his expression: fatigue, melancholy, or both, though not for long. Emotions moved through Ed like tropical weather. They weren't superficial for being fast-changing, only more noticeable for the contrast of one to the next.

"It's Ruth, yes?" Ed asked, hanging down from his height as if to sniff at her. "You look… different. Your hair, is it?"

Ruth didn't answer Ed, though she touched her hair to see how it might have betrayed her.

He tried again: “How is it going here? So far, so good? It’s been, what, about three weeks now?”

The Doctor interceded: “I’ve been meaning to acquaint Ruth with what you do here and elsewhere, Ed, your work—”

Ed looked at the Doctor quizzically. “Doctoring?”

“No, with your area of expertise.”

“Neurology?”

“Yes, that, but what you’ve been focused on here in particular and why. Maybe now’s a good time for us to sit down together for a bit? Why don’t you two come in?”

They did, but not with any enthusiasm.

“Ruth’s never worked in neurology before, or in chronic pain and its management. But she’s learning quickly. Chaudhri’s acquainting her with the finer points, and she’s lately been reading about the digestive system, gut bacteria.”

“Is that right?” Ed was unmoved. He knew what side Ruth had to be playing for. He did not trust her any more than she did him.

“Ed’s not merely a doctor, Ruth, not merely a fine one; he’s a patient, too—mine sometimes, but mostly his own, and he’s had some success with his experiments…” He would tempt his friend into a sermon. “What did E. O. Wilson say again, Ed? There is no greater *high* than discovery? Haven’t you found that?”

Ed let loose a big guffaw at all that Wilson’s quote suggested. “Yes. Yes, I have.”

At that, Ed breathed in, gathering his energies, and looked around the room, to its bright, empty walls and the camera that had been rehung on a shiny new mount in the corner of the Doctor’s office. Maybe Adele or her “security guys” were watching now? If so, they’d get a good show.

“The gut, huh?” Ed began, slowly to start. “You, Ruth, probably know we call it the second brain and that digestive pipes house up to a hundred million neurons? Our famous nerve cells—not just up here, but here—” Ed moved his hand from head to abdomen and held it there, as if its bulk owed to that swelling population of neurons. "That's more than the spinal cord. Right in the tissue lining the esophagus, stomach, intestines. The majority of the body's serotonin is found right here—eighty to ninety percent of it. You'll find all the major neurotransmitters camping here, *all* the happy-making, pain-busting chemicals the nervous system provides: not just serotonin, but dopamine, oxytocin, GABA, endorphins, you name it.

"But I'm getting ahead of myself"—they needed to go back to the brain, he said, where the circuitry was "so damned complex we don't yet fully understand it.

"I bet you've read that each of our *hundreds of billions* of neurons has between a thousand and ten thousand synapses or connections. With trillions in the cerebral cortex alone. But have you tried to *imagine* it, Ruth? That is more than there are stars in the universe. Who can visualize that? No one." Ed was gaining on himself now. "And what about our hundred thousand miles of nerve fibers that begin in the cortex of the brain? Miles *and* miles? Or the endless nerve endings on our outer edges—on yours, Ruth, that *right now* are sensing minute shifts in vibration, sound, temperature. It's too much, isn't it? More than any one of us can imagine. But you can feel it, can't you? The immensity working even on the smallest parts of us? If you close your eyes and let yourself?"

How Ed took you up, to the heights he most preferred and was unafraid of. It didn't matter if you knew what he was saying and doing, as the Doctor did, knew it as performance, at least in part, before it really did become feeling and charged the air around him.

Did Ruth feel the charge? Was she taking in that air? If she could, he knew she would begin to make her way to forgiving Ed the appetites he wore so openly. She'd better understand his carelessness—not with patients, never that, but with living, and at such a volume, not because life wasn't precious but because it *was*, and Ed couldn't believe his luck at being part of it. The Doctor couldn't give Ruth whatever Adele had promised her—money surely and other material improvements in her life—but he could give her this: the wonder in the intricacy of our design, the passion it inspired in people like them, scientists and caregivers and sometimes sensualists. Couldn't it draw out a version of Ruth she could be proud of, whatever Adele's influence?

With his face gleaming, sweat at his temples, and a vein showing in the middle of his forehead like a tulip stem held there, Ed now toured Ruth through the visionaries who'd inspired him, from Marie Curie all the way to the father of cannabis research, Raphael Mechoulam at the Hebrew University. He was coming round to the studies that demonstrated the potential neuroprotective and neurogenerative effects of THC, as well as the anti-inflammatory and anti-seizure benefits of cannabidiol, or CBD.

One thing to cure all ills.

That Ed believed that thing was cannabis went a long way to making it so for him.

It could only affirm the Doctor's new approach with his patients, and that's where the Doctor went in his mind as Ed turned to describe how the body strives for homeostasis, in everything it does for us.

"Right now, at this very moment, Ruth, our systems are working hard to achieve balance. And I wanted to help mine find that balance again. Exertion causes my headaches, you see. Here I was, a man at middle age, and I was suddenly felled by the blood vessels in my very own head: killer migraines caused by any activities that raised my central blood pressure. I wanted to find a treatment that could quiet my system without imposing unnecessary constraints, side effects, and as organically as possible. For me, that treatment has been cannabis. Many growers are focusing on CBD-rich strains now, some on THC. Have you ever tried it, Ruth? The new stuff and all it has to offer?"

Ruth went wide-eyed and hot red, blurted out a no, and then looked to the Doctor for help.

But he couldn't give it: He was there and gone. That sense of promise that his friend was stirring in him, as only Ed could, made him eager to get back to his patients and his own bid for a cure. He saw Ruth and Ed out as soon as he could. Ruth had smiled, hadn't she? Hadn't she said thank you? "I'm glad you've found something that works *for you*," she'd said to Ed, almost prophetically, as if she knew that's where the Doctor had turned his mind's eye, "personalized medicine," *made just for you.*

He spoke to each of his patients now as he should have spoken to Sarah once, to a secret moving in each one of them, a longing for relief that had become too terrible to carry alone: "We analyzed your history, your blood, and have created something tailored just for you. It could be the thing that's been missing, and it has care in it, real care, but you must not give up on your self-care. You see, the new medication works synergistically. It builds on the neurotransmitters in the brain that elevate mood—the treatment needs to act on a landscape that is as friendly, as fruitful, as joyful as is possible. Do you understand?"

His plan was to change their habits, to cause them to want to. They couldn't understand as he did just how plastic their systems could be, how available to learning and so to neurogenesis at any age. Habitual stress and pain limit this opportunity: If you expect pain, studies from several disciplines had shown, you're not only more likely to get it, but the pain will be worse, much worse. A potent self-fulfilling prophecy.

As a condition of continuing to formulate this medication *just for you*, they had to commit to whatever activities had proven beneficial to them in the past—meditation or yoga or sex, magnesium infusions or B vitamins or butterbur, kava, or cannabis—which would support the efficacy of this new remedy, and do so with regularity in the next several weeks, up to forty-five days at least, *please.*

"Give these to yourself, these changes to your routine, and this particular treatment is far more likely to help."

Somewhere near the conclusion of his pitch, he patted their shoulder—maybe it was a double pat to the upper arm—or he gave a firm handshake. To show them he was in it with them, this process, this hope. Eyes meeting theirs: *I will commit to you, if you will to me, here and now.* He hoped they would not merely hear his intentions but feel them.

There was an eeriness in the gaining purity of the transactions he'd been having with his patients, just as there was in this string of days of spring and sun, taking them into June. A kind of benediction that thrilled and scared him.

Maybe he was fooling himself—his luck couldn't hold; nothing did. Maybe he was nothing more than a con man exploiting their devotion to him, but when patients came in squinting from the now persistent light outside, or uptight from their commute to the clinic, or from the pain—a headache coming, or having arrived, or gone now, leaving them drained—he felt he'd opened a door for them that had always been there but no one noticed, not even him, until now. *Can you imagine it? This way, a way out. What could it hurt to try?*

Ruth

Shadows moved on the street in a light evening breeze. There was a man hiding in them, following Ruth.

She'd sensed someone there in the past few days, off and on, but couldn't be sure. Today she swore she saw him: Adam, one of the clinic's patients, barred from the clinic last week when it was discovered he was responsible for some of the thefts. Only two instances could be proven, in fact—were caught by the cameras—but it was enough.

It was Adam's long limbs Ruth had seen on her first visit to the clinic, as he slept in the lounge—as safe there, with a blanket thrown over his head and shoulders, as perhaps he wasn't elsewhere. And she'd since studied his file, all the treatments tried, which had helped his migraines—a gift of a brain injury he'd gotten while serving in the military—though never for long enough. A former intravenous heroin user, he now refused injections, including Botox and some of the more effective long-lasting CGRP antagonists, and cannabis, too, in all forms: "Doesn't trust himself," the Doctor wrote in his notes.

Of course, the Doctor had to be the one to tell Adam that he could no longer come to the clinic—at least temporarily. Ruth hadn't been within earshot when he called, but Sue and others had. The Doctor was conciliatory: No charges would be brought, and if Adam returned what he took, showed some contrition, the Doctor was sure he could change Mrs. Watson's mind about the suspension. But there was yelling, hanging up, more calls put in, which Sue fielded. Threats were made. *He doesn't mean any of it*, the Doctor told them all. *Not to worry.*

And now Ruth had either to run away from Adam as fast as she could or run right to him and into his intentions, whatever they were, show him she wouldn't be intimidated. She'd gotten away from another addict who'd hunted her, hurt her in ways that had not healed, only to come here and attract another. And did Adam know something? Had he seen something he shouldn't have? He couldn't have seen her take Larry's phone, but when she put it back where it would be found later?

No, she'd been careful, but it didn't matter how strategic Ruth thought she'd been in the past weeks, or how well she believed she was juggling what she had to do so that she could do something as simple as use her skills again, she couldn't get away, could she? The ante kept going up and up. When Ruth told Mrs. Watson that the Doctor had taken to locking his desk and putting the key out of reach, that she couldn't be certain if the journal was even in there, Mrs. Watson told her she had any number of keys at her disposal, including to the Doctor's home.

That was where Ruth was walking now, to Brooklyn Heights, to identify the Doctor's apartment building in the row of them and pick out which windows were his in that building's face. *And what a lovely building it is,* Mrs. Watson told Ruth, *on a lovely block. Go have a look.* But Ruth wasn't alone on her walk. Adam was in between the spaces where the light grew long before it angled away and soon would be gone as the night came on. He'd threatened that everyone at the clinic would "get what's coming to them." It sounded so much like the threats made against Ruth online, the last one from only weeks ago: *Justice is coming for U.* She didn't doubt it was coming. Ever. And she'd been running from it as best she could—was this where the race ended for her?

Adrenaline's sickly flush took her heart, her hands, the muscles of her legs, which were twitching now, but she didn't know which way to go and, stuck there, between fight and flight, nowhere, really, with the smell of moist soil sharp in her nose from the raked-over plot of a nearby tree, and of those spring lilacs, too, coming to her in that same ever-so-light breeze, from where she couldn't see, she cried out, screamed, not so much for her life as *at it*. She screamed for help.

The Doctor

A bright curtain of fog pulled across the Doctor's vision. Adam's words caught in it: "This is bullshit. *You're* bullshit!"

But it was Izzy who sat before him. He could see only one side of her gray curls as she appealed to him. His mind dulling, becoming fog. A numbness in his left arm. It was not a stroke, but a visual or ocular migraine, his mother's genetic gift to him. His triggers: stress and too little sleep. He'd had trouble getting decent rest before he was forced to confront Adam, and since then it had only gotten worse.

"You must talk to her," Izzy said to the Doctor now. "I think you are the only person Adele trusts anymore. Well... Marie, of course. But Adele admires you. She thinks you are a paragon. She's been looking for one for a long time now."

The Doctor had incidents like this one so infrequently these days that when they came he had to remind himself, as he would one of his patients, that in twenty to thirty minutes he'd be able to see again, and in an hour or so, though fatigued, he'd be left with a slight headache and the aphasia would subside; words would be less cumbersome, not only to find but to fathom.

"I'm glad to have Orson at home with me," Izzy continued, "for however long he needs. He can breathe easier at my place. I have no expectations of him. None. I never have. And it's a godsend to have him nearby in these days. So unpredictable."

The Doctor couldn't put what she said in the right context. She admitted to having had a cancer scare—the breast. But all was well now. He couldn't tell if she was wanting him to comfort her or maybe Orson: "He needs more good men in his life." No, it was the church that was the cause of her coming to him: "A glorious fortress. Just what the architect intended."

"She changed the locks upstairs, of course, but Orson's already found a way around that. Got his hands on his own set of keys. It's a game they're stuck in. She shuts him out, he finds a way in. He goes away, has had enough, then goes back when she needs him. He can't go far. Despite what he says, he adores her, and he's not terribly sure of his own powers, though that doesn't keep him from asserting them. Like his father. Poor Adele! Our father was a selfish man. But he could be very kind. My mother brought that out in him. Mom and I took him as he was. That's the key to so much, but Adele, she made demands. Who could blame her after losing her own mother so young? But our father ran out of patience with it, and she hasn't stopped *demanding*. She's always required that I be someone else, anyone else but me, if I wanted her affection, but I couldn't do it for her: I love her, but I can't do that. *How?*"

Izzy shuddered at the thought of it—or perhaps at what came next: "But have you ever met anyone more alive than she is? Orson is like her in that way and is drawn to it. And the beauty. She *is* beautiful. And so destructive. I'm trying to contain the damage now. Not just for her, but for all of us too, every single one of us. This church should be protected. Someone has to stand up for it. I have a petition here, Doctor—"

He couldn't see the petition or whether she was holding it up, not through the boiling and shimmering of the fog and how it silvered and threatened to become a full rainbow of colors, too bright. He wanted to close his eyes.

"I'd like to share it with my friends here, to enlist them. They've come to love this place, just as I have. I know they're patients—yours, and Adele's, too, in a way—but they are also *my* friends, my compatriots. I wanted to be up-front with you about this, of course."

"Yes," he managed to say, and then, "I understand," which he plucked from the increasing swirl of words and shocks that he couldn't organize and so could not defend himself from.

"It's not fair. Don't I get my day in court?" Adam was saying to him again, the conversation looping.

"I understand, Adam, I do. It isn't fair—"

"You're no different from any of them, are you? From that fucking drug dealer you were married to? Nope, no fucking different. You're nothing but a liar, *a goddamned liar*. It's bullshit. You're ..."

He'd tried to calm Adam and himself—his own anger rioting through him against the effort to contain it and speak reason to Adam, who had hung up, called back, hung up, called again.

"What I did I *had* to do, for my brothers," Adam told the Doctor. "There are thousands of us. You gonna keep us all out? Was it Sue or that new nurse? Did she complain about me? What, did she see me in front of the meds closet? So the fuck what? I didn't take anybody's fucking phone. I took some food—nothing much. And I needed the Narcan, okay?"

"I would have given you some, if you'd asked, Adam. I would have. They have it on video, the cameras—"

"Narcan keeps my brothers alive. They fought. They're still fighting for their lives right here. And what are you doing? What are you all doing? Nothing, man. *Nothing*. You are *nothing*. And you get to throw me away? You get to say who's in, who's out? *You?*"

Ruth

She had gone to her knees. She managed to look up to see a man approaching, getting closer. Her panic fooled her into believing he'd climbed down from a tree, as if he'd been hiding there all this time, moving behind her from city tree to tree, until the time was right to jump down, on this empty bit of side street. She struggled to get up before he could get to her, but his hand was already under her upper arm.

"Ruth, is it? From the clinic?"

It wasn't Adam.

Someone else, gentler.

Helping her to her feet.

Dirt under his fingernails and on his clothes and boots. Skin weathered by sun and wind but not yet old or fragile-seeming. Durable instead. A patient from the clinic. Jeff, she remembered. She'd sat in on his exam with Chaudhri and seen him using a crownlike TENS device more than once, and when he had it on his head, he looked like a prince lately reclaimed from some faraway frontier.

"Are you all right?" he asked her.

She took in every bit of him to regain herself—at this distance she could make out the smells of sweat, mulch, and leather coming from him. Sunlight and debris pulled through his brown hair, which was thick and full enough to fall in his eyes. His muscles were long, unostentatious, roping, even in his jaw and forehead. There was a narrowing look in his eyes, of a man accustomed to concentrating on one task until it was done. Now he was concentrating on her, touching her as if not to leave marks.

"How awful," she said, letting herself lean into him, breathing him in and out, until she was on both feet.

"What is?"

"I had a start. I thought I saw someone. I was sure—"

"Someone you know?"

She looked around them, for signs of anyone else coming. A jogger and a late commuter, both rigged up in earphones, passed by on the opposite side of the street, blocks from Clinton Street's busy artery. They didn't look her way.

"Yes, someone I know, but—" She was dizzy, embarrassed. She didn't trust herself to say more.

"There's a café close by, just back this way, where I keep some ladders in exchange for pruning their trees. Maybe take a breather? It's not far."

She nodded. He extended his arm and she took it shyly, and they walked back in the direction of the clinic, toward Cobble Hill.

The café was beside a small bench-lined park on a mostly residential block. People crowded into the tables outside the long, open windows of its storefront. Ruth and Jeff sat inside near the far end of the bar, for some quiet. He got them glasses of ice water. She apologized. She'd interrupted his work.

"My work has no end, so it's good when one's forced on me," he said. "And it's good to sit."

It was, and the water was a cold astonishment in her mouth. Voices were being broadcast, at volume, nearby, the radio on in a sound system behind the bar.

"Sue said something about New Hampshire," he said. "You're from there?"

She nodded.

"I have some family there, cousins," he told her.

"Where?"

"Milton. Wolfeboro. Up in the woods."

"The woods," she repeated. Words so inviting against the radio voices, one of which she recognized from Mrs. Watson's:

It was practiced, a storyteller's, good at tempting you to listen. The other voice being broadcast—a guest on the radio show—spoke of a drought in California, flooding in Texas, wildfires in a Georgia swamp, making a sad list: "It's rough all over the country, and then we get word of this hack. Incredible timing, and unfortunate, with this developing weather system. It's a big one…"

Her agitation still quivered through her, through every one of those 100,000 miles of nerve fibers Dr. Konradi, Ed, had described. She had to force herself to focus on Jeff. "Are they in the tree business, too? Your family?"

"No one in my immediate family even thinks about trees, or not much. I actually grew up here mostly, in the city, but I left every chance I could: camp, boarding school, college."

He told her he'd studied forestry and economics in California, at Berkeley. He didn't mean to come back to New York. "Now I can't seem to go. Nature has its challenges everywhere these days. But especially here. The city's hard on its trees and plants. They need friends. Care… I think I'll have a beer. You want one?"

"Yes, sure, one beer, why not? I have money."

"Your money's no good here. Mine isn't either—I know the bartender. Know him well. His uncle owns this place. You have a preference?"

"Of?"

"Beer."

"No, none."

She watched him shake hands with the bartender and heard him ask something about playing some music, *on such a fine night, c'mon.* The radio conversation clicked off and the murmur and clatter of the café grew up like tall grass around her, cars streaming by on the street, the air through the open storefront turning cool, pricking her skin. Then instrumental music moved through the room, a saxophone in the lead; in its sinuousness was an edge of complaint, wildness, calling to

Ruth's nerves. She wouldn't let them answer, and as soon as Jeff set the beer before her, she drank it down in gulps.

"Excuse me," she said when she saw him watching her.

He raised his beer bottle to her in salute and drained half of it. "Nothing like it after a hard day. John"—he inclined his head to the bartender—"thinks he's being funny. That's Coltrane he's playing, because of the title: *A Love Supreme*. Everybody's a comedian, but it's not that kind of love Coltrane was after here—"

"At least it's free," Ruth said.

"The music? Love?"

"The beer."

He laughed. It was warm, his laugh, along with the alcohol in the beer and the buttery light outside, the sun setting now. They didn't talk while they listened to Coltrane's saxophone refusing to touch down, until Jeff asked, "Shall we have another?"

"I should get back to the clinic," she said. "There's a support group tonight I should sit in on."

"I'm going to it, too. Izzy—she's a friend from the clinic—she made a point of ensuring a few of us would be there tonight. Not sure why. But there's still time. We're not far."

Ruth agreed. She swallowed down what remained in her bottle while Jeff went back to the bar to get them two more. As Jeff sat down across from Ruth again, the music changed: Van Morrison this time, "Crazy Love."

"You're an ass, John," Jeff called.

"Beautiful girl, beautiful night," John called back, waving at Ruth. Ruth found herself smiling as her body shifted into his description, the song of it, *beautiful girl, beautiful night*, and into the music now playing, as if these effects were what mattered now, were what was real, and everything before it, all the tension and upheaval of her days since arriving in the city, weren't, or didn't have to be.

"I can't argue with that," Jeff said, grinning at John. "*Won't* argue." And then, confiding to Ruth happily, "But he's still an ass. You feeling better?"

How badly she wanted to tell Jeff everything she could, confess to how out of her depth she was here, how afraid, because she could see he was kind and would try to understand her. And he smelled delicious to her, a man who wrapped himself in and around tree limbs, who would wrap himself around her if she'd let him. It could be that simple, at least for as long as the beer lasted. But no longer than that: He was a patient at the clinic, after all, and she'd become a person who could never share all of what she'd done and where she'd been without risk.

She'd guessed the password to Larry's phone on her fourth try, his birth month and day, which were probably irresistible to him because they were the same backward and forward—1111—and had e-mailed herself the audio files, numbered one to five, from Larry's phone. She then deleted the record of the transmissions from his e-mail outbox and trash. She'd put the phone under one of the lounge couches, obscured by a leg, where it might have fallen. The cleaners had found it and promptly returned it. What would this attractive tree man make of that? That the games she was playing weren't innocent, that she wasn't, that she had a past that was hard to explain and could shame her, if she let it? That defending herself was not merely academic, but a reflex, as with the asshole at the bar the day of the heavy rains. And that taking Larry's phone had excited her? That holding it was holding others' lives in her hand, everything they expected they could keep private? Even now, sitting here with him, it still excited her.

"Can I ask you a favor, Jeff? Can I call you Jeff?"

"Yes, and yes, of course," he said with polite anticipation in his voice.

"Can we keep this between us? You coming upon me like that? On the street?"

"Okay."

"And can I ask you not to ask me about it? I mean, it's that it's hard to explain."

"Okay. But when it's settled some, maybe it would be good to talk about it? That was some scream, and I thought—"

"Of course, I will, but while we finish these, I'd like to talk about something else, if that's okay. Maybe you could tell me more about your work here."

"I'd rather show you. In exchange for my silence?"

Her surprise made her laugh: "Are we bargaining?" He wasn't letting go of their chance meeting and what it could confer that easily.

"I'd just like to show you around some, if you have the time. Take a walk maybe. There's a dawn redwood not far away, in Brooklyn Heights. I'd like to show you that."

"A redwood in New York City? One of those Californian giants? Really?"

"Really."

"Are there many here?"

"No."

"It must be lonely."

"It's holding its own. It's tough."

"Did you happen to hear them mention something about a storm before, on the radio?"

"Yes," he said. "They've been talking about it all day. Another storm—big, chances are. And some hack, the satellites—"

He was interrupted by an eruption of Sinatra singing "Fly Me to the Moon" at volume.

"Dammit, John!" Jeff yelled, and he and Ruth laughed too. They hummed with the song, laughing again, at the idea of spring on another planet entirely—why not Jupiter? why not Mars?—just as the song said, with Sinatra's dangerous velvet insistence ("baby, kiss me") pursuing them outside, into an evening cooling and purpling with the sun's disappearance, all the way back to the clinic.

The Wind Report

We're on the air with Alistair B. Freeman, a professor of meteorology and atmospheric sciences at CUNY—

"Of climatology, not meteorology."

Sorry, right—

"You know the difference?"

No, I'm afraid I don't.

"I should probably have explained that up-front: I don't give seven-day forecasts, though any climatologist could. We study meteorology, too, but we also have to learn the science of looking longer into our past, and based on that, we make predictions for the future, best we can, create models, for months to years to come. We see weather as history—the planet's, yours, mine."

You've been at this for some time?

"More than fifty years. I'm old—"

No, I didn't mean—

"Well, I am—eighty-two. And truth is, I'm pretty tired, but this stuff, it's thrilling. Terrifying, too. I can't look away. Can't retire. It's more eventful than ever out there, with more variables than ever."

Including us? And these hackers?

"What the hackers did was target some supercomputers at the National Weather Service, on which the National Hurricane Center relies. Our GOES, the Geostationary Operational Environmental Satellites. They're responsible for the images you see on your TV news. We have three of these, and for the moment they're not talking. They've gone silent. It's happened before, in 2014, and they fixed it. They will again—they're working on the firewalls now."

We're getting a lot of messages about this new storm, that it's make-believe or man-made? An invention of the hackers?

"It's real, all right, and it was made like most are. Started as a tropical wave off the west coast of Africa. A lot of our big storms start right there, from hot air that flows over the Sahara and hits the cooler, wetter air at the coast. It's a factory. Storms cropping up every two to three days. Something to see—gorgeous, and, like I said, terrifying—but when they hit the cold of the Atlantic, they're generally stopped cold, lose momentum. Though, of course, not always, and hello, Floyd or Ivan, Sandy or Florence. This storm is headed for the Bahamas now. May follow Floyd's path—"

Hurricane Floyd's path?

"Yep, 1999. Straight up the East Coast. Caused one of the largest evacuations in U.S. history, and, thanks to our technology, many fewer deaths. And this latest system is a rough one—already a Category 3. Winds up to—"

Careful with talk about winds around here, Professor.

"Yes, we had some windy days here, didn't we? The jet stream not behaving, and then, you see—I'm sorry, what's your name again?"

Tom, Thomas.

"All atmospheric disturbances, Thomas, like storms—and we can include the wind that hung around so long in this part of the Northeast—these disturbances redistribute heat, and as the planet gets hotter there's more distributing to do. The winds have to work harder. And there's all kinds of evidence that the winds of these big storms are getting stronger faster. They can get to Category 3 some nine or ten hours faster than they used to. And global wind speeds in general have increased: It's windier up there *and* down here. And then, with more water vapor in the atmosphere, the storms are wetter. And they can kick up earlier than they used to—spring and summer. All our models have changed."

But you did say we're better off? Now?

"In terms of forecasts? My, yes. With or without our GOES, we've got plenty of eyes up there—our other satellites—and there's Europe's GOES, India's, Japan's. We've got radar, drones, and manned weather planes. We issue warnings earlier. Just remember what happened with the Galveston storm—did I mention Galveston already?"

Texas?

"Yes. Galveston, Texas. In 1900, eight thousand died, but it may have been as many as twelve thousand. Hard to say for sure. 'Sorry state of affairs'—that's what they called our forecasting back then, and comparatively it was. Comparatively we were blind.

"But the biggest part of what went wrong then was arrogance. We don't know where the storm began, precisely. It hit Cuba as a tropical storm, dumped a lot of rain there. Then it went on its way to the Florida Straits. The Cubans knew what was coming for Galveston. Jesuits, who ran the observatory on the island, were some of the best weather watchers in the world. They could read the clouds. Especially Father Benito Viñes. If we had meteorological saints, he'd be one of them, but our weather bureau, run at the time by a swine named Willis Moore, dismissed Viñes's prediction. Moore and his cohorts had their own ideas. These turned out to be fatal."

Deadly arrogance. And these hackers? Would you charge them with the same thing, Professor?

"They're pretty contemptible, but they can't hurt us like Moore did, not with all the backups we have. Whoever went after our satellites might be looking to make a statement about the climate. Or about chaos. I don't know. I don't, Thomas. We have enough chaos. We have a talent for it."

How about a little music now, Professor? Shall we play something in honor of that cloud-whispering priest? Father—?

"Viñes."

I imagine he helped save a lot of lives.

"He did."

Listen to this, Professor, from Joni Mitchell. Are you familiar with her music?

"I'm old, son, not dead. I was young once. So was she."

Here's "Both Sides Now," my friends, in honor of an unsung Jesuit seer who could read the clouds. Keep your eyes open. And your hearts. We'll be back shortly and will be taking some calls for the Professor.

Ruth

That night's support group had the air of a reunion. The rising energy of a party. There were faces Ruth had never seen, and no sign of Ed or the Doctor. More chairs were dragged in from the waiting room, but no one sat in them yet; people stood, milling, talking, hugging.

"Let's toast to our Izzy's health! *Tout de suite!* Where's that Sancerre, darling?" an elegant man dressed for cocktails at a country club sang over the voices to Izzy.

"Not now, Richard!" Izzy called back while wrapped in the arms of a petite middle-aged woman in a headscarf who seemed to be congratulating Izzy for something.

A patient Ruth knew named Albert, who was tethered to his phone via an earpiece and wearing a fedora, contributed, at some volume, "They're calling it a hurricane now! The Bahamas are bracing for it."

"Do us favor, Al? Not now with this news?" This was Alla, a Russian woman of soft curves, a no-nonsense manner, and teeth so white they were almost blue. "We just have our spring back."

"When we're done here," the man called Richard, perhaps a little drunk already, cheered, "in honor of Izzy and her church, we'll fling off our clothes and run into the streets. It's *all the rage!* Christine? Gayle? Say you will!"

"I don't disrobe for just anyone, Richard, and especially not for sport," retorted a tall Black woman in a crisp linen suit. She had a full oval face, short salted hair, and a wry smile.

"Hear, hear," sighed Christine, a longtime patient of the Doctor's, a lovely redhead who reminded Ruth of a great-aunt she'd dearly loved.

"Why, hello, Jeff! Up for a jog in your birthday suit? Who's your friend? She looks fit as any fiddle!"

Jeff didn't have to answer Richard, because Izzy was asking for their attention: "I'll try not to go on and on. There's just so much to explain to give you all the full picture—"

"What do you think is going on here?" Jeff, sitting beside Ruth, whispered into her ear.

"I don't know exactly. I've only sat in on two of these so far, at the Doctor's urging," Ruth whispered back. "I don't know a lot of these people."

"They're friends of Izzy's and many of them patients, former patients too. I met some at Izzy's place. She has these parties. They go on for hours, so much food *and wine*. Hey," Jeff breathed into her ear, "would you, Ruth?"

"Would I what?"

"Streak?"

Izzy began, "It's easy to forget we're in a church, isn't it?" And Ruth tried hard to listen, but the beer had relaxed her. She imagined taking her clothes off, piece by piece. How long would it take before the group noticed the new nurse stripping down? She leaned one of her knees lightly against Jeff's.

"Originally this was a Catholic church. Built in the 1870s by an Irishman, Bartley T. Murphy. He was born and raised in this city. His parents had their fill of the religious persecution in Ireland, and so, with his mother heavily pregnant, they set sail, only to get a good deal more of the same here."

Jane, who Ruth knew worked for the ACLU, gave a loud snort of recognition.

"Bartley T. Murphy was just a boy when he saw a Catholic church burn. St. Mary's, down on the Lower East Side. Burnt by Protestants mostly, the nativists, who were proud to call themselves that. By then the numbers of Catholics in the city had grown, thanks to Irish immigration. Most were poor, uneducated—"

"And *unwelcome*," added Jane, now sunk into one of the barrel chairs.

"Walls had to be built around every Catholic church. The protection became all the more necessary when an outspoken anti-immigrant candidate by the name of Harper was elected mayor of New York City in 1844. Harper and his brothers, printers by trade, had published an account by a young Canadian nun that claimed she and her sisters were forced to serve the sexual needs of priests. It wasn't true, of course, not a word, and it turns out a man wrote the account—"

"Go figure," said Gayle with singsong derision.

"—but that didn't matter at the time. The story was a bestseller. It funded Harper's campaign and fed the nativist movement's worst fears."

"The dirty papists!" Richard cried.

"Shut up, Richard, please," Gayle directed happily. "Our Izzy is talking."

"The new mayor organized a torchlight parade to burn New York's first Catholic cathedral, St. Patrick's. Not the St. Patrick's in Midtown; that wasn't built yet. This St. Patrick's was downtown, in what was mostly farmland then. But the bishop at the time, John Joseph Hughes, himself the son of poor Irish country farmers, had his own army: the Ancient Order of the Hibernians. Now it's a cultural institution, but then it was a militia, really. Hughes positioned sharpshooters on the walls around the church and sent word to the mayor that if one brick of the cathedral or one head of any Catholic was harmed, he'd see the city turned into 'another Moscow,' which meant it would be ravaged as Napoleon's army had done to Moscow during his invasion. That shut Harper's march down."

"This would make a great film," Jeff whispered again.

"I think it *was* a film," Ruth could barely hide how thrilled she was by the night's unexpected storytelling and Jeff's still being so near to her. Would he take off his clothes and run into the night with her if she asked?

"*The* St. Patrick's, in Midtown? That structure became a centerpiece of the bishop's expansion plans for the city and state. They called it 'Hughes's Folly.' Bartley T. Murphy didn't think any of it folly at all, and this church, St. Gabriel's—*our* church—was inspired by Hughes's ambitions. Years of study too. Fundraising. More sacrifice and hard, hard labor by those who'd already done so much of that.

"St. Gabriel's had its own wall, too. Part of it still stands in the rear of the church, but my sister, Adele, and her contractors tore most of it down. It was simpler than rebuilding it—"

Someone booed—Richard, of course.

There was a catch in Izzy's voice. She cleared it. "Bartley T. Murphy wasn't alone in assuming there'd be a holy war between Catholics and Protestants right here on our streets. Notice the size of this basement: He hoped it would accommodate those in need of sanctuary, not only the dead, with room for a crypt for martyrs and officiates—that was standard, of course—but for the living too, so people could be hidden and smuggled away. And they were, via tunnels under this very floor. It served an important purpose, this place. A heroic one. It shouldn't be lost, forgotten—"

Emotion tipped up in Izzy's voice, and through Ruth too. "A *sanctuary*. And it still is—a stronghold, all load-bearing masonry. Apart from the oak timbers in the roof, it's as fire-resistant as they come. And Bartley T. Murphy departed from what was the popular style at the time—neo-Gothic. Murphy chose neo-Romanesque, to connect to the church's architectural origins in Europe. Its heaviness was part of the idea, you see. No accident—"

"I'm here, Auntie!" Orson burst into the room to stand beside his aunt. "I'm here! What have I missed?"

Izzy looped her arm in Orson's and gripped him tight to her.

"I have a petition here for each of you to sign," Izzy told them. "I need it to persuade Adele to preserve the place—"

Richard led a chorus of boos this time.

"Now, now. Many of you know my mother was Catholic. But my father wasn't, and my sister Adele isn't. She thinks my sentimentality has to do with my Catholicism, but I'm not much of a Catholic, in fact. My politics prevent me from being in step the way the truly devout are. Still, my sister thinks I have trouble seeing the world clearly.

"Maybe it shouldn't matter: not Bartley T. Murphy's commitment or passion. Or how he used the education he had—both formal *and* informal. Or what he witnessed on these streets—horrible, horrible things. That's why he picked the Annunciation: When Gabriel appeared to Mary, he said, 'Do not be afraid.' Murphy made sure those words were built into the church, written into the glass and stone. 'Be not afraid.'" Izzy's voice dissolved into a sound that was as much lament as sob.

Orson put his arms around his aunt and arched over her, tucking her head under his chin.

She sniffed, steadied herself. "Maybe it's because I am getting older, or frailer—"

"Auntie," Orson said, "c'mon now."

"You're our jolly good fellow!" cried Richard.

"—that places like these become more important. It's also another century talking to us, it's part of our cultural identity, and together we can be part of that conversation. It's a responsibility, isn't it? To look back, and with *clarity*, with *care*, so that we might move forward without repeating our mistakes? Its preservation is ours, too. Otherwise it's willful ignorance, isn't it? Smallness?"

"Dear Auntie," Orson crooned at her. He took the petition from her and signed it with a flourish. He held it up and soon everyone was on their feet, one after another taking the pen.

The Doctor

"Won't you join us in a bit?" Izzy said and left his office door open—an invitation—and through it came voices of patients he'd not seen in some time, along with voices of those he had.

A lofting male voice sang out "*Darling, darling!*" Richard: a gazelle of a man rarely seen outside his sports jacket and Italian loafers. He was one of Izzy's dearest friends and a onetime patient for chronic tension headaches. He liked to say that if he were not gay he'd run off with Izzy and spend her money on... what was it? Behind his closed eyes, the Doctor searched for the two or three words he recalled Izzy and Richard saying so often, after which they'd toss their heads back in laughter. But the Doctor couldn't find the words, and when he opened his eyes the show went on, a sheer rainbow of electricity cascading over the objects in his office—the chair Izzy had been sitting in, the camera's blinking red light high in the corner.

He needed to get up and walk in the night air, but to get out he'd have to pass by the lounge without betraying his disorientation.

In his desk he had vials of pills, results of his experiments with Curtis, the compounding pharmacist, in different sizes, weights, and colors. He fumbled with the key to the drawer and plucked out one vial. The pills in this one were round, small, dense, and white as paper, a blank slate onto which the patient could project all they hoped for. It could pass for a generic aspirin or Tylenol, but it was something quite different. *The thing you've been missing.*

He put one in his mouth, and as he felt it sliding down his throat he imagined it could give him back a sense of order, along with his focus, his "clarity"—which was among the words he heard Izzy sending out like beacons to him from the lounge. Along with "sanctuary," "responsibility," "preservation." And she was asking those gathered out there with her for a commitment, just as the Doctor had of many of his patients in the past several days.

Through the current in his eyes he could see the group of them as he slipped past. Anousheh was there, in her hijab and long azure tunic. Her migraines had been caused by a heart condition, the name of which eluded him. And Gayle? Did he see her there, too? A professor at a tony liberal arts college in Connecticut. She blamed allergies and teaching for her headaches and had a term for her students, but he couldn't locate it either. He nodded his hellos to anyone who looked his way, but they were so focused on signing Izzy's petition and on Izzy herself, with Orson's arms around her, they barely noticed him.

By the time he got to the Fulton Ferry Landing, his eyes had begun clearing of the aura. The last time he'd come to this spot, high on Ed's lozenge, the wind had kept the crowds away, but they were back like homing pigeons now, each one equipped with a flashing camera, including a large wedding party, making a backdrop of the Brooklyn Bridge spanning the river, its cables lit up against the dark. Across the river on the Manhattan side was South Street Seaport, its market rebuilt since Hurricane Sandy—with its own constellation of lights flashing, as if signaling back.

In the cityscape just behind the Seaport were the missing towers, and alongside was the new tower, a solemn elegance, its spire a long line of LEDs. At this hour, the river refigured the city's light, took it as if into the gleaming skin of some long, luminous sea creature, forever gliding away and away. Day or night, it could be counted on to run fast and dangerous, just as Mr. Bavicchi had warned him when he slung himself over the railing to get closer to it.

If he dropped Sarah's journal in the water now, it would be carried off by means that couldn't be taken back. He'd still be keeping his promise: *For your eyes only, please.* He had the journal in his shoulder bag now. He'd pointed himself toward the police station tonight but had come here instead, just like everyone else.

The woman called Mathilde had come to the Doctor around this time of night as he made his way home, stopping him on the dark side of a dying streetlight. She was a small part of a large shadow, her every sentence beginning with "Sarah": "Sarah, she asks…" "Sarah, for her, you must promise…" He'd tried to press Mathilde for more information, but she gave none, except that Sarah had left the journal and a note with instructions in her apartment for Mathilde. That night, long before the winds came, he reasoned that promising whatever was asked of him was part of keeping both women safe, that they knew they were in danger. After he'd read the journal, this was still his best answer to why Sarah had to go away.

But as the months accumulated, he'd raised the possibility of Sarah's suicide, only to dismiss it and raise it again, only to reject it again. And murder? He shook it off like a bad dream. Impossible to assemble. Round and round he went, so in the months since Sarah was gone, the length of his leash tying him to his promise had gotten shorter and tighter, chafing, and the hope that he'd restore the journal to Sarah herself someday soon was hard to sustain.

Hadn't he taken all he possibly could from what she'd written—every word, every question—into him so deeply that it lost language, the way hunger did? He'd spent too much time alone with the pages, regretting them, but also reenacting them, insinuating himself into what was not his, justifying just as she had, breathless—no matter how many times he read it—at her every capitulation.

Even now, from the very spot where he stood, he peered into the streets near the Seaport, where Sarah had last been seen alive, gauging the distance of time, to feel there might be some change possible in that distance, only to feel the sorrow that there wasn't.

He was gaining on that clarity he'd wished for when he took the white pill that he and Curtis had made because he could remember it was "derangements and decadences" that Izzy and Richard liked to say they'd live for, just the two of them, *if* things were different, *if* only. Anousheh suffered from PFO: patent foramen ovale—the words came easier now—a gap between two chambers of the heart. Surgery had corrected the problem and her migraines. And Gayle used to call her students "congenitally coddled."

A cry behind him. He turned to see that the bride from the wedding party had toppled over, her legs in the air, one white-stockinged foot without a shoe. Its heel had gotten stuck between the boards of the pier. Her dress was as layered and elaborate as the wedding cake waiting on them somewhere, and its skirt tilted up like a bell, exposing all the works inside it. Cameras turned to her, going off around her like a mass of electronic lightning bugs: another fairy tale in crisis. As the groom and the photographer flanked her to help her to her feet, all three fell into hysterics. The Doctor smiled, too, remembering how much he and Jackie had laughed at their wedding, smashing glasses, ripping the hem of her dress dancing, everything part of an adventure they'd begun together. Everything so new. All this so far away.

That very morning Ed had insisted, "You need a vacation, man, to go away, *far away*."

The Doctor had ached at the sound of it, as he did now. If he could just disentangle himself enough from the imperatives that had him trapped in protecting what and who he could, he could leave. If he let himself.

"I'd like to go see my father. I have to. And soon."

"Go. I'll mind the store."

"She won't allow that."

"Adele? Let's just imagine a world where it doesn't matter what Adele allows and what Adele wants. Doesn't that sound like fun?"

"I'm in the middle of something, Ed, with my patients, the harder cases, then I'll go."

"Are you gonna let me in there? Whatever it is you and Curtis are cooking up?"

"Some magic, I hope," the Doctor said.

"Okay, buddy, *don't* tell me. Just promise me you'll go straight home and jerk off. I'll write you a script for it—"

"Awfully kind, but no," the Doctor laughed. "I can't promise anything these days, Ed. Wish I could."

He took the journal out of his bag. If he dropped it, it would hardly make a sound as it hit the water. No one would notice it; no one had really seen him at all. All the cameras were pointed elsewhere, life drawn to life, like the East River gliding away, as quickly as it came.

Ruth

Ruth was expected at Mrs. Watson's after her workday unless she received a text telling her otherwise. When Izzy's meeting began to break up, she tried to say her goodbyes to Jeff, to thank him, but he put up a hand and said, "I'm going where you are."

"You're going to Mrs. Watson's?"

"I'm walking you to her door, then I'm going home."

There was no refusing, and Adam could still be out there, waiting for her. She didn't imagine it: He'd been there, nearby, but, no stranger to panic, she may have filled in the rest of it, that is, how far Adam had been willing to go. How much trouble did he really want? And how much trouble did Jeff want as he walked with her into the night again? How much could he handle? She could smell him again and feel—against night air that was cool enough to be refreshing but not cold—his warmth, steady beside her. The quiet outside was still startling after so many weeks of wind: They could hear crickets, just a precious few, sounding on and off in the low bushes and trees along the sidewalk, and hear the rush of the city, but at a remove from where they were on Linden Place, and distant voices, echoing and unintelligible, comforting in their going about the business of sounding on and off too. That sweetness in the air, not just of flowers, but of a man walking a woman to a door.

"Do you have to report in every night?" he asked.

"Not every night," she said. "But many."

"Is it a chore?"

To admit that it was or could be was to pretend she had any say in her dealings with Mrs. Watson, so she told him about the parts that surprised her—that a few times they'd listened to the most extraordinary music together, or more recently watched a film, then another, shown in the screening room in the brownstone's finished basement, with food and wine served, and Mrs. Watson gasping through certain scenes of *The Verdict*—like when Paul Newman slaps the woman playing his lover—or *Notorious*—when Cary Grant rescues Ingrid Bergman from a house full of Nazis—insisting on replaying them as she had the opening of *Stabat Mater*, grabbing for Ruth's hand. On other nights when the meetings were brief, cursory, Ruth could go or use the library upstairs.

"You love to read?" he asked, and she could hear the smile in his voice before she saw it on his face.

"Of course. You?"

"Very much," he said.

So it was something he hoped for in others, just as Ruth did. He wasn't the kind of man who feared the richness of others, their intelligence or capacities, that he might be eclipsed by these things, though she could be filling in gaps again. Wishful thinking. How could it be helped on a night like this? Just as she couldn't help telling him about the library at 10 Linden Place—that every time she entered the room, every single time, she was overcome by a crazed feeling of gratitude at the care taken with it, that there were still places in private homes that valued books. Every book a passage to somewhere else, like the tunnels Izzy had described under St. Gabriel's floors, escape hatches each and every one. And that 10 Linden housed the books in a hardwood that told its own story, showing off grains and colors that wandered into yellow and amber, to red and back again, from the herringbone pattern in the polished floor to the shelves that extended to the third story with its slim catwalk, all the way up to the coffered ceiling with its rosettes and flèches and sunken square panels with recessed lights. The room had its own climate control, its own half bath, a long, yawning reading table at its center, and four well-worn leather armchairs with ottomans, silk pillows, cashmere throws.

"Out of another time," he said.

Outside time, she wanted to say, but didn't. She didn't want to mention time at all, because it was running out for them. Despite how slowly they'd walked, they were only steps from 10 Linden Place.

"Yes."

"Maybe it's like a kind of church—for you?" he asked.

"Maybe better."

"And your church?" she asked him. "Where is that?"

"I guess it's always been right here—" He stopped and put his arms out to the night—up to the sky, then out toward the lamplight and the trees.

"What kind of trees are these?" she asked, to detour her thoughts. "Are they lindens?"

"There's more than one kind. That's a linden there. Littleleaf linden. That one's a ginkgo. That over there is a honey locust. Down a little way—looks like another linden. Shall we go look?"

"I should go in—"

He didn't want her to, because he stood there, deciding whether to say more. "Maybe you'll show me that library sometime?"

"Maybe," she whispered, imagining whispering to him in the library, the two of them alone as she led him around that narrow catwalk, inviting him to drag his fingertips over each of the books' bindings. Of course, she knew it would never happen. She had no real rights once she was through those doors. "Goodnight," she said.

"I'll wait till you're inside."

Ruth had been given her own key, because Marie was generally gone by late evening. She climbed the stairs, fumbled with the key, and opened the door, only to run back to Jeff, take his hand, and press it to her face. "Thank you," she urged at him, "thank you," and then fled through both doors into the foyer, past the tolling of the chandelier to the sitting room. It wasn't only because Mrs. Watson was likely to be there at this hour, but because if she didn't keep running away from Jeff, she knew she would run back to him and press her mouth to his.

But she held herself at the room's threshold, not yet seen: Mrs. Watson wasn't alone. She was laughing, in a great jagged burst.

"I'm glad you can see the fun in it, Adele." Dr. Konradi's voice? Yes, it was Ed's. *Ed? Here?*

"I insist you tell me how you got Larry to do it." The jocularity in Mrs. Watson's voice was poor cover for the bitterness there. "To betray me?"

"I already told you, Adele: Who's to say that Larry played a part at all? There's no guarantee there. He lost his phone recently, though he recovered it the next day. You're pretty adept at surveillance, so you know the possibilities here are endless. A copy came to me, landed right in my lap, *unbidden*—"

"If you think I believe that, then you're a bigger fool than—"

Ed boomed through: "The point is, I have the recordings, Adele, and I can make them disappear. If Larry himself recorded them, he had a reason. Maybe he just wanted a memento—or five—of your time together? Or maybe he had other things in mind. Tell me, do you think he felt at all *coerced* by you? Exploited?"

"No! I am not discussing this with you! This is extortion! Solved by one call to the police. Don't you see how ludicrous this is? How dangerous? And I just heard Ruth come in. A witness to this intimidation. She's very devoted to me."

"Is she? Like Larry is? Does she know about you and Larry?"

"Tell me, if it were you, presented with the threat of exposure of something so *very* private, what would you do?"

"Not a good hypothetical, Adele. I have less to lose all around. But that's not what's happening here. No exposure necessary, or no more than this. I can handle it all for you, manage this into a big nothing. Larry likes me, and we can all laugh about it someday. I just want some consideration for my efforts. Not money. What I'd like concerns the clinic, as I've explained, which means the Doc. My friend. Yours. Protecting him—"

"From me? My God, you're a—"

"Yes, yes, *I know*: I'm a fool! A pig! Falstaff, is it?"

"That doesn't begin to cover it. This is *grotesque*. You. *Here*. And it's the same antique storyline, isn't it? Women are not allowed to express their desire, claim it, as men do, not without consequences. *Terrible* consequences."

"Ah, Adele, you are fully at your liberty there, I promise you. It's the stuff of my fantasies, frankly. If a man did what you did with a subordinate, like Larry? These days? He'd be laid to waste. You know that. C'mon, knock off the theater. It's not claiming desire that's objectionable here. It's claiming *people*, their lives, ripping the wheel right from their own hands."

"You sound like my son. Was he part of this too?"

Ed ignored the question. "I'm a good doctor, Adele. Why? Partly because I've discovered I'm especially good at helping people take firm hold of what they need—physically, spiritually, you name it. Desire? Sure, why not? I'm its biggest goddamned proponent. I've pried open any number of floodgates—"

"It's vile to think of—"

"I'm a healer."

"You're *nothing* of the kind. And you're not half the man the Doctor is!"

Ed laughed. "You think I don't know that? I've always known it. *Know your limitations and you're free*. I know mine, so I have a lot more license than he does. He's a moral man.

I'm not. You and I, Adele, I'd venture to say we're very much alike."

"You're flattering yourself. You must be high. To do this—"

"I'm sober as I know how to be, Adele. Clear as a bell to show you, and me too, frankly, the sincerity of my intentions. I admire you. I mean, look at this room! Just look! The glass and the stone. All of it erotic and expensive. A kind of dare. *You* are a dare, aren't you? Imagine if I came here with nothing in my hands? Nothing to bargain with? You'd have dismissed me without a second's—"

"Men! They claim to love women! Honor them! But it's other men they're looking to impress. All variety of tribalism in the world, but men aligning with men against women? That's a story that repeats endlessly!" Mrs. Watson huffed in and out, stepped back from an edge fraying in her voice. "Did you imagine I would just roll over here?"

"I wish you would."

"Do you think I can't harm you?"

"I *know* you can. And I'm guessing you'd enjoy it. But I'm willing to risk it for the Doctor, for his patients. I'm trying to gain him some rights in all this, for the man he needs to be. He's not been himself."

"It's that missing girl. He's lost all sense—"

"No, no, I don't think so, but it's telling, the way she's stuck in him: I think it's some kind of wish to break out."

"He doesn't know about this, these recordings?"

"Not from me, and I don't have to tell him."

"He wouldn't want this."

"Probably not. But like I said, men like him wreck themselves for other people—they believe in codes and right and wrong. So men like me, we sometimes have to do the dirty work."

"You've made a mistake here."

"I've made them before—"

"And imagine that I debated funding your marijuana research. Helping to rehabilitate you. I'll see you never practice medicine again."

"Let me say this again: All I'm asking, in exchange for my help here, to make this all go away, is to let the Doctor decide who he treats and how he treats them, who's barred from the clinic, whether it's Adam or anyone else—"

"Adam?! Is that what this is about? A thief?"

"Stop imposing so many conditions. Stop screwing with the man and his work—"

"You disgust me—"

"—otherwise I can't guarantee the recordings of your *sessions* won't get out there. That special music coming out of your mouth, Adele! The things you say. It's not just the usual fare, is it? Larry is a whole lot stouter than I thought—"

"Ruth! Ruth! Are you out there? Ruth! Come here!"

"This doesn't have to be adversarial. I'll keep your secrets, Adele. Keep them *close.* I'm on your side. Think of me as a fixer, your fixer—"

"*Ruth!*" A crack of lightning.

Ruth crossed into the room.

"There you are! Where have you been?"

"I was waiting, outside, down the hall. I didn't want to interrupt—"

"Interrupt?! I needed you! This so-called doctor here"—Mrs. Watson did not take her eyes from Ed; she cornered him with them—"he means to humiliate me. I want you to be my witness: time and date. So when I go to the authorities, it won't only be my word against his—"

Mrs. Watson and Ed were both standing now. Mrs. Watson's posture was hunched, all her limbs clenched, while Ed appeared shiny in a pressed dress shirt and chinos, enlivened by the showdown.

"Hello, Ruth. Not to worry. Adele—Mrs. Watson—is overstating things. Some information has come my way that could be problematic for all of you at the clinic. The whole enterprise. Adele's in shock, understandably upset—"

"Get out before I call the police. Get out—now."

"Ruth, will you be all right? Here?" Ed asked. "You've gone white as—"

"Ruth is in no danger, and she knows it."

"Ruth?" he queried with his eyes, moved them to the door and back, an invitation to go with him. She wished she'd never downloaded those recordings. She'd had nothing to do with Ed having them—she couldn't have—but did he know she had taken them? Had she left some trace of the transfer on Larry's phone? She hadn't listened to them—she couldn't bring herself to—but it was too late now to admit that, because she'd have to concede that she'd withheld this from her employer, and it could soon be a matter for the police.

She looked away from Ed, to the floor.

"We'll talk soon, Adele. Very soon. Goodnight, ladies."

They didn't move or speak as they listened to his unhurried steps, then the front doors clattering shut. Ruth put her hand to her cheek where Jeff's hand had just been.

"Please, Ruth, please get us something to drink... "

From bottles that were within reach on top of the liquor cabinet, Ruth grabbed for the Glen-something. Scottish. Twenty-four years old. She poured it into a highball glass, neat, and handed it to Mrs. Watson.

"Don't make me drink alone."

Ruth poured for herself.

"I'm having trouble breathing—the windows, the windows—"

Ruth shoved the layers of velvet curtains aside and pulled up the shades to get to the two double-hung windows at one end of the room, on the street side. A nearby streetlight, alert in what was now, at nearly nine o'clock, fully night, cast into the room, and that cool air, once the windows were open, sighed through the screens.

Ruth took her glass, assumed her post across the table from her employer, on that petrified chair, and watched Mrs. Watson empty her glass. She could see, in the soft light from the metalwork lamp on the sofa's side table, that Mrs. Watson's face was hard-drawn with tension. She lifted her sharp chin and pushed it out, in a kind of defiant pout.

"He said he had some information?" Ruth ventured. "What was he talking about?" The thinness of her voice, made thinner by the lie in it.

Mrs. Watson either didn't hear or ignored the question. "I need leverage, Ruth. Now more than ever. Whatever I can get, and *quickly*. Are you up to helping me? If you're not, you must tell me. I can't be disappointed. Not now." A whine in her voice: "I just *can't* be disappointed anymore."

Ruth started to say, "Of course. Whatever you—" but wasn't able to finish, because Mrs. Watson looked up with eyes round and flaring green and threw her glass across the room with a shriek that finished with glass shattering against walnut paneling.

"I'm sorry," Mrs. Watson said after several moments in which all Ruth could hear was her own rabbit pulse. "I scared you... It's that I can't bear it, you see, can't let it happen, to be made a joke of."

Mrs. Watson curled herself into the sofa, tucked her head into its corner, as if to hide. "*You* talk, Ruth. Speak, about anything."

"I came to tell you about tonight, but you've probably had enough—"

She turned to look at Ruth. "I'll decide when I've had enough."

"Izzy was at the clinic tonight, for group. Asking patients to sign a petition to designate St. Gabriel's a historical landmark. She brought friends, former patients—"

"And they signed?"

"Most of them."

"And you? You signed it?"

"No, not me."

"Why not, Ruth?"

Mrs. Watson would make her tell her. Not just act her part, but speak the lines so both women could hear them.

"Because it wasn't appropriate. Because I work for you."

"And the Doctor? Was he there?"

"He passed through but didn't stop." It was as if he wasn't all there, like he was giving a good imitation of himself.

"He signed?"

"Not that I saw."

"Isabelle! Dear Lord, *Isabelle*... She played our father's pet. That's how he thought of her. But me? I made him see me as an equal. He taught me not to back down. 'Never be anyone's victim,' he told me. Not particularly original from a father to a daughter, is it? But, you see, I began by refusing to be *his* victim, my father's. His moods—how he used his disapproval like a hammer poised right over your head. He resented me for it at times, but he respected me. Of course, he made me the executor of his estate—not my stepmother, and certainly not my half sister. What an utter disaster that would have been! Taking care of the whole world's needs, and ghosts, too. A dead Irish architect! *Dear God!* My father left her money, but she gives, what, half of it away? I'd venture to say *at least* half. In love with a gay man all these years. Was he there? Richard? Looking like a yacht-club gigolo?"

"Yes."

"Of course. An alcoholic. She collects causes. Pets of her own. She thinks Orson a cause, *my* son—"

Twice the son, Ruth remembered Orson saying to her on their first meeting. He'd have to be, or try—

"—and though he's a grown man, or should be by now, he's happy to let her take him in. I assume he was there?"

"Only at the end."

"Of course. Well, the two of them I can handle. The law's on my side there, too. She can collect all the signatures she wants. Let her. I have this new *matter* to contend with. They say if you want to make peace with your enemies, work with them. Who said that? Mandela? I can't recall, can you?"

Ruth shook her head, drank her whisky. It was stronger than she'd suspected. Her eyes watered.

"You give the appearance of it, anyway, working together. In this age of ours, more than most, it's about what you *appear* to be doing. No one knows what's in your heart—if you're really capitulating—do they? Or changing course at all?"

"No."

"Ruth"—Mrs. Watson sat up and leaned toward her—"I am going to need more than that journal now, do you see? I'm going to need *anything* you can find for me, including things that might implicate others, Dr. Konradi included. Anything out of the ordinary. Anything that can persuade him to keep the course—"

"I'm sorry, persuade who?"

"The Doctor. He is so very crucial to the clinic's success."

"Yes."

"Have more whisky, Ruth. I startled you. And get me another."

She poured for both of them.

"Sit beside me."

Ruth hadn't eaten enough that day, only what was on offer at the clinic's kitchen, and she'd had beer that evening—two beers, to calm her down, though it was really Jeff who'd done that for her. And now the whisky, to which she was not accustomed. Her mind softened and hummed with its own imperatives: The weather was to change again; she wanted to rest, to get home and rest and get off this ride, but she had to concentrate on what Mrs. Watson was saying there beside her on the sofa, something about the horrible timing: "That vile swamp animal coming here now when there's news of the girl. My detective says she's been spotted in Vermont, near Bennington. *Vermont!* That can't be an accident—her going there, where Louis grew up, and hiding out all this time—"

Mrs. Watson's commentary slowed; her sentences began but did not finish. A few syllables dropped off.

Was it true? Sarah in Vermont? Or was it just another manipulation? More theater, and for whom? And was Ed pretending? Of course he'd put Larry up to the recordings. Who else had that kind of nose for something so untoward?

"A storm is coming, they say, a bad one," Ruth struggled to put in, judging that they were two women commiserating now, side by side again, allies. The timing so horrible; these things that kept coming.

But Mrs. Watson turned toward her abruptly, wide awake as a bell just rung, and scolded: "A storm is always coming, Ruth. *Always.* You have to be equal to it. Don't you understand that by now? *Can't* you?"

Part IV

Blow, winds, and crack your cheeks! rage! blow!
You cataracts and hurricanoes, spout
Till you have drench'd our steeples, drown'd the cocks!

—Shakespeare, *King Lear*

The wind is a horse:
hear how he runs
through the sea, through the sky.

He wants to take me: listen
how he roves the world
to take me far away.

Hide me in your arms
just for this night,
while the rain breaks against sea and earth
its innumerable mouth.

—Pablo Neruda,
"Wind on the Island"

The Doctor

The air hadn't changed yet, and the sun carried on scouring everything it could, but TV and computer screens showed images of weather that if it made its way up to the mid-Atlantic would twist the city, heave the waters up around it, fill its underground lungs. There was near-constant chatter in the clinic about what would or would not happen, and when, whether to stay or go, and go where. It was fed by the weather apps, streaming broadcasts and podcasts, and social media posts multiplying. But with nothing but untroubled blue sky overhead, it all had the feel of a game.

In a follow-up appointment, it was young Gus who assured the Doctor that the malfunctioning weather satellites in the news were no big deal. He talked excitedly about new weather drones out there, and especially the manned weather planes, "the Lockheed WC-130, up there *right* now. They fly *right* into the eye."

Gus and his mother had been trying the Doctor's new pills.

"What's in them exactly?" Lydia asked. The Doctor talked in generalities of crucial supplements, minerals like magnesium, mentioned an herb that had benefited her before, and a mild analgesic, without confirming a thing. Of Gus's pill, he said, with a smile, that he'd expressly put some joy into it, "to go along with the fun he should be having."

The boy hadn't had a headache that one of the Doctor's white pills, a glass of water, and closing his eyes for a little while hadn't resolved, and Lydia, having started getting the weekly massages prescribed for her with either Larry or Jill, along with the blue pills taken up to three times daily, hadn't had anything but mild attacks. "I almost can't believe it," she said.

Neither could Jane. "I'm better," she said, and threw her hands up. Along with the silver-flecked yellow pills he'd given her, she'd been doing biofeedback and meditation regularly, as she'd promised him. "But it can't last, right? With this body? And this weather? You and I know that, right, Doctor?"

"Do we?" the Doctor asked.

Jane looked as rested and robust as the Doctor had ever seen her. Her eyes and skin were clear. She may have gained weight.

Jeff came in worried for his trees. He didn't know how he'd protect them from the weather coming up the coast, or his own head from the distress growing there. He'd heard about the personalized medicines from Ruth, though the Doctor had excluded her from the actual prescribing and follow-up appointments, for the sake of the confidence established, the agreement made between patient and doctor. Ruth didn't complain, though she still hovered much too much by his door.

Lately she was there when he shut it and there when he opened it again.

That very afternoon, as the Doctor was finishing up his pitch to Jeff, asking him to commit to constructive habits to help the new treatment along, the phone rang. It was five o'clock or thereabouts. Sue sent it through. The Doctor didn't pick up. He and Jeff were in the middle of a handshake, making their pact. Sue's voice suddenly erupted on the intercom: "Sorry, Doctor. It's Mrs. Watson. She says she needs you."

"Tell her I'll call her right back. I'm with a patient."

"I told her that already."

"Tell her again."

Sue breathed at him, stayed on the line, refusing without saying a word.

"Put her on hold then."

When Jeff left his office with his portion of pills, Ruth was posted only feet from his now open door, a look of worried anticipation on her face. It was likely Adele had contacted her too. He knew she often called or texted Ruth when she didn't get the response she wanted from the Doctor or Sue.

He didn't shut his door when he returned to the phone. Why bother?

"I'm unwell," Adele complained. "And, worse, I'm out of the loop, Louis. Did you mean to keep your latest advances from me?"

"I was waiting to see if the approach had any effect, if it was doing anyone any good."

Ruth held her position, appearing to read through some notes in her blue notebook.

"What time should I expect you tonight?" Adele asked.

"I have more patients to see, some paperwork," he said.

"How many?"

"Two or three."

"You'll be busy until roughly seven o'clock, then?"

"Seven or just about," he confirmed, loud enough for Ruth to hear.

"Then you'll come here?"

"Seven o'clock it is, Adele."

Only then did he shut his door against Ruth's watching and waiting.

"Bring some of those pills for me. After all, I'm your patient, too. Don't I suffer?"

Ruth

The light in the Doctor's Brooklyn Heights apartment was brackish. Ruth's eyes were surfeited with the bright day, and the blinds were drawn down over the half-open windows. When two of the blinds caught a fluffing current, one then the other, she started and nearly ran back out to the street. But she waited until the blinds settled and the daylight again etched stark seams around them. She didn't put on the light, not yet. When she got Mrs. Watson's text, confirming that the Doctor would be tied up and then visiting at 10 Linden until well into the evening, and that Ruth should go, ASAP, with the keys provided, she had felt nauseated, weak in her legs. Yet there was also a kind of inescapable momentum building in Ruth and, she sensed, in everyone around her, as if the approaching storm, a hurricane, was already inside all of them, stirring, before it had even made landfall.

Less than an hour ago, she'd resolved to tell the Doctor how far Mrs. Watson was asking her to go. She'd waited by his door to do just that, because Mrs. Watson wouldn't stop. Of course, Ruth had kept her apprised of Orson's latest activities, how frequently he'd been in and out of the clinic, studiously avoiding Ruth. She'd told Mrs. Watson that deliveries arrived, box after box, not in his name but in his mother's—as if daring her to interfere. One item was as big as a refrigerator—a backup generator, Sue explained to Ruth, just in case.

But Mrs. Watson didn't care, or for only so long. Her focus scattered and reassembled around Ed, the Doctor, and Larry, all while the storm moved closer. It was forecast to hit Maryland, then Delaware, then New Jersey. It was a Category 3, then 2, then 3 again. Mrs. Watson was poised to fire Larry, call the police, and have Ed hauled off, then she retreated. She needed more information—who was involved, who had put whom up to what. "Let them think they've won, let that son of a bitch get cocky," she said.

At the Doctor's apartment Ruth was to look for whatever she could find there, "to better assess the terrain, something to tell us of the Doctor's loyalties, his state of mind. Yes, Ruth?"

Ruth said yes when she meant no, or did mean it until, while waiting by the Doctor's door, she heard Ed's voice swell toward her: "Not to worry, Sue! The Lady Adele knows all about it. I spoke to her myself. It's all on the up-and-up. Adam's come to make amends."

Ruth tried to step back out of seeing but was too late.

"Oh, Ruth, so glad you're here. Adam's back," Ed said with a wink. He didn't reference their meeting at Mrs. Watson's—he didn't have to—only that Adam wanted a word. "Do you have a sec for a little contrition before the flood? A little mea culpa before the apocalypsis—"

Before she could say no, Adam loomed behind them and Ed set off down one of the halls to the treatment rooms, in search of more staff.

Adam stepped in to bend close to her ear, so that only she'd hear what he had to say: "I went for you for no good reason but that you're new here. But I don't know you, you know? And you don't know me."

They weren't alone. Where Ruth stood near the Doctor's closed door was just off the far edge of the lounge—in it were Gus and Lydia and a schoolteacher whose name Ruth couldn't recall. She hoped they would look her way.

"I'm sorry I did that. I just wanted to tell you. I tried—on the street. A few times. I tried to talk to you. To tell you it wasn't fair. I'm fucked up sometimes—I mean, what I think is *fucked up*."

"I understand," she said, and she did, better than he could know. She couldn't think what else to say and didn't have to, because Ed emerged from the hall with Larry. Close behind was Alla, rosy from a massage, then Sally, the nutritionist.

Ed had the air of a man who was fresh from a win. Maybe he was, but what Ruth felt, concretely and absolutely, was that she had to get out of there, and quickly.

"I didn't take your phone, man," Adam called to Larry.

Ruth wanted to tell them she was the one who took it, and she *would* tell them if she didn't leave them as soon as she could. She'd show them all just how fucked up *she* could be. No better—and maybe worse—than Adam, who'd at least had the courage to come clean to them. She didn't belong there, and she didn't deserve his apologies.

"Ruth, Ruth, please, join us here for a moment," Ed directed. She did join them, but once Adam and Ed had said all they could, cleared what air they could, she made the excuse of having to meet someone.

"So glad to have you back, Adam," she put in before leaving them at just before five.

Besides some noise echoing from outside, voices rising, cars accelerating, there was a heavy silence in the Doctor's apartment. There was a smell of antiques in the room, coming from objects that had known damp and dry, been through heat and cold. The silence struck her as antique too, belonging to a place where a secret or secrets could be kept, and for as long as they needed. To open the blinds seemed too impolite: In the past few days, it had been hotter than it had been in weeks, and the Doctor had taken what precautions he could against it. She found a switch beside the door to an overhead light and snapped it on to see furniture better suited to an old New England home, or a bed-and-breakfast. It was another century's country elegant, shapely and heavy.

There wasn't much of it: a couch of blue wool fabric with a wooden frame and arms, a coffee table, two chairs. A small flat-screen TV was consigned to a corner.

And there were precious few things hung on the walls, no sign of the personal life of the man who lived here—no pillow on the couch having conformed to the shape of his head, no book or magazine left open on a table. There were no dishes or glasses in the sink or crumbs on the kitchen counter, which was really just an island with stools that divided the rest of the large living room from an open kitchen area. He hadn't settled in here, hadn't let himself. Or maybe he simply wasn't there enough to achieve that.

She moved closer to a photograph hung between the first two of three windows in the room—it was another image of the wagon on the hill belonging to that series of photos in the entryway to the clinic, except that it was in full color, showing September maybe, green foliage beginning to give way to yellows. Between the next two windows was a trim watercolor of a picturesque white farmhouse with green shutters, framed with some care, in a distressed gilt. His family home? Under the painting and the photograph were bookcases. In one, the top shelf was dedicated to works by the neurologist Oliver Sacks, whom the Doctor was given to quoting; a couple of titles by another physician, Lewis Thomas; a Norton's critical edition of Darwin's *On the Origin of Species*; and just one novel, George Eliot's *Middlemarch*. When she ran her fingers over these books, there was practically no dust on any of them, unlike those shelved below.

She planned not only to look at as many of the books as she could, but to look through them, to see any notations or what might fall out. She wanted to know all she could of him now that she was there—the thrill of the trespass urging her on—to draw out every fragment of what he kept hidden, in drawers, a bureau or desk somewhere, a closet, and in the next room, the bedroom on the other end of the long rectangle of this apartment. It was even darker in that room, the shades drawn over its two windows. She made out a large bed with a wooden frame, a bureau, a rocking chair with something stacked tall in it, laundry, or bedding maybe, and, in a corner, what she took for a small desk.

When she reached for the light switch to turn it on, nothing happened. She tried again.

"That light needs a new bulb," a voice said to her. A man's. "There's a lamp here. Let me turn it on for you." A soft yellow light filled the room. "Does that help, Ruth? Can you see now?"

That bedding in the rocking chair was not bedding at all. It was the Doctor, arms crossed over his chest, a pillow on his lap.

"Doctor—" Her voice faltering, small. "I'm sorry, I knocked. I—"

He waited for her to say more, but she couldn't. She couldn't lie to him. In the lamp's light, she saw there was a baseball bat leaning against the wall next to him. Maybe he saw her see it. Maybe he didn't. She couldn't look at him. And just as the heat in the apartment gained with his silence and seemed suddenly unbearable to Ruth, he stood up, said, "Let's go."

In the living room he motioned for her to sit on one of the wooden chairs. He lowered himself onto the far end of his couch. Its proportions were not right for such a tall, straight man. It was as if he were sitting in someone else's living room.

"How did you know?" she asked first, from all the questions proliferating with her ragged pulse. "That I'd come?"

"I guessed. The look on your face. Adele's call. And something in the air, too. I slipped out when you were all in the lounge greeting Adam. I imagine you know something about that, about his return?"

"Yes."

"And I gather you read the journal in my office? Sarah's. Do I have that right, Ruth?"

"Yes." And when he didn't speak, she added, "Not *all* of it."

Inside her, things moved as if in those winds she knew when she first came to the city, everything tossing. She sat on her hands so he wouldn't see them shake. He could marshal great calm and was using it now, thinking, making decisions. He held her at a cliff's edge with his silence. Time was not the same thing to either of them now, in that room.

"Are you going to call the police?"

"You know the answer to that, don't you?"

She could see him sleeping next to her again, keeping her company in the clinic the night of the heavy rains, how he'd arranged her hairpins in a little pile for her. He'd caught her in her first transgression then. But she had to remember she didn't know him well, and she'd been bitterly wrong in her character judgments before.

"Will you insist that I be let go?"

"Do you want something to drink? Water? I think that's all I have here."

"No."

The muddy half-light of his living room, its quiet and *his*, and the heat all squeezed at her lungs now, while the day rattled lightly at the blinds, wanting to come in.

"I… I wouldn't blame you if you did. I *am* sorry. I—"

He got up. He stood miles above her, it seemed. She expected he would yell at her at last, then she worried that he would simply open the door and ask her to go, with no more said. She imagined him doing it, and her legs went waxy and weak. Instead he opened the blind farthest from them and opened that window wider. Then did the same with the next window. The room expanded and surrendered details—the honey in the wood floors, the cinnamon in the wood furniture, a bumpiness in the old plaster on the walls, the dust swirling in the column of light now coming in at the other end of the room. An antique trunk there, at that end, that she'd not seen at first, and a photo, too, that had been in shadow on one of the bookshelves, nearer that window, of a woman and a boy, all long limbs, both of them with that same deep-set, haunted look around the eyes.

"She asked you to do this? Adele? She gave you keys to the building, my apartment?" he asked as he reseated himself.

Ruth nodded.

"Why?"

He had to know why.

"She thinks she's at war. Has to be ready—"

"*War?*" A roar in the word. "*War?* With who? Me?"

"Yes, sort of." She got up the nerve to say, without looking at him, "She's in love with you. You must know that."

"She's persuaded herself to it. I am her doctor, a business partner—no other kind."

"We see what we want to see. You said that to me."

"I said we see things, Ruth, not as they are but as *we* are, but that was about pain—"

"But it's the same thing with love, isn't it?"

He sighed. "Maybe."

It moved her how he did this—considered other points of view. Especially now. This generosity of his. Even as his patience was being so sorely tested.

"We are *fooled*," he spat at Ruth, and then composed his voice to continue, "over and over, and *want* to be. We want to be *in* love, inside that feeling, all the possibilities and sensations it tempts us with, the *high* of it. To start. Up here." He tapped the top of his forehead. "But the work of love—the effort, the tedium? The compromise? No. We don't want that."

He sighed again, this time caving in with it, like a man who'd heard the same story too many times, about a problem with no solution.

"Adele sees," he went on, "exactly what she wants to see and no more. Is that what you mean, then—a war of perspectives, a war of wills?"

"Someone is threatening her, she says," Ruth explained. "And she's protecting herself. She thinks she's protecting you, too."

"*Who* is threatening her?"

"I shouldn't say."

"I've caught you here red-handed, Ruth, and you *won't* say?"

"It's that I don't really know the whole story, Doctor, and it's not my business—"

"I expected you to say to me you had no choice, that you *had* to do this, come here, to my home. That Adele forced you."

"I had a choice—*choices*. It's just that none of them are pleasant, really, and I wanted—" She stopped herself.

"Wanted *what*?" he asked, his head snapping in her direction. A signal of the impatience he was trying to master. "Wanted *what*, Ruth?"

That deranging smallness that she'd known so much in this city found her again. She was a bit player in all this. She never meant to change the course of anything. She wrapped her arms around herself. If she could just stop talking.

"This is all my parents' old furniture," he told her, after a time, "made from trees that my father brought down—old or sick or inconvenient trees. My dad knew lots of woodworkers, carpenters. This table is red elm, hard elm. Its texture is very distinctive. Those chairs are oak, the frame of this couch is pine. The old trunk over there is pine, too, I think. My wife took all our good furniture when we separated. I was home in Vermont not long after, and my father was ready to get rid of this, so I took it. Funny old stuff. Not comfortable at all, is it?"

Ruth's phone buzzed like an angry wasp in her bag. It made her jump, her heart too, as if up her throat.

"Is that her? Adele?" he asked.

"Probably. She's expecting you to come to her—"

"I didn't have any more appointments tonight. I left so I could get here first. I asked Chaudhri to go to her in my place."

"That will upset her."

"Yes, I imagine it will." He snorted. "*Imagine* the theatrics." A gleeful vengefulness in his voice briefly, then gone. "Yes, well, we're both her creatures, Ruth."

"It's not the same, Doctor. You know that. She needs you"—Ruth barely suppressed the whine in her voice—"you're indispensable. And, then, you know it's more than that."

"Evidently, Ruth, she needs you too. For some things. Breaking and entering?"

She didn't argue with him.

"But I made my own bargain with her, so I could treat my patients any way I deem necessary. That's the idea. The deal. Otherwise I'd probably be angrier."

Ruth deserved more of his anger; she deserved what was coming to her.

"And what is it that you want, Ruth? From Adele? A job? Income? You could have all that elsewhere."

"Not as easy as you think, given my past. At the hospital, I was let go. She's willing to pay—pay *a lot*. I really need the money." She could hear her desperation and was as disdainful of it as she imagined he was. He waited for her to continue. She tried hard not to, but she was speaking already: "And, then, as you must know, she's got this vantage on things. She talks about life, all the reversals, upsets, disappointments, failures, like they're, I don't know, something bigger, like it's all art or music. As beautiful somehow as it is ugly. And she can step back and appraise it—"

"So you're saying you admire her?"

"We listen to music. We drink wine. She's this small woman who seems, like, *immense*—I've just never really met anyone like her, with that kind of will. It's like she's daring someone, or life—yeah, maybe life itself—to knock her down."

"You do admire her, then. And you want to *please* her?"

"Things have happened in my life. She knows, if not everything, then *a lot*. She knows I'm on my own. I don't have many friends out there anymore. And I know things about her. I think I understand why she has to be who she is, like it's all clay in her hands. But she's not the only reason why I came here today."

She looked into those deeply socketed eyes of his, and he looked at her as he always did, as if he could see inside her to how pathetic it all was.

"Is that your mother there in the photo?" she asked.

"Yes. She had migraines. I can't remember if I told you that… She wanted me to be near her. Often. And I was. On hand. My father was always working, so I had to be."

That was where it began, then, for him, Ruth decided. The subduing of himself, the waiting on others. The patience. So very young.

"How is she now?"

"Dead. A stroke. When I was in college—"

"I'm sorry."

"You should go, Ruth. If you have nothing else to tell me. And I'll take those keys, please."

Leave and go where? How would she explain what had happened here to Mrs. Watson? Her every word seemed to dissolve in her mouth as she tried to speak, betraying her panic, but she had to get them out. "I came in part because I'd like to read the rest of the journal. I want to know what happened to her, to Sarah."

If he considered this, he didn't show it. Only said, "The keys? Can I have them, please?"

She got up to hand them to him.

"I tried to hire a locksmith," he said, "but the guy I called, he's leaving the city. The storm."

"Will you leave too?" Ruth asked.

"Doubtful."

He looked past her, maybe to the window. He was managing his disgust.

"If you want my help in any form, you have to tell me what I need to know, Ruth, so that I know what to do here. About Adele. And you, too. I don't have to tell you, do I? That you shouldn't be in this situation? That none of us should? That it's not productive? Not *right*?"

She shook, then nodded, her head. No, then yes.

"Ruth," he pressed.

So, sitting back down on the edge of the chair, she told him. Told him it was his friend Doctor Konradi, Ed, who had come across some information about Mrs. Watson and her massage therapist Larry that would embarrass her if it got out into the world. Ed offered to prevent that. When the Doctor asked her what Ed hoped to achieve by this, she told him Dr. Konradi seemed to be doing this for the Doctor, as an exchange, to give him more freedom and control in the practice, to bring Adam back into the clinic just as the Doctor had hoped. And it had worked—so far—hadn't it?

The Doctor gave another of his sad, emptying sighs, saying to no one in particular, "This all would have remedied itself in time. That's all that was needed here—time."

"And the pills, she knows about them, too, that you seem to be having some success there. What's in them, Doctor? They seem to be miraculous—"

"That's not how this works, Ruth. I ask, you answer. Tell me what happened at the hospital up north—why exactly were you let go?"

"It wasn't just one thing. I mean, it *was*, on paper. There was a child, a preemie, a boy. The mother wouldn't touch the child. Wouldn't hold him. I knew the mother a little before she got pregnant. My husband's cousin; she was at our wedding." Alysia, a bone-thin brunette, barely twenty, who smoked and drank through her pregnancy. "I just wanted to help—"

Ruth heard herself making excuses. She couldn't help it: They ran like a current in her, along with the self-pity. It began long before that day in the NICU. She had to explain, but her tears, coming too, were making it hard. She'd been valued at the hospital for years. She was a good nurse. Among the best they had. She was, wasn't she? Then her husband, so altered, kept showing up, looking for her, seething, snatching at her. It began to poison the very air around her. Such gossip in hospitals. There were bruises, too—on her skin, her arms, her neck, for everyone to see. Why didn't she just leave him? A question that hung in the poison air she breathed at the hospital and everywhere else. One thing could not have happened without the other—the violence.

Only five minutes sooner and she would have made it out of their house in Seabrook. She *was* leaving her husband, this time for good. Nathaniel came at her, rushing up the stairs at midday, when he'd usually be working: "Where do you think you're going?" She wasn't going to run from him ever again. Not cower. "Cunt. You spoiled fucking cunt." With her arms out, she pushed, her palms impacting his chest. He didn't expect it, didn't brace himself. She ran at him and pushed through him and he flew up and back and away, and she almost went with him—*almost*. She grabbed the banister just in time, but, *oh, God,* the room spun, the hall with its long stairwell, Nathaniel a heap at the bottom of it: *traumatic brain injury*.

She explained that for a time everyone told her she was heroic. A fighter. A survivor. There was a consensus. Those were the words used for that consensus. And *lucky*—she'd been lucky. For a time, she had the support of even her husband's family—Alysia, that young cousin, too, with whom Nathaniel was never really close. But when he recovered from his wounds, though not from the changes to his brain, Nathaniel, vacant and mild-mannered now and confused sometimes to tears, started walking the streets, like a bum; and when people began pitying him, she became the brute, not him. They could see it with their own eyes now, though it had taken at least a year to see it and for the whispers to turn into a kind of corrosive hiss.

She decided to work harder, to know better, be better. The Doctor understood that, didn't he? At the hospital she would be the very best she could be, as courageous as she could be, as she'd once failed to be by not leaving her husband sooner, and so she had dared to take another woman's baby in her arms, and not just that: take the child to her body, undoing buttons, one, then two, for that vital skin-to-skin contact, when the mother refused to, was afraid to, to touch so fragile and unformed a life, so easy to break. Ruth could still feel that windup-squirrel pulse against her. She was protecting the tiny creature as no one had protected her. And when the baby later died from respiratory failure, barely two weeks after Ruth had tried to warm him against her chest, someone had to be blamed, and Ruth was overdue, along with the doctor on call in the ward. She had nothing to do with what killed the child, but there was video of her holding the child to her heart as a mother might. And she was no mother, was she? *Bitch, murderer, whore.*

The Doctor

Once Ruth had confessed all she could, he sat listening to her sniffle and her phone humming at intervals and remembered the night at the pier, suspending the notebook over the water. He'd bent to ease it down to the river, his arm between the railings, his head nearly against it. On that railing were inscribed lines from Whitman's "Crossing Brooklyn Ferry," addressing the "countless crowds of passengers" who had crossed, would cross, pulling the view out so wide to stretch outside Whitman's time—all time, in fact—the tides of human coming and going always moving, uncentering each one of us from ourselves alone. As if we could be *un*-self-centered—if only the Doctor could—by simply letting go.

He got up and went to the bedroom. His bag was on the floor by the chair he'd been sitting in when Ruth came in, and next to it was the old baseball bat his uncle Kenneth had made for him. Mixed wood. He'd been good at baseball in high school and enjoyed the feeling of his team counting on him, something he'd found again with his patients.

Ruth's eyes were round and wet when he returned to her. She was ready to run from him. He half-hoped she would.

"Take it." He handed the journal to her.

"Take it?" she repeated. Stunned. Her nose was running.

"Finish it. Keep it safe."

"*Safe?*"

"I made a promise not to share it with anyone—"

"To Sarah?"

"Yes, I thought so. The woman who brought it to me, she made me promise for Sarah. Sarah writes about her. At the end—you'll see. That's why I never shared the notebook with the police. It was wrong of me. But I wasn't able to keep that promise anyway, was I? But maybe it has things to say to you and you alone, Ruth. Benefits to you. Her experience. I've taken all I can from it—"

"No, *please*, don't give it to me. *Don't*—I'll read it here and leave it here, *with you*."

"No, Ruth. Tell Adele I destroyed it. I nearly did, but I couldn't. Please."

Apparently Ruth didn't trust herself with it, but the Doctor knew she had to. She had to be brave, not for Adele or him but for herself. Didn't she know she was more than a tale of woe to be confessed and by which to be excused?

"I should have explained: I *copied* some pages for Mrs. Watson. I hesitated to hand them over—I did, really—but when I did give what I had to her, she told me she'd already read it. I don't know if it's true or how much she read, but she knew what was in the journal even before I did."

He looked at her to see if she was telling the truth. She nodded emphatically. Panic as well as apology on her face.

"When? How long ago?" he asked, marveling.

But before Ruth could answer him, something tickled inside him. What? The realization of the absurdity? He let out one laugh and then another and couldn't stop them coming, bulging up out of him. His knees went rubbery and he dropped back onto the couch. How ridiculous it was! How ridiculous *he* was, his reverence for his oath, to keep *the secrets confided in me*. The solemnity with which he'd protected this book. Its skin like his skin. Sarah's. He'd absorbed every word, written to him—*for* him, him alone, he thought—knew them by heart, tortured himself with his own failure, his desire, when *nothing* could be kept private, *nothing* sacred.

"My God!" he shrieked. "Why?!"

"She seems to see Sarah as a kind of rival for your attention." He saw that one side of Ruth's mouth formed a slight smile. She wasn't sure whether she had permission to find any of this as funny as he did. "She says what Sarah wrote has become an obsession for you, that you're too distracted from the work?"

The Doctor laughed into his hands, his back shook, his head too. It hurt. The anger there. The disbelief.

"Are you all right?" she asked him. "Doctor?"

He wanted to slap her as hard as he could. Slap her for her weakness, for his. But in the state he was in, those blows became, in his mind's eye, something comic, like staged Three Stooges slaps, cracking in the air, useless as they were exaggerated, for an audience, always watching. Insatiable.

"What a goddamned mess!" He struggled to recover himself. "It's like a baton in some *fucking* race! This is a woman's life! Her pain! All I have ever wanted is to do my duty as a doctor. To be practically invisible as a man, so I could help—"

"But you're not! You're *not* invisible. *Nothing* about you is," she gushed. "*No one* thinks that. They all think you're a hero—Dr. Konradi, Mrs. Watson, your staff. Sarah did, too, didn't she? That's why she wrote this to you?"

"A hero?! In these days? These *faithless* days? In this *godforsaken* place? Me? You know *nothing* about me or what I've done." This made him laugh again, but through a sneer. For weeks now he'd been waiting for the police to come for him for beating a man. The Doctor didn't regret it. He'd do it again, wouldn't he? Each and every one of them so trapped in smallness.

"And you, Ruth? Why should you know all this about me? Why should Adele?"

She stood up and inched around the back of her chair.

"And why on earth should Adele share it with you? *Any* of it? You two making a meal out of me? As what? Some kind of *entertainment*? *I'm* obsessed? *I'm* the one? Why do *you* have the right—who are you, Ruth, to *say* these things to me, to be here now *in my home*? Who are *you*?"

"I'm sorry, Doctor. I'm not a part of this. I shouldn't be. Like you said I—" She started backing up, toward the door.

"But you *are* a part of it now, aren't you? You broke into my home! My God! No more excuses! No more fucking apologies! Not one fucking more—"

He slammed his hand on the coffee table, then he crossed the distance to her in no time, a few inches away, and stood over her, deciding. It would have been easy to take her by the neck and shake her. Instead he shoved the journal into her hands, with a force he dared her to counter.

"Why not take this to her, then? Your boss? Finish the job, Ruth. You are at least a competent spy, an able messenger, aren't you? *At least that?* Now get the hell away from me, do you understand? And from my patients. *Far* away! Don't come back. Never let me lay eyes on you again. Never again!"

Ruth

She wasn't running, not yet, but already she couldn't catch her breath. Cars everywhere around her inching, honking to hurry, but stuck in the swell, many with their belongings tied to their roofs. All the taxis she saw were filled with passengers. It was a Friday, but that wasn't it. It was the storm, chasing them. She'd forgotten about it.

In her bag was her phone from her other life, with its New Hampshire number, carried like a dead thing. Muted. The phone given to her by Mrs. Watson, however, was alive, expectant with message after message waiting on Ruth for a reply. From this phone Ruth texted, "He was there. Waiting for me. He knows."

There was no reply, or none that came quickly enough when she needed to get away from the glare here—from the sun, still shining into evening, and the agitation, the terrible urge to flee the city, its noise and worry.

She typed another text: "I can't do this anymore, forgive me." Then she deleted the last two words, letter by letter. It wasn't Mrs. Watson's forgiveness she needed most. *No more fucking apologies.*

She sent the message and turned off that phone. Her hands shook as she did. She would throw it away, but she didn't have the strength. Not yet. Only to go home, or what passed for home now, her apartment. She ran then, and kept running.

The Wind Report

"The power in this kind of storm? Let me put it this way, Thomas: Compared to a hurricane, an atom bomb is puny, like a firecracker on the Fourth of July. A hurricane is a lot closer to an H-bomb, a thermonuclear bomb, but one that goes off, say, every sixty seconds—"

And what kind of explosion are we looking at here with this hurricane, Professor Freeman? Beatrice, they're calling it—

"Beatrice was moving at twenty miles per hour, then thirty, then, as recently as an hour ago, forty and climbing. It's clocked about two thousand miles to get to the East Coast, drawing fuel along the way from the warmer air and water to the south. That bone-chilling cold you feel when you swim in the North Atlantic? That's a gift. It's protection. It usually slows these storms, but this one is compact. It's coiled, and it got around this mass of dense, dry air that usually—"

The Bermuda high?

"Yes, very good, Thomas—the Bermuda high is legendary in its own right. A wall of dry air that pushes storms out to sea, but not this time. And there are other factors, too: There's a strong upper trough on the other side, from the west, also pulling it north. And then the global winds aren't in our favor: The jet stream's not playing its part to break up those strong upper winds. It's weak. It's pretty unlikely we'll see a Category 5 or even 4 in the Northeast, but not impossible. No one can say it's impossible. And we're seeing another front that's forming off the coast here, pretty unstable. It's come in with this heat. Beatrice might meet up with it en route. I'm worried about that, frankly—that Beatrice might absorb it. That guarantees more energy. But I can't say for sure. Time will tell."

We're getting lots of calls. You're something of a celebrity among weather watchers. And the oddsmakers? I had no idea people bet on the weather.

"It's a pure bet, Thomas. Can't be rigged—not like sports."

Or an election?

"Sure."

We're going to take one of those calls now, from Seline. Hello, Seline, you're on the air with Professor Alistair Freeman.

"Hello? Yes. Thank you. I am on with you?"

Yes, go ahead, Seline.

"I am new to this country. I lived here only a year, in Arkansas, now New York City. I am from the Marshall Islands. Do you know about my home, Professor?"

"Of course, Seline. Of course."

"You know about the water?"

Can you fill our listeners in, Professor?

"What I think Seline means is that sea levels in the South Pacific have risen about a foot over the last three or four decades. It's rising faster there than elsewhere because of changing global trade winds in that part of the ocean, and the islands are only feet above sea level and in some areas it's only inches. Which island are you from, Seline?"

"Majuro—a neighborhood called Jenrok. But my father was born on Bikini Island, so we were promised a place here in the U.S., to work and live."

How old are you, Seline?

"Fifteen."

"Some of your listeners may not know, Thomas, that the U.S. government did nuclear testing near the Bikini Islands, in the 1940s and '50s. The residents were relocated to the Marshall Islands. They survived all that, but the sea is another matter. There are plans to try to raise the islands up, but it requires funding, and they don't have it. In the meantime, those originally from the Bikini Islands and their families have a standing offer of residence from the U.S., as compensation for moving them. Seline's parents evidently took them up on it. Is that right, Seline?"

"Yes. We saw my grandparents' graves washed away. The sea comes into your home. Even our drinking water tasted of sea."

"It's a rare place. Paradise. I'm sorry, Seline. Very sorry."

"Do you know about the ghost in the wave, Professor?"

"No, I'm afraid I don't."

"We are taught that there is a ghost in the wave that wants to come to land, to drown the land. You cannot look at it. That will only anger it. Look away, get away from it, far away from the shore, even if the water has come to your home, or else the wave will take you and you will then travel in the waves too, angry too, and always reaching for the land. For the home you lost."

Ruth

When Ruth stopped, it was because her head and lungs ached with decisions made and then unmade with every stride she took. City workers and community volunteers were posted near the subway entrances. They handed out bottles of water, flyers, maps. She'd avoided them until now. She took a bottle, read the flyers. There'd be a preemptive shutdown of the electrical grid in low-lying areas. Subways and tunnels would be closed by noon the next day, Saturday. *Know your BFE!* they called. *Find the evacuation centers and shelters near you! Know your BFE!*

"BFE?" she asked a volunteer.

"Base flood elevation. Look at the map. Go for higher ground."

Her apartment, on the fourth floor, would have to be high enough for now.

In it, the air was heavy as wool. What wind there was came hot as engine exhaust. She'd never made the time to buy an air-conditioning unit.

She opened her windows. Pulled the shades against the sun that had begun only now to fade, the clouds gathering. She took off her scrubs, through which she'd sweated, and left them on the floor. Then she stood there, deciding still. Stay or go?

She couldn't risk checking her messages, in case Mrs. Watson was chasing her there, and in case family or friends from home were looking for her, or in case they weren't.

The storm, if it came as forecast, would separate her from everyone. It would decide things for her. She sampled the radio stations she could stream on her personal phone for more information. One station reported that updated weather models were pointing to the hurricane first making landfall on Long Island, another on New Jersey.

Then she heard the voice of a radio host she'd heard before—at Mrs. Watson's and the bar—then an older man's voice talking of an island disappearing into the ocean. It was this voice that made her listen. A kind voice. Calm, as she was not. On her bed, she curled around it, or around her phone from which it spoke to her, to let its kindness touch her if it could: "Seline," the man said, "if you're still listening. Seline, I know it's hard, that you miss your home… "

There was time to get more supplies, time even for finding shelter somewhere. Ruth couldn't bring herself to open the journal now, which she'd shoved into her bag as she fled the Doctor's. It was one thing to have read it, even part of it, another to be responsible for it. For Sarah. She didn't dare tell the Doctor that Sarah might be alive, per Mrs. Watson's detective. He was too angry, and there was no guarantee it was true. She couldn't tell what was true here and what was done for effect, gamesmanship. She had to decide not to be part of it. From here on in.

Outside, the sound of horns continued, and hammering: windows being boarded up. Voices yelling, directing, quarreling, laughing. In her fatigue, she told herself they were building a great big set for a play, something not meant to last beyond the first few performances.

"From up high," the kindly voice on the radio went on, "in those photos taken from space, what you see of this planet is the blue—blue water. Water covers more than seventy percent of the planet's surface. Billions of us make our livelihood from it and are fed by it. And then there's water in us, of course. It's half of our composition. It's not an accident: We came from the water, didn't we? Maybe that's the source of that myth of the ghost in the wave—we came out of a wave, in a way. A science writer—Loren Eiseley is his name—he wrote that we are a way water travels, 'beyond the reach of rivers,' he said.

"And maybe you've heard about what the Dutch have done, Seline? How enterprising they've been? They've been beating back the encroaching water for centuries: Much of their country is *below* sea level. They've spent their treasure to make room for it in an effort actually called 'Room for the River.' It's a lovely name, don't you think? Room for the River? They've evacuated floodplains, moved dikes, homes, farms, even built floating houses, some high up on stilts. It's not a matter of debate that the seas are rising, and you've seen it firsthand, haven't you, Seline? You are proof of that. Welcome proof, if you're still listening, Seline, that we are all in this together, you see. We have to be. You are an invitation to make room."

Ruth fell asleep wrapped around the man's words: *welcome, together, invitation…*

She woke to the dark and heat and her phone dead. There was a moment of confusion, but her mind burst through it—a thousand things restored—and shook her. The Doctor's tirade. Her mortification so acute she felt it in her teeth, on the skin of her face. The Doctor's eyes trying to burn through her: *Who are you?* The only response she had was to get up, find Sarah's journal in her bag, and carry it back to her damp bed.

Mathilde. She got me out, back to my apartment.

I let her come and go as she pleases.

I sometimes worry she won't come back. I wouldn't blame her. We're strangers, pretty much.

I saw her first. In the halls of P.'s building, vacuuming the carpets.

He noticed her too, that she looks like a girl, because she's all delicate bones. Her eyes are oil dark and big on a small face, but she's careful with them. They look at you and then away, quickly, the long lids coming down like gates, like she's seen things she doesn't want to see again.

P. suggested we hire her to clean his office. But of course it wasn't an office at all. I told him not to, but he asked her anyway and she agreed.

There wasn't any hiding what went on in there. The room held on to the smell and heat of us, and some days it rotted and we rotted with it. Sweat and perfume, body parts open and wet. An asshole licked clean has its own smell. So does desire, and ours had grit in it, felt everywhere in that room, of something broken. Something that wouldn't stop breaking once it started.

I shouldn't tell you everything that went on in there, Doctor, who touched me, or how many, how many I allowed to—because that's the truth: I allowed it. With my blindfold on. Or off. With eyes closed, anyway. Not seeing what I didn't want to see. I'd given in. To the feeling—not seeing. And to being seen. Watched. I was watched. And not just by him. Because he had to keep pushing it, that was part of the game, too. To gauge how far we could go. This "friend" or that, for a "little fun." He'll contribute funds, this friend, help us keep it all going if he can just… or she can, just this once… It's expensive, an enterprise like this. He acted like this put-upon bookkeeper, but it's true about the cost—sex workers have to be paid. And the best of them are performers, artists, daredevils. Among them my whispering friend whose body was as soft and hairless as any woman's. He taught me my body would do what I thought it couldn't if it was touched with intention and focus, for long enough, his breath in my ear, his lips to the skin there, and once I knew that, I knew too much and felt too much to go back.

I was never hurt. Not physically. Safety—he'd say the word. I would, too, though there was no such thing between us. It was code that linked to other things, words, and acts, that made that room and what went on in it possible. We lost the light in there. Perspective.

By October his plans took shape and found a kind of pace, at nights and on weekends. He'd signed a lease on the office by then, and we were high on this terrible wonderful shocking newness. Like cold water after warm. Warm after cold. And the days were so lovely, one after another. There was light still, or I could see it, and believe in it, though the days were getting shorter. But, as if with every act of pleasure we dared, every bit of new skin that was given me, it was like some light was taken away. I can't say exactly when I stopped seeing it altogether or only that light made in my own head when the migraine came, the fucking auras. There were no more seasons. And now, just after New Year's, it's so very dark. I don't know how I got through Christmas at my parents'. Their faces showing concern. Mine smiling at them, while behind it all I wanted was to get back to him and the others.

And to the bar he kept raising: "This time she wants to touch you a little. Just a little. She thinks you're the most beautiful thing she's ever seen." But I know it wasn't me that woman he was talking about saw. It was surrender. Like a foreign country that his friends could leave and return to if P. said so. But I was tied there, in exile.

And that Russian man was coming again. He'd come once before. But I was wrong: He wasn't Russian. He was Latvian.

I raised my eyebrows because his wife, Nadya, and her father are Latvian. A friend of a friend, he said. Nothing to worry about. A supporter of our project here. An ally. Discreet.

And now the nausea is a slick inside me. It comes with or without headaches and stays. A sense of ashes that doesn't go away. I taste them every day. Some of it is withdrawal—from the drugs, and from him. Mathilde doesn't know I have pills stashed here from P. and the others. This will fix you up. This makes me feel so good. This will relax you. You'll love this. My sister took this after surgery, she didn't feel a thing.

They don't know that I'm not like them, that my body isn't, though it might appear to be. How could they know when I've held it wide open to them? Gave it like a meal? Like I had nothing at all to hide or to protect. Like I was as free as I pretended to be?

And now I can't do anything but lie here. Even when I'm too sick to pick up a pen, I keep on writing to you in my head, desperate things I'm not sure I could stomach seeing on paper.

Is it four or five days since I've seen him?

We were to make a show of it on that last afternoon, a Sunday: Charlie (he asked me to call him Charlie, though I don't know if that's his real name) arrived on schedule with his smooth skin and whispers for me alone, part of our conspiracy. He brought another woman, someone we hadn't seen before but heard about for the lengths she'd go to. She told us to call her Lia. The Latvian man was supposed to come that day. But he didn't show, and P. was agitated, and me? My body refused to play before I did or could. P. was impatient and gave me something to calm me down. But my body still refused: I lay there, the other two playing all the parts instead. They kissed me. Each of them. I feared my mouth had soured not just from the pill dissolving in it but from the pain that had come to that familiar point at my temple, drilling through and into my eye, and I turned away and Lia cooed at me, caressed my hair, "Poor baby. Poor thing. You're all wrung out."

They were not monsters, these people who did this for hire. By comparison, they were innocent.

I don't know if P. enjoyed them that day, if they enjoyed each other. I couldn't see even if I chose to. The pill P. gave me dissolved, and the murmuring came from inside me as Lia purred things that floated away into the murmuring. What was real? What wasn't? She asked P., "Do you want to touch me, maestro? I feel so good." Already there was that awful, awful light, bands of it, sparks flaring through it, and other voices, more demanding than anything else in that room. The drug numbed me into lethargy. I wasn't fully awake, but I wasn't asleep either. Through every part of me I was negotiating with sensation. Not now. No more.

When did P. climb on top of me? By then we were alone in the room. That salty chocolate smell of his rolling over me. He would yank me back to him. He said to me—his lips, no one else's, right up against my ear—"I need you, I love you, I'm sorry, I'm so sorry," while he was spreading my legs wide, pushing them up, and saying, "Please, let me"—and he said my name, Sarah, which sounded as false as saying "love" or "safety" did by then. "Let me have this. I need it." The two of us weren't supposed to anymore. He'd made me promise him. It couldn't be love. That was the point of the game, those were the rules now. And the game had taken over: He couldn't even force himself inside me, though he tried. He couldn't get an erection. This made him hit the bed beside my head and cry out, "You gave me God and then you took it away. How could you do that?!"

Did he say God? When I'd given him every perversity he asked for?

He used his legs to keep mine open. He put his hands on my arms, holding them down. But it was playacting, because I couldn't resist him. I couldn't move. But he didn't matter then, you see. He was absorbed into my seasickness. He couldn't hurt me more than I was already hurting. I could barely feel the pressure in the places he touched me because of the pressure inside me.

But Mathilde didn't know this when she burst in the room. What she saw with those big, knowing eyes of hers did not look consensual and she threw herself at him. She hit him with what I think was a broom, and with her hands. She swore at him in English and French, in all the ways she could, and she chased him out with screams and threats of the police… And when he was gone, she cried beside me, as if over a corpse. A stranger's. Her sobs thundering in my head.

And the smells on her—ammonia, lavender, and citrus, the cleaning products—these traveled like vines made from teeth from her into me, and I imagined I was climbing away on them into death, because every time it hurt this badly, the body and its blood turning into this sensate concrete, it's death you believe in most, that you feel must be a friend. It seems like the only lightness possible. But I wasn't dead, and to demonstrate, I vomited—on the bed. I don't think she cleaned it up.

When she comes to my apartment now, she changes out of her cleaning clothes right away, because I had to tell her about my sensitivity to smells—fuck, to everything. She always puts on other clothes that she brings with her in a shopping bag. Soft T-shirts and jeans. Sometimes she showers. She won't take any money for the food she brings. She is Moroccan but lived in Ecuador with a man whom she left. She says things first in French, then English, translating. I don't know if this man from Ecuador hurt her. But someone or something must have. She has scars on her arms and legs and said that many men will be pigs, "si on les laisse"—if one lets them. As I did. How could I explain, after what she saw, that he cured me once? That he was the cure for me.

I thought he would have tried to find me by now. Or called. To say the words we always say, even if they're hollow. To close the distance between us or just stop it from growing and growing. But he doesn't come or call and I don't go or call. I stay still and feel cold. Leaden. And I shiver. When she comes, Mathilde sometimes lies beside me and tries to warm me.

She says, "Medecin, il faut qu'on y va." I understand French from years at school: It's necessary one goes to the doctor. I have only one doctor who matters. Your name and number are on my prescription bottles in my bathroom. She asks, "Telephone?" No, I tell her. Not yet. When I'm stronger.

How could I come to you now without explaining how far I am from the girl you treated? Me, who's been stretched to contain all these appetites? And the loneliness now, so cold and so vast. I don't know which is worse: this loneliness or the shame. I waited all these years for someone to choose me. He did. To help with the pain for which I'm wired. I had to take every risk for that. But no one warned me about this kind of pain.

Ruth

Outside Ruth's window, day was breaking in layer after layer of phosphorescent red. Everything in its foreground looked black and singed, but not the clouds clustered there, so many taking on the color and substance of lava. Raised by the sea, Ruth knew the old sailor's warning: *Red sky at night, sailor's delight. Red sky in morning, sailors take warning.*

If she went soon, she could get away. Leave the city altogether. There was still time. She washed her face and mouth, put on deodorant, a kettle for some tea, slipped on clean clothes. She found her large suitcase with the wheels, found her raincoat, some rain boots she used to wear in the worst New Hampshire weather. Was it so easy just to vanish? Sarah would tell her.

Sarah

Today I'm going to find him. But I'm weak as if I haven't moved in months, not just days. Like a woman whose body is a punishment. If ever I had those chemicals in my brain you told me about, Doctor, that gave me relief, they've abandoned me. So I had to take something. A Percocet, they gave me. Or maybe it's Adderall. Don't know what it is for sure. But I'm waiting for it to chase the ashes away. Give me courage. Luck.

Mathilde came in the early evening before I could leave. She brought groceries: a roasted chicken, slices of mango from a street vendor, and yellow roses. She was surprised to see me up, showered and dressed. She was nervous. At first she wouldn't tell me why, but I got it out of her: Someone's outside the building. Someone she's seen there before. A Russian man—he dresses like a Russian, she says, like a European would but plus voyant, plus doré, which she translates as "with more shininess, golden." Flashier, she means. She has seen him before. She says he didn't try to hide. "He wants me to see him. He is not afraid."

I hug Mathilde to me, because now she is afraid. I could feel the long wire of her backbone, the beating of her ribs and chest against me. Is she younger than me or older? I never asked. She says she can't go to the police. She's not legal here. But I can call. I tell her there's no need—we are fine here. I comfort her after all these days of her comforting me. I want to kiss her eyelids, but instead I read to her as P. once read to me, and feel the gray in my mind loosening. When Mathilde leaves, I'll go wait for him in the room. I'll clean it as Mathilde would—better, order his books, his things. He said I took God from him. Did he mean love? Or inspiration? Freedom? If I took it, I must be able to give it back. Somehow. Find it for him. And me. We went too far but now we know the dangers. We can make a new agreement to steady us again, protect each other from the other. Put up the boundaries you tried to show me, Doctor, didn't you? Boundaries can be love, can't they? Health. I know you know. Have known.

I lost my job. Of course. I just stopped going. What choice did I have? But there are other jobs.

I'll call my parents, tell them again that I've been unwell in these last days but now I'm so much better. "I just didn't want to worry you," I'll say. Knock, knock. Who's there? Me, right here. I have a new friend, and I've read George Eliot to her. My mother's favorite novelist. And I did so not just because I miss my mother, and I do, but because Eliot understood how limited we are and will remain if we don't keep adapting and stretching outside ourselves to survive, to know, know better, that there's strength and salvation in that. As my mother often says, we can't transcend our limitations until we first accept them in ourselves and others. I have never really understood the real generosity in that until now.

When I gave you a copy of Eliot's Middlemarch, Doctor, I circled a passage I love, dog-eared the page. Did you see it? "If we had a keen vision and feeling of all ordinary human life, it would be like hearing the grass grow and the squirrel's heart beat, and we should die of that roar which lies on the other side of silence. As it is, the quickest of us walk about well wadded with stupidity."

I try to translate this into French for Mathilde, but "we walk about well wadded with stupidity"? I don't have the vocabulary. So I put the blanket around me, covering my head, my ears, but not my face, and I smile like a fool, walking into things. But I'm wide-eyed and startled at every sound and sight when I take the blanket off. The best pantomime I can do for her, and we laugh. It feels so good to laugh and then to see her go. I watch her leave from the window, get safely into a cab that I insist she take, for which I make her take some money.

I've got to rush now. I have to go while I can, while I have the strength. But what I must say to you is that I have heard it, that roar, inside and out, felt that undone by sensation, that exposed. And I have survived it, haven't I? When what was so ordinary became so inhospitable. And so very frightening.

And I am here, on the other side. I made it.

Ruth

When Ruth turned the page, there was nothing there. Nothing more was written. There were nearly as many blank pages left as filled ones. It was a shock, as if Sarah had been yanked out of her, so that she didn't notice right away that her shades were moving—not frantically, but steadily. The wind was picking up.

She went back to the journal to check once more that there was nothing more to read, shaking it to see if anything would fall out, scanning the insides of the back and front covers for something more. She held it to her chest as if to feel its heartbeat but only felt her own, beginning to race again, making her sweat with the heat inside her and heavy around her. On the other side? Of all that intense feeling? Where was that? Oblivion? And going and returning hadn't been painless for Sarah. Not like Wharton's *House of Mirth* heroine Lily Bart. To slip the body and its hungers, the world bearing down, Lily had killed herself: Whether by accident or on purpose, she'd taken too much of a sleeping narcotic and she hadn't come back. And Sarah—had she actually survived? That blank page told Ruth nothing, nothing at all.

She went to the window and pulled the shade up. A thick veil had fallen over the sky. Not red at all anymore, but a glowing yellow color, inflected with a steely pewter that was static and swelling all at once, electric with threat. If there'd been a window of time in which to leave, it was closed or closing now. She was alone in a city that was still so strange to her. A shelter nearby would let her in, surely, before the lights went out. It wasn't too late. She had those flyers to direct her.

She was going to find them, rushing now, when someone knocked on her door. No buzzer from downstairs first, as would normally be the case—someone was right outside the door. A city volunteer? A concerned neighbor? Or someone sent by Mrs. Watson? Her detective, if he in fact existed, hunting Ruth now too? Marie? Or the Doctor, pursuing her here?

The knock came again. It wasn't harried. It was polite. Pretended to be, anyway. It terrified her. She willed it to go away, but it came again. Measured. What did she have in the apartment that could double as a weapon? Or if she just kept still… But the kettle—the water had come to a boil and sang out those first notes of its signal.

"Ruth?" She didn't recognize the voice at first. She snatched the kettle off the burner, grabbed a kitchen knife. "Ruth? I'm sorry to show up like this. Someone was going out downstairs—they let me in. I got your address from Sue. Is everything okay? Are you?… Ruth, are you there?"

"Jeff?"

"Yes."

"Um—let me just—" She got rid of the knife, picked her scrubs up off the floor, smoothed her bed.

"I came to see if you'd come to St. Gabriel's?" Jeff pressed through the door. "No one has heard from you or the Doctor since yesterday, and since you're new in town, we wanted to make sure you were okay. And Orson has the church—you know, above the clinic—all set up. It's pretty elaborate. He asked after you, too—"

"Orson?"

Was this a trap? Would she find the Doctor out there, too? The police?

"He may need some medical support there. People might need help, a nurse. And it's not just that; everybody at the clinic, they've been saying what a big help—"

The peephole in her door gave her a view of Jeff, and Jeff alone. She began to unlock the door—one lock, then two. She didn't know what she could say to him, about the Doctor, Sarah and her lover, even Lily Bart—that, like Lily Bart and Sarah, Ruth was in exile, maybe forever. But he was just as shy as she was, and once he saw her, he lost his thread while they blinked at each other, then found it:

"Yes, what a big help you are at the clinic, how much you contribute—"

His brown hair was stuck to his forehead, all of it damp. The rain must have begun, and he hadn't bothered to put up the hood of the long nylon tarp poncho he had on. He had one earphone in, connecting him to the latest news; the other dangled against his chest.

Under his poncho he was outfitted with high boots meant for touring disasters, made from rubber nearly as dense as tires, with treads inches thick. On his back was a knapsack sizable enough to hold a child. Ruth knew it was packed with everything he or she might anticipate needing, his best effort at preparedness. She wanted to throw her arms and legs around him.

"You okay?" he asked, peering at her as if she was made of bright light and checking behind her to make sure she was alone.

"Yes," she told him, because it was what he wanted to hear.

He came no further than her doorframe and, with an uncertainty that touched her, he asked, "You coming?" He wouldn't force her. "It could be bad, and soon—"

She remembered the Doctor's ordering her not to go near his patients. She'd have to try to explain to Jeff why she couldn't go. Shouldn't. That she'd be fine here or at some other shelter. But she didn't.

"Let me get a few things," she said, "then we'll go."

The Doctor

The flags and awnings that were put back up after the winds had calmed were coming down again for the storm, one after another steel gates snapping shut that Friday night, as if to hassle him. As he walked away from Brooklyn Heights, he cursed all of it, and behind his twitching face he felt intoxicated by the curses, a stream of them building in him, then gone in his forward motion. He moved with the pace of his heart, too fast, and remembered a thousand things and then forgot them.

At Flatbush Avenue, it assailed him again that he'd had Sarah within reach once and, as quickly, he lost sight of that and of her, waiting for him in the park on a painfully beautiful day in September. He forgot that regret almost as soon as it pierced his diaphragm, forgot his clinical detachment, forgot that he was never very good at it anyway, forgot his empathy. He forgot order and how impossible it was. He forgot disorder and how it pursued him. It went like this for blocks, even as he entered Prospect Park and saw the homeless men and women being chased from their territories there, a voice over a loud-speaker yelling that this was no dress rehearsal, as the sunset's afterglow faded and emergency lights blossomed around them. After he passed the long line of idling Con Ed trucks up and down Prospect Park South, looking like an invading force awaiting orders, he forgot them, too, lengthening his strides, despite the ache in his knees that traveled to his hips.

He forgot to be polite or to talk at all when a young woman in an orange vest asked where he lived, where he planned to go. And not long after, on Ocean Parkway, he forgot to thank a young man, also made official by a city-issued baseball cap and vest, who offered him a bottle of water and spoke of mandatory evacuation in *these zones*. He forgot to look at the map the young man showed him or listen as it was explained to him that those who failed to leave low-lying areas of the city would be detained, by force if necessary.

He couldn't explain to the young man that he was walking out of every sickroom he'd ever been in, letting go of every hand. He was walking away from Ruth's face as he roared at it that day and its fright and guilt, as his anger took the future from them both, brought another gate down.

Voices, like bird after bird in his head—Ruth's, Adele's, Adam's, Ed's, Jackie's, Sarah's, and her lover's, screeching at him as if in too small a garden—were silenced one by one in the walking and forgetting.

It was the sight of Nathan's, the hot dog place, that reminded him where he was now, after so many hours—five, six? longer? he didn't know—Coney Island. He'd been drawn by lights casting into the low, murky night sky and by habit. He'd walked here before to see old New York and how it hung on—the few freak shows stubborn as weeds alongside the arcade games, the ancient jerking Cyclone, the defunct Parachute Jump from the 1939 World's Fair, the persistent smell of fried food and salt air, the boardwalk against the expanse of sea and sand.

Tonight the park's array of neon was extinguished and was taken over by other lights: the emergency vehicles' colors pulsing over everything; tall portable light towers, aiming to illuminate the low sky; the headlights of a few bulldozers and a half dozen trucks, rumbling on and off, moving sand and sandbags in and out.

Behind them, the Wonder Wheel started for an interval, stopped, moved again. They were taking the cars off.

"You gonna stand there, *hombre*, or help?" someone called to him from a nearby group of men, passing sandbags to a pile where other men were putting them on dollies and onto other trucks.

"Park's closed to tourists!" the same voice called again.

"He's come to see the Eiffel Tower," another voice put in. Faces flickered at him as they laughed, but not for long. They kept moving the bags.

"Don't pay them any attention," said someone coming up behind him, speaking musically, and then, at volume, "Just a bunch of broke-ass Mexicans."

"Like you, eh, Pedro?"

"Mexican *American*, and I'm rich, as you can see, in friends and associates," said a young man, stretching an open hand toward them and the Doctor. Pedro, if that was his name, was all smiles, in his own city-issued vest and cap, though his cap was on backwards and his bare arms were muscled and slick with sweat. He held a clipboard. "How are you tonight, sir?"

"Taking a break, eh, Pedro?"

More laughter.

The Doctor nodded his hello and felt a throbbing from his feet to his ears. His body had to keep moving or else it would start telling him in every way about its age and what he'd put it through to get to this spot. Pedro said he was from the Hurricane Specialist Unit and that this was Zone A, and only those working for the city could stay.

"We're here by order of the governor and the mayor. Between us, they don't like each other much, but for this they mean to show the world we're ready, and we will—"

"You here to chat with tourists, Pedro?"

"We'll show them all how it's done here in New York City." Pedro spoke like a convert. "We're taking the lessons learned from Katrina and Sandy and Puerto Rico—"

"*Revolu!*" someone cried.

"No mames, *culero*!"

"By tomorrow we'll have evacuated over four hundred thousand people. Do you have a shelter picked out, sir?"

The Doctor stepped into the line behind the man he took to be the one who'd first called out to him.

"No tourist, this one!"

They made room for him and tossed him a bag, which he tossed on.

"Okay, sir," Pedro said, coming up beside him. "Okay! You're lending a hand. But I'm going to need your name for my records here. We have to keep it all official."

"Louis," he said. "Louis Berger."

The Doctor hunched, and soon the bags, sheathed in plastic, went in and out of his sweating hands at a rhythm so brisk that it was as if he and these men were joined in lifting something alive, snaking through their hands. He stole a look at the chalky, starless sky above them and nearly laughed as he heard Adele taunting him: "Are you up there, Ophiuchus? Can you hear me?"

"No," he said, out loud. No one heard him. Engines exerted themselves around them. On the beach, sloping down to a shore that he couldn't see from where he stood, bulldozers shoved the sand into defensive shapes, and behind this there was the outbreath of the surf, building.

Ruth

When she and Jeff emerged from the subway, the rain came down as if poured, and steam rose from the hot pavement. It was hard to see clearly or get a full breath. In the heaviest of it, Jeff seized on to Ruth's hand and, over the din, yelled to tell her how many street trees had fallen during Hurricane Sandy: eight thousand. Now the trees were as sodden and slouching as she and Jeff were, but intact, and she was giddy when she knew she shouldn't be.

She still was when they climbed the stairs to the first set of doors into the church's entry area. And walking through the next set of doors was like climbing into warm light: pools of light, overlapping, splashing, and there was music too, some sort of singing that was also chanting—Gregorian maybe, or an update of it, women's voices only—making for more pools inside the pools of light, causing the colors in the stone to open up; rose streaked through its dinginess, along with tinges of a deeper red, a cream softening through.

What was ripped up, boarded up, crumbling, and absent inside St. Gabriel's—statuary, pews, organ pipes—was visible, but these wounds were now matched by what was there, too. In the lights, the granite columns, which supported the ceiling's heavy groin vaults and arches, recovered some of their original sheen and flesh there in their tans and browns.

At the top of each column, twenty to thirty feet up on either side, there were sculpted blank-eyed faces, full-cheeked children's faces of indeterminate sex, and men's faces, with and without beards, these of apostles maybe, or saints, anchored into a pattern of acanthus leaves. The faces appeared resigned, forbearing, as if they understood disaster would come.

Jeff and Ruth heard Izzy before they realized she was upon them, fizzing with the pleasure of playing hostess: "I'm so glad you came, Ruth! Jeff volunteered to find you! It's safer here with us. So much better. Why don't you take off your boots. Leave them over there." She pointed to a standing army of paired boots and shoes to one side of the church doors.

"Or you can carry them with you to whatever spot you stake out. We have these wonderful socks you can put on, with rubber treads, nonslip on the wet floor. We have to think about these things, so *many* things—"

Ruth and Jeff had let go of each other's hands as if by instinct when Izzy approached. Jeff bent to unlace his boots, and while Ruth shimmied hers off, she was stuck wondering what Izzy meant: Ruth was safer here than where? At another shelter, or maybe at Mrs. Watson's? Was this yet a competition, a game? Won, say, with a show of supplies? And what a show it was: Along one of the far walls, down an aisle, there were at least a dozen crates overflowing with apples, shining and durable.

"Oh, you look amazed, Ruth. And you're right to be. It *is* amazing. All that Orson has done—"

Five-gallon containers of water lined the opposite wall and, like the apples, seemed to shore it up.

"Yes, there's food. Water. He's aiming for a gallon a day for every person who comes and stays, but he's fretting already whether he has enough. There are dehumidifiers—he has four—"

There was a soft whooshing under the music: from white machines, one not far from where they stood, working to pull the damp chill from a place that had long been damp and chilled. The smell of incense and age hung on, but it mixed with smells of food and an undercurrent of lemon from cleaning products. What they could scrub clean, they had.

"And a generator—it's magnificent. If you ask him about it, be prepared to hear every specification. He thinks he's an expert, and maybe he is!" Izzy laughed. "And he was so particular about the lights. He looked into every battery-operated light he could find, like the votives—"

These lights flickered with their imitation flames and were set in groups on tables and on the thick stone window insets. It was far brighter than the last time she was here, because the church's limited lights were burning, too: sconces on the walls and three large metal pendant fixtures hanging down the center aisle, combined with several portable lights, stark but effective as theater lights in spotlighting and lifting shadows.

"Of course, he has an army of USB phone chargers, and all kinds of radios: crank, two-way, satellite. He's spent simply hour upon hour considering the psychological side of things, of being stranded"—Izzy's voice dropped, confiding—"*trapped*, you know? But she veered back to cheer: "And look at that table up there—it's a banquet of food. Everything's here to make a point, he says—"

Thermal blankets were draped around people's shoulders or abandoned over the backs of pews. Their aluminized coating caught the light and glowed as Izzy listed more items made ready for their refugees: wipes, diapers, hand sanitizer, feminine hygiene products, even those little kits with toothbrushes and tiny toothpastes that you get on airplanes.

"And over there, look, there's two massage chairs and a couple of masseuses somewhere. Can you believe it? And there's a man who teaches juggling—that's him up on the altar getting some food. There's lasagna. And quiche, too: root vegetables and chèvre. It's so gorgeous!"

Izzy was nearly breathless with delight. Orson's vision was hers as well, and that he'd articulated it in ways she didn't anticipate made it all the more exciting: with puzzles and coloring books, board games, packs of playing cards, hula hoops, jump ropes. Orson wanted as complete a world as he could fashion, not just a refuge but an ideal, an alternate world. That every window in the church was already boarded up fit: Nothing of the storming day could mix with Orson's set piece, and none of life's regular drears, either—its everyday transactions and hierarchies and expectations. He'd use the suspension the extreme weather forced on those who came to the church to remind them of what pleasures he could, and of eccentricity and sensuality, too.

Ruth spied a young couple, in their late teens or early twenties, under a glowing blanket, at one end of a far pew, kissing open-mouthed and with a slowness that matched the music filling in around them. For the moment, anyway, they weren't afraid. They were lulled. Ruth felt this, too. She wanted to leave Izzy's descriptions—now about the cots on offer, and the pillows (which were real pillows, not puny travel pillows)—and take Jeff to a corner and eat one of those shining apples. He'd use his own pocketknife to cut it into sections for them. He'd offer her one and she'd take it, only to hold it to his lips.

"We have first aid kits at the ready and duct tape, all kinds of antiseptic and analgesics, and now *you*, Ruth, a capable professional here. What a godsend to have you among us—"

Izzy then grabbed Ruth to her, hugging her to her excitement. Ruth was wet from the rain, and the tote bag that was on her shoulder slipped down to the crook of her arm. It had also gotten wet, but before leaving her apartment she'd wrapped its contents hurriedly in plastic grocery bags—her toothbrush and underwear, a few shirts, jeans, the two phones she had, and Sarah's journal.

Behind Izzy, Jane was approaching.

"Ruth?" Jane called as she closed the distance between them. "Is that you? And Jeff?"

"Yes!" Izzy gushed. "They're here! You see, Ruth, so many of the Doctor's patients are here. Our *friends*, safe: Alla; Albert and his partner; Larry and Jill are here somewhere. Anousheh and her husband came for support. I insisted Gayle stay in Connecticut, of course. Richard went out to the Hamptons and got stuck out there. He can be *such* a fool—"

"Where is he, Ruth—the Doctor?" Jane asked, pleading in her voice.

"I don't know," Ruth said. "I haven't seen him since yesterday."

"Dr. Konradi, he was here," Jane reported. "He's worried. Sue is, too. She even went to his place. His apartment door wasn't even locked, and he left his cellphone there. Wherever he is, he doesn't have a way to call—"

"Sue's since left the city," Izzy put in. "Her husband took their family inland, as far from the coast as they could go—"

Jane broke in: "It's not like him, not to be in touch. Under the circumstances, you know? I called him last night, and he always gets back to me. *Always*, like within an hour or so. I don't have enough of the new pills with me. I can feel the pressure in my head already. He knows how the weather affects me—*all of us*—so I assumed he'd be here to help, *want* to be. I know he has more pills downstairs, but his office, it's locked. You can get us in, can't you, Ruth? And it's not just me." Jane's eyes followed Lydia walking toward them with her son. "You must know where Sue keeps the keys—"

"Oh, good, it's you, Ruth," Lydia said on arriving, with a squinting half smile, a squint in her voice, too. Gus stood beside her, looking far more at ease than his mother. "Do you know if the Doctor's coming? Gus isn't feeling so well—"

"I feel fine," Gus said.

"I didn't know animals would be allowed—" Lydia began.

Izzy cut in, explaining to Ruth, "They need somewhere to go, too. We couldn't refuse people's pets, could we?"

Ruth, for the first time, recognized the moving forms of small dogs' backs—two from her vantage—and the wafting tail of an orange cat, there and then gone into a space between pews.

"Gus is allergic," Lydia said to Ruth, over Izzy's explanations.

Albert hailed Ruth and Jeff. "Oh, hello, you two! I thought that was you! I want you to meet my mother and my guy—my *guy* is here. There he is, over there—"

But no one looked, because there came a clatter, then what was more like a fusillade. Doors burst open and banged, the first set then the second as someone bulleted through them, but it was the wind that held the doors apart and sent them clacking, surface against surface, echoing at everyone who'd turned to watch as what had seemed impassable was now forced open, the storm announcing itself. A new intensity.

"No!" a man hollered. It was Orson, running down the aisle at the doors and the person who'd let the weather in.

"Adam!" he yelled. Was that Adam coming in, or was Orson calling for Adam's help? "Adam! The doors!"

A smallish hooded figure in a shiny, squeaking watermelon-rind-green raincoat ran past Ruth and the rest of them and collided with Orson, pushing him back on his heels and melting into him, arms around him, holding on with all of her. He stiffened, regained his footing, and soon realized—by way of her coat or her height and then her hood falling back—it was Letty. He embraced her, as hard, with the same desperation.

"Daddy!" Letty howled. "Daddy!"

"It's okay, baby. It's okay. You're here. *I'm* here."

At their distance, those standing with Ruth couldn't miss Orson comforting the girl, and some portion of them, for whom the relationship was news, had to be surprised: Orson had a daughter. Ruth herself thought, *Of course*. She knew all the parts supporting this fact but hadn't had the right focus to put them all together. The picture was completed by someone else—someone who'd struggled, along with others, including Adam, to close the doors against the wind: Marie. She now stood some feet away from Letty and the man who had been and maybe still was her lover. Dripping with rain, her own coat's hood off, she watched them through her steamed-up glasses; the rest of her face a frown.

The Doctor

At dawn under a red sky, the Doctor stopped moving the bags to drink some bitter coffee they'd handed out and followed after a few others to the boardwalk to see the wall of high dunes built in the night as they'd worked. He let himself sit on a bench and, as he was telling himself the coffee was reviving him, he fell asleep sitting upright, coffee in his hand. It was still in his hand when he woke, but it was cold, and the sky hung with the yellow and green of jaundice and waves thundered on the other side of the dunes.

To walk was pain. To break the cement in his every joint. Sarah was there in the waking and walking. She spoke to him again, and he was too tired to do anything about it. He thought he would circle back to say his farewells to the men, but the sky was lowering, the dense air smothering, and he knew the pain showed in his face. Some hard-won paces away from what was left of the group he'd joined in the night, he lifted his hand in goodbye and yelled out, "Good luck! God speed!"

In reply he heard, "You had enough, old man? You going home to the wife and kids?"

Pedro, it had to be, called to him about a shelter, an address lost in the air between them. "Mr. Berger, it's not far—"

He worried the young man would jog over to him, press the point, but with all he had to manage, he let the Doctor go into rain that was only a drizzle and, as he walked, became heavier. He could see fewer bodies and fewer vehicles around him, and these were emergency vehicles, one or two belonging to the National Guard. What taxis there were weren't open for business. As the downpour found momentum, so did a weakness in him, starting in his legs, climbing into his mind, where reproaches populated. He could not cover the eleven or so miles he'd walked last night. When a truck pulled up beside him, huffing and shaking like an angry bull, he took it for a trick or a joke. "You want a ride, old man?" It was a Mack truck, like those he'd helped load and unload all night. Did Pedro send it after him? Was the driver's face now angling down at him among those he'd worked with in the dark? He wasn't sure and didn't ask. The face directed at him, however young, was grim and impatient. He climbed in.

There was another man in the cab, also Latino, blank-faced with fatigue, and no more than twenty-five. Beyond telling him they were heading to Dumbo with their sandbags, the men didn't speak. They listened to the radio, which reported that on the Jersey Shore the winds were already gusting to a hundred miles per hour. High tide had come and gone, but it would come again later, at force.

They dropped him on a street a block from his apartment. The driver barely looked at him as he barked, "You shouldn't be out here. You got that? Time is running out on this shit."

When he opened his apartment door, the dark inside was total, the air close. If he'd left any lights on, someone had since turned them off, and his windows had since been slapped over with boards from the outside. Once he flipped the switch, he saw someone had picked up his phone and placed it on the counter, on top of a paper torn from a yellow pad—not his but Sue's. She'd been there, looking for him, and must have found his door unlocked. She'd written, in her tidy print/script combination, "Please call. Let us know you're okay." This was restrained for Sue: few words. No exclamations, underscores, or teasing. He had no other phone line to call with—he wasn't there enough to justify one—and his cellphone was dead. He connected it to a charger, then showered.

As he was dressing, the electricity went out.

His hair wet to his head, his phone still of no use to him, he walked back outside into the wind. The screaming of the wires reassured him: It was familiar and told him that there were some things yet connected, holding on. But just as he turned a corner onto Clinton Street, he heard a hollow sound that seemed to rise in one long groan, then a reverberating exhalation, as if from the pit of the earth to the sky. Was that notice of the rending? Was that when the sky fell at last and made it impossible to see?

He was thrust back and nearly off his feet several times, and he should have gone back, but he told himself the church wasn't far, a half mile at most; he could make it as he had so many times before, even as his adrenaline told him that there was no before this swirling and slashing and perhaps no after.

He had to bend his back, turn his head away from the tearing of the world. Branches, splintering, were no longer branches, roof shingles weren't shingles, or traffic lights lights—all of it was shrapnel flying at him.

Let us know you are okay. Sue wanted him to know that the lines of care and duty ran both ways between him and his colleagues and patients—Sue coming to find him when she had her own family to look after.

You shouldn't be out here. Time is running out on this shit.

But he had no choice, and there was a rightness in it: the storm abrading him and every one of his assumptions and misdirections, because, even nearly blinded, he could so clearly distinguish the privilege of having had a place among those at the clinic so that his every day had had purpose. To fight for others was fighting for himself. His own sense of worth. There was vanity in it, *his*—of course there was. So many quarrels and strategies were born from it, but how plainly precious even these were to him, too—to believe in a code of conduct sufficiently to fight for it or in the methods that could remedy pains. He had almost let himself lose sight of it. *Do no harm*: That was his idea of what love was, even if it had kept him from romantic love all these years since his marriage. From the pain of it. And from the violence—yearning that reverberated and could shatter. But of course there would be pain, of course there was dislocation, failure, loss. Did he really believe it could be otherwise? There was no outrunning it, and how pain connected us one to the other, to the other, as much as it separated us. He could protect no one, but he couldn't help but try, even for Sarah in her absence. It was the kind of risk in human life about which there was no choice for him, even if it meant he was a fool, and that made him pick himself up as the wind and rain twisted him off-balance and pushed him back hard onto his ass, and then, soaked through, as depleted as he'd ever been, and as alive, he lowered himself onto all fours into the water coursing down the street. He would crawl there if he had to.

Ruth

The doors of the church wouldn't hold. The wind kept bullying through them, flinging in with it more people.

Nearly a dozen had been cut by the wreckage carried in the storm. A girl, no more than nine, had badly twisted her ankle; one man had a facial wound, and probably a concussion. Some talked too much, others barely at all, but charging the air caught in the church, as its population swelled to more than a hundred people, were too many twitching eyes and mouths spreading rumors about how high the storm surge was in New Jersey and Long Island, how fast the winds spinning toward them.

There were several calls to bolt the entry doors against anything or anyone else coming in. Orson directed his friend to juggle, the massage therapists to persuade people into their chairs. The music was changed, restricted to the upbeat, but with the voices in the church and the storm outside growing louder with every moment, all that could be heard of Orson's playlist was a tempo that in other settings would be cheerful but here felt frantic.

Ruth cared for those she could with what they had on hand: disinfectant, ice packs, fluids, bandages. There were now far more faces gathered that Ruth didn't know than ones she did, and in them there was need that she remembered from her days at the hospital, more of it than she knew she could address well. But she didn't stop, and trained calm into her voice and movements. She was asked a few times if there was a priest or pastor on duty and had to explain that to her knowledge there hadn't been one at St. Gabriel's in a long time.

She skirted the clinic's patients as best she could as she walked the ranks. The inquiries about the Doctor and his whereabouts had clenched her insides with a familiar sense of fault.

She couldn't help noticing Adam moving through the assembled, too, as if he were on patrol, head up on a tense neck, shoulders back. He barely spoke to anyone save for a few words exchanged with Orson, as though giving or getting an official report.

Jeff had been enlisted in directing arrivals and handing out supplies, and when he could, he looked for Ruth, nodded so she would nod back at him, and she did.

Gus had taken to following her. He wanted a reprieve from his mother's attentions. He asked Ruth only once whether she thought the Doctor was okay, and she told him yes, though she couldn't know, and as she wrapped the little girl's ankle in an Ace bandage, she wished that she'd never have to see the man again.

The little girl, whose name was Chitra, so far refused to remove her own blue rain poncho or let Ruth dry her dripping pigtails, but Gus's presence seemed to soften her. Chitra reported directly to Gus that she'd seen a bird outside, its wings outstretched, unable to stop, then plummet.

He told her, "On other planets, like Neptune, the winds are *way* faster, faster than anything around here. And it's got a whole lot of moons, fourteen, but this one moon it has, Triton, and *only* this one, it orbits backwards, I mean in a direction *opposite* than the way Neptune moves. That's *crazy*."

Chitra nodded, eyes wide with understanding.

"And our moon?" he went on. "It was formed out of a collision between earth and this big rock, like the size of Mars, called Theia. *Bam!* It's got all kinds of scars. Like a soldier would."

"Or a witch," Chitra whispered.

At that, the electricity died. The battery-powered light that continued to illuminate the church's interior was thin. And without the music or the dehumidifiers' hum, the furious churning outside had no cover and seemed to press nearer.

Orson had to feel scores of eyes on him, but he said nothing, only waited, counting the seconds until his generator would behave as anticipated.

When a portion, though not all, of the lights returned with barely a flicker, there was a vague cheer.

An earphone in his ear, Albert stood up on a pew near the front of the church, and with his partner beside him, smiling up at him, he announced, "They downgraded Beatrice to a Category 2 and they're saying it's on its way to 1, *Category 1*!"

Another meager cheer went up, but it dissipated into murmuring: A deep, weary male voice rejoined within Ruth's hearing that Hurricane Sandy had been only a Category 1 and *look what it did*. Someone repeated that comment, then someone else, and so on. Orson's radios were out of sight for now, but from those who carried their own or the lucky few who still were able to get signals on their phones, reports quickly circulated that, just as forecast, contact with land had absorbed much of the storm's force. Dunes were leveled, houses lifted away, but how many houses and how many people were injured or worse? No one could say for sure, and that was when a scattering of calls to bolt the church doors came again.

Orson then persuaded Letty to sing and set up a portable speaker and microphone at the front of the church, where she'd performed the last time Ruth had been here. Letty launched into "You Are My Sunshine," but she was no match for the agitation in the room, her own included—her mother had left only moments after she'd arrived. There'd been a brief argument, and Ruth had heard Marie say, "She won't come here, and she *cannot* be left alone, do you understand?!" She had to have meant Mrs. Watson. Marie had tried to take Letty back out with her, before the storm got worse, but the girl had refused to move from her father's side: "Daddy needs me!" Her mother then marched right back out into the day alone. Now Ruth watched as the girl wavered in her song and seemed to be growing younger before her eyes.

"They can't bolt the doors. They *can't*." Adam suddenly was speaking passionately to the side of Ruth's head, as if taking up a debate that Ruth had some say in. She turned to see the tall man's head bobbing, eyes ticking as if scanning for signs of an attack. His pupils were small, or so they seemed to Ruth in the light that could no longer be described as bright, but he was too jittery and heightened to be high on opioids. Was it the anxiety of a soldier, a traumatized one, or some sort of amphetamine he was on?

"They want to do it, a bunch of people back there. We can't let them. Ed's out there. You know that, right? Ed went out—" He paused to make sure no one else was listening and bent down to Ruth's ear, as he had before, heating it with his fast breath. "Ed went out to find the Doc, do you get me? He's *out there*."

"Tell them you'll guard the door, Adam. They can bolt the front doors if need be, but you'll be there if anyone wants in, if anyone comes, you'll be right there. You'll know."

He slid his jaw out, considering, then gave one wild assenting jerk of his head and barreled his way back to the church doors.

She couldn't see if he'd made it all the way back to the doors when a blast came: a shock wave on the northeast side of the church. Boards over one of the three great windows were dashed away. Then came, barely an instant later, a crack, not superficial but deep, of something foundational, as if of dense lake ice sundering just underfoot. Dust sifted down from the window, and through a fissure came a whistling that was only a minor note in what was now an orchestra of sounds and motion so forceful that Ruth imagined it as separate waterways surging at them, intent on merging and reshaping the world.

Around her, everyone shrank, and Gus and Chitra huddled into her. And, as if all their heartbeats had voices, yelling broke out. Was it about the door? Fear finding a ready outlet in that dispute?

"Get the fuck back, do you *fucking* hear me? *Get back!* Get out of the way!" Adam commanded. "Let me! Let *me*!"

Then another man's voice: "No! Dammit, *no*!"

When Adam emerged up the center aisle, fists clenched, it was as if he were brandishing himself, daring anyone to challenge him as he kicked coats and bags out of his way. This obscured for a moment that another figure trailed right behind him, and that person was carrying someone—wilted and waterlogged. Ed, half-wobbling, labored to lift the length of a man to him, one arm pressing the man's upper body to him the best he could, the other scooping him aloft under his knees.

Cries went up at the recognition of Ed with the Doctor in his arms. With Izzy in the lead, Jeff, Jane, and Alla, as well as Jill and Larry (whom Ruth had not seen until just now), even Mr. Bavicchi, hurried to them. Ed would not or maybe could not stop, in order to preserve whatever momentum or strength he had left, and Adam shielded him, forcing the oncomers behind them and into a strange procession in the chaos.

Ruth didn't move. She gripped the children all the tighter to her as more shock waves went through the church and more voices broke out:

"That's no goddamn Category 1!"

"Who is that man?"

"Is he dead?"

"I have no signal! Does anyone have a signal?!"

"Is he... *dead*?" Gus whispered to Ruth. "The Doctor, he's not, is he?"

Ruth closed her eyes for as long as she could. Not long. There was another blast. Another length of plywood torn away now from the middle of those three grand windows. Then glass falling and falling. Gus pulled free of Ruth and made for his mother, a boy dodging through a shower of stained glass.

The Doctor

He was in a dream he couldn't wake from. He was inside a vault, flickering with a thousand birthday candles. He knew relief so intense it became joy. Then, no: Near him, he heard people crying. The wind towering around them, acting a tsunami. The wind that hated them. Someone—Orson?—demanded, "Ruth! Ruth! Come now!" Someone else—Adam, was it?—alerted them, "Look, look, his eyes are open!" An appeal for fluids went out. Once "delirious" was spoken, it licked around him and made him doubt what he heard from farther away, another word circling: "tornadoes," repeating.

But it was a hurricane, the Doctor remembered, that was overwhelming the city, or had that been a dream, too? It had to be—all of it. Why else couldn't he move his tongue to talk or raise his limbs? And why else were so many people he knew and cared for there on hand? There was Orson, Izzy, Alla, Lydia, Gus, Albert, and Mr. Bavicchi holding a child—whose? A grandchild? Adam hovering, and Ed, who was crying the soft, shaking cry of a man emptied out. He expected to see Chaudhri and Jackie, too, with that look of hers, a mix of avidity and disappointment. Instead it was Ruth's stricken face that bent toward his—he spoke to her, to say what he knew he had to, but it came out as babbling.

There was the searing feeling of a split at the back of his head, out of which things were pouring now. Had he had a stroke? But how could that be when he could understand things around him so clearly, better than he ever had?

Around them he saw brooms and mops moving, buckets carried to and fro, full of the sky that had finally fallen with water and wind and glass, and there they were, already putting what they could back together, working with one another. He wanted so desperately to tell them that this strange place, with so many people gathered and striving—surviving together—was the very expression of the wholeness he believed in for them, that they all had been searching for, whether they knew it or not, for which, in this dream, he'd gotten down on hands and knees in a flooded city street.

It was not just *in* them, he wanted to shout at them, that hidden wholeness—not only there in the body's capacities to be mined, to heal—but it was *between* them, too, *right now*, for each of them to know and to see, here at the end of the world.

They were joined now, weren't they? Through all of it, Ruth, so near to him he could touch her: human mind after mind working in concert, not only within those discrete parts that made up each of their nervous systems, but between people, reaching, reshuffling, adapting, *right now*.

Could Ruth see or feel it all as she put the IV in his arm, piercing his skin?

Ed, if he would just stop crying, could explain it, as he had before. He knew all about the caudate nucleus, that large territory of the brain that oversees a range of behaviors that depend on trust—communication, learning, cooperation, even love. Darwin marveled at human altruism, that as a species we were nearly singular in our drive to share food and resources, with strangers as well as our own communities, as here, in this beautiful, beautiful dream.

"There is grandeur in this view of life": That was Darwin expressing the glory in how a few life forms became many, but through that same evolution there emerged in us and between us a collaboration—not the kind Adele was selling, but an adaptability away from self-interest only.

Every day, every hour, didn't we all travel between insecurity and security, fear and courage, between dark and light, from deprivation and such bitter aloneness to an abundance of feeling, of sustenance of one kind or another, and the rewards of companionship? Could Ruth feel this as he did? This alchemy? Versions of ourselves proliferating, and with these our connections to each other altering, too?

His patients believed in him, and time was running out, as it had for Sarah. What choice did he have but to use that belief, let it be the cure in the pills he'd made and prescribed for them. This was his own reaching for God, wasn't it? This was the love he knew how to give. He could trust himself in this, at least—*at least* that, yes—to help them to believe they didn't carry life's physical and emotional burdens alone. *Abide with me, help of the helpless, abide with me.*

He wished he could have explained it to Sarah, so now he had to tell Ruth. Tell her everything. It no longer mattered to him how or why anyone else had read Sarah's journal. What mattered was that Sarah had misunderstood her place in things, let pain and its shames narrow her choices. He hadn't known how to stop it until it was too late, but he couldn't let Ruth do the same—to be isolated, desperate, or think herself forced out, beyond hope and connection, by him or by anyone else.

She was putting a cool hand to his hot forehead. She was speaking to him over the shrieking of the wind, her lips touching his ear—*I'm sorry*, she said. *I was wrong. I shouldn't have*—her mind and his circling the same territory, going to the same places. Of course! Consciousness was a performance the brain put on every day, and hadn't they shared days and circumstances, and now this bright dream together in this old church?

I should have told you, but I wasn't sure that it was true. I'm not sure of anything here. And I was afraid. She could be alive and well, Sarah could be. Or there's a report—I don't know how reliable it is—she's been seen in Vermont, near where your home was, where I think your father still is…

His home? His father? What was Ruth saying? His father, with his own mind going and full of dreams that were as real to the old man as any reality he'd once agreed on, and had shared with others. What had his father told him—that his mother was back, alive and young again? And now Sarah, too? Was nothing as it had been? Everything wrenched free and up out of the ground, in motion, the order we knew disordered? Were there no rules at all?

Even the dead would not stay dead.

Ruth pushed something between the blankets he'd been buried under. *If she's out there, if there's a chance, you'll find her and give it back to her, to finish it.* The journal, with its soft skin. *It's hers, her story. Not mine, Doctor.*

But nothing is ours alone, he wanted to say to her, or never for long—not even this dream of his—but he couldn't. He was able to compel his hand to touch her. The sensation of her warm skin, a pulse there—he swore he could feel it jumping through him, as real as anything he'd known in the past twenty-four hours, and then nothing and everything went out. He heard nothing and saw and felt nothing. Asleep or dead. There was no saying.

Ruth

The Doctor slept as the church shuddered.

And Ed, who remained anxious for his friend, even after he himself had rested and hydrated, asked Ruth more than once, in a whisper, if the Doctor might be dipping into a coma. Ed knew better, but still Ruth reassured him: The Doctor had a bad knock on his head, had swelling, but his pupils were even in size and responsive to light, and he roused when she checked his pulse or shook him lightly, only to sink away again, away from the tiles on the roof clacking, the remaining plywood on the windows shaking, ransacked by the wind.

Not far from where the Doctor slept, Albert cleaved to his transistor radio. A few people, like Izzy's friend Anousheh and her husband, collected around him for what news he could get. Albert wore his helmet. He wasn't alone, particularly since two of the three stained-glass windows had fractured. Both windows illustrated the story of the nativity, and now were only partially there, their story partially told, and let in the rain.

No one, Gus included, had been seriously injured by the falling glass. Just minor cuts and scrapes. There wasn't wood enough to reboard the windows, so the holes between the lead frames were stuffed with pillows and blankets, and with a few of the life jackets that Orson had ordered just in case. Everything that could be was moved away from the broken side of the church—cots and food and of course people, who restored their headgear and rainwear and put their backs to the brush of the wind and rain.

Izzy took it upon herself to pluck what good news she could from what Albert shared: What a blessing that it wasn't high tide when Beatrice advanced on the city. Of course there was flooding, but it was not nearly as damaging as it could have been. And while by now most everyone had heard that this storm was faster and more compact than other recent hurricanes, Sandy included, Izzy pointed out that this meant it wouldn't—just couldn't—stay long, and was surely speeding away by now.

She didn't mention that that intensity had an unexpected consequence: tornadoes. They weren't all that uncommon in hurricanes that circulated over land and met, at full tilt, with other air masses—just as Beatrice had done over Long Island, especially in the Hamptons, on its East End. At least two had spun out of her eye wall as it traveled west, then north.

Only a handful of people, like Albert, understood what could be coming for them at the church—one of Beatrice's angry, blindly whirling children. Radar had spotted one on the southwest side of Brooklyn, buzzing its way north. Another was headed for Lower Manhattan.

When any of Izzy's cohort asked after her dear friend Richard, who'd holed up in the Hamptons—where twenty people had been confirmed dead so far—Izzy just pointed a finger to the long church walls to either side, up above the rounded arches, to what at first glance looked like a motif carved into them. But it was words—stylized and hard to make out in the light and under the grime. Ruth assumed it was Bible verse, probably in Latin. But squinting between shadows, stepping back for a better perspective, she could see that carved there, in more than one language and in more than one alphabet, was BE NOT AFRAID, the words the angel Gabriel spoke to Mary when he appeared to her. It was inscribed in Latin, French, German, Italian, Gaelic, Arabic, and Hebrew, from what Ruth recognized; and of course, at either end of the line, English. Izzy said nothing more on the subject.

But so many refugees in the church, a group of any number of races, of longtime New Yorkers and recent arrivals, sometimes both in the same family—they were afraid. And those same walls designed to protect them also held them captive. Arguments broke out over who got what and why—cots, blankets, food and water—and just who was in charge here, and they quieted just as quickly: the drama inside was no match for what they were hearing outside.

It wasn't quite eight o' clock when the pressure and racket around them began to ease, and even those who couldn't sit still finally rested: children; a whimpering dog that kept shitting on the floor; Albert and his radio; an elderly woman, Mrs. Santos, who, since her arrival at the church, just shook her head and wept and smiled, smiled and wept.

Larry and Jill, who kept moving in and out of sight, finally made a nest of each other on a pew, and Izzy and Orson and Letty huddled up together as well.

Adrenaline fell all around: Gus put his head on his mother's lap. Alla wrapped Jane in a blanket and another around them both. Rather than claim a cot, Anousheh and her husband sat deeply in two of the barrel chairs that had been carried up hours ago from the clinic's waiting room. They held hands even as they slept.

Mr. and Mrs. Bavicchi, who'd been watching one of their neighbors' children, were now free of that duty, and pushed their cots together and locked arms.

Ruth sat down at Jeff's insistence. "Stop for a minute," he said. "Just stop." He positioned her next to him and then arranged her head against his neck. She told him she couldn't but was asleep again before he could insist.

It was Ed, his boots on again and his windbreaker zipped up to his throat, who woke Ruth to say the Doctor was fully conscious, and wanting a word. "Now. Come with me." They were preparing to leave.

"Leave?"

She didn't understand. How long had she been asleep? Not long enough for things, as she had understood them, to change so drastically.

The National Guard was not far away, only a few blocks, Ed explained, and Adam had contacts among them who would get Ed and the Doctor, with Adam's help, to St. Mary's Hospital, where both men used to work and had friends, access to anything they needed.

"There's a CT scan with your name on it up there, right, Doc?"

The Doctor, no longer tethered to an IV, sat upright on his cot. He didn't object. His eyes were so small and deep in their swollen sockets that they looked like they were retreating into his head.

"Yes, Ed. But I'm fine. Just fine," he said, though the faintness of his voice betrayed him. "Can you sit with me, Ruth?" With effort, he inched over to make room for her beside him. "Ed, can you give us a moment?"

His breath was sour, his skin bloodless; there was a lopsidedness to his head as it sat on his neck. He was waking into himself, finding his way back to wherever he was now.

"This place," he said, "it's transformed, isn't it? I didn't think it could be real. But it is? Real?"

Ruth nodded.

"Is she here?"

Who did he mean?

"*Adele?* Did she come?"

Ruth shook her head. "At home. With Marie. Marie wouldn't leave her."

"Does she know about this?

"As much as she'll let herself, yes. Did Dr. Konradi ask you the usual questions, Doctor? Date? President's name? Your name?"

"All that, yes," he said. "I seem to know where I am. And who I am. Or enough of it. But I think I was dreaming before, a good dream. You gave me the journal back—"

He touched his side, where he must have slipped it under the waistband of his pants.

"And did you say that Sarah was seen?"

"Yes," she said, but in a whisper.

"I thought I'd made it up, and that everyone was here. And you, too, ministering to me? It had to be a dream—"

She thought he was scolding her, reminding her of his warning to her. She broke in: "I know I shouldn't be here—you told me to stay away. I didn't expect to see you again, and you were in bad shape. And I shouldn't have said anything about Sarah; I'm sorry. I was just so worn out. What matters right now is that you rest. Please, Doctor, *please*, lie back. Don't go yet—it's just too soon. You shouldn't—"

"Stop, Ruth. Stop." He half-raised his hand, but it took effort. "*All* of us shouldn't do this or that, should we, Ruth? But we do, we do. And we're all so very damned sorry about it. Eventually. Or most of us. I'm sorry myself, *all* the time. I—" He huffed out what was meant to be a laugh, maybe. His voice, so full of gravel, came slow. "I got things wrong, very wrong, and it was a shock. I overreacted—"

"No, don't—please, don't apologize to me, Doctor—"

"*Listen*. Just listen." He moved next to her. "Time's running out."

His side to her side, without looking at her directly, he admitted that he shouldn't have come to the church in the storm but he'd had no choice. He hoped he could find a way to explain it to her: He said he was *indebted*. Did she understand? That he was tied—and so much more than he knew—to this place, these people. And Orson, creating all this? It was no ordinary shelter. No ordinary anything. *Look at it.*

"There's something here, Ruth—is it radiance? Do you know what I mean?" She did, even as she knew he must be delirious. "And a kind of… abundance around us, *real abundance*. It starts here"—he tapped his head—"as a dream, and then ends up here, all around us, in an old church, a tomb, transformed. Adele's not here, but in a way she is, isn't she?" he said, wonder warming the hoarseness of his voice, angling his inflection up. "That's the surprise of it. Mother and son will always be in conversation, won't they? Like it or not. Even when they're apart or at odds? She *is* here. Orson's taken up the very best of his mother, made it his, and given it back to us in this place."

Around them, in disjointed rows, were sleeping figures, many covered from head to toe in the shining thermal blankets. The table of food on the altar had been ravaged and replenished and ravaged again, utensils and plates and napkins left on the floor around it.

He asked her if she could feel it, too—that everything had changed. And it would change again, at any moment, and she had to be ready. Or try. She remembered—didn't she?—about human habits? He had told her about that? Formed in the brain, in its very physical architecture, in the synapses? The brain reinforcing and refining its processes, including pain processes, shaping and reshaping itself.

"But there is architecture right here, around us, Ruth—between us, too."

If this was delirium, it was not like any Ruth had encountered in a patient. Could she be the one who was dreaming?

"It's visible and it's invisible, an expression of what's in our minds and between them—between *us*, so that we might find our way to each other. We shape each other. Change together. That's the opportunity we have to offer each other, and it's happening here, now. Can you feel it?"

He grabbed hold of her hand, hard. His hand was too cold. The grip of a dead man come back to life.

"You've heard people talk about the synaptic gaps, as if there's an emptiness there, in the clefts," he said. "But of course it's not an emptiness at all—it's as active as the sea in those spaces. Messengers traveling in that salty fluid. Charges. Sparks. Sparking."

He shook her hand as if the charge was there in his grip.

"And Sarah's journal? It spoke to you, didn't it? All that life in her needing life, and connection, even with her gone?"

She told him yes, because she had to. But she was only half-awake herself, her own breath bad. Dampness, which had overwhelmed the church when the rain came in through the two windows, ran all through her clothes and hair. Then the chill of him—it made her shiver. She wished she could just go back to sleep for a while longer, and that the Doctor would, too, that he could rest some more, but he had to keep waking to whoever he had to be in order to stand and leave after struggling so hard to get to them. He needed to account for all that was in his head, however addled, find the words to translate it for her, and he wouldn't let her go until he did.

"And Sarah was seen *alive*?"

"Yes, Mrs. Watson said a detective she hired told her. Tracked her to Vermont. I don't know if it's true. Any of it. Do you?"

"You'd like it to be, though?"

"Yes," she said, and she did, earnestly.

"Maybe, Ruth"—and he whispered this, from awe, she thought, not merely from his fatigue or frailty now, but from hope that she felt rising in her too—"maybe she did get through, made it to the other side? Maybe we can too, Ruth—"

He was exhilarating her. Ed eyed them, communicated, *C'mon, let's go,* but the Doctor couldn't go. Not yet. His patients needed him. "The pills, Doctor? Some have been asking me for more—they're afraid to go without. They're working so well—"

"The pills?" he asked, as if trying to connect who he'd been to who he was now, as if he was surprised Ruth would ask. "Placebo, Ruth. That's all they are. There's a supply in my office, and there's more where those came from. Maybe I should have told them. I thought it better I didn't at first, to let them decide if they could trust me, the care I gave—*we* gave, yes, Ruth, *we* gave—and that they can give themselves. Inspire them to make better habits, so they could support themselves, believe in their own capacities to control—"

But he didn't say more, because Adam was shouting. Someone had come up behind him and Ed, and it had set Adam off like an alarm. Adam had Larry in a headlock. Only then did the Doctor stand, wavering once he was on his feet;

Ruth inserted her shoulder under his arm to bracket him up. But the squall passed quickly. Adam let Larry go, apologized: "You surprised me, man. You surprised me," and Larry, red-faced, mewled that he was only trying to say hello.

"What the fuck is wrong with you?" he hissed.

The prone bodies in the cots and pews stirred, but not much else. And Ed said, "It's time to go. Adam, help me here," and they came to take the Doctor away, but he wouldn't let them yet. He faced Ruth. His eyes drove what they could of his strength into hers, his hands on either side of her upper arms now, pressing in so that she would feel every one of his long fingers, even after he was gone, as he said something with an urgency that seemed misplaced at the time: "You are a part of things here now, Ruth. You are welcome here. *And* you are your own—all yours. Do you understand me, what I'm saying?"

She nodded for him, and with Ed inserting himself between him and Ruth, and Adam on the Doctor's other side, he was whisked away, and already there was the question forming in her head: "When are you coming back?"

Jane tried to approach the Doctor as the men were exiting down the center aisle and was rebuffed by Ed: "He needs treatment, dammit! Can't you see that?! Can't you see?"

"He'll be all right," Ruth told Jane to reassure her. "He's left you all plenty of medicine until he comes back. He'll be back soon."

And Ruth believed it.

Then she let herself slip back beside Jeff and slept again.

When daylight filtered in through the uncovered windows and around the seams of the patch job, the wind and rain had quit at last. Orson and Izzy put out coffee and hot cocoa, milk and honey, and tea and hot water in electric urns.

Izzy set after reading from the stack of children's books they had at the ready. She struck on a pace that was neither fast nor slow, allowing lavish pauses to show every picture from *My Life with the Wave,* or *The Giving Tree*, or *Grandmother's*

Pigeon. But it wasn't just her delivery that drew kids and adults to her, that soothed them, Ruth knew. It was that the stories had beginnings, middles, and endings, which recalled a kind of order they were all eager to have restored to them. They were no longer suspended by the storm in time or place or in their prayers.

Very few of them noticed that the generator had gone out again or thought much of it—Izzy's voice mesmerized them, and the light and warmth kept gaining. It was a June morning, after all. But Orson noticed. He looked tired but energized, too; he had managed to keep them all as safe as anyone could. He bent to speak to Izzy, for her alone, and to kiss her on the temple. "Isn't my aunt magnificent?" he said, as if to himself, for himself, and then kissed Letty, who sat cross-legged on the floor close to Izzy's knee. He went away then, to check, Ruth guessed, on the generator.

No one went to search for Orson when he didn't come back right away. People ate and drank and began to trade reports about the damage outside but in lowered voices, so as not to spook the feeling in the church: yes, a new day with new light, a lovely summer morning from the looks of it, one they recognized, or hoped they did.

It was Jeff who went to see if Orson might need help when he hadn't returned to them. Jeff understood generators. He understood how dangerous they could be. It was Jeff who discovered Orson on the floor of the church's boiler room, in no more than an inch of water, just enough that he hadn't been grounded when he flipped the generator's transfer switch on the electrical panel. The volts he took burned his hand and the soles of his feet, in water he may not have fully registered was there yet, and stopped his heart. Orson was dead.

The Wind Report

"It was *arrogance*, those people not leaving. What, they thought their money would protect them? Now they're paying—"

They're paying way too much, Dan: nearly thirty people dead in the Hamptons alone, many more missing, and here in the city, what, a dozen fatalities reported so far?

"If you don't mind my saying to… Dan, is it?"

Yes, Professor, we've got Dan on the line.

"In 1938, we had one of the biggest and deadliest storms we've seen up this way, the Great New England Hurricane. Why? Because of too little information, too little warning given. Here what we had was too *much* information, lots of conflicting reports—along with a few satellites on the blink. A lot of people out there just didn't believe it would be much more than a passing squall. Storms this strong, up here? And this early in the hurricane season? It's rare. No one wants to believe it—how things have changed for us—and who can blame them?"

"Wants" is the operative word here, right, Professor? It's like we're engaged in some kind of magical thinking—

"But it's not easy, is it, Thomas? To make room in us for the worst? Prepare for it? For irregularities like we've never seen? Weather that's making up rules as it goes, for the sake of that equilibrium the planet requires and will get sooner or later, with or without us?"

Like the tornadoes? They just don't happen here, do they? Like this? In Lower Manhattan they're reporting that the spire on St. Paul's Chapel is gone. And Brooklyn's Williamsburgh Savings Bank building? Half its tower just crumpled. Amazing there weren't more fatalities.

"Always is—how we survive. And tornadoes *do* happen here, though on a smaller scale. In Brooklyn in 2007, a tornado hit Sunset Park and Bay Ridge and traveled nine miles. And that's right where the vertical shear in the northeast part of Beatrice's eye wall was the strongest and formed its own tornado, all these years later. It moved faster and traveled longer, so it did more damage than in 2007. The one let loose in Lower Manhattan was weaker, but not by much, didn't travel as far but still did a job—"

But you knew, you predicted it—the possibility of these tornadoes. You mentioned another weather front?

"I worried it could be a possibility, yes, depending on the path of the storm and what systems it did or didn't encounter—unstable air. We saw it with Irma in 2017—tornadoes in Florida."

Some people bet on you, Professor, and won.

"I read the information that was available against what these systems have whipped up before, that's all. That doesn't make me a hero, or only if our standards for heroes are lower than ever. Don't we all want to do our best by each other and this planet of ours? This beautiful, goddamned terrifying place? If we can? Know *all* we can? If it's not too late? And if not, what the hell's wrong with us?"

But it's behind us now, Professor? Beatrice has gone up north. It's on its way to New England. Some flooding there, I understand?

"That's right. Eerie similarities to 1938. They say lightning doesn't strike twice. They should stop saying that."

Ruth

Izzy wasn't fit to do it, but still she insisted that she be the one to tell Mrs. Watson and Marie about Orson. In shock, Izzy shivered and hiccuped, and her gaze slipped from the faces around her to nothing, so it was agreed that Ruth should go with her.

Standing in the foyer of 10 Linden Place, once Izzy got out all the words, Mrs. Watson hit her half sister across the face with the back of her hand. Izzy, dazed, did nothing to protect herself. She didn't recoil, didn't object as the glass chandelier overhead shook and sang. When Mrs. Watson drew her arm back again, Ruth stepped between the women. Behind her, Izzy slumped to the floor and sobbed, her head against the back of Ruth's knees.

"Is she making this up?" Mrs. Watson asked Ruth.

"No," Ruth said.

Marie stood there with them, until, without a sound, she bolted from the brownstone to Letty and Orson, his body still at the church now at just before twelve noon. There would be no police or ambulances available for many hours.

"I won't hear that," Mrs. Watson said, pointing to her sister crying on the floor. "Get her out of here or else I can't say what I'll do—"

Ruth helped Izzy to her feet.

"Doesn't she want to see him? *Adele?*" She angled around Ruth: "Won't you come? You can see all he did there. You can see how brilliant it was, how truly ingenious he—" Izzy let out another sob that sent Mrs. Watson racing away and down the hall.

Izzy recovered herself enough to say, "I'll stay with him until she comes."

And once she assured Ruth she could walk, Ruth let her go, out into the unblinking sunlight, and then Ruth was stranded there, at 10 Linden Place, just as Mrs. Watson was, with the landlines not yet restored, cellphone signals still unreliable, and a generator that functioned precisely as expected.

She found Mrs. Watson leaning over her liquor cabinet, as if over a toilet. She wanted the Doctor. *Now.* She needed him. Where was he? Ruth *had* to get him. She couldn't go to the church without him.

Ruth explained that the Doctor had been injured in the storm. She expected he'd be fine, just fine. She didn't tell Mrs. Watson that Ed had taken the Doctor away, or what the Doctor had told her. The conversation wasn't digested in Ruth's mind, was part of a dream—his to begin with, but now it felt like hers alone and something to be guarded.

"Everything is upside down out there," Ruth said, and then she asked if there was any damage here, to the house, the garden. But she got no answer, only:

"He'll come. I'll explain everything. He'll forgive us. We'll wait for him."

Mrs. Watson poured herself a tall drink of something clear. Vodka or gin. No ice, no mixer. Once she'd swallowed it, she asked Ruth to tell her who'd been at the church, how many people, and what it was that Izzy was referring to, that Orson had done. Ruth supplied details that seemed improbable now—the attention taken with the light and food, that Orson had forgotten nothing: games, a juggler, those apples, so many apples, and special socks, nonslip—

"Socks?" Mrs. Watson asked with disbelief. "*Socks*?"

Orson had been found wearing only socks. No shoes. Something Izzy had chosen to share with her sister.

Ruth struggled to say, "They had the very best intentions. The worst of the weather had passed, and we were all so relieved—" but Mrs. Watson stopped her.

"What we need now, *right now*, is *real* news," and she searched through the radio sources available through her sound system. But what they learned from WNYC was just as implausible: how the steeple of a church in downtown Manhattan had not so much fallen as been carried away, leaving those who'd been sheltering inside shocked and terrified but alive, with survivable injuries. And how dozens upon dozens of buildings in Battery Park City were twisted, too. One side of the new Trade Center tower had lost its wall of glass, its steel skeleton exposed and its tall lobby drafted into the swirling.

Outside the city, they heard that many of the great mansions of South and East Hampton, new and old, were without roofs and chimneys and gazebos, a few having fallen in like soufflés. Several simply drifted off their foundations.

After public radio, Mrs. Watson landed on *The Wind Report*, but, in no time, it became unbearable to her: It wasn't just the latest tallies of the dead or missing that they were giving, but that, Ruth guessed, Orson had listened to the program in these very rooms regularly.

Tears tracked down Mrs. Watson's face, dripped from her chin, as if she did not know they were there. She wouldn't eat, and she couldn't get drunk, though she kept drinking. Could she lie down for a moment? They went up to her room and she slid her into her great bed, its rock-salt wall glowing behind it. But before Ruth could leave the room, Mrs. Watson was out again, following her down the stairs.

Of course she couldn't settle, and she talked about Orson as if nothing was determined yet: "Why is it he was born without a *shred* of common sense? Why does he think he can do anything he wants, *when* he wants it? Just like his father. Why can't he listen?"

The fact of his death couldn't be absorbed in hour after hour at 10 Linden, which did not move so much as swell with their own injury. What time was it? Ruth guessed it was late afternoon, nearly evening, when the bell sounded.

"It must be the Doctor finally! Or Marie come back with Letty! Doesn't she have her key? Go, Ruth, please go! Let them in, and *hurry*!"

But it was Ed. He'd come at Izzy's urging.

Mrs. Watson refused to see him, wouldn't leave her sitting room. She told Ruth to send him away.

"Get the Doctor. Or tell *him* to. I need the Doctor."

But that was why Ed had come, even as he understood he may not be welcome. The Doctor wouldn't be coming. At St. Mary's—the hospital still functional but overwhelmed—they'd declared the Doctor fit, or fit enough, concussed thanks to an injury to the back of his head but lucky to be alive, given what might have happened, and then he'd left them, slipped away, even though Ed had forbidden it, and was on his way, probably with Adam's help, to see about his father in Vermont, where the storm, or its remnants, were projected to hit later. He'd been meaning to go for months and months.

"I couldn't talk him out of it. He kept saying there was no time to lose."

The Doctor was gone before he could have heard about Orson, but Ed was sure that when he found out, he'd be in touch as soon as he could, when the phones were all working, the power grid restored. Then, Ed's eyes round, his mouth open to say something more, helplessness overtook his face. He yelled, to fill the whole house: "I'm sorry, Adele! Do you hear me? I put Larry up to it. *Me!* But that's done now. I loved that boy! I loved Orson …" The lament in his voice carried and cracked his words. "We all did! I came back to the church to see if everyone made it through—Jesus, I'm sorry. Adele?! I'm so goddamned sorry—"

"No!" Mrs. Watson yelled back. "No! Stop that! Ruth, make him stop! Ruth!" She repeated Ruth's name so as not to hear anything more until it was lost in a sudden crashing of glass, things breaking.

"I have to go to her," Ruth said to Ed.

Ed teetered, his hands out. A supplicant.

"*Please.*" Ruth urged him away, her instinct, one she knew well, from habit, only to protect her patient: *I am a trained nurse.* She hurried back to Mrs. Watson, who threw a coaster at her, then a book, then a pillow.

Ruth grabbed her arms. "Stop it, *please*!"

"To *hell* with you! Where is the Doctor?!"

"He left. That's why Ed came—to tell you. He left the city to check on his father."

"Father?" Mrs. Watson stopped struggling so that she might understand. "Where? *How?*"

"Vermont, Ed said. Vermont. Because of the storm. Earlier today. I don't know how he got out, if he did. Adam, maybe—"

Mrs. Watson became a fit then and tried to wrestle Ruth and this latest news off of her. She swore and spit, but Ruth was stronger, though not by much. She dragged Mrs. Watson to the sofa, and when she freed one hand to slap at Ruth's neck, Ruth pushed her over onto one side and got behind her, mooring the older woman to her with her arms, applying pressure as the paroxysms came now, tears that bled from her with anger and accusations and soaked them both.

"Why isn't it Isabelle? She could die a martyr! She'd love that! Or why not that ape, that piece of offal? He thinks he can come here and say sorry now? *Now?* Why is he still alive? Why not make them stand in that electrified water in their socks! Socks?! How could that possibly be? How could he survive a hurricane and fucking tornadoes and then die from sheer carelessness? They helped him with that shelter business—against my wishes! They killed him! And why was there any water in that room? It should have held! The foundation! In any fucking weather! It was repaired! I paid good money, and I will sue! I will sue! Ruin them, every single one of them! And that redoubt! That stone monstrosity! I will raze it, raze it to the ground! I'll make them watch it fall—"

Ruth had wanted to run from this place once before, the first time she came here, and she did again now. This woman, in grief so fresh, was more frightening than ever, but everything she uttered and exerted, Ruth felt inside her and understood, though she wished she didn't. Why not them? Why not you? Why me?

And why did it have to be Ruth here? Because there was no one else, or no one Mrs. Watson would accept, save Ruth, and then only barely, because what choice did she have? And what choice did Ruth have? Human pains—Ruth understood how they could bend even the strongest among us, as they had Ruth herself.

The last thing the Doctor had said to her was that she was a part of things now. If that hadn't been true when he said it, she judged it was now: She'd been swallowed up by a game in these past weeks, the rules and stakes of which had not been of her own making, but Mrs. Watson's or Ed's or the Doctor's, even Sarah's. Yet now every bit of it had been rearranged, annulled, reassembled. Ruth, too. In flux. All of them at the mercy of things outside their control. And the Doctor said things would change again and she had to be ready, but how?

Back at St. Gabriel's that morning, Ruth hadn't thought much of it when Jeff emerged from the clinic downstairs to get Mr. Bavicchi, who Jeff knew was a retired electrician and could address whatever currents and other dangers there might still be. And she barely remarked it when Jeff had gone to retrieve his rubber boots. Why would he need them in the clinic? But when Jeff emerged again and, uttering something barely audible about an accident, escorted Ruth away from the group listening to Izzy read and back down the stairs, he appeared to have stiffened from the inside out, every string in him pulled taut. The two men had carried Orson from the wet floor of the boiler room and onto the table of the nearest treatment room. They didn't need a nurse, but they thought they did, so that they could be certain of what they saw: the waxy pallidness setting in already, the faint smell of burnt skin, and of his bowels having let go. She closed Orson's eyes, but his jaw, slack as the rest of him, kept pulling his mouth open as if he had one last thing to say.

"Don't leave me, please," Mrs. Watson entreated when Ruth tried to move away from her, to give her room now that she'd tired herself and calmed some. Here was the vulnerability Ruth knew she should expect under the circumstances, but it unsettled her more than the woman's anger did. A new woman in a new woman's body.

It had been only weeks since Mrs. Watson first lectured Ruth while listening to Stabat Mater, but it seemed like years ago, because time wasn't the same anymore: Either it ran too fast, too thin, or somehow not at all, festering with real and imagined threats, and ghosts, even of her and Mrs. Watson's former selves. How sure Mrs. Watson had been when insisting in their first meeting that no one could accomplish anything in this life unless they were willing to risk themselves. How indomitable she was that day. As if it was her gift and hers alone to turn ugliness into triumph. As if it was easy.

Ruth, swallowing back panic now, reached over Mrs. Watson for the remote control to the sound system. It had a keyboard and a small window, like a smartphone. She dialed in S-T-A and Stabat Mater appeared. She selected it.

"No," Mrs. Watson groaned.

"Sshhhh. Listen and breathe. Please."

The music began, as it did, with the one voice, piercing, the other voice following—a ladder of sound that the two voices built together, to achieve such heights. Could Mrs. Watson hear it? She must have, because, though she wept, her breaths slowed and were less shallow. So Ruth let the music keep opening to them, through all the movements, from that deliberate starkness at first, its evocation of silence with sound, until the voices declared themselves and consoled—hear me—joining the composition's fullness with so many voices now, men's voices, too, impervious as they sang faster and faster: *Magnificat, magnificat.*

"This is wrong," Mrs. Watson told Ruth through tears, sniffling.

"I'll turn it off—"

"No, no, dammit. I mean the music—it was written as a duet. The choir was added later, by someone else. It's wrong. It's too much."

And though Mrs. Watson cringed, she didn't pull away. Instead she pushed her body back into Ruth's, anchored still behind her. Ruth tightened herself around Mrs. Watson, against the enormity the music had struck on. This surely was some of what the Doctor had meant about architecture, visible and invisible, between people. Carried and made real in music like this. In the feelings it evoked and that bound us together. As with Sarah's journal. Hadn't that been the same? Ruth might never meet Sarah, but what she'd dared to write about, things so very private and true—how the pain could come and blot everything else out, Sarah included, and how she'd do anything to stop it, now and forever, along with its frightening confinements—all that she wrote about seemed to speak directly to Ruth. And Sarah had been cured, hadn't she? If only for a time? Even if her love and all the pleasures that attended it had betrayed her in the end? The isolation had lifted, as she'd helped to lift Ruth's own? By sharing what had trapped her but also freed her? In word after word, she must have come to understand, finally, that she had to be her own remedy.

Would the Doctor, if he ever found Sarah, find her free, or freer? Having known that roar, on the other side of silence? Having survived it?

"No," Mrs. Watson said again, in conversation with herself but out loud. "I shouldn't have allowed it. I could have stopped it. It's my fault. All of it."

"It was an accident," Ruth corrected. "An accident." And she looked for other comforts to bridge the distance between her and the woman in her arms, made that much greater suddenly by fault assigned—your fault, hers, his, mine.

"The Doctor, when I saw him only hours ago, said your son had taken the best of you into that shelter. That you were there. That Orson made the inside of that old place into a kind of radiance. That's the word he used, because it glowed in there—it did. And abundance: He talked about that, too, about Orson's gifts, and yours."

Ruth spoke directly into the heat and salt between them. She spoke of the pills the Doctor had made for her—*designed just for you*. He wanted me to tell you. He wouldn't leave you out. There would be some of him there for her. His good work. Until he was back. Ruth wouldn't tell his secret about what was in them. That wasn't the point. Compassion had to be. Faith.

"Why didn't he come? Come here first? And when is he coming back, Ruth? When?"

"Soon," she said, but she didn't know, and the question she herself kept asking expanded, with "if" as much as "when," as the last movement ended.

"I should go. To the church. I should see my son."

"Yes," said Ruth, though she knew that what waited for Mrs. Watson in the church wasn't her son anymore.

"But we'll play it just one last time. The first movement?"

She needed it for courage. So did Ruth.

The first syllable—*stah*—launched again and soared: an invitation to stand and sing up and out of our despair—the mother stood sorrowing—to try to be equal to what comes—loss, the love we cannot help, the betrayals and reversals, the pain and pleasure—however we can.

Then the second voice arrived, precisely as they expected and needed it to: supporting the first, then leading, then both voices intertwined in their dizzying ascent to remind us we are all well met there, in our sorrows. No one is immune: I love, I long, I ache, I grieve, I fear. There was no defense from any of it, but there was reprieve in things that connect us one to another, however briefly, closing all the distances between us—dead to living, living to dead, life to life.

"Judith Raskin," Mrs. Watson recited. "She was from Yonkers. This was recorded in Naples."

"Yes," Ruth said, "from Yonkers to Naples," and to Brooklyn now, where two women held on to each other as they climbed.

Acknowledgements

This book began thanks in part to a lonely church: Strong Place Baptist Church, built in 1851, designed by renowned architect Minard Lafever. Except for a daycare in its basement, it had been abandoned by its congregation for decades when I used to walk to it from my place in downtown Brooklyn to the corner of Strong Place and DeGraw in Cobble Hill. I'd find myself going there often just to be alongside something so elegant and imposing, built with great care and ambition, and now deserted and dull with time. It's been converted into high-end condos since, but the silence in and around it back then, the density of shadows inside (felt even on the outside), and that quality of waiting for its fate to be decided, one way or another, was where this novel began.

It was helped along by a review of my last novel, for which I'm enormously grateful too. Marion Winik in *Newsday* wrote that *The Affairs of Others* "recalls those occasions when a substance one has just ingested is a whole lot stronger than expected" and that "those who look for their experiences of altered consciousness through the legal drug of fiction will be well satisfied."

I've been a heavy consumer of the legal drug of fiction my entire life, particularly those books that derange and can rearrange your experience of the world as you read and after. But that "altered consciousness" is also something that comes with my predisposition to migraines, which I've lived with all my life, a painful affliction caused, according to most theories, by an electrical storm in the brain. This storm does many of the things I write about in *The Pain of Pleasure*, including heightening the senses, making you see and feel things that aren't there, and affecting your mood, bringing it low but also, sometimes, sending it to heights that, as George Eliot put it, can make you feel "dangerously well."

These extremes that I've known (along with some forty million others in the U.S.) seemed to me irresistibly rich metaphorical territory for a novel, and all the more so given the altered states Americans have been living with since roughly 2016. In these years of stark political and economic divide, made worse by a deadly pandemic and a series of climate crises, we've all been made to feel the pain of the human condition, personally and as a collective. Through all the distractions, this book got long. It became a refuge, as well as a means to achieve some catharsis—so the thanks due to my earliest readers is even greater than it might be otherwise.

To that end, thank you, Cody Melville, who never says die, who hears the music and believes in it—mine, his, yours—and whose artistic soul is regenerative for him and anyone lucky enough (like me) to be in his company; beloved sister Meredith Loyd-Marshall, always one of my first and most dogged readers and proofers, who understood the big, messy heart of this novel from the get-go and wasn't afraid, kept the faith; intrepid voyager David Slocum, who always reminds me of the boons of good hard work, that there is solace and strength and discoveries, too, in one foot in front of the other, one sentence after another; and Jess Walter, whose discipline and commitment to writing, never mind his enormous talent and know-how, astound and renew me both as an editor who's worked with him over the years and as a writer. His kindness to me is all the more remarkable for his honesty about what he thinks is working in my writing and what's not. Will Blythe, too, can't help but tell it to me straight and understands the imperatives and challenges of creative output better than most. He is my editor in chief, my companion and colleague as an editor and writer, and a brilliant badass. And thanks to Rebecca Rotert, a gorgeous soul and fearless writer, poet, and painter, who told me that, while all the science the Doctor of the story is hiding behind is fascinating, it could stand trimming. I took her advice and that of her uncle and my old friend, Ron Hansen, who reminded me how tough I am, and who's a glory on the page and a mensch everywhere else.

The size of the novel's first few drafts also owed to the books, articles, and podcasts I was relying on in order to write persuasively from a neurologist's point of view and to better understand the brain's capacities for pain and pleasure, as well as the effects of climate change in NYC and elsewhere. They helped to shore up the world of the book and my confidence in it. Among them: *The Pain Chronicles*, by Melanie Thernstrom; *Migraine: Understanding a Common Disorder*, by Oliver Sacks (and, inevitably, a few of his other books in which he tackles consciousness and the brilliance of William James); *A Brain Wider Than the Sky: A Migraine Diary*, by Andrew Levy; *The Brain That Changes Itself: Stories of Personal Triumph from the Frontiers of Brain Science*, by Norman Doidge; *Reaching Down the Rabbit Hole*, by Dr. Allen H. Ropper and Brian David Burrell; *Synaptic Self: How Our Brains Become Who We Are*, by Joseph LeDoux; *Sudden Sea: The Great Hurricane of 1938*, by R. A. Scotti; *A Furious Sky: The Five-Hundred-Year History of America's Hurricanes*, by Eric Jay Dolan; *Scientific American* (several pieces, especially a 2015 special collector's edition devoted to the mind and the power of placebo); Radiolab; and *The New York Times*'s science coverage.

When you think your book is ready for an agent or editor, there's another gathering of forces required as you look to confirm that you've accomplished what you set out to do and have something of value to show. The readers who helped me at this stage: Maggie Noble, stalwart sister from another mister, who is not just one of the sharpest readers around but one of the finest minds, and who reminded me not to step back an inch from how literary this book was and from the ideas that make it go; Charles Yu, a writer of subversive imagination, humor, and great economy with so much heart it's a wonder he can contain it; Abby Higgins, whose passions and creativity when it comes to love, reading and writing, and art truly help keep hope alive; Carolyn Cure, a devoted and wide-ranging reader who's the captain of her ship in more than one way—her courage gives me courage; Kathy Burch, fellow migraine sufferer, fighter, teacher, firecracker—she's an invitation to live and laugh (hard); Marie Aronsohn, a former student and friend who's taught me much about enduring and taking to heart my own lessons on honoring one's intentions for a given work, whatever may come; Maggie of the Sea Calderwood, who's one of the hardest, and through-and-through creative, workers I know and whose enthusiasm for this book completely revived my own; and Christopher Goddamn Napolitano, the most capable and inventive publishing professional I've had the pleasure to work with and a lover of fiction; his support for this book has been thrilling and affirming.

But a confession is due here before I add to my lists: I didn't send this book to a single mainstream trade publisher, literary or otherwise. I knew, given the flux happening in publishing and how literary fiction in particular is being affected, that I wanted to go another way, where I'd have more say in the process, the shape of the final product, and how it's sold. Anna DeVries, cherished friend and my excellent former editor at Picador, helped me find my bravery on this front, and so did Lidia Yuknavitch, a mermaid/siren and visionary, whose rebellion is her art, her art rebellion.

Then enter agitator for art and indie bookseller Jaime Clarke; he suggested I submit the novel to the publisher with which he collaborates as an editor and writer of iconoclastic fiction: Roundabout Press, which is aptly named, it seems to me, for this era in literary publishing. He and Dan Pope (another accomplished writer and editor) welcomed the novel, and I'm proud to embark with them on their mission to provide "a forum that is free from corporate or conglomerate concerns" and publish work "that challenges the status quo."

And I'd have been utterly lost without Will Palmer: I've worked with some of the most talented copy editors in the business, from Norton and *The New Yorker* to New York Review of Books Classics and *Playboy* (no kidding), and he's a giant among them and my dear friend. His thoroughness made me feel as bulletproof as one can when publishing a novel, which is all kinds of uphill.

The ingenious Rex Bonomelli designed exactly the cover that I was dreaming of: one that conveys the intersection between pain and pleasure, the sacred and the secular, represented in these pages. He wowed us all. And Elissa Von Letkemann lent her design savvy and smarts to the creation of my website and her two cents to this book's evolution.

Finally, to my parents, Suzanne and Jerry Loyd, my founders and friends, whose imagination and moxie is the source of my own and who understood that the road to publishing this novel would be full of detours and were game for the ride. They've taught me that nothing worth doing is easy and that the bears in our hearts, full of wild longings and stubbornness, must absolutely be respected.

Photograph by Susannah Bothe

Amy Grace Loyd is an editor, teacher, and author of the novel *The Affairs of Others*, a BEA Buzz Book and Indie Next selection. She began her career at independent book publisher W.W. Norton & Company and *The New Yorker*, in the magazine's fiction and literary department. She was the associate editor on the New York Review Books Classics series and the fiction and literary editor at *Playboy* magazine and later at *Esquire*. She's also worked in digital publishing, as an executive editor at e-singles publisher Byliner and as an acquiring editor and content creator for Scribd Originals. She has been an adjunct professor at the Columbia University MFA writing program and a MacDowell and Yaddo fellow. She lives between New York and New Hampshire.